The Lilac Sunbonnet
A Love Story

by

S. R. Crockett

The Lilac Sunbonnet
A Love Story
by S. R. Crockett

ISBN: 978-93-63052-49-9

Published by

DOUBLE 9 BOOKS

2/13-B, Ansari Road
Daryaganj, New Delhi – 110002
info@double9books.com
www.double9books.com
Tel. 011-40042856

ABOUT THE AUTHOR

Samuel Rutherford Crockett was a Scottish novelist who published under the pen name "S. R. Crockett". He was born on September 24, 1859, in Little Duchrae, Balmaghie, Kirkcudbrightshire, Galloway, as the illegitimate son of dairymaid Annie Crocket. His Cameronian grandparents nurtured him on the tenanted farm until the family relocated to Cotton Street, Castle Douglas in 1867 (later fictionalized as Cairn Edward). In 1876, he obtained the Galloway bursary at Edinburgh University, where he earned an MA. He began his journalistic career in 1877 to support his bursary by writing for journals. He left the university in April 1879 without receiving a diploma. From 1879 to 1881, he traveled throughout Europe as a tutor before returning to Edinburgh's New College to prepare for the ministry. The Crocketts had four children: Maisie Rutherford, Philip Hugh Barbour, George Milner, and Margaret Douglas, all of whom appeared in his children's stories. In 1906, the family relocated from Bank House in Penicuik to Torwood House in Peebles, but Crockett spent much of the year overseas and made frequent trips back to Galloway. In 1886, he released a volume of poetry under the alias Ford Brereton, titled Dulce Cor (Latin for Sweet Heart). Dulce Cor is a ruined abbey in Galloway. In the late 1880s, he was a regular contributor to The Christian Leader magazine, edited by W.H. Wylie.

CONTENTS

CHAPTER I
THE BLANKET-WASHING

Ralph Peden lay well content under a thorn bush above the Grannoch water. It was the second day of his sojourning in Galloway—the first of his breathing the heather scent on which the bees grew tipsy, and of listening to the grasshoppers CHIRRING in the long bent by the loch side. Yesterday his father's friend, Allan Welsh, minister of the Marrow kirk in the parish of Dullarg, had held high discourse with him as to his soul's health, and made many inquiries as to how it sped in the great city with the precarious handful of pious folk, who gathered to listen to the precious and savoury truths of the pure Marrow teaching. Ralph Peden was charged with many messages from his father, the metropolitan Marrow minister, to Allan Welsh—dear to his soul as the only minister who had upheld the essentials on that great day, when among the assembled Presbyters so many had gone backward and walked no more with him.

"Be faithful with the young man, my son," Allan Welsh read in the quaintly sealed and delicately written letter which his brother minister in Edinburgh had sent to him, and which Ralph had duly delivered in the square, grim manse of Dullarg, with a sedate and old-fashioned reverence which sat strangely on one of his years. "Be faithful with the young man," continued the letter; "he is well grounded on the fundamentals; his head is filled with godly lear, and he has sound views on the Headship; but he has always been a little cold and distant even to me, his father according to the flesh. With his companions he is apt to be distant and reserved. I am to blame for the solitude of our life here in James's Court, but to you I do not need to tell the reason of that. The Lord give you his guidance in leading the young man in the right way."

So far Gilbert Peden's letter had run staidly and in character like the spoken words of the writer. But here it broke off. The writing, hitherto fine as a hair, thickened; and from this point became crowded and difficult, as though the floods of feeling had broken some dam. "O man Allan, for my sake, if at all you have loved me, or owe me anything, dig deep and see if the lad has a heart. He shews it not to me."

So that is why Ralph Peden lies couched in the sparce bells of the ling, just where the dry, twisted timothy grasses are beginning to overcrown the purple bells of the heather. Tall and clean-limbed, with a student's pallor of clear-cut face, a slightly ascetic stoop, dark brown curls clustering over a white forehead, and eyes which looked steadfast and true, the young man was sufficient of a hero. He wore a broad straw hat, which he had a pleasant habit of pushing back, so that his clustering locks fell over his brow after a fashion which all women thought becoming. But Ralph Peden heeded not what women thought, said, or did, for he was trysted to the kirk of the Marrow, the sole repertory of orthodox truth in Scotland, which is as good as saying in the wide world—perhaps even in the universe.

Ralph Peden had dwelt all his life with his father in an old house in James's Court, Edinburgh, overlooking the great bounding circle of the northern horizon and the eastern sea. He had been trained by his father to think more of a professor's opinion on his Hebrew exercise than of a woman's opinion on any subject whatever. He had been told that women were an indispensable part of the economy of creation; but, though he accepted word by word the Westminster Confession, and as an inexorable addition the confessions and protests of the remnant of the true kirk in Scotland (known as the Marrow kirk), he could not but consider woman a poor makeshift, even as providing for the continuity of the race. Surely she had not been created when God looked upon all that he had made and found it very good. The thought preserved Ralph's orthodoxy.

Ralph Peden had come out into the morning air, with his note-book and a volume which he had been studying all the way from Edinburgh. As he lay at length among the grass he conned it over and over. He referred to passages here and there. He set out very calmly with that kind of determination with which a day's work in the open air with a book is often begun. Not for a moment did he break the monotony of his study. The marshalled columns of strange letters were mowed down before him.

A great humble-bee, barred with tawny orange, worked his way up from his hole in the bank, buzzing shrilly in an impatient, stifled manner at finding his dwelling blocked as to its exit by a mountainous bulk. Ralph Peden rose in a hurry. The beast seemed to be inside his coat. He had instinctively hated bees and everything that buzzed ever since as a child he had made experiments with the paper nest of a tree-building wasp. The humble-bee buzzed a little more, discontentedly, thought of going back, crept out at last from beneath the Hebrew Lexicon, and appeared to comb his hair with his feeler. Then he slowly mounted along the broad blade of a meadow fox-tail grass, which bent under him as if to afford him an elastic send-off upon his flight. With a spring he lumbered up, taking his way over the single field which separated his house from the edge of the Grannoch water—where on the other side, above the glistening sickle-sweep of sand which looked so inviting, yet untouched under the pines by the morning sun, the hyacinths lay like a blue wreath of peat smoke in the hollows of the wood.

But there was a whiff of real peat smoke somewhere in the air, and Ralph Peden, before he returned to his book, was aware of the murmur of voices. He moved away from the humble-bee's dwelling and established himself on a quieter slope under a bush of broom. A whin-chat said "check, check" above him, and flirted a brilliant tail; but Ralph Peden was not afraid of whin-chats. Here he settled himself to study, knitting his brows and drumming on the ground with the toe of one foot to concentrate his attention. The whin-chat could hear him murmuring to himself at intervals, "Surely that is the sense—it must be taken this way." Sometimes, on the contrary, he shook his head at Luther's Commentary, which lay on the short, warm turf before him, as if in reproof. Ralph was of opinion that Luther, but for his great protective reputation, and the fact that he had been dead some time, might have been served with a libel for heresy—at least if he had ministered to the Marrow kirk.

Then after a little he pulled his hat over his eyes to think, and lay back till he could just see one little bit of Loch Grannoch gleaming through the trees, and the farm of Nether Crae set on the hillside high above it. He counted the sheep on the green field over the loch, numbering the lambs twice because they frisked irresponsibly about, being full of frivolity and having no opinions upon Luther to sober them.

Gradually a haze spun itself over the landscape, and Ralph Peden's head slowly fell back till it rested somewhat sharply upon a spikelet of prickly whin. His whole body sat up instantly, with an exclamation which was quite in Luther's manner. He had not been sleeping. He rejected the thought; yet he acknowledged that it was nevertheless passing strange that, just where the old single-arched bridge takes a long stride over the Grannoch lane, there was now a great black pot a-swing above a blinking pale fire of peats and fir-branches, and a couple of great tubs set close together on stones which he had not seen before. There was, too, a ripple of girls' laughter, which sent a strange stirring of excitement along the nerves of the young man. He gathered his books to move away; but on second thoughts, looking through the long, swaying tendrils of the broom under which he sat, he resolved to remain. After all, the girls might be as harmless as his helper of yesterday.

"Yet it is most annoying," he said; "I had been quieter in James's Court."

Still he smiled a little to himself, for the broom did not grow in James's Court, nor the blackbirds flute their mellow whistle there.

Loch Grannoch stretched away three miles to the south, basking in alternate blue and white, as cloud and sky mirrored themselves upon it. The first broad rush of the ling [Footnote: Common heath (Erica tetralix).] was climbing the slopes of the Crae Hill above —a pale lavender near the loch-side, deepening to crimson on the dryer slopes where the heath-bells grew shorter and thicker together. The wimpling lane slid as silently away from the sleeping loch as though it were eloping and feared to awake an angry parent. The whole range of hill and wood and water was drenched in sunshine. Silence clothed it like a garment—save only for the dark of the shadow under the bridge, from whence had come that ring of girlish laughter which had jarred upon the nerves of Ralph Peden.

Suddenly there emerged from the indigo shade where the blue spruces overarched the bridge a girl carrying two shining pails of water. Her arms were bare, her sleeves being rolled high above her elbow; and her figure, tall and shapely, swayed gracefully to the movement of the pails. Ralph did not know before that there is an art in carrying water. He was ignorant of many things, but even with his views on woman's place in the economy of the universe, he could not but be satisfied with the fitness and the beauty of the girl who came up the path, swinging her pails with the compensatory sway of lissom body, and that strong outward flex of the elbow which kept the brimming cans swinging in safety by her side.

Ralph Peden never took his eyes off her as she came, the theories of James's Court notwithstanding. Nor indeed need we for a little. For this is Winifred, better known as Winsome Charteris, a very important young person indeed, to whose beauty and wit the poets of three parishes did vain reverence; and, what she might well value more, whose butter was the best (and commanded the highest price) of any that went into Dumfries market on Wednesdays.

Fair hair, crisping and tendrilling over her brow, swept back in loose and flossy circlets till caught close behind her head by a tiny ribbon of blue— then again escaping it went scattering and wavering over her shoulders wonderingly, like nothing on earth but Winsome Charteris's hair. It was small wonder that the local poets grew grey before their time in trying to find a rhyme for "sunshine," a substantive which, for the first time, they had applied to a girl's hair. For the rest, a face rather oval than long, a nose which the schoolmaster declared was "statuesque" (used in a good sense, he explained to the village folk, who could never be brought to see the difference between a statue and an idol—the second commandment being of literal interpretation along the Loch Grannoch side), and eyes which, emulating the parish poet, we can only describe as like two blue waves when they rise just far enough to catch a sparkle of light on their crests. The subject of her mouth, though tempting, we refuse to touch. Its description has already wrecked three promising reputations.

But withal Winsome Charteris set her pails as frankly and plumply on the ground, as though she were plain as a pike-staff, and bent a moment over to look into the gypsy-pot swung on its birchen triangle. Then she made an impatient movement of her hand, as if to push the biting fir-wood smoke aside. This angered Ralph, who considered it ridiculous and ill-ordered that a gesture which showed only a hasty temper and ill-regulated mind should be undeniably pretty and pleasant to look upon, just because it was made by a girl's hand. He was angry with himself, yet he hoped she would do it again. Instead, she took up one pail of water after the other, swung them upward with a single dexterous movement, and poured the water into the pot, from which the steam was rising. Ralph Peden could see the sunlight sparkle in the water as it arched itself solidly out of the pails. He was not near enough to see the lilac sprig on her light summer gown; but the lilac sunbonnet which she wore, principally it seemed in order that it might hang by the strings upon her shoulders, was to Ralph a singularly attractive piece of colour in the landscape. This he did not resent, because it is always safe to admire colour.

Ralph would have been glad to have been able to slip off quietly to the manse. He told himself so over and over again, till he believed it. This process is easy. But he saw very well that he could not rise from the lee of the whin bush without being in full view of this eminently practical and absurdly attractive young woman. So he turned to his Hebrew Lexicon with a sigh, and a grim contraction of determined brows which recalled his father. A country girl was nothing to the hunter after curious roots and the amateur of finely shaded significances in Piel and Pual.

"I WILL not be distracted!" Ralph said doggedly, though a Scot, correct for once in his grammar; and he pursued a recalcitrant particle through the dictionary like a sleuthhound.

A clear shrill whistle rang through the slumberous summer air.

"Bless me," said Ralph, startled, "this is most discomposing!"

He raised himself cautiously on his elbow, and beheld the girl of the water-pails standing in the full sunshine with her lilac sunbonnet in her hand. She wared it high above her head, then she paused a moment to look right in his direction under her hand held level with her brows. Suddenly she dropped the sunbonnet, put a couple of fingers into her mouth in a manner which, if Ralph had only known it, was much admired of all the young men in the parish, and whistled clear and loud, so that the stone-chat fluttered up indignant and scurried to a shelter deeper among the gorse. A most revolutionary young person this. He regretted that the humble-bee had moved him nearer the bridge.

Ralph was deeply shocked that a girl should whistle, and still more that she should use two fingers to do it, for all the world like a shepherd on the hill. He bethought him that not one of his cousins, Professor Habakkuk Thriepneuk's daughters (who studied Chaldaeic with their father), would ever have dreamed of doing that. He imagined their horror at the thought, and a picture, compound of Jemima, Kezia, and Kerenhappuch, rose before him.

Down the hill, out from beneath the dark green solid foliaged elder bushes, there came a rush of dogs.

"Save us," said Ralph, who saw himself discovered, "the deil's in the lassie; she'll have the dogs on me!"—an expression he had learned from John Bairdison, his father's "man," [Footnote: Church officer and minister's servant.] who in an unhallowed youth had followed the sea.

Then he would have reproved himself for the unlicensed exclamation as savouring of the "minced oath," had he not been taken up with watching the dogs. There were two of them. One was a large, rough deerhound, clean cut about the muzzle, shaggy everywhere else, which ran first, taking the hedges in his stride. The other was a small, short-haired collie, which, with his ears laid back and an air of grim determination not to be left behind, followed grimly after. The collie went under the hedges, diving instinctively for the holes which the hares had made as they went down to the water for their evening drink. Both dogs crossed to windward of him, racing for their mistress. When they reached the green level where the great tubs stood they leaped upon her with short sharp barks of gladness. She fended them off again with gracefully impatient hand; then bending low, she pointed to the loch-side a quarter of a mile below, where a herd of half a dozen black Galloway cows, necked with the red and white of the smaller Ayrshires, could be seen pushing its way through the lush heavy grass of the water meadow.

"Away by there! Fetch them, Roger!" she cried. "Haud at them—the kye's in the meadow!"

The dogs darted away level. The cows continued their slow advance, browsing as they went, but in a little while their dark fronts were turned towards the dogs as after a momentary indecision they recognized an enemy. With a startled rush the herd drove through the meadow and poured across the unfenced road up to the hill pasture which they had left, whose scanty grasses had doubtless turned slow bovine thoughts to the coolness of the meadow grass, and the pleasure of standing ruminant knee-deep in the river, with wavy tail nicking the flies in the shade.

For a little while Ralph Peden breathed freely again, but his satisfaction was short-lived. One girl was discomposing enough, but here were two. Moreover the new-comer, having arranged some blankets in a tub to her satisfaction, calmly tucked up her skirts in a professional manner and got bare-foot into the tub beside them. Then it dawned upon Ralph, who was not very instructed on matters of household economy, that he had chanced upon a Galloway blanket-washing; and that, like the gentleman who spied upon Musidora's toilet, of whom he had read in Mr. James Thomson's Seasons, he might possibly see more than he had come out to see.

Yet it was impossible to rise composedly and take his way manseward. Ralph wished now that he had gone at the first alarm. It had become so much more difficult now, as indeed it always does in such cases. Moreover, he was certain that these two vagabonds of curs would return. And they would be sure to find him out. Dogs were unnecessary and inconvenient beasts, always sniffing and nosing about. He decided to wait. The new-comer of the kilts was after all no Naiad or Hebe. Her outlines did not resemble to any marked degree the plates in his excellent classical dictionary. She was not short in stature, but so strong and of a complexion so ruddily beaming above the reaming white which filled the blanket tub, that her mirthful face shone like the sun through an evening mist.

But Ralph did not notice that, in so far as she could, she had relieved the taller maiden of the heavier share of the work; and that her laugh was hung on a hair trigger, to go off at every jest and fancy of Winsome Charteris. All this is to introduce Miss Meg Kissock, chief and favoured maidservant at the Dullarg farm, and devoted worshipper of Winsome, the young mistress thereof. Meg indeed, would have thanked no one for an introduction, being at all times well able (and willing) to introduce herself.

It had been a shock to Ralph Peden when Meg Kissock walked up from the lane-side barefoot, and when she cleared the decks for the blanket tramping. But he had seen something like it before on the banks of the water of Leith, then running clear and limpid over its pebbles, save for a flour-mill or two on the lower reaches. But it was altogether another thing when, plain as print, he saw his first goddess of the shining water-pails sit calmly down on the great granite boulder in the shadow of the bridge, and take one small foot in her hand with the evident intention of removing her foot-gear and occupying the second tub.

The hot blood surged in responsive shame to Ralph Peden's cheeks and temples. He started up. Meg Kissock was tramping the blankets rhythmically, holding her green kirtle well up with both hands, and singing with all her might. The goddess of the shining pails was also happily unconscious, with her face to the running water. Ralph bent low and hastened through a gap in the fence towards the shade of the elder bushes on the slope. He did not run—he has never acknowledged that; but he certainly came almost indistinguishably near it. As soon, however, as he was really out of sight, he actually did take to his heels and run in the direction of the manse, disconcerted and demoralized.

The dogs completed his discomfiture, for they caught sight of his flying figure and gave chase—contenting themselves, however, with pausing on the hillside where Ralph had been lying, with indignant barkings and militant tails high crested in air.

Winsome Charteris went up to the broom bushes which fringed the slope to find out what was the matter with Tyke and Roger. When she got there, a slim black figure was just vanishing round the white bend of the Far Away Turn. Winsome whistled low this time, and without putting even one finger into her mouth.

CHAPTER II
THE MOTHER OF KING LEMUEL

It was not till Ralph Peden had returned to the study of the manse of the Marrow kirk of Dullarg, and the colour induced by exercise had had time to die out of his naturally pale cheeks, that he remembered that he had left his Hebrew Bible and Lexicon, as well as a half-written exegesis on an important subject, underneath the fatal whin bush above the bridge over the Grannoch water. He would have been glad to rise and seek it immediately—a task which, indeed, no longer presented itself in such terrible colours to him. He found himself even anxious to go. It would be a serious thing were he to lose his father's Lexicon and Mr. Welsh's Hebrew Bible. Moreover, he could not bear the thought of leaving the sheets of his exposition of the last chapter of Proverbs to be the sport of the gamesome Galloway winds—or, worse thought, the laughing-stock of gamesome young women who whistled with two fingers in their mouths.

Yet the picture of the maid of the loch which rose before him struck him as no unpleasant one. He remembered for one thing how the sun shone through the tangle of her hair. But he had quite forgotten, on the other hand, at what part of his exegesis he had left off. It was, however, a manifest impossibility for him to slip out again. Besides, he was in mortal terror lest Mr. Welsh should ask for his Hebrew Bible, or offer to revise his chapter of the day with him. All the afternoon he was uneasy, finding no excuse to take himself away to the loch-side in order to find his Bible and Lexicon.

"I understand you have been studying, with a view to license, the last chapter of the Proverbs of Solomon?" said Gilbert Welsh, interrogatively, bending his shaggy brows and pouting his underlip at the student.

The Marrow minister was a small man, with a body so dried and twisted ("shauchelt" was the local word) that all the nerve stuff of a strong nature had run up to his brain, so that when he walked he seemed always on the point of falling forward, overbalanced by the weight of his cliff-like brow.

"Ralph, will you ground the argument of the mother of King Lemuel in this chapter? But perhaps you would like to refer to the original Hebrew?" said the minister.

"Oh, no," interrupted Ralph, aghast at the latter suggestion, "I do not need the text—thank you, sir."

But, in spite of his disclaimer, he devoutly desired to be where the original text and his written comment upon it were at that moment—which, indeed, was a consummation even more devoutly to be wished than he had any suspicion of. The Marrow minister leaned his head on his hand and looked waitingly at the young man.

Ralph recalled himself with an effort. He had to repeat to himself that he was in the manse study, and almost to pinch his knee to convince himself of the reality of his experiences. But this was not necessary a second time, for, as he sat hastily down on one of Allen Welsh's hard-wood chairs, a prickle from the gorse bush which he had brought back with him from Loch Grannoch side was argument sharp enough to convince Bishop Berkeley.

"Compose yourself to answer my question," said the minister, with some slight severity. Ralph wondered silently if even a minister of the Marrow kirk in good standing, could compose himself on one whin prickle for certain, and the probability of several others developing themselves at various angles hereafter.

Ralph "grounded" himself as best as he could, explaining the views of the mother of King Lemuel as to the woman of virtue and faithfulness. He seemed to himself to have a fluency and a fervour in exposition to which he had been a stranger. He began to have new views about the necessity for the creation of Eve. Woman might possibly, after all, be less purely gratuitous than he had supposed.

"The woman who is above rubies," said he, "is one who rises early to care for the house, who oversees the handmaids as they cleanse the household stuffs—in a" (he just saved himself from saying "in a black pot")—"in a fitting vessel by the rivers of water."

"Well put and correctly mandated," said Mr. Welsh, very much pleased. There was unction about this young man. Though a bachelor by profession, he loved to hear the praises of good women; for he had once known one.

"She openeth her mouth with wisdom; and—"

Here Ralph paused, biting his tongue to keep from describing the picture which rose before him.

"And what," said the minister, tentatively, leaning forward to look into the open face of the young man, "what is the distinction or badge of true beauty and favour of countenance, as so well expressed by the mother of King Lemuel?"

"A LILAC SUNBONNET!" said Ralph Peden, student in divinity.

CHAPTER III
A TREASURE-TROVE

Winsome CHARTERIS was a self-possessed maid, but undeniably her heart beat faster when she found on the brae face, beneath the bush of broom, two books the like of which she had never seen before, as well as an open notebook with writing upon it in the neatest and delicatest of hands. First, as became a prudent woman of experience, she went up to the top of the hill to assure herself that the owner of this strange treasure was not about to return. Then she carefully let down her high-kilted print dress till only her white feet "like little mice" stole in and out. It did not strike her that this sacrifice to the conventions was just a trifle belated.

As she returned she said "Shoo!" at every tangled bush, and flapped her apron as if to scare whatever curious wild fowl might have left behind it in its nest under the broom such curious nest- eggs as two great books full of strange, bewitched-looking printing, and a note-book of curious and interesting writings. Then, with a half sigh of disappointment, Winsome Charteris sat herself down to look into this matter. Meg Kissock from the bridge end showed signs of coming up to see what she was about; but Winsome imperiously checked the movement.

"Bide where you are, Meg; I'll be down with you presently."

She turned over the great Hebrew Bible reverently. "A. Welsh" was written on the fly-leaf. She had a strange idea that she had seen it before. It seemed somehow thrillingly familiar.

"That's the minister's Hebrew Bible book, no doubt," she said. "For that's the same kind of printing as between the double verses of the hundred-and-nineteenth Psalm in my grandfather's big Bible," she continued, sapiently shaking her head till the crispy ringlets tumbled about her eyes, and she had impatiently to toss them aside.

She laid the Bible down and peeped into the other strange-looking book. There were single words here of the same kind as in the other, but the most part was in ordinary type, though in a language of which she could make nothing. The note-book was a resource. It was at least readable, and Winsome Charteris began expectantly to turn it over. But something stirred reprovingly in her heart. It seemed as if she were listening to a conversation not meant for her. So she kept her finger on the leaf, but did not turn it.

"No," she said, "I will not read it. It is not meant for me." Then, after a pause, "At least I will only read this page which is open, and then look at the beginning to see whose it is; for, you know, I may need to send it back to him." The back she had seen vanish round the Far Away Turn demanded the masculine pronoun.

She lifted the book and read:

"Alas!" (so ran the writing, fluent and clear, small as printer's type, Ralph Peden's beautiful Hellenic script), "alas, that the good qualities of the housewives of Solomon's days are out of date and forgotten in these degenerate times! Women, especially the younger of them, are become gadabouts, chatterers in the public ways, idle, adorners of their vain selves, pamperers of their frail tabernacles—"

Winsome threw down the book and almost trod upon it as upon a snake.

"'Tis some city fop," she said, stamping her foot, "who is tired of the idle town dames. I wonder if he has ever seen the sun rise or done a day's work in his life? If only I had the wretch! But I will read no more!"

In token of the sincerity of the last assertion, she picked up the note-book again. There was little more to read. It was at this point that the humble-bee had startled the writer.

But underneath there were woids faintly scrawled in pencil: "Must concentrate attention"—"The proper study of mankind is"—this last written twice, as if the writer were practising copy-lines absently. Then at the very bottom was written, so faintly that hardly any eyes but Winsome's could have read the words:

"Of all colours I do love the lilac. I wonder all maids do not wear gear of that hue!"

"Oh!" said Winsome Charteris quickly.

Then she gathered up the books very gently, and taking a kerchief from her neck, she folded the two great books within it, fastening them with a cunning knot. She was carrying them slowly up towards the farm town of Craig Ronald in her bare arms when Ralph Peden sat answering his catechism in the study at the manse. She entered the dreaming courtyard, and walked sedately across its silent sun-flooded spaces without a sound. She passed the door of the cool parlour where her grandfather and grandmother sat, the latter with her hands folded and her great tortoiseshell spectacles on her nose, taking her afternoon nap. A volume of Waverley lay beside her.

Into her own white little room Winsome went, and laid the bundle of books in the bottom of the wall-press, which was lined with sheets of the Cairn Edward Miscellany. She looked at it some time before she shut the door.

"His name is Ralph," she said. "I wonder how old he is—I shall know tomorrow, because he will come back; but—I would like to know tonight."

She sighed a little—so light a breath that it was only the dream of a sigh. Then she looked at the lilac sunbonnet, as if it ought to have known.

"At any rate he has very good taste," she said.

But the lilac sunbonnet said never a word.

CHAPTER IV
A CAVALIER PURITAN

The farm town of Craig Ronald drowsed in the quiet of noon. In the open court the sunshine triumphed, and only the purple-grey marsh mallows along the side of the house under the windows gave any sign of life. In them the bees had begun to hum at earliest dawn, an hour and a half before the sun looked over the crest of Ben Gairn. They were humming busily still. In all the chambers of the house there was the same reposeful stillness. Through them Winsome Charteris moved with free, light step. She glanced in to see that her grandfather and grandmother were wanting for nothing in their cool and wide sitting-room, where the brown mahogany-cased eight- day clock kept up an unequal ticking, like a man walking upon two wooden legs of which one is shorter than the other.

It said something for Winsome Charteris and her high-hearted courage, that what she was accustomed to see in that sitting-room had no effect upon her spirits. It was a pleasant room enough, with two windows looking to the south—little round-budded, pale- petalled monthly roses nodding and peeping within the opened window-frames. Sweet it was with a great peace, every chair covered with old sprigged chintz, flowers of the wood and heather from the hill set in china vases about it. The room where the old folk dwelt at Craig Ronald was fresh within as is the dew on sweetbrier. Fresh, too, was the apparel of her grandmother, the flush of youth yet on her delicate cheek, though the Psalmist's limit had long been passed for her.

As Winsome looked within,

"Are ye not sleeping, grandmother?" she said.

The old lady looked up with a resentful air.

"Sleepin'! The lassie's gane gyte! [out of her senses]. What for wad I be sleepin' in the afternune? An' me wi' the care o' yer gran'faither—sic a handling, him nae better nor a bairn, an' you a bit feckless hempie wi' yer hair fleeing like the tail o' a twa- year-auld cowt! [colt]. Sleepin' indeed! Na, sleepin's nane for me!"

The young girl came up and put her arms about her grandmother.

"That's rale unceevil o' ye, noo, Granny Whitemutch!" she said, speaking in the coaxing tones to which the Scots' language lends itself so easily, "an' it's just because I hae been sae lang at the blanket-washin', seein' till that hizzy Meg. An' ken ye what I saw!-ane o' the black dragoons in full retreat, grannie; but he left his camp equipage ahint him, as the sergeant said when—Ye ken the story, grannie. Ye maun hae been terrible bonny in thae days!"

"'Deed I'm nane sae unbonny yet, for a' yer helicat flichtmafleathers, sprigget goons, an' laylac bonnets," said the old lady, shaking her head till the white silk top-knots trembled. "No, nor I'm nane sae auld nayther. The gudeman in the corner there, he's auld and dune gin'ye like, but no me—no me! Gin he warna spared to me, I could even get a man yet," continued the lively old lady, "an' whaur wad ye be then, my lass, I wad like to ken?"

"Perhaps I could get one too, grannie," she said. And she shook her head with an air of triumph. Winsome kissed her grandmother gently on the brow.

"Nane o' yer Englishy tricks an' trokin's," said she, settling the white muslin band which she wore across her brow wrinkleless and straight, where it had been disarrayed by the onslaught of her impulsive granddaughter.

"Aye," she went on, stretching out a hand which would have done credit to a great dame, so white and slender was it in spite of the hollows which ran into a triangle at the wrist, and the pale- blue veins which the slight wrinkles have thrown into relief.

"An' I mind the time when three o' his Majesty's officers—nane o' yer militia wi' horses that rin awa' wi' them ilka time they gang oot till exerceese, but rale sodgers wi' sabre-tashies to their heels and spurs like pitawtie dreels. Aye, sirs, but that was before I married an elder in the Kirk o' the Marrow. I wasna twenty-three when I had dune wi' the gawds an' vanities o' this wicked world."

"I saw a minister lad the day—a stranger," said Winsome, very quietly.

"Sirce me," returned her grandmother briskly; "kenned I e'er the like o' ye, Winifred Chayrteris, for licht-heedit-ness an' lack o' a' common sense! Saw a minister an' ne'er thocht, belike, o' sayin' cheep ony mair nor if he had been a wutterick [weasel]. An' what like was he, na? Was he young, or auld—or no sae verra auld, like mysel'? Did he look like an Establisher by the consequence o' the body, or—"

"But, grannie dear, how is it possible that I should ken, when all that I saw of him was but his coat-tails? It was him that was running away."

"My certes," said grannie, "but the times are changed since my day! When I was as young as ye are the day it wasna sodger or minister ayther that wad hae run frae the sicht o' me. But a minister, and a fine, young-looking man, I think ye said," continued Mistress Walter Skirving anxiously.

"Indeed, grandmother, I said nothing—" began Winsome.

"Haud yer tongue, Deil's i' the lassie, he'll be comin' here. Maybes he's comin' up the loan this verra meenit. Get me my best kep [cap], the French yin o' Flanders lawn trimmed wi' Valenceenes lace that Captain Wildfeather, of his Majesty's—But na, I'll no think o' thae times, I canna bear to think o' them wi' ony complaisance ava. But bring me my kep—haste ye fast, lassie!"

Obediently Winsome went to her grandmother's bedroom and drew from under the bed the "mutch" box lined with pale green paper, patterned with faded pink roses. She did not smile when she drew it out. She was accustomed to her grandmother's ways. She too often felt the cavalier looking out from under her Puritan teaching; for the wild strain of the Gordon blood held true to its kind, and Winsome's grandmother had been a Gordon at Lochenkit, whose father had ridden with Kenmure in the great rebellion.

When she brought the white goffered mutch with its plaits and puckers, granny tried it on in various ways, Winsome meanwhile holding a small mirror before her.

"As I was sayin', I renounced thinkin' aboot the vanities o' youth langsyne. Aye, it'll be forty years sin'—for ye maun mind that I was marriet whan but a lassie. Aye me, it's forty-five years since Ailie Gordon, as I was then, wed wi' Walter Skirving o' Craig Ronald (noo o' his ain chammer neuk, puir man, for he'll never leave it mair)," added she with a brisk kind of acknowledgment towards the chair of the semi-paralytic in the corner.

There silent and unregarding Walter Skirving sat—a man still splendid in frame and build, erect in his chair, a shawl over his knees even in this day of fervent heat, looking out dumbly on the drowsing, humming world of broad, shadowless noonshine, and often also on the equable silences of the night.

"No that I regret it the day, when he is but the name o' the man he yince was. For fifty years since there was nae lad like Walter Skirving cam into Dumfries High Street frae Stewartry or frae Shire. No a fit in buckled shune sae licht as his, his weel-shapit leg covered wi' the bonny 'rig-an'-fur' stockin' that I knitted mysel' frae the cast on o' the ower-fauld [over-fold] to the bonny white forefit that sets aff the blue sae weel. Walter Skirving could button his knee-breeks withoot bendin' his back—that nane could do but the king's son himsel'; an' sic a dancer as he was afore guid an' godly Maister Cauldsowans took hand o' him at the tent, wi' preachin' a sermon on booin' the knee to Baal. Aye, aye, its a' awa'—an' its mony the year I thocht on it, let alane thocht on wantin' back thae days o' vanity an' the pride o' sinfu' youth!"

"Tell me about the officer men, granny," said Winsome.

"'Deed wull I no. It wad be mair tellin' ye gin ye were learnin' yer Caritches" [Westminster Catechism].

"But, grandmammy dear, I thought that you said that the officer men ran away from you—"

"Hear till her! Rin frae me? Certes, ye're no blate. They cam' frae far an' near to get a word wi' me. Na, there was nae rinnin' frae a bonny lass in thae days. Weel, there was three o' them; an' they cam' ower the hill to see the lasses, graund in their reed breeks slashed wi' yellow. An' what for no, they war his Majesty's troopers; an' though nae doot they had been on the wrang side o' the dyke, they were braw chiels for a' that!"

"An' they cam' to see you, granny?" asked Winsome, who approved of the subject.

"What else—but they got an unco begunk [cheat]. Ye see, my faither had bocht an awfu' thrawn young bull at the Dumfries fair, an' he had been gaun gilravagin' aboot; an' whaur should the contrary beast betak' himsel' to but into the Roman camp on Craig Ronald bank, where the big ditch used to be? There we heard him routin' for three days till the cotmen fand him i' the hinderend, an' poo'ed him oot wi' cart-rapes. But when he got oot—certes, but he was a wild beast! He got at Jock Hinderlands afore he could climb up a tree; an', fegs, he gaed up a tree withoot clim'in', I'se warrant, an' there he hung, hanket by the waistband o' his breeks, baa-haain' for his minnie to come and lift him doon, an' him as muckle a clampersome [awkward] hobbledehoy as ever ye saw!

"Then what did Carlaverock Jock do but set his heid to a yett [gate] and ding it in flinders; fair fire-wood he made o't; an' sae, rampagin' into the meadow across whilk," continued the old lady, with a rising delight in her eye, "the three cavalry men were comin' to see me, wi' the spurs on them jangling clear. Reed breeks did na suit Jock's taste at the best o' times, and he had no been brocht up to countenance yellow facin's. So the three braw King George's sodgers that had dune sic graund things at Waterloo took the quickest road through the meadow. Captain St. Clair, he trippit on his sword, an' was understood to cry oot that he had never eaten beef in his life. Ensign

Withershins threw his shako ower his shoother and jumpit intil the water, whaur he expressed his opinion o' Carlaverock Jock stan'in' up to his neck in Luckie Mowatt's pool—the words I dinna juist call to mind at this present time, which, indeed, is maybe as weel; but it was Lieutenant Lichtbody, o' his Majesty's Heavy Dragoons, that cam' aff at the waurst. He made for the stane dyke, the sven-fite march dyke that rins up the hill, ye ken. Weel, he made as if he wad mak' ower it, but Boreland'a big Heelant bull had heard the routin' o' his friend Carlaverock Jock, an' was there wi' his horns spread like a man keppin' yowes [catching sheep]. Aye, my certes!" here the old lady paused, overcome by the humour of her recollections, laughing in her glee a delightfully catching and mellow laugh, in which Winsome joined.

"Sae there was my braw beau, Lieutenant Lichtbody, sittin' on his hunkers on the dyke tap girnin' at Carlaverock Jock an' the Boreland Hielantman on baith sides o' him, an' tryin' tae hit them ower the nose wi' the scabbard o' his sword, for the whinger itsel' had drappit oot in what ye micht ca' the forced retreat. It was bonny, bonny to see; an' whan the three cam' up the loanin' the neist day, 'Sirs,' I said, 'I'm thinkin' ye had better be gaun. I saw Carlaverock Jock the noo, fair tearin' up the greensward. It wudna be bonny gin his Majesty's officers had twice to mak' sae rapid a march to the rear—an' you, Lieutenant Lichtbody, canna hae a'thegither gotten the better o' yer lang sederunt on the tap o' the hill dyke. It's a bonny view that ye had. It was a peety that ye had forgotten yer perspective glasses.'

"And wad ye believe it, lassie, the threesome turned on the braid o' their fit an' marched doon the road withoot as muckle as Fair- guid-e'en or Fair-guid-day!"

"And what said ye, grannie dear?" said Winsome, who sat on a low seat looking up at her granny.

"O lassie, I juist set my braid hat ower my lug wi' the bonny white cockade intil't an' gied them 'The Wee, Wee German Lairdie' as they gaed doon the road, an' syne on the back o't:

"'Awa, Whigs, awa'!
Ye're but a pack— —'"

But the great plaid-swathed figure of Winsome's grandfather turned at the words of the long-forgotten song as though waking from a deep sleep. A slumberous fire gleamed momentarily in his eye.

"Woman," he said, "hold your peace; let not these words be heard in the house of Walter Skirving!"

Having thus delivered himself, the fire faded out of his eyes dead as black ashes; he turned to the window, and lost himself again in meditation, looking with steady eyes across the ocean of sunshine which flooded the valley beneath.

His wife gave him no answer. She seemed scarce to have heard the interruption. But Winsome went across and pulled the heavy plaid gently off her grandfather's shoulder. Then she stood quietly by him with one hand upon his head and with the other she gently stroked his brow. A milder light grew in his dull eye, and he put up his hand uncertainly as if to take hers.

"But what for should I be takin' delicht in speakin' o' thae auld unsanctified regardless days," said her grandmother, "that 'tis mony a year since I hae ta'en ony pleesure in thinkin' on? Gae wa', ye hempie that ye are!" she cried, turning with a sudden and uncalled-for sparkle of temper on her granddaughter; "There's nae time an' little inclination in this hoose for yer flichty conversation. I wonder muckle that yer thouchts are sae set on the vanities o' young men. And such are all that delight in them." She went on somewhat irrelevantly, "Did not godly Maister Cauldsowans redd up [settle] the doom o' such—'all desirable young men riding upon horses—'"

"An' I'll gae redd up the dairy, an' kirn the butter, grannie!" said Winsome Charteris, breaking in on the flow of her grandmother's reproaches.

CHAPTER V
A LESSON IN BOTANY

No lassie in all the hill country went forth more heart-whole into the June morning than Winsome Charteris. She was not, indeed, wholly a girl of the south uplands. Her grandmother was never done reminding her of her "Englishy" ways, which, according to that authority, she had contracted during those early years she had spent in Cumberland. From thence she had been brought to the farm town of Craig Ronald, soon after the death of her only uncle, Adam Skirving—whose death, coming after the loss of her own mother, had taken such an effect upon her grandfather that for years he had seldom spoken, and now took little interest in the ongoings of the farm.

Walter Skirving was one of a class far commoner in Galloway sixty years ago than now. He was a "bonnet laird" of the best type, and his farm, which included all kinds of soil—arable and pasture, meadow and moor, hill pasture and wood—was of the value of about L300 a year, a sum sufficient in those days to make him a man of substance and consideration in the country.

He had been all his life, except for a single year in his youth when he broke bounds, a Marrow man of the strictest type; and it had been the wonder and puzzle of his life (to others, not to himself) how he came to make up to Ailie Gordon, the daughter of the old moss-trooping Lochenkit Gordons, that had ridden with the laird of Redgauntlet in the killing time, and more recently had been out with Maxwell of Nithsdale, and Gordon of Kenmure, to strike a blow for the "King-over-the-Water." And to this very day, though touched with a stroke which prevented her from moving far out of her chair, Ailie Skirving showed the good blood and high-hearted lightsomeness that had won the young laird of Craig Ronald upon the Loch Grannoch side nearly fifty years before.

It was far more of a wonder how Ailie Gordon came to take Walter Skirving. It may be that she felt in her heart the accent of a true man in the unbending, nonjuring elder of the Marrow kirk. Two great heart-breaks had crossed their lives: the shadow of the life story of Winsome's mother, that earlier Winsome whose name had not been heard for twenty years in the house of Craig Ronald; and the more recent death of Adam, the strong, silent, chivalrous-natured son who had sixteen years ago been killed, falling from his horse as he rode home alone one winter's night from Dumfries.

It was a natural thing to be in love with Winsome Charteris. It seemed natural to Winsome herself. Ever since she was a little lass running to school in Keswick, with a touse of lint-white locks blowing out in the gusts that came swirling off Skiddaw, Winsome had always been conscious of a train of admirers. The boys liked to carry her books, and were not so ashamed to walk home with her, as even at six years of age young Cumbrians are wont to be in the company of maids. Since she came to Galloway, and opened out with each succeeding year, like the bud of a moss rose growing in a moist place, Winsome had thought no more of masculine admiration than of the dull cattle that "goved" [stared stupidly] upon her as she picked her deft way among the stalls in the byre. In all Craig Ronald there was nothing between the hill and the best room that did not bear the mark of Winsome's method and administrative capacity. In perfect dependence upon Winsome, her granny had gradually abandoned all the management of the house to her, so that at twenty that young woman was a veritable Napoleon of finance and capacity. Only old Richard Clelland of the Boreland, grave and wise pillar of the kirk by law established, still transacted her market business and banked her siller—being, as he often said, proud to act as "doer" for so fair a principal. So it happened that all the reins of government about this tiny lairdship of one farm were in the strong and capable hands of a girl of twenty.

And Meg Kissock was her true admirer and faithful slave—Winsome's heavy hand, too, upon occasion; for all the men on the farm stood in awe of Meg's prowess, and very especially of Meg's tongue. So also the work fell mostly upon these two, and in less measure upon a sister of Meg's, Jess Kissock, lately returned from England, a young lady whom we have already met.

During the night and morning Winsome had studied with some attention the Hebrew Bible, in which the name Allan Welsh appeared, as well as the Latin Luther Commentary, and the Hebrew Lexicon, on the first page of which the name of Ralph Peden was written in the same neat print hand as in the note-book.

This was the second day of the blanket-washing, and Winsome, having in her mind a presentiment that the proprietor of these learned quartos would appear to claim his own, carried them down to the bridge, where Meg and her sister were already deep in the mysteries of frothing tubs and boiling pots. Winsome from the broomy ridge could hear the shrill "giffgaff" [give and take] of their colloquy. She sat down under Ralph's very broom bush, and absently turned over the leaves of the note-book, catching sentences here and there.

"I wonder how old he is?" she said, meditatively; "his coat-tails looked old, but the legs went too lively for an old man; besides, he likes maids to be dressed in lilac—" She paused still more thoughtfully. "Well, we shall see." She bent over and pulled the milky-stalked, white-seeded head of a dandelion. Taking it between the finger and thumb of her left hand she looked critically at it as though it were a glass of wine. "He is tall, and he is fair, and his age is—"

Here she pouted her pretty lips and blew.

"One—ha, ha!—he was an active infant when he ran from the blanket-tramping—two, three, four—"

Some tiny feather-headed spikelets disengaged themselves unwillingly from the round and venerable downpolled dandelion. They floated lazily up between the tassels of the broom upon the light breeze.

"Five, six, seven, eight—faith, he was a clean-heeled laddie yon. Ye couldna see his legs or coat-tails for stour as he gaed roon' the Far Away Turn."

Winsome was revelling in her broad Scots. She had learned it from her grandmother.

"Nine, ten, eleven, twelve, thirteen, fourteen, fifteen—I'll no can set the dogs on him then—sixteen, seventeen, eighteen—dear me, this is becoming interesting."

The plumules were blowing off freely now, like snow from the eaves on a windy day in winter.

"Nineteen, twenty, twenty-one—I must reverence my elders. If I don't blow stronger he'll turn out to be fifty—twenty-three, twenty-f—"

A shadow fell across the daintily-held dandelion and lay a blue patch on the grass. Only one pale grey star stood erect on the stem, the vacant green sheathing of the calyx turning suddenly down.

"TWENTY-FOUR!—" said Ralph Peden quietly, standing with his hat in his hand and an eager flush on his cheek. The last plumule floated away.

Winsome Charteris had risen instinctively, and stood looking with crimson cheeks and quicker-coming breath at this young man who came upon her in the nick of time.

He was startled and a little indignant. So they stood facing one another while one might count a score—silent and drinking each the other in, with that flashing transference of electric sympathy possible only to the young and the innocent.

It was the young man who spoke first. Winsome was a little indignant that he should dare to come upon her while so engaged. Not, of course, that she cared for a moment what he thought of her, but he ought to have known better than to have stolen upon her while she was behaving in such a ridiculous, childish way. It showed what he was capable of.

"My name is Ralph Peden," he said humbly. "I came from Edinburgh the day before yesterday. I am staying with Mr. Welsh at the manse."

Winsome Charteris glanced down at the books and blushed still more deeply. The Hebrew Bible and Lexicon lay harmlessly enough on the grass, and the Luther was swinging in a frivolous and untheological way on the strong, bent twigs of broom. But where was the note-book? Like a surge of Solway tide the remembrance came over her that, when she had plucked the dandelion for her soothsaying, she had thrust it carelessly into the bosom of her lilac-sprigged gown. Indeed, a corner of it peeped out at this moment. Had he seen it?—monstrous thought! She knew young men and the interpretations that they put upon nothings! This, in spite of his solemn looks and mantling bashfulness, was a young man.

"Then I suppose these are yours," said Winsome, turning sideways towards the indicated articles so as to conceal the note-book. The young man removed his eyes momentarily from her face and looked in the direction of the books. He seemed to have entirely forgotten what it was that had brought him to Loch Grannoch bridge so early this June morning. Winsome took advantage of his glance to feel that her sunbonnet sat straight, and as her hand was on its way to her clustering curls she took this opportunity of thrusting Ralph's note-book into more complete concealment. Then her hands went up to her head only to discover that her sunbonnet had slipped backward, and was now hanging down her back by the strings.

Ralph Peden looked up at her, apparently entirely satisfied. What was a note-book to him now? He saw the sunbonnet resting upon the wavy distraction of the pale gold hair. He had a luxurious eye for colour. That lilac and gold went well together, was his thought.

Trammelled by the fallen head-gear, Winsome threw her head back, shaking out her tresses in a way that Ralph Peden never forgot. Then she caught at the strings of the errant bonnet.

"Oh, let it alone!" he suddenly exclaimed.

"Sir?" said Winsome Charteris—interrogatively, not imperatively. Ralph Peden, who had taken a step forward in the instancy of his appeal, came to himself again in a moment.

"I beg your pardon," he said very humbly, "I had no right—"

He paused, uncertain what to say.

Winsome Charteris looked up quickly, saw the simplicity of the young man, in one full eye-blink read his heart, then dropped her eyes again and said:

"But I thought you liked lilac sunbonnets!"

Ralph Peden had now his turn to blush. Hardly in the secret of his own heart had he said this thing. Only to Mr. Welsh had his forgetful tongue uttered the word that was in his mind, and which had covered since yesterday morn all the precepts of that most superfluous wise woman, the mother of King Lemuel.

"Are you a witch?" asked Ralph, blundering as an honest and bashful man may in times of distress into the boldest speech.

"You want to go up and see my grandmother, do you not?" said Winsome, gravely, for such conversation was not to be continued on any conditions.

"Yes," said the young man, perjuring himself with a readiness and facility most unbecoming in a student desiring letters of probation from the Protesting and Covenant-keeping Kirk of the Marrow.

Ralph Peden lightly picked up the books, which, as Winsome knew, were some considerable weight to carry.

"Do you find them quite safe?" she asked.

"There was a heavy dew last night," he answered, "but in spite of it they seem quite dry."

"We often notice the same thing on Loch Grannoch side," said Winsome.

"I thought—that is, I was under the impression—that I had left a small book with some manuscript notes!" said the young man, tentatively.

"It may have dropped among the broom," replied the simple maid.

Whereupon the two set to seeking, both bareheaded, brown cropped head and golden wilderness of tresses not far from one another, while the "book of manuscript notes" rose and fell to the quickened heart-beating of that wicked and deceitful girl, Winsome Charteris.

CHAPTER VI
CURLED EYELASHES

Now Meg Kissock could stand a great deal, and she would put up with a great deal to pleasure her mistress; but half an hour of loneliness down by the washing was overly much for her, and the struggle between loyalty and curiosity ended, after the manner of her sex, in the victory of the latter. As Ralph and Winsome continued to seek, they came time and again close together and the propinquity of flushed cheek and mazy ringlet stirred something in the lad's heart which had never been touched by the Mistresses Thriepneuk, who lived where the new houses of the Plainstones look over the level meadows of the Borough Muir. His father had often said within himself, as he walked the Edinburgh streets to visit some sick kirk member, as he had written to his friend Adam Welsh, "Has the lad a heart?" Had he seen him on that broomy knowe over the Grannoch water, he had not doubted, though he might well have been fearful enough of that heart's too sudden awakening.

Never before had the youth come within that delicate AURA of charm which radiates from the bursting bud of the finest womanhood. Ralph Peden had kept his affections ascetically virgin. His nature's finest juices had gone to feed the brain, yet all the time his heart had waited expectant of the revealing of a mystery. Winsome Charteris had come so suddenly into his life that the universe seemed newborn in a day. He sprang at once from the thought of woman as only an unexplained part of the creation, to the conception of her (meaning thereby Winsome Charteris) as an angel who had not lost her first estate.

It was a strange thing for Ralph Peden, as indeed it is to every true man, to come for the first time within the scope of the unconscious charms of a good girl. There is, indeed, no better solvent of a cold nature, no better antidote to a narrow education, no better bulwark of defence against frittering away the strength and solemnity of first love, than a sudden, strong plunge into its deep waters.

Like timid bathers, who run a little way into the tide and then run out again with ankles wet, fearful of the first chill, many men accustom themselves to love by degrees. So they never taste the sweetness and strength of it as did Ralph Peden in these days, when, never having looked upon a maid with the level summer lightning of mutual interest flashing in his eyes, he plunged into love's fathomless mysteries as one may dive upon a still day from some craggy platform among the westernmost isles into Atlantic depths.

Winsome's light summer dress touched his hand and thrilled the lad to his remotest nerve centres. He stood light-headed, taking in as only they twain looked over the loch with far-away eyes, that subtle fragrance, delicate and free, which like a garment clothed the maid of the Grannoch lochside.

"The water's on the boil," cried Meg Kissock, setting her ruddy shock of hair and blooming, amplified, buxom form above the knoll, wringing at the same time the suds from her hands, "an' I canna lift it aff mysel'."

Her mistress looked at her with a sudden suspicion. Since when had Meg grown so feeble?

"We had better go down," she said simply, turning to Ralph, who would have cheerfully assented had she suggested that they should together walk into the loch among the lily beds. It was the "we" that overcame him. His father had used the pronoun in quite a different sense. "WE will take the twenty-ninth chapter of second Chronicles this morning, Ralph—what do WE understand by this peculiar use of VAV CONVERSIVE?"

But it was quite another thing when Winsome Charteris said simply, as though he had been her brother:

"We had better go down!"

So they went down, taking the little stile at which Winsome had meditated over the remarks of Ralph Peden concerning the creation of Eve upon their way. Meg Kissock led the van, and took the dyke vigorously without troubling the steps, her kirtle fitting her for such exercises. Winsome came next, and Ralph stood aside to let her pass. She sprang up the low steps light as a feather, rested her fingertips for an appreciable fraction of a second on the hand which he instinctively held out, and was over before he realized that anything had happened. Yet it seemed that in that contact, light as a rose-leaf blown by the winds of late July against his cheek, his past life had been shorn clean away from all the future as with a sharp sword.

Ralph Peden had dutifully kissed his cousins Jemima, Kezia, and Kerenhappuch; but, on the whole, he had felt more pleasure when he had partaken of the excellent bannocks prepared for him by the fair hands of

Kerenhappuch herself. But this was wholly a new thing. His breath came suddenly short. He breathed rapidly as though to give his lungs more air. The atmosphere seemed to have grown rarer and colder. Indeed, it was a different world, and the blanket-washing itself was transferred to some deliciously homely outlying annex of paradise.

Yet it seemed the most natural thing in the world that he should be helping this girl, and he went forward with the greatest assurance to lift the black pot off the fire for her. The keen, acrid swirls of wood-smoke blew into his eyes, and the rank steam of yellow home-made soap, manufactured with bracken ash for lye, rose to his nostrils. Now, Ralph Peden was well made and strong. Spare in body but accurately compacted, if he had ever struggled with anything more formidable than the folio hide-hound Calvins and Turretins on his father's lower shelf in James's Court, he had been no mean antagonist.

But, though he managed with a great effort to lift the black pot off its gypsy tripod, he would have let the boiling contents swing dangerously against his legs had not Winsome caught sharply at his other hand and leaned over, so balancing the weight of the boiling water. So they walked down the path to where the tubs stood under the shade of the great ash-trees, with their sky-tossing, dry- rustling leaves. There Ralph set his burden down. Meg Kissock had been watching him keenly. She saw that he had severely burned his hand, and also that he said nothing whatever about it. He was a man. This gained for the young man Meg's hearty approval almost as much as his bashfulness and native good looks. What Meg Kissock did not know was that Ralph was altogether unconscious of the wound in his hand. It was a deeper wound which was at that time monopolising his thoughts. But this little incident was more than a thousand certificates in the eyes of Meg Kissock, and Meg's friendship was decidedly worth cultivating. Even for its own sake she did not give it lightly.

Before Winsome Charteris could release her hand, Ralph turned and said:

"Do you know you have not yet told me your name?"

Winsome did know it very well, but she only said, "My name is Winsome Charteris, and this is Meg Kissock."

"Winsome Charteris, Winsome Charteris," said Ralph's heart over and over again, and he had not even the grace to say "Thank you"; but Meg stepped up to shake him by the hand.

"I'm braw an' prood to ken ye, sir," said Meg. "That muckle sumph [stupid], Saunders Mowdiewort, telled me a' aboot ye comin' an' the terrible store o' lear [learning] ye hae. He's the minister's man, ye ken, an' howks the graves ower by at the parish kirk-yard, for the auld betheral there winna gang ablow three fit deep, and them that haes ill-tongued wives to haud doon disna want ony mistake—"

"Meg," said her mistress, "do not forget yourself."

"Deil a fear," said Meg; "it was auld Sim o' Glower-ower-'em, the wizened auld hurcheon [hedgehog], that set a big thruch stane ower his first wife; and when he buried his second in the neist grave, he just turned the broad flat stone. 'Guid be thankit!' he says, 'I had the forethocht to order a stane heavy eneuch to hand them baith doon!'"

"Get to the washing, Meg," said Winsome.

"Fegs!" returned Meg, "ye waur in nae great hurry yersel' doon aff the broomy knowe! What's a' the steer sae sudden like?"

Winsome disdained an answer, but stood to her own tub, where some of the lighter articles—pillow-slips, and fair sheets of "seventeen-hundred" linen were waiting her daintier hand.

As Winsome and Meg washed, Ralph Peden carried water, learning the wondrous science of carrying two cans over a wooden hoop; and in the frankest tutelage Winsome put her hand over his to teach him, and the relation of master and pupil asserted its ancient danger.

It had not happened to Winsome Charteris to meet any one to whom she was attracted with such frank liking. She had never known what it was to have a brother, and she thought that this clear-eyed young man might be a brother to her. It is a fallacy common among girls that young men desire them as sisters. Ralph himself was under no such illusion, or at least would not have been, had he had the firmness of mind to sit down half a mile from his emotions and coolly look them over. But in the meanwhile he was only conscious of a great and rising delight in his heart.

As Winsome Charteris bent above the wash-tub he was at liberty to observe how the blood mantled on the clear oval of her cheek. He had time to note—of course entirely as a philosopher—the pale purple shadow under the eyes, over which the dark, curling lashes came down like the fringe of the curtain of night.

"Why—I wonder why?" he said, and stopped aghast at his utterance aloud of his inmost thought.

"What do you wonder?" said Winsome, glancing up with a frank dewy freshness in her eyes.

"I wonder why—I wonder that you are able to do all this work," he said, with an attempt to turn the corner of his blunder.

Winsome shook her head.

"Now you are trying to be like other people," she said; "I do not think you will succeed. That was not what you were going to say. If you are to be my friend, you must speak all the truth to me and speak it always." A thing which, indeed, no man does to a woman. And, besides, nobody had spoken of Ralph Peden being a friend to her. The meaning was that their hearts had been talking while their tongues had spoken of other things; and though there was no thought of love in the breast of Winsome Charteris, already in the intercourse of a single morning she had given this young Edinburgh student of divinity a place which no other had ever attained to. Had she had a brother, she thought, what would he not have been to her? She felt specially fitted to have a brother. It did not occur to her to ask whether she would have carried her brother's college note-book, even by accident, where it could be stirred by the beating of her heart.

"Well," Ralph said at last, "I will tell you what I was wondering. You have asked me, and you shall know: I only wondered why your eyelashes were so much darker than your hair."

Winsome Charteris was not in the least disturbed.

"Ministers should occupy their minds with something else," she said, demurely. "What would Mr. Welsh say? I am sure he has never troubled his head about such things. It is not fitting," Winsome said severely.

"But I want to know," said this persistent young man, wondering at himself.

"Well," said Winsome, glancing up with mischief in her eye, "I suppose because I am a very lazy sort of person, and dark window- blinds keep out the light."

"But why are they curled up at the end?" asked unblushingly the author of the remarks upon Eve formerly quoted.

"It is time that you went up and saw my grandmother!" said Winsome, with great composure.

"Juist what I was on the point o' remarkin' mysel'!" said Meg Kissock.

CHAPTER VII
CONCERNING TAKING EXERCISE

Winsome and Ralph walked silently and composedly side by side up the loaning under the elder-trees, over the brook at the watering- place to which in her hoydenish girlhood Winsome had often ridden the horses when the ploughmen loosed Bell and Jess from the plough. In these days she rode without a side-saddle. Sometimes she did it yet when the spring gloamings were gathering fast, but no one knew this except Jock Forrest, the ploughman, who never told any more than he could help.

Silence deep as that of yesterday wrapped about the farmhouse of Craig Ronald. The hens were all down under the lee of the great orchard hedge, chuckling low to themselves, and nestling with their feathers spread balloon-wise, while they flirted the hot summer dust over them. Down where the grass was in shadow a mower was sharpening his blade. The clear metallic sound of the "strake" or sharpening strop, covered with pure white Loch Skerrow sand set in grease, which scythemen universally use in Galloway, cut through the slumberous hum of the noonday air like the blade itself through the grass. The bees in the purple flowers beneath the window boomed a mellow bass, and the grasshoppers made love by millions in the couch grass, chirring in a thousand fleeting raptures.

"Wait here while I go in," commanded Winsome, indicating a chair in the cool, blue-flagged kitchen, which Meg Kissock had marked out in white, with whorls and crosses of immemorial antiquity—the same that her Pictish forefathers had cut deep in the hard Silurian rocks of the southern uplands.

It was a little while before, in the dusk of the doorway Winsome appeared, looking paler and fairer and more infinitely removed from him than before. Instinctively he wished himself out with her again on the broomy knowe. He seemed somehow nearer to her there. Yet he followed obediently enough.

Within the shadowed "ben"-room of Craig Ronald all the morning this oddly assorted pair of old people had been sitting—as indeed every morning they sat, one busily reading and often looking up to talk; while the other, the master of the house himself, sat silent, a majestic and altogether pathetic figure, looking solemnly out with wide-open, dreamy eyes, waking to the actual world of speech and purposeful life only at rare intervals.

But Walter Skirving was keenly awake when Ralph Peden entered. It was in fact he, and not his partner, who spoke first—for Walter Skirving's wife had among other things learned when to be silent— which was, when she must.

"You honour my hoose," he said; "though it grieves me indeed that I canna rise to receive yin o' your family an' name! But what I have is at your service, for it was your noble faither that led the faithful into the wilderness on the day o' the Great Apostasy!"

The young man shook him by the hand. He had no bashfulness here. He was on his own ground. This was the very accent of the society in which he moved in Edinburgh.

"I thank you," he said, quietly and courteously, stepping back at once into the student of divinity; "I have often heard my father speak of you. You were the elder from the south who stood by him on that day. He has ever retained a great respect for you."

"It WAS a great day," Walter Skirving muttered, letting his arm rest on the little square deal table which stood beside him with his great Bible open upon it—"a great day—aye, Maister Peden's laddie i' my hoose! He's welcome, he's mair nor welcome."

So saying, he turned his eyes once more on the blue mist that filled the wide Grannoch Valley, and the bees hummed again in the honey-scented marshmallows so that all heard them.

"This is my grandmother," said Winsome, who stood quite quiet behind her chair, swinging the sunbonnet in her hand. From her flower-set corner the old lady held out her band. With a touch of his father's old-fashioned courtesy he stooped and kissed it. Winsome instinctively put her hand quickly behind her as though he had kissed that. Once such practices have a beginning, who knows where they may end? She had not expected it of him, though, curiously, she thought no worse of him for his gallantry.

But the lady of Craig Ronald was obviously greatly pleased.

"The lad has guid bluid in him. That's the minnie [mother] o' him, nae doot. She was a Gilchrist o' Linwood on Nithsdale. What she saw in your faither to tak' him I dinna ken ony mair than I ken hoo it cam' to pass that I am the mistress o' Walter Skirving's hoose the day.—Come oot ahint my chair, lassie; dinna be lauchin' ahint folks's backs. D'ye think I'm no mistress o' my ain hoose yet, for a' that ye are sic a grand hoosekeeper wi' your way o't."

The accusation was wholly gratuitous. Winsome had been grave with a great gravity. But she came obediently out, and seated herself on a low stool by her grandmother's side. There she sat, holding her hand, and leaning her elbow on her knee. Ralph thought he had never seen anything so lovely in his life—an observation entirely correct. The old lady was clad in a dress of some dark stiff material, softer than brocade, which, like herself, was more beautiful in its age than even in youth. Folds of snowy lawn covered her breast and fell softly about her neck, fastened there by a plain black pin. Her face was like a portrait by Henry Raeburn, so beautifully venerable and sweet. The twinkle in her brown eyes alone told of the forceful and restless spirit which was imprisoned within. She had been reading a new volume of the Great Unknown which the Lady Elizabeth had sent her over from the Big House of Greatorix. She had laid it down on the entry of the young man. Now she turned sharp upon him.

"Let me look at ye, Maister Ralph Peden. Whaur gat ye the 'Ralph'? That's nae westland Whig name. Aye, aye, I mind—what's comin' o' my memory? Yer grandfaither was auld Ralph Gilchrist; but ye dinna tak' after the Gilchrists—na, na, there was no ane o' them weel faured—muckle moo'd [large-mouthed] Gilchrists they ca'ed them. It'll be your faither that you favour."

And she turned him about for inspection with her hand.

"Grandmother—" began Winsome, anxious lest she should say something to offend the guest of the house. But the lady did not heed her gentle monition.

"Was't you that ran awa' frae a bonny lass yestreen?" she queried, sudden as a flash of summer lightning.

It was now the turn of both the younger folk to blush. Winsome reddened with vexation at the thought that he should think that she had seen him run and gone about telling of it. Ralph grew redder and redder, and remained speechless. He did not think of anything at all.

"I am fond of exercise," he said falteringly.

The gay old lady rippled into a delicious silver stream of laughter, a little thin, but charmingly provocative. Winsome did not join, but she looked up imploringly at her grandmother, leaning her head back till her tresses swept the ground.

When Mistress Skirving recovered herself,

"Exerceese, quo' he, heard ye ever the like o' that? In their young days lads o' speerit took their exerceese in comin' to see a bonny lass—juist as I was sayin' to Winifred yestreen nae faurer gane. Hoot awa', twa young folk! The simmer days are no lang. Waes me, but I had my share o' them! Tak' them while they shine, bankside an' burnside an' the bonny heather. Aince they bloomed for Ailie Gordon. Once she gaed hand in hand alang the braes, where noo she'll gang nae mair. Awa' wi' ye, ye're young an' honest. Twa auld cankered carles are no fit company for twa young folks like you. Awa' wi' ye; dinna be strange wi' his mither's bairn, say I—an' the guid man hae's spoken for the daddy o' him."

Thus was Ralph Peden made free of the Big Hoose of Craig Ronald.

CHAPTER VIII
THE MINISTER'S MAN ARMS EOR CONQUEST

Saunders Mowdiewort, minister's man and grave-digger, was going a sweethearting. He took off slowly the leathern "breeks" of his craft, sloughing them as an adder casts his skin. They collapsed upon the floor with a hideous suggestion of distorted human limbs, as Saunders went about his further preparations. Saunders was a great, soft-bodied, fair man, of the chuby flaxen type so rare in Scotland—the type which looks at home nowhere but along the south coast of England. Saunders was about thirty-five. He was a widower in search of a wife, and made no secret of his devotion to Margaret Kissock, the "lass" of the farm town of Craig Ronald.

Saunders was slow of speech when in company, and bashful to a degree. He was accustomed to make up his mind what he would say before venturing within the range of the sharp tongue of his well- beloved—an excellent plan, but one which requires for success both self-possession and a good memory. But for lack of these Saunders had made an excellent courtier.

Saunders made his toilet in the little stable of the manse above which he slept. As he scrubbed himself he kept up a constant sibilant hissing, as though he were an equine of doubtful steadiness with whom the hostler behooved to be careful. First he carefully removed the dirt down to a kind of Plimsoll load-line midway his neck; then he frothed the soap-suds into his red rectangular ears, which stood out like speaking trumpets; there he let it remain. Soap is for putting on the face, grease on the hair. It is folly then to wash either off. Besides being wasteful. His flaxen hair stood out in wet strands and clammy tags and tails. All the while Saunders kept muttering to himself:

"An' says I to her: 'Meg Kissock, ye're a bonny woman,' says I. 'My certie, but ye hae e'en like spunkies [will-o'-the-wisps] or maybes," said Saunders in a meditative tone. "I had better say 'like whurlies in a sky-licht.' It micht be considered mair lovin' like!"

"Then she'll up an' say: 'Saunders, ye mak' me fair ashamed to listen to ye. Be mensefu' [polite], can ye no?'"

This pleased Saunders so much that he slapped his thigh so that the pony started and clattered to the other side of his stall.

"Then I'll up an' tak' her roun' the waist, an' I'll look at her like this—" (here Saunders practised the effect of his fascinations in the glass, a panorama which was to some extent marred by the necessary opening of his mouth to enable the razor he was using to excavate the bristles out of the professional creases in his lower jaw. Saunders pulled down his mouth to express extra grief when a five-foot grave had been ordered. His seven-foot manifestations of respect for the deceased were a sight to see. He held the opinion that anybody that had no more 'conceit o' themsel'' [were so much left to themselves] than to be buried in a three-foot grave, did not deserve to be mourned at all. This crease, then, was one of Saunders's assets, and had therefore to be carefully attended to. Even love must not interfere with it.)

"Sae after that, I shall tak' her roun' the waist, juist like this—" said he, insinuating his left arm circumferentially. It was an ill-judged movement, for, instead of circling Meg Kissock's waist, he extended his arm round the off hindleg of Birsie, the minister's pony, who had become a trifle short tempered in his old age. Now it was upon that very leg and at that very place that, earlier in the day, a large buzzing horse-fly had temporarily settled. Birsie was in no condition, therefore, for argument upon the subject. So with the greatest readiness he struck straight out behind and took Saunders what he himself called a "dinnle on the elbuck." Nor was this all, for the razor suddenly levered upwards by Birsie's hoof added another and entirely unprofessional wrinkle to his face.

Saunders uprose in wrath, for the soap was stinging furiously in the cut, and expostulated with Birsie with a handful of reins which he lifted off the lid of the corn-chest.

"Ye ill-natured, thrawn, upsettin' blastie, ye donnart auld deevil!" he cried.

"Alexander Mowdiewort, gin ye desire to use minced oaths and braid oaths indiscriminately, ye shall not use them in my stable. Though ye be but a mere Erastian and uncertain in yer kirk membership, ye are at least an occasional hearer, whilk is better than naething, at the kirk o' the Marrow; and what is more to the point, ye are my own hired servant, and I desire that ye cease from makin' use o' any such expressions upon my premises."

"Weel, minister," said Saunders, penitently, "I ken brawly I'm i' the wrang; but ye ken yersel', gin ye had gotten a dinnle i' the elbuck that garred ye loup like a troot i' Luckie Mowatt's pool, or gin ye had cuttit yersel' wi' yer ain razor, wad 'Effectual Callin',' think ye, hae been the first word i' yer mooth? Noo, minister, fair Hornie!"

"At any rate," said the minister, "what I would have said or done is no excuse for you, as ye well know. But how did it happen?"

"Weel, sir, ye see the way o't was this: I was thinkin' to mysel', 'There's twa or three ways o' takin' the buiks intil the pulpit— There's the way consequential—that's Gilbert Prettiman o' the Kirkland's way. Did ever ye notice the body? He hauds the Bibles afore him as if he war Moses an' Aaron gaun afore Pharaoh, wi' the coat-taillies o' him fleein' oot ahint, an' his chin pointin' to the soon'in'-board o' the pulpit."

"Speak respectfully of the patriarchs," said Mr. Welsh sententiously. Saunders looked at him with some wonder expressed in his eyes.

"Far be it frae me," he said, "to speak lichtly o' ony ane o' them (though, to tell the truth, some o' them war gye boys). I hae been ower lang connectit wi' them, for I hae carriet the buiks for fifteen year, ever since my faither racket himsel' howkin' the grave o' yer predecessor, honest man, an' I hae leeved a' my days juist ower the wa' frae the kirk."

"But then they say, Saunders," said the minister, smilingly, "'the nearer the kirk the farther frae grace.'"

"'Deed, minister," said Saunders, "Grace Kissock is a nice bit lassie, but an' Jess will be no that ill in a year or twa, but o' a' the Kissocks commend me till Meg. She wad mak' a graund wife. What think ye, minister?"

Mr. Welsh relaxed his habitual severe sadness of expression and laughed a little. He was accustomed to the sudden jumps which his man's conversation was wont to take.

"Nay," he said, "but that is a question for you, Saunders. It is not I that think of marrying her."

"The Lord be thankit for that! for gin the minister gaed speerin', what chance wad there be for the betheral?"

"Have you spoken to Meg herself yet?" asked Mr. Welsh.

"Na," said Saunders; "I haena that, though I hae made up my mind to hae it oot wi' her this verra nicht—if sae it micht be that ye warna needin' me, that is—" he added, doubtfully, "but I hae guid reason to hope that Meg—"

"What reason have you, Saunders? Has Margaret expressed a preference for you in any way?"

"Preference!" said Saunders; "'deed she has that, minister; a maist marked preference. It was only the last Tuesday afore Whussanday [Whitsunday] that she gied me a clour [knock] i' the lug that fair dang me stupid. Caa that ye nocht?"

"Well, Saunders," said the minister, going out, "certainly I wish you good speed in your wooing; but see that you fall no more out with Birsie, lest you be more bruised than you are now; and for the rest, learn wisely to restrain your unruly member."

"Thank ye, minister," said Saunders; "I'll do my best endeavours to obleege ye. Meg's clours are to be borne wi' a' complaisancy, but Birsie's dunts are, so to speak, gratuitous!"

CHAPTER IX
THE ADVENT OF THE CUIF

"Here's the Cuif!" said Meg Kissock, who with her company gown on, and her face glowing from a brisk wash, sat knitting a stocking in the rich gloaming light at the gable end of the house of Craig Ronald. Winsome usually read a book, sitting by the window which looked up the long green croft to the fir-woods and down to the quiet levels of Loch Grannoch, on which the evening mist was gathering a pale translucent blue. It was a common thing for Meg and Jessie Kissock to bring their knitting and darning there, and on their milking-stools sit below the window. If Winsome were in a mood for talk she did not read much, but listened instead to the brisk chatter of the maids. Sometimes the ploughmen, Jock Forrest and Ebie Farrish, came to "ca' the crack," and it was Winsome's delight on these occasions to listen to the flashing claymore of Meg Kissock's rustic wit. Before she settled down, Meg had taken in the three tall candles "ben the hoose," where the old people sat—Walter Skirving, as ever, silent and far away, his wife deep in some lively book lent her by the Lady Elizabeth out of the library of Greatorix Castle.

A bank of wild thyme lay just beneath Winsome's window, and over it the cows were feeding, blowing softly through their nostrils among the grass and clover till the air was fragrant with their balmy breath.

"Guid e'en to ye, 'Cuif,'" cried Meg Kissock as soon as Saunders Mowdiewort came within earshot. He came stolidly forward tramping through the bog with his boots newly greased with what remained of the smooth candle "dowp" with which he had sleeked his flaxen locks. He wore a broad blue Kilmarnock bonnet, checked red and white in a "dam-brod" [draught-board] pattern round the edge, and a blue-buttoned coat with broad pearl buttons. It may be well to explain that there is a latent meaning, apparent only to Galloway folk of the ancient time, in the word "cuif." It conveys at once the ideas of inefficiency and folly, of simplicity and the ignorance of it. The cuif is a feckless person of the male sex, who is a recognized butt for a whole neighbourhood to sharpen its wits upon.

The particular cuif so addressed by Meg came slowly over the knoll.

"Guid e'en to ye," he said, with his best visiting manners.

"Can ye no see me as weel, Saunders?" said Jess, archly, for all was grist that came to her mill.

Saunders rose like a trout to the fly.

"Ow aye, Jess, lass, I saw ye brawly, but it disna do to come seekin' twa lasses at ae time."'

"Dinna ye be thinkin' to put awa' Meg, an' then come coortin' me!" said Jess, sharply.

Saunders was hurt for the moment at this pointed allusion both to his profession and also to his condition as a "seekin'" widower.

"Wha seeks you, Jess, 'ill be sair ill-aff!" he replied very briskly for a cuif.

The sound of Meg's voice in round altercation with Jock Gordon, the privileged "natural" or innocent fool of the parish, interrupted this interchange of amenities, which was indeed as friendly and as much looked for between lads and lasses as the ordinary greeting of "Weel, hoo's a' wi' ye the nicht?" which began every conversation between responsible folks.

"Jock Gordon, ye lazy ne'er-do-weel, ye hinna carried in a single peat, an' it comin' on for parritch-time. D'ye think my maister can let the like o' you sorn on him, week in, week oot, like a mawk on a sheep's hurdie? Gae wa' oot o' that, lyin' sumphin' [sulking] an' sleepin' i' the middle o' the forenicht, an' carry the water for the boiler an' bring in the peats frae the stack."

Then there arose a strange elricht quavering voice—the voice of those to whom has not been granted their due share of wits. Jock Gordon was famed all over the country for his shrewd replies to those who set their wits in contest with his. Jock is remembered on all Deeside, and even to Nithsdale. He was a man well on in years at this time, certainly not less than forty-five. But on his face there was no wrinkle set, not a fleck of gray upon his bonnetless fox-red shock of hair, weather-rusted and usually stuck full of feathers and short pieces of hay. Jock Gordon was permitted to wander as a privileged visitor through the length and breadth of the south hill country. He paid long visits to Craig Ronald, where he had a great admiration and reverence for the young mistress, and a hearty detestation for Meg Kissock, who, as he at all times asserted, "was the warst maister to serve atween the Cairnsmuirs."

"Richt weel I'll do yer biddin', Meg Kissock," he answered in his shrill falsetto, "but no for your sake or the sake o' ony belangin' to you. But there's yae bonny doo [dove], wi' her hair like gowd, an' a fit that she micht set on Jock Gordon's neck, an' it wad please him weel. An' said she, 'Do the wark Meg Kissock bids ye,' so Jock Gordon, Lord o' Kelton Hill an' Earl o' Clairbrand, will perform a' yer wull. Otherwise it's no in any dochter o' Hurkle-backit [bent-backed] Kissock to gar Jock Gordon move haund or fit."

So saying, Jock clattered away with his water-pails, muttering to himself.

Meg Kissock came out again to sit down on her milking-stool under the westward window, within which was Winsome Charteris, reading her book unseen by the last glow of the red west.

Jess and Saunders Mowdiewort had fallen silent. Jess had said her say, and did not intend to exert herself to entertain her sister's admirer. Jess was said to look not unkindly on Ebie Farrish, the younger ploughman who had recently come to Craig Ronald from one of the farms at the "laigh" end of the parish. Ebie had also, it was said, with better authority, a hanging eye to Jess, who had the greater reason to be kind to him, that he was the first since her return from England who had escaped the more BRAVURA attractions of her sister.

"Can ye no find a seat guid eneuch to sit doon on, cuif?" inquired Meg with quite as polite an intention as though she had said, "Be so kind as to take a seat." The cuif, who had been uneasily balancing himself first on one foot and then on the other, and apologetically passing his hand over the sleek side of his head which was not covered by the bonnet, replied gratefully:

"'Deed I wull that, Meg, since ye are sae pressin'."

He went to the end of the milk-house, selected a small tub used for washing the dishes of red earthenware and other domestic small deer, turned it upside down, and seated himself as near to Meg as he dared. Then he tried to think what it was he had intended to say to her, but the words somehow would not now come at call. Before long he hitched his seat a little nearer, as though his present position was not quite comfortable.

But Meg checked him sharply.

"Keep yer distance, cuif," she said; "ye smell o' the muils" [churchyard earth].

"Na, na, Meg, ye ken brawly I haena been howkin' [digging] since Setterday fortnicht, when I burriet Tarn Rogerson's wife's guid- brither's auntie, that leeved grainin' an' deein' a' her life wi' the rheumatics an' wame disease, an' died at the last o' eatin' swine's cheek an' guid Cheddar cheese thegither at Sandy Mulquharchar's pig-killin'."

"Noo, cuif," said Meg, with an accent of warning in her voice, "gin ye dinna let alane deevin' [deafening] us wi' yer kirkyaird clavers, ye'll no sit lang on my byne" [tub].

From the end of the peat-stack, out of the dark hole made by the excavation of last winter's stock of fuel, came the voice of Jock Gordon, singing:

"The deil he sat on the high lumtap,
HECH HOW, BLACK AN' REEKY!
Gang yer ways and drink yer drap,
Ye'll need it a' whan ye come to stap
IN MY HOLE SAE BLACK AN' REEKY, O!
HECH HOW, BLACK AN' REEKY!

"Hieland kilt an' Lawland hose,
Parritch-fed an' reared on brose,
Ye'll drink nae drap whan ye come tae stap
IN MY HOLE SAE BLACK AN' REEKY, O!
HECH HOW, BLACK AN' REEKY!"

Meg Kissock and her sweetheart stopped to listen. Saunders Mowdiewort smiled an unprofessional smile when he heard the song of the natural. "That's a step ayont the kirkyaird, Meg," he said. "Gin ye hae sic objections to hear aboot honest men in their honest graves, what say ye to that elricht craitur scraichin' aboot the verra deil an' his hearth-stane?"

Certainly it sounded more than a trifle uncanny in the gloaming, coming out of that dark place where even in the daytime the black Galloway rats cheeped and scurried, to hear the high, quavering voice of Jock Gordon singing his unearthly rhymes.

By-and-bye those at the house gable could see that the innocent had climbed to the top of the peat-stack in some elvish freak, and sat there cracking his thumbs and singing with all his might:

"HECH HOW, BLACK AN' REEKY! IN MY HOLE SAE BLACK AN' REEKY, O!"

"Come doon oot o' that this meenit, Jock Gordon, ye gomeral!" cried Meg, shaking her fist at the uncouth shape twisting and singing against the sunset sky like one demented.

The song stopped, and Jock Gordon slowly turned his head in their direction. All were looking towards him, except Ebie Farrish, the new ploughman, who was wondering what Jess Kissock would do if he put his arm around her waist.

"What said ye?" Jock asked from his perch on the top of the peat- stack.

"Hae ye fetched in the peats an' the water, as I bade ye?" asked Meg, with great asperity in her voice. "D'ye think that ye'll win aff ony the easier in the hinnerend, by sittin' up there like yin o' his ain bairns, takkin' the deil's name in vain?"

"Gin ye dinna tak' tent to [care of] yersel', Meg Kissock," retorted Jock, "wi' yer eternal yammer o' 'Peats, Jock Gordon, an' 'Water, Jock Gordon,' ye'll maybes find yersel' whaur Jock Gordon'll no be there to serve ye; but the Ill Auld Boy'll keep ye in routh o' peats, never ye fret, Meg Kissock, wi' that reed-heed [red head] o' yours to set them a-lunt [on fire]. Faith an' ye may cry 'Water! water!' till ye crack yer jaws, but nae Jock Gordon there— na, na—nae Jock Gordon there. Jock kens better."

But at this moment there was a prolonged rumble, and the whole party sitting by the gable end (the "gavel," as it was locally expressed) rose to their feet from tub and hag-clog and milking- stool. There had been a great land-slip. The whole side of the peat-stack had tumbled bodily into the great "black peat-hole" from which the winter's peats had come, and which was a favourite lair of Jock's own, being ankle-deep in fragrant dry peat "coom" — which is, strange-to say, a perfectly clean and even a luxurious bedding, far to be preferred as a couch to "flock" or its kindred abominations.

All the party ran forward to see what had become of Jock, whose song had come to so swift a close.

Out of the black mass of down-fallen peat there came a strange, pleading voice.

"O guid deil, O kind deil, dinna yirk awa' puir Jock to that ill bit—puir Jock, that never yet did ye ony hairm, but aye wished ye weel! Lat me aff this time, braw deil, an' I'll sing nae mair ill gangs aboot ye!"

"Save us!" exclaimed Meg Kissock, "the craitur's prayin' to the Ill Body himsel'."

Ebbie Farrish began to clear away the peat, which was, indeed, no difficult task. As he did so, the voice of Jock Gordon mounted higher and higher:

"O mercy me, I hear them clawin' and skrauchelin'! Dinna let the wee yins wi' the lang riven taes and the nebs like gleds [beaks like kites] get haud o' me! I wad rayther hae yersel', Maister o' Sawtan, for ye are a big mensefu' deil. Ouch! I'm dune for noo, althegither; he haes gotten puir Jock! Sirce me, I smell the reekit rags o' him!"

But it was only Ebie Farrish that had him by the roll of ancient cloth which served as a collar for Jock's coat. When he was pulled from under the peats and set upon his feet, he gazed around with a bewildered look.

"O man, Ebie Farrish," he said solemnly, "If I didna think ye war the deil himsel'—ye see what it is to be misled by ootward appearances!"

There was a shout of laughter at the expense of Ebie, in which Meg thought that she heard an answering ripple from within Winsome's room.

"Surely, Jock, ye were never prayin' to the deil?" asked Meg from the window, very seriously. "Ye ken far better than that."

"An' what for should I no pray to the deil? He's a desperate onsonsy chiel yon. It's as weel to be in wi' him as oot wi' him ony day. Wha' kens what's afore them, or wha they may be behaudin' to afore the morrow's morn?" answered Jock stoutly.

"But d'ye ken," said John Scott, the theological herd, who had quietly "daundered doon" as he said, from his cot-house up on the hill, where his bare-legged bairns played on the heather and short grass all day, to set his shoulder against the gable end for an hour with the rest.

"D'ye ken what Maister Welsh was sayin' was the new doctrine amang thae New Licht Moderates—'hireling shepherds,' he ca'd them? Noo I'm no on mysel' wi' sae muckle speakin' aboot the deil. But the minister was sayin' that the New Moderates threep [assert] that there's nae deil at a'. He dee'd some time since!"

"Gae wa' wi' ye, John Scott! wha's gaun aboot doin' sae muckle ill then, I wad like to ken?" said Meg Kissock.

"Dinna tell me," said Jock Gordon, "that the puir deil's deed, and that we'll hae to pit up wi' Ebie Farrish. Na, na, Jock's maybe daft, but he kens better than that!"

"They say," said John Scott, pulling meditatively at his cutty, "that the pooer is vested noo in a kind o' comy-tee [committee]!"

"I dinna haud wi' comy-tees mysel'," replied Meg; "it's juist haein' mony maisters, ilka yin mair cankersome and thrawn than anither!"

"Weel, gin this news be true, there's a heep o' fowk in this parish should be mentioned in his wull," said Jock Gordon, significantly. "They're near kin till him—forby a heep o' bairns that he has i' the laich-side o' the loch. They're that hard there, they'll no gie a puir body a meal o' meat or the shelter o' a barn."

"But," said Ebie Farrish, who had been thinking that, after all, the new plan might have its conveniences, "gin there's nae deil to tempt, there'll be nae deil to punish."

But the herd was a staunch Marrow man. He was not led away by any human criticism, nor yet by the new theology.

"New Licht here, New Licht there," he said; "I canna' pairt wi' ma deil. Na, na, that's ower muckle to expect o' a man o' my age!"

Having thus defined his theological position, without a word more he threw his soft checked plaid of Galloway wool over his shoulders, and fell into the herd's long swinging heather step, mounting the steep brae up to his cot on the hillside as easily as if he were walking along a level road.

There was a long silence; then a ringing sound, sudden and sharp, and Ebie Farrish fell inexplicably from the axe-chipped hag-clog, which he had rolled up to sit upon. Ebie had been wondering for more than an hour what would happen if he put his arm round Jess Kissock's waist. He knew now.

Then, after a little Saunders Mowdiewort, who was not unmindful of his prearranged programme nor yet oblivious of the flight of time, saw the stars come out, he knew that if he were to make any progress, he must make haste; so he leaned over towards his sweetheart and whispered, "Meg, my lass, ye're terrible bonny."

"D'ye think ye are the first man that has telled me that, cuif?" said Meg, with point and emphasis.

Jock Forrest, the senior ploughman—a very quiet, sedate man with a seldom stirred but pretty wit, laughed a short laugh, as though he knew something about that. Again there was a silence, and as the night wind began to draw southward in cool gulps of air off the hills, Winsome Charteris's window was softly closed.

"Hae ye nocht better than that to tell us, cuif?" said Meg, briskly, "nocht fresh-like?"

"Weel," said Saunders Mowdiewort, groping round for a subject of general interest, his profession and his affection being alike debarred, "there's that young Enbra' lad that's come till the manse. He's a queer root, him."

"What's queer aboot him?" asked Meg, in a semi-belligerent manner. A young man who had burned his fingers for her mistress's sake must not be lightly spoken of.

"Oh, nocht to his discredit ava, only Manse Bell heard him arguin' wi' the minister aboot the weemen-folk the day that he cam'. He canna' bide them, she says."

"He has but puir taste," said Ebie Farrish; "a snod bit lass is the bonniest work o' Natur'. Noo for mysel'—"

"D'ye want anither?" asked Jess, without apparent connection.

"He'll maybe mend o' that opeenion, as mony a wise man has dune afore him," said Meg, sententiously. "Gae on, cuif; what else aboot the young man?"

"Oh, he's a lad o' great lear. He can read ony language back or forrit, up or doon, as easy as suppin' sowens. He can speak byordinar' graund. They say he'll beat the daddy o' him for preachin' when he's leecensed. He rade Birsie this mornin' too, after the kickin' randie had cuist me aff his back like a draff sack."

"Then what's queer aboot him?" said Jess.

Meg said nothing. She felt a draft of air suck into Winsome's room, so that she knew that the subject was of such interest that her mistress had again opened her window. Meg leaned back so far that she could discern a glint of yellow hair in the darkness.

The cuif was about to light his pipe. Meg stopped him.

"Nane o' yer lichts here, cuif," she said; "it's time ye were thinkin' aboot gaun ower the hill. But ye haena' telled us yet what's queer aboot the lad."

"Weel, woman, he's aye write—writin', whiles on sheets o' paper, and whiles on buiks."

"There's nocht queer aboot that," says Meg; "so does ilka minister."

"But Manse Bell gied me ane o' his writings, that she had gotten aboot his bedroom somewhere. She said that the wun' had blawn't aff his table, but I misdoot her."

"Yer ower great wi' Manse Bell an' the like o' her, for a man that comes to see me!" said Meg, who was a very particular young woman indeed.

"It was cuttit intil lengths like the metre psalms, but it luikit gye an' daft like, sae I didna' read it," said the cuif hastily. "Here it's to ye, Meg. I was e'en gaun to licht my cutty wi't."

Something shone gray-white in Saunders's hand as he held it out to Meg, It passed into Meg's palm, and then was seen no more.

The session at the house end was breaking up. Jess had vanished silently. Ebie Farrish was not. Jock Forrest had folded his tent and stolen away. Meg and Saunders were left alone. It was his supreme opportunity.

He leaned over towards his sweetheart. His blue bonnet had fallen to the ground, and there was a distinct odour of warm candle- grease in the air.

"Meg," he said, "yer maist amazin' bonny, an' I'm that fond o' ye that I am faain' awa' frae my meat! O Meg, woman, I think o' ye i' the mornin' afore the Lord's Prayer, I sair misdoot! Guid forgie me! I find mysel' whiles wonderin' gin I'll see ye the day afore I can gang ower in my mind the graves that's to howk, or gin Birsie's oats are dune. O Meg, Meg, I'm that fell fond o' ye that I gruppit that thrawn speldron Birsie's hint leg juist i' the fervour o' thinkin' o' ye."

"Hoo muckle hae ye i' the week?" said Meg, practically, to bring the matter to a point.

"A pound a week," said Saunders Mowdiewort, promptly, who though a cuif was a business man, "an' a cottage o' three rooms wi' a graun' view baith back an' front!"

"Ow aye," said Meg, sardonically, "I ken yer graund view. It's o' yer last wife's tombstane, wi' the inscriptions the length o' my airm aboot Betty Mowdiewort an' a' her virtues, that Robert Paterson cuttit till ye a year past in Aprile. Na, na, ye'll no get me to leeve a' my life lookin' oot on that ilk' time I wash my dishes. It wad mak' yin be wantin' to dee afore their time to get sic-like. Gang an' speer [ask] Manse Bell. She's mair nor half blind onyway, an' she's fair girnin' fain for a man, she micht even tak' you."

With these cruel words Meg lifted her milking-stool and vanished within. The cuif sat for a long time on his byne lost in thought. Then he arose, struck his flint and steel together, and stood looking at the tinder burning till it went out, without having remembered to put it to the pipe which he held in his other hand. After the last sparks ran every way and flickered, he threw the glowing red embers on the ground, kicked the pail on which he had been sitting as solemnly as if he had been performing a duty to the end of the yard, and then stepped stolidly into the darkness.

The hag-clog was now left alone against the wall beneath Winsome's window, within which there was now the light of a candle and a waxing and waning shadow on the blind as some one went to and fro. Then there was a sharp noise as of one clicking in the "steeple" or brace of the front door (which opened in two halves), and then the metallic grit of the key in the lock, for Craig Ronald was a big house, and not a mere farm which might be left all night with unbarred portals.

Winsome stepped lightly to her own door, which opened without noise. She looked out and said, in a compromise between a coaxing whisper and a voice of soft command:

"Meg, I want ye."

Meg Kissock came along the passage with the healthy glow of the night air on her cheeks, and her candle in her hand. She seemed as if she would pause at the door, but Winsome motioned her imperiously within. So Meg came within, and Winsome shut to the door. Then she simply held out her hand, at which Meg gazed as silently.

"Meg!" said Winsome, warningly.

A queer, faint smile passed momentarily over the face of Winsome's handmaid, as though she had been long trying to solve some problem and had suddenly and unexpectedly found the answer. Slowly she lifted up her dark-green druggit skirt, and out of a pocket of enormous size, which was swung about her waist like a captured leviathan heaving inanimate on a ship's cable, she extracted a sheet of crumpled paper.

Winsome took it without a word. Her eye said "Good-night" to Meg as plain as the minister's text.

Meg Kissock waited till she was at the door, and then, just as she was making her silent exit, she said:

"Ye'll tak' as guid care o't as the ither yin ye fand. Ye can pit them baith thegither."

Winsome took a step towards her as if with some purpose of indignant chastisement. But the red head and twinkling eyes of mischief vanished, and Winsome stood with the paper in her hand. Just as she had begun to smooth out the crinkles produced by the hands of Manse Bell who could not read it, Saunders who would not, and Meg Kissock who had not time to read it, the head of the last named was once more projected into the room, looking round the edge of the rose-papered door.

"Ye'll mak' a braw mistress o' the manse, Mistress—Ralph— Peden!" she said, nodding her head after each proper name.

CHAPTER X
THE LOVE-SONG OF THE MAVIS

Winsome stamped her little foot in real anger now, and crumpling the paper in her hand she threw it indignantly on the floor. She was about to say something to Meg, but that erratic and privileged domestic was in her own room by this time at the top of the house, with the door barred.

But something like tears stood in Winsome's eyes. She was very angry indeed. She would speak to Meg in the morning. She was mistress of the house, and not to be treated as a child. Meg should have her warning to leave at the term. It was ridiculous the way that she had taken to speaking to her lately. It was clear that she had been allowing her far too great liberties. It did not occur to Winsome Charteris that Meg had been accustomed to tease her in something like this manner about every man under forty who had come to Craig Ronald on any pretext whatever—from young Johnnie Dusticoat, the son of the wholesale meal-miller from Dumfries, to Agnew Greatorix, eldest son of the Lady Elizabeth, who came over from the castle with books for her grandmother rather oftener than might be absolutely necessary, and who, though a papist, had waited for Winsome three Sabbath days at the door of the Marrow kirk, a building which he had never previously entered during his life.

Winsome went indignant to bed. It was altogether too aggravating that Meg should take on so, she said to herself.

"Of course I do not care a button," she said as she turned her hot cheek upon the pillow and looked towards the pale gray-blue of the window-panes, in which there was already the promise of the morning; though yet it was hardly midnight of the short midsummer of the north.

"It would be too ridiculous to suppose that I should care for anybody whom I have only seen twice. Why, it was more than a year before I really cared for dear old grannie! Meg might know better, and it is very silly of her to say things like that. I shall send back his book and paper to-morrow morning by Andrew Kissock when he goes to school." Still even after this resolution she lay sleepless.

"Now I will go to sleep," said Winsome, resolutely shutting her eyes. "I will not think about him any more." Which was assuredly a noble and fitting resolve. But Winsome had yet to discover in restless nights and troubled morrows that sleep and thought are two gifts of God which do not come or go at man's bidding. In her silent chamber there seemed to be a kind of hushed yet palpable life. It seemed to Winsome as if there were about her a thousand little whispering voices. Unseen presences flitted everywhere. She could hear them laughing such wicked, mocking laughs. They were clustering round the crumpled piece of paper in the corner. Well, it might lie there forever for her.

"I would not read it even if it were light. I shall send it back to him tomorrow without reading it. Very likely it is a Greek exercise, at any rate."

Yet, for all these brave sayings, neither sleep nor dawn had come, when, clad in shadowy white and the more manifest golden glimmer of her hair, she glided to the windowseat, and drawing a great knitted shawl about her, she sat, a slender figure enveloped from head to foot in sheeny white. The shawl imprisoned the pillow tossed masses of her rippling hair, throwing them forward about her face, which, in the half light, seemed to be encircled with an aureole of pale Florentine gold.

In her hand Winsome held Ralph Peden's poem, and in spite of her determination not to read it, she sat waiting till the dawn should come. It might be something of great importance. It might only be a Greek exercise. It was, at all events, necessary to find out, in order that she might send it back.

It was a marvellous dawning, this one that Winsome waited for. Dawn is the secret of the universe. It thrills us somehow with a far-off prophecy of that eternal dawning when the God That Is shall reveal himself—the dawning which shall brighten into the more perfect day.

It was just the slack water—the water-shed of the night. So clear it was this June night that the lingering gold behind the western ridge of the Orchar Hill, where the sun went down, was neither brighter nor yet darker than the faint tinge of lucent green, like the colour of the inner curve of the sea-wave just as it bends to break, which had begun to glow behind the fir woods to the east.

The birds were waking sleepily. Chaffinches began their clear, short, natural bursts of song. "CHURR!" said the last barn owl as he betook himself to bed. The first rook sailed slowly overhead from Hensol wood. He was seeking the early worm. The green lake in the east was spreading and taking a roseate tinge just where it touched the pines on the rugged hillside.

Beneath Winsome's window a blackbird hopped down upon the grass and took a tentative dab or two at the first slug he came across; but it was really too early for breakfast for a good hour yet, so he flew up again into a bush and preened his feathers, which had been discomposed by the limited accommodation of the night. Now he was on the topmost twig, and Winsome saw him against the crimson pool which was fast deepening in the east.

Suddenly his mellow pipe fluted out over the grove. Winsome listened as she had never listened before. Why had it become so strangely sweet to listen to the simple sounds? Why did the rich Tyrian dye of the dawn touch her cheek and flush the flowering floss of her silken hair? A thrush from the single laurel at the gate told her:

> "There—there—there—" he sang,
> "Can't you see, can't you see, can't you see it?
> Love is the secret, the secret!
> Could you but know it, did you but show it!
> Hear me! hear me! hear me!
> Down in the forest I loved her!
> Sweet, sweet, sweet!
> Would you but listen,
> I would love you!
> All is sweet and pure and good!
> Twilight and morning dew,
> I love it, I love it,
> Do you, do you, do you?"

This was the thrush's love-song. Now it was light enough for Winsome to read hers by the red light of the midsummer's dawn. This was Ralph's Greek exercise:

> "Sweet mouth, red lips, broad unwrinkled brow,
> Sworn troth, woven hands, holy marriage vow,
> Unto us make answer, what is wanting now?
> Love, love, love, the whiteness of the snow;
> Love, love, love, and the days of long ago.

> "Broad lands, bright sun, as it was of old;
> Red wine, loud mirth, gleaming of the gold;
> Something yet a-wanting—how shall it be told?
> Love, love, love, the whiteness of the snow;
> Love, love, love, and the days of long ago.

"Large heart, true love, service void of sound,
Life-trust, death-trust, here on Scottish ground,
As in olden story, surely I have found—
  Love, love, love, the whiteness of the snow,
  Love, love, love, and the days of long ago."

The thrush had ceased singing while Winsome read. It was another voice which she heard—the first authentic call of the springtime for her. It coursed through her blood. It quickened her pulse. It enlarged the pupil of her eye till the clear germander blue of the iris grew moist and dark. It was a song for her heart, and hers alone. She felt it, though no more than a leaf blown to her by chance winds. It might have been written for any other, only she knew that it was not. Ralph Peden had said nothing. The poem certainly did not suggest a student of divinity in the Kirk of the Marrow. There were a thousand objections—a thousand reasons— every one valid, against such a thing. But love that laughs at locksmiths is equally contemptuous of logic. It was hers, hers, and hers alone. A breath from Love's wing as he passed came again to Winsome. The blackbird was silent, but a thrush this time broke in with his jubilant love-song, while Winsome, with her love-song laid against a dewy cheek, paused to listen with a beating heart and a new comprehension:

"Hear! hear! hear!
  Dear! dear! dear!
Far away, far away, far away,
  I saw him pass this way,
Tirrieoo, tirrieoo! so tender and true,
  Chippiwee, chippiwee, oh, try him and see!
Cheer up! cheer up! cheer up!
  He'll come and he'll kiss you,
  He'll kiss you and kiss you,
And I'll see him do it, do it, do it!"

"Go away, you wicked bird!" said Winsome, when the master singer in speckled grey came to this part of his song. So saying, she threw, with such exact aim that it went in an entirely opposite direction, a quaint, pink seashell at the bird, a shell which had been given her by a lad who was going away again to sea three years ago. She was glad now, when she thought of it, that she had kissed him because he had no mother, for he never came back any more.

"Keck, keck!" said the mavis indignantly, and went away.

Then Winsome lay down on her white bed well content, and pillowed her cheek on a crumpled piece of paper.

CHAPTER XI
ANDREW KISSOCK GOES TO SCHOOL

Love is, at least in maidens' hearts, of the nature of an intermittent fever. The tide of Solway flows, but the more rapid his flow the swifter his ebb. The higher it brings the wrack up the beach, the deeper, six hours after, are laid bare the roots of the seaweed upon the shingle. Now Winsome Charteris, however her heart might conspire against her peace, was not at all the girl to be won before she was asked. Also there was that delicious spirit of contrariness that makes a woman even when won, by no means seem won.

Besides, in the broad daylight of common day she was less attuned and touched to earnest issues than in the red dawn. She had even taken the poem and the exercise book out of the sacred enclosure, where they had been hid so long. She did not really know that she could make good any claim to either. Indeed, she was well aware that to one of them at least she had no claim whatever. Therefore she had placed both the note-book and the poem within the same band as her precious housekeeping account-book, which she reverenced next her Bible—which very practical proceeding pleased her, and quite showed that she was above all foolish sentiment. Then she went to churn for an hour and a half, pouring in a little hot water critically from time to time in order to make the butter come. This exercise may be recommended as an admirable corrective to foolish flights of imagination. There is something concrete about butter-making which counteracts an overplus of sentiment— especially when the butter will not come. And hot water may be overdone.

Now Winsome Charteris was a hard-hearted young woman—a fact that may not as yet have appeared; at least so she told herself. She had come to the conclusion that she had been foolish to think at all of Ralph Peden, so she resolved to put him at once and altogether out of her mind, which, as every one knows, is quite a simple matter. Yet during the morning she went three times into her little room to look at her housekeeping book, which by accident lay within the same band as Ralph Peden's lost manuscripts.

First, she wanted to see how much she got for butter at Cairn Edward the Monday before last; then to discover what the price was on that very same day last year. It is an interesting thing to follow the fluctuations of the produce market, especially when you churn the butter yourself. The exact quotation of documents is a valuable thing to learn. Nothing is so likely to grow upon one as a habit of inaccuracy. This was what her grandmother was always telling her, and it behooved Winsome to improve. Each time as she strapped the documents together she said, "And these go back to-day by Andra Kissock when he goes to school." Then she took another look, in order to assure herself that no forgeries had been introduced within the band while she was churning the butter. They were still quite genuine.

Winsome went out to relieve Jess Kissock in the dairy, and as she went she communed with herself: "It is right that I should send them back. The verses may belong to somebody else—somebody in Edinburgh—and, besides, I know them by heart."

A good memory is a fine thing.

The Kissocks lived in one of the Craig Ronald cot-houses. Their father had in his time been one of the herds, and upon his death, many years ago, Walter Skirving had allowed the widow and children to remain in the house in which Andrew Kissock, senior, had died. Mistress Kissock was a large-boned, soft-voiced woman, who had supplied what dash of tenderness there was in her daughters. She had reared them according to good traditions, but as she said, when all her brood were talking at the same time, she alone quietly silent:

"The Kissocks tak' efter their faither, they're great hands to talk—a' bena [except] An'ra'."

Andrew was her youngest, a growing lump of a boy of twelve, who was exceeding silent in the house. Every day Andra betook himself to school, along the side of Loch Grannoch, by the path which looked down on the cloud-flecked mirror of the loch. Some days he got there, but very occasionally.

His mother had got him ready early this June morning. He had brought in the kye for Jess. He had helped Jock Gordon to carry water for Meg's kitchen mysteries. He had listened to a brisk conversation proceeding from the "room" where his very capable sister was engaged in getting the old people settled for the day. All this was part of the ordinary routine. As soon as the whole establishment knew that Walter Skirving was again at the window over the marshmallows, and his wife at her latest book, a sigh of satisfaction went up and the wheels of the day's work revolved. So this morning it came time for Andra to go to school all too soon. Andra did not want to stay at home from school, but it was against the boy's principle to appear glad to go to school, so Andra made it a point of honour to make a feint of wanting to stay every morning.

"Can I no bide an' help ye wi' the butter-kirnin' the day, Jess?" said Andra, rubbing himself briskly all over as he had seen the ploughmen do with their horses. When he got to his bare red legs he reared and kicked out violently, calling out at the same time:

"Wad ye then, ye tairger, tuts—stan' still there, ye kickin' beast!" as though he were some fiery untamed from the desert.

Jess made a dart at him with a wet towel.

"Gang oot o' my back kitchen wi' yer nonsense!" she said. Andra passaged like a strongly bitted charger to the back door, and there ran away with himself, flourishing in the air a pair of very dirty heels. Ebie Farrish was employed over a tin basin at the stable door, making his breakfast toilet, which he always undertook, not when he shook himself out of bed in the stable loft at five o'clock, but before he went in to devour Jess with his eyes and his porridge in the ordinary way. It was at this point that Andra Kissock, that prancing Galloway barb, breaking away from all restrictions, charged between Ebie's legs, and overset him into his own horse-trough. The yellow soap was in Ebie's eyes, and before he got it out the small boy was far enough away. The most irritating thing was that from the back kitchen came peal on peal of laughter.

"It's surely fashionable at the sea-bathin' to tak' a dook [swim] in the stable-trough, nae less!"

Ebie gathered himself up savagely. His temperature was something considerably above summer heat, yet he dared not give expression to his feelings, for his experiences in former courtships had led him to the conclusion that you cannot safely, having regard to average family prejudice, abuse the brothers of your sweetheart. After marriage the case is believed to be different.

Winsome Charteris stood at the green gate which led out of the court-yard into the croft, as Andra was making his schoolward exit. She had a parcel for him. This occasioned no surprise, nor did the very particular directions as to delivery, and the dire threatenings against forgetfulness or failure in the least dismay Andra. He was entirely accustomed to them. From his earliest years he had heard nothing else. He never had been reckoned as a "sure hand," and it was only in default of a better messenger that Winsome employed him. Then these directions were so explicit that there did not appear to be any possibility of mistake. He had only to go to the manse and leave the parcel for Mr. Ralph Peden without a message.

So Andrew Kissock, nothing loath, promised faithfully. He never objected to promising; that was easy. He carried the small, neatly wrapped parcel in his hand, walking most sedately so long as Winsome's eyes were upon him. He was not yet old enough to be under the spell of the witchery of those eyes; but then Winsome's eye controlled his sister Meg's hand, and for that latter organ he had a most profound respect.

Now we must take the trouble to follow in some detail the course of this small boy going to school, for though it may be of no interest in itself save as a study in scientific procrastination, a good deal of our history directly depends upon it.

As soon as Andrew was out of sight he pulled his leather satchel round so that he could open it with ease, and, having taken a handful of broken and very stale crumbs out of it for immediate use, he dropped Winsome's parcel within. There it kept company with a tin flask of milk which his mother filled for him every morning, having previously scalded it well to restore its freshness. This was specially carefully done after a sad occasion upon which his mother, having poured in the fine milk for Andra's dinner fresh from Crummie the cow, out of the flask mouth there crawled a number of healthy worms which that enterprising youth had collected from various quarters which it is best not to specify. Not that Andra objected in the least. Milk was a good thing, worms were good things, and he was above the paltry superstition that one good thing could spoil another. He will always consider to his dying day that the very sound licking which his mother administered to him, for spoiling at once the family breakfast and his own dinner, was one of the most uncalled-for and gratuitous, which, even in his wide experience, it had been his lot to recollect.

So Andra took his way to school. He gambolled along, smelling and rooting among the ragged robin and starwort in the hedges like an unbroken collie. It is safe to say that no further thought of school or message crossed his mind from the moment that the highest white steading of Craig Ronald sank out of view, until his compulsory return. Andra had shut out from his view so commonplace and ignominious facts as home and school.

At the first loaning end, where the road to the Nether Crae came down to cross the bridge, just at the point where the Grannoch lane leaves the narrows of the loch, Andra betook himself to the side of the road, with a certain affectation of superabundant secrecy.

With prodigious exactness he examined the stones at a particular part of the dyke, hunted about for one of remarkable size and colour, said "Hist! hist!" in a mysterious way, and ran across the road to see that no one was coming.

As we have seen, Andra was the reader of the family. His eldest brother had gone to America, where he was working in New York as a joiner. This youth was in the habit of sending across books and papers describing the terrible encounters with Indians in the Boone country—the "dark and bloody land" of the early romancers. Not one in the family looked at the insides of these relations of marvels except Andra, who, when he read the story of the Indian scout trailing the murderers of his squaw across a continent in order to annihilate them just before they entered New York city, felt that he had found his vocation—which was to be at least an Indian scout, if indeed it was too late for him to think of being a full-blooded Indian.

The impressive pantomime at the bridge was in order to ascertain whether his bosom companion, Dick Little, had passed on before him. He knew, as soon as he was within a hundred yards of the stone, that he had NOT passed. Indeed, he could see him at that very moment threading his way down through the tangle of heather and bog myrtle, or, as he would have said, "gall busses opposite." But what of that?—For mighty is the power of make-believe, and in Andra, repressed as he was at home, there was concentrated the very energy and power of some imaginative ancestry. He had a full share of the quality which ran in the family, and was exceeded only by his brother Jock in New York, who had been "the biggest leer in the country side" before he emigrated to a land where at that time this quality was not specially marked among so many wielders of the long bow. Jock, in his letters, used to frighten his mother with dark tales of his hair-breadth escapes from savages and desperadoes on the frontier, yet, strangely enough, his address remained steadily New York.

Now it is not often that a Galloway boy takes to lying; but when he does, a mere Nithsdale man has no chance with him, still less a man from the simple-minded levels of the "Shire."[Footnote: Wigtonshire is invariably spoken of in Galloway as the Shire, Kirkcudbrightshire as the Stewardry.] But Andra Kissock always lied from the highest motives. He elevated the saying of the thing that was not to the height of a principle. He often lied, knowing that he would be thrashed for it—even though he was aware that he would be rewarded for telling the truth. He lied because he would not demean himself to tell the truth.

It need not therefore surprise us in the least that when Dick Little came across the bridge he was greeted by Andra Kissock with the information that he was in the clutches of The Avenger of Blood, who, mounted upon a mettle steed with remarkably dirty feet, curveted across the road and held the pass. He was required to give up a "soda scone or his life." The bold Dick, who had caught the infection, stoutly refused to yield either. His life was dear to him, but a soda scone considerably dearer. He had rather be dead than hungry.

"Then die, traitor!" said Andra, throwing down his bag, all forgetful of Winsome Charteris's precious parcel and his promises thereanent. So these two brave champions had at one another with most surprising valour.

They were armed with wooden swords as long as themselves, which they manoeuvred with both hands in a marvellously savage manner. When a blow did happen to get home, the dust flew out of their jackets. But still the champions fought on. They were in the act of finishing the quarrel by the submission of Dick in due form, when Allan Welsh, passing across the bridge on one of his pastoral visitations, came upon them suddenly. Dick was on his knees at the time, his hands on the ground, and Andra was forcing his head determinedly down toward the surface of the king's highway. Meanwhile Dick was objecting in the most vigorous way.

"Boys," said the stern, quiet voice of the minister, "what are you doing to each other? Are you aware it is against both the law of God and man to fight in this way? It is only from the beasts that perish that we expect such conduct."

"If ye please, sir," answered Andra in a shamefaced way, yet with the assurance of one who knows that he has the authorities on his side, "Dick Little wull no bite the dust."

"Bite the dust!—what do you mean, laddie?" asked the minister, frowning.

"Weel sir, if ye please, sir, the Buik says that the yin that got his licks fell down and bit the dust. Noo, Dick's doon fair aneuch. Ye micht speak till him to bite the dust!"

And Andra, clothed in the garments of conscious rectitude, stood back to give the minister room to deliver his rebuke.

The stern face of the minister relaxed.

"Be off with you to school," he said; "I'll look in to see if you have got there in the afternoon."

Andra and Dick scampered down the road, snatching their satchels as they ran. In half an hour they were making momentary music under the avenging birch rod of Duncan Duncanson, the learned Dullarg schoolmaster. Their explanations were excellent. Dick said that he had been stopped to gather the eggs, and Andra that he had been detained conversing with the minister. The result was the same in both cases—Andra getting double for sticking to his statement. Yet both stories were true, though quite accidentally so, of course. This is what it is to have a bad character. Neither boy, however, felt any ill-will whatever at the schoolmaster. They considered that he was there in order to lick them. For this he was paid by their parents' money, and it would have been a fraud if he had not duly earned his money by dusting their jackets daily. Let it be said at once that he did most conscientiously earn his money, and seldom overlooked any of his pupils even for a day.

Back at the Grannoch bridge, under the parapet, Allan Welsh, the minister of the Kirk of the Marrow, found the white packet lying which Winsome had tied with such care. He looked all round to see whence it had come. Then taking it in his hand, he looked at it a long time silently, and with a strange and not unkindly expression on his face. He lifted it to his lips and kissed the handwriting which addressed it to Master Ralph Peden. As he paced away he carefully put it in the inner pocket of his coat. Then, with his head farther forward than ever, and the immanence of his great brow overshadowing his ascetic face, he set himself slowly to climb the brae.

CHAPTER XII
MIDSUMMER DAWN

True love is at once chart and compass. It led Ralph Peden out into a cloudy June dawning. It was soft, amorphous, uncoloured night when he went out. Slate-coloured clouds were racing along the tops of the hills from the south. The wind blew in fitful gusts and veering flaws among the moorlands, making eddies and back-waters of the air, which twirled the fallen petals of the pear and cherry blossoms in the little manse orchard.

As he stepped out upon the moor and the chill of dawn struck inward, he did not know that Allan Welsh was watching him from his blindless bedroom. Dawn is the testing-time of the universe. Its cool, solvent atmosphere dissolves social amenities. It is difficult to be courteous, impossible to be polite, in that hour before the heart has realized that its easy task of throwing the blood horizontally to brain and feet has to be exchanged for the harder one of throwing it vertically to the extremities.

Ralph walked slowly and in deep thought through the long avenues of glimmering beeches and under the dry rustle of the quivering poplars. Then, as the first red of dawn touched his face, he looked about him. He was clear of the trees now, and the broad open expanse of the green fields and shining water meadows that ring in Loch Grannoch widened out before him. The winds sighed and rumbled about the hill-tops of the Orchar and the Black Laggan, but in the valley only the cool moist wind of dawn drew largely and stately to and fro.

Ralph loved Nature instinctively, and saw it as a townbred lad rarely does. He was deeply read in the more scientific literature of the subject, and had spent many days in his Majesty's botanic gardens, which lie above the broad breast of the Forth. He now proved his learning, and with quick, sure eye made it real on the Galloway hills. Every leaf spoke to him. He could lie for half a day and learn wisdom from the ant. He took in the bird's song and the moth's flight. The keepers sometimes wondered at the lights which flashed here and there about the plantations, when in the coolness of a moist evening he went out to entrap the sidelong- dashing flutterers with his sugar-pots.

But since he came to Galloway, and especially since he smelled the smell of the wood-fire set for the blanket-washing above the Crae Water bridge, there were new secrets open to him. He possessed a voice that could wile a bird off a bought. His inner sympathy with wild and tame beasts alike was such that as he moved quietly among a drowsing, cud-chewing herd on the braes of Urioch not a beast moved.

Among them a wild, untamed colt stood at bay, its tail arched with apprehension, yet sweeping the ground, and watched him with flashing eyes of suspicion. Ralph held out his hand slowly, more as if it were growing out of his side by some rapid natural process than as if he were extending it. He uttered a low "sussurrus" of coaxing and invitation, all the while imperceptibly decreasing his distance from the colt. The animal threw back its head, tossed its mane in act to flee, thought better of it and dropped its nose to take a bite or two of the long coarse grass. Then again it looked up and continued to gaze, fascinated at the beckoning and caressing fingers. At last, with a little whinny of pleasure, the colt, wholly reassured, came up and nestled a wet nose against Ralph's coat. He took the wild thing's neck within the arch of his arm, and the two new friends stood awhile in grave converse.

A moment afterwards Ralph bent to lay a hand upon the head of one of the placid queys [Footnote: Young—cows.] that had watched the courtship with full, dewy eyes of bovine unconcern. Instantly the colt charged into the still group with a wild flourish of hoofs and viciously snapping teeth, scattering the black-polled Galloways like smoke. Then, as if to reproach Ralph for his unfaithfulness, he made a circle of the field at a full, swinging gallop, sending the short turf flying from his unshod hoofs at every stride. Back he came again, a vision of floating mane and streaming tail, and stopped dead three yards from Ralph, his forelegs strained and taut, ploughing furrows in the grass. As Ralph moved quietly across the field the colt followed, pushing a cool moist nose over the young man's shoulder. When at last Ralph set a foot on the projecting stone which stood out from the side of the grey, lichen-clad stone dyke, the colt stood stretching an eager head over as though desirous of following him; then, with a whinny of disappointment, he rushed round the field, charging at the vaguely wondering and listlessly grazing cattle with head arched between his forelegs and a flourish of widely distributed heels.

Over the hill, Craig Ronald was still wrapped in the lucid impermanence of earliest dawn, when Winsome Charteris set her foot over the blue flagstones of the threshold. The high tide of darkness, which, in these northern summer mornings never rose very high or lasted very long, had ebbed long ago. The indigo grey of the sky was receding, and tinging towards the east with an imperceptibly graded lavender which merged behind the long shaggy outline of the piny ridge into a wash of pale lemon yellow.

The world paused, finger on lip, saying "Hush!" to Winsome as she stepped over the threshold from the serenely breathing morning air, from the illimitable sky which ran farther and farther back as the angels drew the blinds from the windows of heaven.

"Hush!" said the cows over the hedge, blowing fragrant breaths of approval from their wide, comma-shaped nostrils upon the lush grass and upon the short heads of white clover, as they stood face to the brae, all with their heads upward, eating their way like an army on the march.

"Hush! hush!" said the sheep who were straggling over the shorter grass of the High Park, feeding fitfully in their short, uneasy way—crop, crop, crop—and then a pause, to move forward their own length and begin all over again.

But the sheep and the kine, the dewy grass and the brightening sky, might every one have spared their pains, for it was in no wise in the heart of Winsome Charteris to make a noise amid the silences of dawn. Meg Kissock, who still lay snug by Jess in a plump-cheeked country sleep, made noise enough to stir the country side when, rising, she set briskly about to get the house on its morning legs. But Winsome was one of the few people in this world —few but happy—to whom a sunrise is more precious than a sun set —rarer and more calming, instinct with message and sign from a covenant-keeping God. Also, Winsome betook her self early to bed, and so awoke attuned to the sun's rising.

What drew her forth so early this June day was no thought or hope or plan except the desire to read the heart of Nature, and perhaps that she might not be left too long alone with the parable of her own heart. A girl's heart is full of thought which it dares not express to herself—of fluttering and trembling possibilities, chrysalis-like, set aside to await the warmth of an unrevealed summer. In Winsome's soul the first flushing glory of the May of youth was waking the prisoned life. But there were throbs and thrillings too piercingly sweet to last undeveloped in her soul. The bursting bud of her healthful beauty, quickened by the shy radiance of her soul, shook the centres of her life, even as a laburnum-tree mysteriously quivers when the golden rain is in act to break from the close-clustered dependent budlets.

Thus it was that, at the stile which helps the paths be tween the Dullarg and Craig Ronald to overleap the high hill dyke, Ralph met Winsome. As they looked into one another's eyes, they saw Nature suddenly dissolve into confused meaninglessness. There was no clear message for either of them there, save the message that the old world of their hopes and fears had wholly passed away. Yet no new world had come when over the hill dyke their hands met. They said no word. There is no form of greeting for such. Eve did not greet Adam in polite phrase when he awoke to find her in the dawn of one Eden day, a helpmeet meet for him. Neither did Eve reply that "it was a fine morn ing." It is always a fine morning in Eden. They were silent, and so were these two. Their hands lay within one another a single instant. Then, with a sense of something wanting, Ralph sprang lightly over the dyke as an Edin burgh High-School boy ought who had often played hares and hounds in the Hunter's Bog, and been duly thrashed therefor by Dr. Adam [Footnote: The Aery famous master of the High School of Edinburgh.] on the following morning.

When Ralph stood beside her upon the sunny side of the stile he instinctively resumed Winsome's hand. For this he had no reason, certainly no excuse. Still, it may be urged in excuse that it was as much as an hour or an hour and a half before Winsome remembered that he needed any. Our most correct and ordered thoughts have a way of coming to us belated, as the passenger who strolls in confidently ten minutes after the platform is clear. But, like him, they are at least ready for the next train.

As Winsome and Ralph turned towards the east, the sun set his face over the great Scotch firs on the ridge, whose tops stood out like poised irregular blots on the fire centred ocean of light.

It was the new day, and if the new world had not come with it, of a surety it was well on the way.

CHAPTER XIII
A STRING OF THE LILAC SUNBONNET

For a long time they were silent, though it was not long before Winsome drew away her hand, which, however, continued to burn consciously for an hour afterwards. Silence settled around them. The constraint of speech fell first upon Ralph, being town-bred and accustomed to the convenances at Professor Thriepneuk's.

"You rise early," he said, glancing shyly down at Winsome, who seemed to have forgotten his presence. He did not wish her to forget. He had no objection to her dreaming, if only she would dream about him.

Winsome turned the bewildering calmness of her eyes upon him. A gentleman, they say, is calm-eyed. So is a cow. But in the eye of a good woman there is a peace which comes from many generations of mothers—who, every one Christs in their way, have suffered their heavier share of the Eden curse.

Ralph would have given all that he possessed—which, by the way, was not a great deal—to be able to assure himself that there was any hesitancy or bashfulness in the glance which met his own. But Winsome's eyes were as clearly and frankly blue as if God had made them new that morning. At least Ralph looked upon their Sabbath peace and gave thanks, finding them very good.

A sparkle of laughter, at first silent and far away, sprang into them, like a breeze coming down Loch Grannoch when it lies asleep in the sun, sending shining sparkles winking shoreward, and causing the wavering golden lights on the shallow sand of the bays to scatter tremulously. So in the depths of Winsome's eyes glimmered the coming smile. Winsome could be divinely serious, but behind there lay the possibility and certainty of very frank earthly laughter. If, as Ralph thought, not for the first time in this rough island story, this girl were an angel, surely she was one to whom her Maker had given that rarest gift given to woman— a well-balanced sense of humour.

So when Ralph said, hardly knowing what he said, "You rise early," it was with that far-away intention of a smile that Winsome replied:

"And you, sir, have surely not lagged in bed, or else you have come here in a great hurry."

"I rose," returned Ralph, "certainly betimes—in fact, a great while before day; it is the time when one can best know one's self."

The sententiousness, natural to his years and education, to some extent rebuked Winsome, who said more soberly:

"Perhaps you have again lost your books of study?"

"I do not always study in books," answered Ralph.

Winsome continued to look at him as though waiting his explanation.

"I mean," said Ralph, quickly, his pale cheek touched with red, "that though I am town-bred I love the things that wander among the flowers and in the wood. There are the birds, too, and the little green plants that have no flow ers, and they all have a message, if I could only hear it and understand it."

The sparkle in Winsome's eyes quieted into calm.

"I too—" she began, and paused as if startled at what she was about to say. She went on: "I never heard any one say things like these. I did not know that any one else had thoughts like these except myself."

"And have you thought these things?" said Ralph, with a quick joy in his heart.

"Yes," replied Winsome, looking down on the ground and playing with the loose string of the lilac sunbonnet. "I used often to wonder how it was that I could not look on the loch on Sabbath morning without feeling like crying. It was often better to look upon it than to go to Maister Welsh's kirk. But I ought not to say these things to you," she said, with a quick thought of his profession.

Ralph smiled. There were few things that Winsome Charteris might not say to him. He too had his experiences to collate.

"Have you ever stood on a hill-top as though you were suspended in the air, and when you seem to feel the earth whirling away from beneath you, rushing swiftly eastward towards the sunrise?"

"I have heard it," said Winsome unexpectedly.

"Heard it?" queried Ralph, with doubt in his voice.

"Yes," said Winsome calmly, "I have often heard the earth wheeling round on still nights out on the top of the Craigs, where there was no sound, and all the house was asleep. It is as if some Great One were saying 'Hush!' to the angels—I think God himself!"

These were not the opinions of the kirk of the Marrow; neither were they expressed in the Acts Declaratory or the protests or claims of right made by the faithful contending remnant. But Ralph would not at that moment have hesitated to add them to the Westminster Confession.

It is a wonderful thing to be young. It is marvellously delightful to be young and a poet as well, who has just fallen—nay, rather, plunged fathoms—deep in love. Ralph Peden was both. He stood watching Winsome Charteris, who looked past him into a distance moistly washed with tender ultramarine ash, like her own eyes too full of colour to be gray and too pearly clear to be blue.

An equal blowing wind drew up the loch which lay be neath flooded with morning light, the sun basking on its broad expanse, and glittering in a myriad sparkles on the, narrows beneath them beside which the blanket-washing had been. A frolicsome breeze blew down the hill towards them in little flicks and eddies. One of these drew a flossy tendril of Winsome's golden hair, which this morning had red lights in it like the garnet gloss on ripe wheat or Indian corn, and tossed it over her brow. Ralph's hand tingled with the desire to touch it and put it back under her bonnet, and his heart leaped at the thought. But though he did not stir, nor had any part of his being moved save the hidden thought of his heart, he seemed to fall in his own estimation as one who had attempted a sacrilege.

"Have you ever noticed," continued Winsome, all unconscious, going on with that fruitful comparison of feelings which has woven so many gossamer threads into three-fold cords, "how everything in the fields and the woods is tamer in the morning? They seem to have forgotten that man is their natural enemy while they slept."

"Perhaps," said Ralph theologically, "when they awake they forget that they are not still in that old garden that Adam kept."

Winsome was looking at him now, for he had looked away in his turn, lost in a poet's thought. It struck her for the first time that other people might think him handsome. When a girl forgets to think whether she herself is of this opinion, and begins to think what others will think on a subject like this (which really does not concern her at all), the proceedings in the case are not finished.

They walked on together down by the sunny edge of the great plantation. The sun was now rising well into the sky, climbing directly upward as if on this midsummer day he were leading a forlorn hope to scale the zenith of heaven. He shone on the russet tassels of the larches, and the deep sienna boles of the Scotch firs. The clouds, which rolled fleecy and white in piles and crenulated bastions of cumulus, lighted the eyes of the man and maid as they went onward upon the crisping piny carpet of fallen fir-needles.

"I have never seen Nature so lovely," said Ralph, "as when the bright morning breaks after a night of shower. Everything seems to have been new bathed in freshness."

"As if Dame Nature had had her spring cleaning," answered Winsome, "or Andrew Kissock when he has had his face washed once a week," who had been serious long enough, and who felt that too much earnestness even in the study of Nature might be a dangerous thing.

But the inner thought of each was something quite different. This is what Ralph thought within his heart, though his words were also perfectly genuine:

"There is a dimple on her chin which comes out when she smiles," so he wanted her to smile again. When she did so, she was lovely enough to peril the Faith or even the denomination.

Ralph tried to recollect if there were no more stiles on this hill path over which she might have to be helped. He had taken off his hat and walked beside her bareheaded, carrying his hat in the hand farthest from Winsome, who was wondering how soon she would be able to tell him that he must keep his shoulders back.

Winsome was not a young woman of great experience in these matters, but she had the natural instinct for the possibilities of love without which no woman comes into the world—at once armour defensive and weapon offensive. She knew that one day Ralph Peden would tell her that he loved her, but in the meantime it was so very pleasant that it was a pity the days should come to an end. So she resolved that they should not, at least not just yet. If to-morrow be good, why confine one's self to to-day? She had not yet faced the question of what she would say to him when the day could be no longer postponed. She did not care to face it. Sufficient unto the day is the good thereof, is quite as excellent a precept as its counterpart, or at least so Winsome Charteris thought. But, all the same, she wished that she could tell him to keep his shoulders back.

A sudden resolve sprang full armed from her brain. Winsome had that strange irresponsibility sometimes which comes irresistibly to some men and women in youth, to say something as an experiment which she well knew she ought not to say, simply to see what would happen. More than once it had got her into trouble.

"I wish you would keep back your shoulders when you walk!" she said, quick as a flash, stopping and turning sideways to face Ralph Peden.

Ralph, walking thoughtfully with the student stoop, stood aghast, as though not daring to reply lest his ears had not heard aright.

"I say, why do you not keep your shoulders back?" repeated Winsome sharply, and with a kind of irritation at his silence.

He had no right to make her feel uncomfortable, whatever she might say.

"I did not know—I thought—nobody ever told me," said Ralph, stammering and catching at the word which came uppermost, as he had done in college when Professor Thriepneuk, who was as fierce in the class-room as he was mild at home, had him cornered upon a quantity.

"Well, then," said Winsome, "if every one is so blind, it is time that some one did tell you now."

Ralph squared himself like a drill-sergeant, holding himself so straight that Winsome laughed outright, and that so merrily that Ralph laughed too, well content that the dimple on her cheek should play at hide and seek with the pink flush of her clear skin.

So they had come to the stile, and Ralph's heart beat stronger, and a nervous tension of expectation quivered through him, bewildering his judgment. But Winsome was very clear-headed, and though the white of her eyes was as dewy and clear as a child's, she was no simpleton. She had read many men and women in her time, for it is the same in essence to rule Craig Ronald as to rule Rome.

"This is your way," she said, sitting down on the stile. "I am going up to John Scott's to see about the lambs. It will be breakfast-time at the manse before you got back."

Ralph's castle fell to the ground.

"I will come up with you to John Scott's," he said with an undertone of eagerness.

"Indeed, that you will not," said Winsome promptly, who did not want to arrive at seven o'clock in the morning at John Scott's with any young man. "You will go home and take to your book, after you have changed your shoes and stockings," she said practically.

"Well, then, let me bid you good-bye, Winsome!" said Ralph.

Her heart was warm to hear him say Winsome—for the first time. It certainly was not unpleasant, and there was no need that she should quarrel about that. She was about to give him her hand, when she saw something in his eye.

"Mind, you are not to kiss it as you did grannie's yesterday; besides, there are John Scott's dogs on the brow of the hill," she said, pointing upward.

Poor Ralph could only look more crestfallen still. Such knowledge was too high for him. He fell back on his old formula:

"I said before that you are a witch—"

"And you say it again?" queried Winsome, with careless nonchalance, swinging her bonnet by its strings. "Well, you can come back and kiss grannie's hand some other day. You are something of a favourite with her."

But she had presumed just a hair-breadth too far on Ralph's gentleness. He snatched the lilac sunbonnet out of her hands, tearing, in his haste, one of the strings off, and leaving it in Winsome's hand. Then he kissed it once and twice outside where the sun shone on it, and inside where it had rested on her head. "You have torn it," she said complainlngly, yet without anger.

"I am very glad," said Ralph Peden, coming nearer to her with a light in his eye that she had never seen before.

Winsome dropped the string, snatched up the bonnet, and fled up the hill as trippingly as a young doe towards the herd's cottage. At the top of the fell she paused a moment with her hand on her side, as if out of breath. Ralph Peden was still holding the torn bonnet-string in his hand.

He held it up, hanging loose like a pennon from his hand. She could hear the words come clear up the hill:

-- "I'm very—glad—that—I—tore—it, and I will come and—see— your—grandmother!"

"Of all the—" Winsome stopped for want of words, speaking to herself as she turned away up the hill—"of all the insolent and disagreeable—"

She did not finish her sentence, as she adjusted the outraged sunbonnet on her curls, tucking the remaining string carefully within the crown; but as she turned again to look, Ralph Peden was calmly folding tip the string and putting it in a book.

"I shall never speak to him again as long as I live," she said, compressing her lips so that a dimple that Ralph had never seen came out on the other side. This, of course, closed the record in the case. Yet in a little while she added thoughtfully: "But he is very handsome, and I think he will keep his shoulders back now. Not, of course, that it matters, for I am never to speak to him any more!"

John Scott's dogs were by this time leaping upon her, and that worthy shepherd was coming along a steep slope upon the edges of his boot-soles in the miraculous manner, which is peculiar to herds, as if he were walking on the turnpike.

Winsome turned for the last time. Against the broad, dark sapphire expanse of the loch, just where the great march dyke stepped off to bathe in the summer water, she saw something black which waved a hand and sprang over lightly.

Winsome sighed, and said a little wistfully yet not sadly:

"Who would have thought it of him? It just shows!" she said. All which is a warning to maids that the meekest worm may turn.

CHAPTER XIV
CAPTAIN AGNEW GREATORIX

Greatorix Castle sat mightily upon a hill. It could not be hid, and it looked down superciliously upon the little squiredom of Craig Ronald, as well as upon farms and cottages a many. In days not so long gone by, Greatorix Castle had been the hold of the wearers of the White Cockade, rough riders after Lag and Sir James Dalzyell, and rebels after that, who had held with Derwentwater and the prince. Now there was quiet there. Only the Lady Elizabeth and her son Agnew Greatorix dwelt there, and the farmer's cow and the cottager's pig grazed and rooted unharmed—not always, however, it was whispered, the farmer's daughter, for of all serfdoms the droit du seignior is the last to die. Still, Greatorix Castle was a notable place, high set on its hill, shires and towns beneath, the blue breath of peat reek blowing athwart the plain beneath and rising like an incense about.

Here the Lady Elizabeth dwelt in solemn but greatly reduced state. She was a woman devoted to the practice of holiness according to the way of the priest. It was the whole wish of her life that she might keep a spiritual director, instead of having Father Mahon to ride over from Dumfries once a month.

Within the castle there were many signs of decay—none of rehabilitation. The carpets were worn into holes where feet had oftenest fallen, and the few servants dared not take them out to be beaten in the due season of the year, for indubitably they would fall to pieces. So the curtains hung till an unwary stranger would rest upon them with a hand's weight. Then that hand plucked a palmbreadth away of the rotten and moth-eaten fabric.

There was an aged housekeeper at Greatorix Castle, who dwelt in the next room to the Lady Elizabeth, and was supposed to act as her maid. Mistress Humbie, however, was an exacting person; and being an aged woman, and her infirmities bearing upon her, she considered it more fitting that the Lady Elizabeth should wait upon her. This, for the good of her soul, the Lady Elizabeth did. Two maids and a boy, a demon boy, in buttons, who dwelt below- stairs and gave his time to the killing of rats with ingenious catapults and crossbows, completed the household—except Agnew Greatorix.

The exception was a notable one. Save in the matter of fortune, Nature had not dealt unhandsomely with Agnew Greatorix; yet just because of this his chances of growing up into a strong and useful man were few. He had been nurtured upon expectations from his earliest youth. His uncle Agnew, the Lady Elizabeth's childless brother, who for the sake of the favour of a strongly Protestant aunt had left the mother church of the Greatorix family, had been expected to do something for Agnew; but up to this present time he had received only his name from him, in lieu of all the stately heritages of Holywood in the Nith Valley hard by Lincluden, and Stennesholm in Carrick.

So Agnew Greatorix had grown up in the midst of raw youths who were not his peers in position. He companied with them till his mother pointed out that it was not for a Greatorix to drink in the Blue Bell and at the George with the sons of wealthy farmers and bonnet lairds. By dint of scraping and saving which took a long time, and influence which, costing nothing, took for a Greatorix no time at all, the Lady Elizabeth obtained for her son a commission in the county yeomanry. There he was thrown with Maxwells of the Braes, Herons from the Shireside, and Gordons from the northern straths—all young men of means and figure in the county. Into the midst of these Agnew took his tightly knit athletic figure, his small firmly set head and full-blooded dark face—the only faults of which were that the eyes were too closely set together and shuttered with lids that would not open more than half way, and that he possessed the sensual mouth of a man who has never willingly submitted to a restraint. Agnew Greatorix could not compete with his companions, but he cut them out as a squire of dames, and came home with a dangerous and fascinating reputation, the best-hated man in the corps.

So when Captain Agnew clattered through the village in clean-cut scarlet and clinking spurs, all the maids ran to the door, except only a few who had once run like the others but now ran no more. The captain came often to Craig Ronald. It was upon his way to kirk and market, for the captain for the good of his soul went occasionally to the little chapel of the Permission at Dumfries. Still oftener he came with the books which the Lady Elizabeth obtained from Edinburgh, the reading of which she shared with Mistress Walter Skirving, whose kinship with the Lochinvars she did not forget, though her father had been of the moorland branch of that honourable house, and she herself had disgraced her ancient name by marrying with a psalm-singing bonnet laird. But the inexplicability of saying whom a woman may not take it into her head to marry was no barrier to the friendship of the Lady Elizabeth, who kept all her religion for her own consumption and did not even trouble her son with it—which was a great pity, for he indeed had much need, though small desire, thereof.

On the contrary, it was a mark of good blood sometimes to follow one's own fancy. The Lady Elizabeth had done that herself against the advice of the countess her mother, and that was the reason why she dwelt amid hangings that came away in handfuls, and was waiting-maid to Mistress Humbie her own housekeeper.

Agnew Greatorix had an eye for a pretty face, or rather for every pretty face. Indeed, he had nothing else to do, except clean his spurs and ride to the market town. So, since the author of Waverley began to write his inimitable fictions, and his mother to divide her time between works of devotion and the adventures of Ivanhoe and Nigel, Agnew Greatorix had made many pilgrimages to Craig Ronald. Here the advent of the captain was much talked over by the maids, and even anticipated by Winsome herself as a picturesque break in the monotony of the staid country life. Certainly he brought the essence of strength and youth and athletic energy into the quiet court-yard, when he rode in on his showily paced horse and reined him round at the low steps of the front door, with the free handling and cavalry swing which he had inherited as much from the long line of Greatorixes who had ridden out to harry the Warden's men along the marches, as from the yeomanry riding-master.

Now, the captain was neither an obliging nor yet a particularly amiable young man, and when he took so kindly to fetching and carrying, it was not long before the broad world of farm towns and herds' cot-houses upon which Greatorix Castle looked down suspected a motive, and said so in its own way.

On one occasion, riding down the long loaning of Craig Ronald, the captain came upon the slight, ascetic figure of Allan Welsh, the Marrow minister, leaning upon the gate which closed the loaning from the road. The minister observed him, but showed no signs of moving. Agnew Greatorix checked his horse.

"Would you open the gate and allow me to pass on my way?" he said, with chill politeness. The minister of the Marrow kirk looked keenly at him from under his grey eyebrows.

"After I have had a few words with you, young sir," said Mr. Welsh.

"I desire no words with you," returned the young man impatiently, backing his horse.

"For whom are your visits at Craig Ronald intended?" said the minister calmly. "Walter Skirving and his spouse do not receive company of such dignity; and besides them there are only the maids that I know of."

"Who made you my father confessor?" mocked Agnew Greatorix, with an unpleasant sneer on his handsome face.

"The right of being minister in the things of the Spirit to all that dwell in Craig Ronald House," said the minister of the Marrow firmly.

"Truly a pleasant ministry, and one, no doubt, requiring frequent ministrations; yet do I not remember to have met you at Craig Ronald," he continued. "So faithful a minister surely must be faithful in his spiritual attentions."

He urged his horse to the side of the gate and leaned over to open the gate himself, but the minister had his hand firmly on the latch.

"I have seen you ride to many maids' houses, Agnew Greatorix, since the day your honoured father died, but never a one have I seen the better of your visits. Woe and sorrow have attended upon your way. You may ride off now at your ease, but beware the vengeance of the God of Jacob; the mother's curse and the father's malison ride not far behind!"

"Preach me no preachments," said the young man; "keep such for your Marrow folk on Sundays; you but waste your words."

"Then I beseech you by the memory of a good father, whom, though of another and an alien communion, I shall ever respect, to cast your eyes elsewhere, and let the one ewe lamb of those whom God hath stricken alone."

The gate was open now, and as he came through, Agnew Greatorix made his horse curvet, pushing the frail form of the preacher almost into the hedge.

"If you would like to come and visit us up at the castle," he said mockingly, "I dare say we could yet receive you as my forefathers, of whom you are so fond, used to welcome your kind. I saw the thumbikins the other day; and I dare say we could fit you with your size in boots."

"The Lord shall pull down the mighty from their seats, and exalt them that are of low estate!" said the preacher solemnly.

"Very likely," said the young man as he rode away.

CHAPTER XV
ON THE EDGE OF THE ORCHARD

But Agnew Greatorix came as often as ever to Craig Ronald. Generally he found Winsome busy with her household affairs, sometimes with her sleeves buckled above her elbows, rolling the tough dough for the crumpy farles of the oat-cake, and scattering handfuls of dry meal over it with deft fingers to bring the mass to its proper consistency for rolling out upon the bake-board. Leaving his horse tethered to the great dismounting stone at the angle of the kitchen (a granite boulder or "travelled stone," as they said thereabouts), with an iron ring into it, he entered and sat down to watch. Sometimes, as to-day, he would be only silent and watchful; but he never failed to compass Winsome with the compliment of humility and observance. It is possible that better things were stirring in his heart than usually brought him to such places. There is no doubt, indeed, that he appreciated the frankness and plain speech which he received from the very practical young mistress of Craig Ronald.

When he left the house it was Agnew Greatorix's invariable custom to skirt the edge of the orchard before mounting. Just in the dusk of the great oak-tree, where its branches mingle with those of the gean [wild cherry], he was met by the slim, lithe figure of Jess Kissock, in whose piquant elvishness some strain of Romany blood showed itself.

Jess had been waiting for him ever since he had taken his hat in his hand to leave the house. As he came in sight of the watcher, Agnew Greatorix stopped, and Jess came closer to him, motioning him imperiously to bring his horse close in to the shadow of the orchard wall. Agnew did so, putting out his arm as if he would kiss her; but, with a quick fierce movement, Jess thrust his hand away.

"I have told you before not to play these tricks with me—keep them for them that ye come to Craig Ronald to see. It's the mistress ye want. What need a gentleman like you meddle with the maid?"

"Impossible as it may seem, the like has been done," said Agnew, smiling down at the black eyes and blowing elf locks.

"Not with this maid," replied Jess succinctly, and in deed slhe looked exceedingly able to take care of herself, as became Meg Kissock's sister.

"I'll go no further with Winsome," said Greatorix gloomily, breaking the silence. "You said that if I consulted her about the well-being of the poor rats over at the huts, and took her advice about the new cottages for the foresters, she would listen to me. Well, she did listen, but as soon as I hinted at any other subject, I might as well have been talking to the old daisy in the sitting-room with the white band round her head."

"Did anybody ever see the like of you menfolk?" cried Jess, throwing up her hands hopelessly; "d'ye think that a bonny lass is just like a black ripe cherry on a bough, ready to drap into your mooth when it pleases your high mightinesses to hold it open?"

"Has Winsome charteris any sweetheart?" asked the captain.

"What for wad she be doing with a sweetheart? She has muckle else to think on. There's a young man that's baith braw an' bonny, a great scholar frae Enbra' toon that comes gye an' aften frae the manse o' Dullarg, whaur he's bidin' a' the simmer for the learnin'. He comes whiles, an' Winsome kind o' gies him a bit convoy up the hill."

"Jess Kissock," said the young man passionately, "tell me no lies, or—"

"Nane o' yer ill tongue for me, young man; keep it for yer mither. I'm little feared o' ye or ony like ye. Ye'll maybe get a bit dab frae the neb o' a jockteleg [point of a sheath-knife] that will yeuk [tickle] ye for a day or twa gin ye dinna learn an' that speedily, as Maister Welsh wad say, to keep yer Han's aff my faither's dochter." Jess's good Scots was infinitely better and more vigorous than the English of the lady's maid.

"I beg your pardon, Jess. I am a passionate, hasty man. I am sure I meant no harm. Tell me more of this hulking landlouper [intruder], and I'll give you a kiss."

"Keep yer kisses for them that likes them. The young man's no landlouper ony mair nor yersel'—no as mickle indeed, but a very proper young man, wi' a face as bonny as an angel—"

"But, Jess, do you mean to say that you are going to help him with Winsome?" asked the young man.

"Feint a bit!" answered the young woman frankly. "She'll no get him gin I can help it. I saw him first and bid him guid-day afore ever she set her een on him. It's ilka yin for hersel' when it comes to a braw young man," and Jess tossed her gipsy head, and pouted a pair of handsome scarlet lips.

Greatorix laughed. "The land lies that way, does it?" he said. "Then that's why you would not give me a kiss to-day, Jess," he went on; "the black coat has routed the red baith but an' ben—but we'll see. You cannot both have him, Jess, and if you are so very fond of the parson, ye'll maybe help me to keep Winsome Charteris to myself."

"Wad ye mairry her gin ye had the chance, Agnew Greatorix?"

"Certainly; what else?" replied the young man promptly.

"Then ye shall hae her," replied Jess, as if Winsome were within her deed of gift,

"And you'll try for the student, Jess?" asked the young man. "I suppose he would not need to ask twice for a kiss?"

"Na, for I would kiss him withoot askin'—that is, gin he hadna the sense to kiss ME," said Jess frankly.

"Well," said Greatorix, somewhat reluctantly, "I'm sure I wish you joy of your parson. I see now what the canting old hound from the Dullarg Manse meant when he tackled me at the loaning foot. He wanted Winsome for the young whelp."

"I dinna think that," replied Jess; "he disna want him to come aboot here ony mair nor you."

"How do you know that, Jess?"

"Ou, I juist ken."

"Can you find out what Winsome thinks herself?"

"I can that, though she hasna a word to say to me—that am far mair deservin' o' confidence than that muckle peony faced hempie, Meg, that an ill Providence gied me for a sister. Her keep a secret?—the wind wad waft it oot o' her." Thus affectionately Jess.

"But how can you find out, then?" persisted the young man, yet unsatisfied.

"Ou fine that," said Jess. "Meg talks in her sleep."

Before Agnew Greatorix leaped on to his horse, which all this time had stood quiet on his bridle-arm, only occasion ally jerking his head as if to ask his master to come away, he took the kiss he had been denied, and rode away laugh ing, but with one cheek much redder than the other, the mark of Jess's vengeance.

"Ye hae ower muckle conceit an' ower little sense ever to be a richt blackguard," said Jess as he went, "but ye hae the richt intention for the deil's wark. Ye'll do the young mistress nae hurt, for she wad never look twice at ye, but I cannot let her get the bonny lad frae Embra'-na, I saw him first, an' first come first served!"

"Where have you been so long," asked her mistress, as she came in.

"Juist drivin' a gilravagin' muckle swine oot o' the or chard!" replied Jess with some force and truth.

CHAPTER XVI
THE CUIF BEFORE THE SESSION

"Called, nominate, summoned to appear, upon this third citation, Alexander Mowdiewort, or Moldieward, to answer for the sin of misca'in' the minister and session o' this parish, and to show cause why he, as a sectary notour, should not demit, depone, and resign his office of grave digger in the kirk-yard of this parish with all the emoluments, benefits, and profits thereto appertaining.—Officer, call Alexander Mowdiewort!"

Thus Jacob Kittle, schoolmaster and session clerk of the parish of Dullarg, when in the kirk itself that reverent though not revered body was met in full convocation. There was presiding the Rev. Erasmus Teends himself, the minister of the parish, looking like a turkey-cock with a crumpled white neckcloth for wattles. He was known in the parish as Mess John, and was full of dignified discourse and excellent taste in the good cheer of the farmers. He was a judge of nowt [cattle], and a connoisseur of black puddings, which he considered to require some Isle of Man brandy to bring out their own proper flavour.

"Alexander Moldieward, Alexander Moldieward!" cried old Snuffy Callum, the parish beadle, going to the door. Then in a lower tone, "Come an' answer for't, Saunders."

Mowdiewort and a large-boned, grim-faced old woman of fifty-five were close beside the door, but Christie cried past them as if the summoned persons were at the top of the Dullarg Hill at the nearest, and also as if he had not just risen from a long and confidential talk with them.

It was within the black interior of the old kirk that the session met, in the yard of which Saunders Mowdiewort had dug so many graves, and now was to dig no more, unless he appeased the ire of the minister and his elders for an offence against the majesty of their court and moderator.

"Alexander Moldieward!" again cried the old "betheral," very loud, to some one on the top of the Dullarg Hill—then in an ordinary voice, "come awa', Saunders man, you and your mither, an' dinna keep them waitin'— they're no chancy when they're keepit."

Saunders and his mother entered.

"Here I am, guid sirs, an' you Mess John," said the grave-digger very respectfully, "an' my mither to answer for me, an' guid een to ye a'."

"Come awa', Mistress Mowdiewort," said the minister. "Ye hae aye been a guid member in full communion. Ye never gaed to a prayer- meetin' or Whig conventicle in yer life. It's a sad peety that ye couldna keep your flesh an' bluid frae companyin' an' covenantin' wi' them that lichtly speak o' the kirk."

"'Deed, minister, we canna help oor bairns—an' 'deed ye can speak till himsel'. He is of age—ask him! But gin ye begin to be ower sair on the callant, I'se e'en hae to tak' up the cudgels mysel'."

With this, Mistress Mowdiewort put her hands to the strings of her mutch, to feel that she had not unsettled them; then she stood with arms akimbo and her chest well forward like a grenadier, as if daring the session to do its worst.

"I have a word with you," said Mess John, lowering at her; "it is told to me that yon keepit your son back from answering the session when it was his bounden duty to appear on the first summons. Indeed, it is only on a warrant for blasphemy and the threat of deprivation of his liveli hood that he has come to-day. What have you to say that he should not be deprived and also declarit excommunicate?"

"Weel, savin' yer presence, Mess John," said Mistress Mowdiewort, "ye see the way o't is this: Saunders, my son, is a blate [shy] man, an' he canna weel speak for him sel'. I thought that by this time the craiter micht hae gotten a wife again that could hae spoken for him, an' had he been worth the weight o' a bumbee's hind leg he wad hae had her or this—an' a better yin nor the last he got. Aye, but a sair trouble she was to me; she had juist yae faut, Saunders's first wife, an' that was she was nae use ava! But it was a guid thing he was grave-digger, for he got her buriet for naething, an' even the coffin was what ye micht ca' a second-hand yin—though it had never been worn, which was a wunnerfu' thing. Ye see the way o't was this: There was Creeshy Callum, the brither o' yer doitit [stupid] auld betheral here, that canna tak' up the buiks as they should (ye should see my Saunders tak' them up at the Marrow kirk)—"

"Woman," said the minister, "we dinna want to hear—"

"Very likely no—but ye hae gien me permission to speak, an' her that's stannin afore yer honourable coort, brawly kens the laws. Elspeth

Mowdiewort didna soop yer kirk an wait till yer session meetings war ower for thirty year in my ain man's time withoot kennin' a' the laws. A keyhole's a most amazin' convenient thing by whiles, an' I was suppler in gettin' up aff my hunkers then than at the present time."

"Silence, senseless woman!" said the session clerk.

"I'll silence nane, Jacob Kittle; silence yersel', for I ken what's in the third volume o' the kirk records at the thirty second page; an' gin ye dinna haud yer wheesht, dominie, ilka wife in the pairish'll ken as weel as me. A bonny yin you to sit cockin' there, an' to be learnin' a' the bairns their caritches [catechism]."

The session let her go her way; her son meantime stood passing an apologetic hand over his sleek hair, and making deprecatory motions to the minister, when he thought that his mother was not looking in his direction.

"Aye, I was speakin' aboot Creeshy Callum's coffin that oor Saunders — the muckle tongueless sumph there got dirt cheap — ye see Greeshy had been measured for't, but, as he had a short leg and a shorter, the joiner measured the wrang leg — joiners are a' dottle stupid bodies — an' whan the time cam' for Creeshy to be streekit, man, he wadna fit — na, it maun hae been a sair disappointment till him — that is to say — gin he war in the place whaur he could think wi' ony content on his coffin, an' that, judgin' by his life an' conversation, was far frae bein' a certainty."

"Mistress Mowdiewort, I hae aye respectit ye, an' we are a' willin' to hear ye noo, if you have onything to say for your son, but you must make no insinuations against any members of the court, or I shall be compelled to call the officer to put you out," said the minister, rising impressively with his hand stretched towards Mistress Elspeth Mowdiewort.

But Elspeth Mowdiewort was far from being impressed.

"Pit me oot, Snuffy Oallum; pit me, Eppie Mowdiewort, oot! Na, na, Snuffy's maybe no very wise, but he kens better nor that. Man, Maister Teends, I hae kenned the hale root an' stock o' thae Callums frae first to last; I hae dung Greeshy till he couldna stand — him that had to be twice fitted for his coffin; an' Wull that was hangit at Dumfries for sheep-stealin'; an' Meg that was servant till yersel — aye, an' a bonny piece she was as ye ken yersel'; an' this auld donnert carle that, when he carries up the Bibles, ye can hear the rattlin' o' his banes, till it disturbs the congregation — I hae dung them a' heeds ower heels in their best days — an' to tell me at the hinner end that ye wad ca' in the betheral to pit oot Elspeth Mowdiewort! Ye maun surely hae an awsome ill wull at the puir auld craitur!"

"Mither," at last said Saunders, who was becoming anxious for his grave-diggership, and did not wish to incense his judges further, "I'm willin' to confess that I had a drap ower muckle the ither night when I met in wi' the minister an' the dominie; but, gin I confess it, ye'll no gar me sit on the muckle black stool i' repentance afore a' the fowk, an' me carries up the buiks i' the Marrow kirk."

"Alexander Mowdiewort, ye spak ill o' the minister an' session, o' the kirk an' the wholesome order o' this parish. We have a warrant for your apprehension and appearance which we might, unless moved by penitence and dutiful submission, put in force. Then are ye aware whaur that wad land you—i' the jail in Kirkcudbright toon, my man Saunders."

But still it was the dread disgrace of the stool of repentance that bulked most largely in the culprit's imagination.

"Na, na," interjected Mistress Mowdiewort, "nae siccan things for ony bairns o' mine. Nae son o' mine sall ever set his hurdies on the like o't."

"Be silent, woman!" said the minister severely; "them that will to black stool maun to black stool. Rebukit an' chastised is the law an' order, and rebukit and chastised shall your son be as weel as ithers."

"'Deed, yer nae sae fond o' rebukin' the great an' the rich. There's that young speldron frae the castle; its weel kenned what he is, an' hoo muckle he's gotten the weight o'."

"He is not of our communion, and not subject to our discipline," began the minister.

"Weel," said Elspeth, "weel, let him alane. He's a Pape, an' gaun to purgatory at ony gate. But then there's bletherin' Johnnie o' the Dinnance Mains—he's as fu' as Solway tide ilka Wednesday, an' no only speaks agin minister an' session, as maybe my Saunders did (an' maybe no), but abuses Providence, an the bellman, an' even blasphemes agin the fast day—yet I never heard that ye had him cockit up on the black henbauks i' the kirk. But then he's a braw man an' keeps a gig!"

"The law o' the kirk is no respecter of persons," said Mess John.

"No, unless they are heritors," said Cochrane of the Holm, who had a pew with the name of his holding painted on it.

"Or members o' session," said sleeky Carment of the Kirkland, who had twice escaped the stool of repentance on the ground that, as he urged upon the body, "gleds [hawks] shouldna pike gleds een oot."

"Or parish dominies," said the session clerk, to give solidarity to his own position.

"Weel, I ken juist this if nae mair: my son disna sit on ony o' yer stools o' repentance," said Eppie Mowdiewort, demonstrating the truth of her position with her hand clenched at the dominie, who, like all clerks of ecclesiastical assemblies, was exceedingly industrious in taking notes to very small purpose. "Mair nor that, I'm maybe an unlearned woman, but I've been through the Testaments mair nor yince—the New Testament mair nor twice—an' I never saw naethin' aboot stools o' repentance in the hoose o' God. But my son Saunders was readin' to me the ither nicht in a fule history buik, an' there it said that amang the Papists they used to hae fowk that didna do as they did an' believe as they believed. Sae wi' a lang white serk on, an' a can'le i' their hands, they set them up for the rabble fowk to clod at them, an' whiles they tied them to a bit stick an' set lunt [fire] them—an that's the origin o' yer stool o' repentance. What say ye to that?"

Mrs. Mowdiewort's lecture on church history was not at all appreciated by the session. The minister rose.

"We will close this sederunt," he said; "we can mak' nocht o' these two. Alexander Mowdiewort, thou art removed from thy office of grave-digger in the parish kirkyard, and both thysel' and thy mother are put under suspension for contumacy!"

"Haith!" said Elspeth Mowdiewort, pushing back her hair; "did ye ever hear the mak' o' the craitur. I haena been within his kirk door for twenty year. It's a guid job that a body can aye gang doon to godly Maister Welsh, though he's an awfu' body to deave [deafen] ye wi' the Shorter Quastions."

"An it's a guid thing," added Saunders, "that there's a new cemetery a-makkin'. There's no room for anither dizzen in yer auld kailyaird onyway—an' that I'm tellin' ye. An' I'm promised the new job too. Ye can howk yer ain graves yersel's."

"Fash na yer heid, Saunders, aboot them," said the old betheral at the door; "it's me that's to be grave-digger, but ye shall howk them a' the same in the mornin', an' get the siller, for I'm far ower frail—ye can hae them a' by afore nine o'clock, an' the minister disna pu' up his bedroom blind till ten!"

Thus it was that Saunders Mowdiewort ended his connection with an Erastian establishment, and became a true and complete member of the Marrow kirk. His mother also attended with exemplary diligence, but she was much troubled with a toothache on the days of catechising, and never quite conquered her unruly member to the last. But this did not trouble herself much—only her neighbours.

CHAPTER XVII
WHEN THE KYE COMES HAME

That night Saunders went up over the hill again, dressed in his best. He was not a proud lover, and he did not take a rebuff amiss; besides, he had something to tell Meg Kissock. When he got to Craig Ronald, the girls were in the byre at the milking, and at every cow's tail there stood a young man, rompish Ebie Farrish at that at which Jess was milking, and quiet Jock Forrest at Meg's. Ebie was joking and keeping up a fire of running comment with Jess, whose dark-browed gipsy face and blue-black wisps of hair were set sideways towards him, with her cheek pressed upon Lucky's side, as she sent the warm white milk from her nimble fingers, with a pleasant musical hissing sound against the sides of the milking-pail.

Farther up the byre, Meg leaned her head against Crummy and milked steadily. Apparently she and Jock Forrest were not talking at all. Jock looked down and only a quiver of the corner of his beard betrayed that he was speaking. Meg, usually so outspoken and full of conversation, appeared to be silent; but really a series of short, low-toned sentences was being rapidly exchanged, so swiftly that no one, standing a couple of yards away, could have remarked the deft interchange.

But as soon as Saunders Mowdiewort came to the door, Jock Forrest had dropped Crummy's tail, and slipped silently out of the byre, even before Meg got time to utter her usual salutation of—

"Guid een to ye, Cuif! Hoo's a' the session?"

It might have been the advent of Meg's would-be sweetheart that frightened Jock Forrest away, or again he might have been in the act of going in any case. Jock was a quiet man who walked sedately and took counsel of no one. He was seldom seen talking to any man, never to a woman—least of all to Meg Kissock. But when Meg had many "lads" to see her in the evening, he could he observed to smile an inward smile in the depths of his yellow beard, and a queer subterranean chuckle pervaded his great body, so that on one occasion Jess looked up, thinking that there were hens roosting in the baulks overhead.

Jess and Ebie pursued their flirtation steadily and harmlessly, as she shifted down the byre as cow after cow was relieved of her richly perfumed load, rumbling and clinking neck chains, and munching in their head-stalls all the while. Saunders and Meg were as much alone as if they had been afloat on the bosom of Loch Grannoch.

"Ye are a bonny like man," said Meg, "to tak' yer minny to speak for ye before the session. Man, I wonder at ye. I wonder ye didna bring her to coort for ye?"

"War ye ever afore the Session, Meg?"

"Me afore the session—ye're a fule man, but ye dinna ken what yer sayin'—gin I thocht ye did—"

Here Meg became so violently agitated that Flecky, suffering from the manner in which Meg was doing her duty, kicked out, and nearly succeeded in overturning the milk-pail. Meg's quickness with hand and knee foiled this intention, but Flecky succeeded quite in planting the edge of her hoof directly on the Cuif's shin-bone. Saunders thereupon let go Flecky's tail, who instantly switched it into Meg's face with a crack like a whip.

"Ye great muckle senseless hullion!" exclaimed Meg, "gin ye are nae use in the byre, gang oot till ye can learn to keep haud o' a coo's tail! Ye hae nae mair sense than an Eerishman!"

There was a pause. The subject did not admit of discussion, though Saunders was a cuif, he knew when to hold his tongue—at least on most occasions.

"An' what brocht ye here the nicht, Cuif?" asked Meg, who, when she wanted information, knew how to ask it directly, a very rare feminine accomplishment.

"To see you, Meg, my dawtie," replied Saunders, tenderly edging nearer.

"Yer what?" queried Meg with asperity; "I thocht that ye had aneuch o' the session already for caa'in' honest fowk names; gin ye begin wi' me, ye'll get on the stool o' repentance o' yer ain accord, afore I hae dune wi' ye!"

"But, Meg, I hae telled ye afore that I am sair in need o' a wife. It's byordinar' [extraordinary] lonesome up in the hoose on the hill. An' I'm warned oot, Meg, so that I'll look nae langer on the white stanes o' the kirkyaird."

"Gin ye want a wife, Saunders, ye'll hae to look oot for a deef yin, for it's no ony or'nar' woman that could stand yer mither's tongue. Na, Saunders, it wad be like leevin' i' a corn-mill rinnin' withoot sheaves."

"Meg," said Saunders, edging up cautiously, "I hae something to gie ye!"

"Aff wi' ye, Cuif! I'll hae nae trokin' wi' lads i' the byre—na, there's a time for everything—especial wi' widowers, they're the warst o' a'—they ken ower muckle. My granny used to say, gin Solomon couldna redd oot the way o' a man wi' a maid, what wad he hae made o' the way o' a weedower that's lookin' for his third?"

CHAPTER XVIII
A DAUGHTER OF THE PICTS

The Cuif put his hands in his pockets as if to keep them away from the dangerous temptation of touching Meg. He stood with his shoulder against the wall and chewed a straw.

"What's come o' Maister Peden thae days?" asked Meg.

"He's maist michty unsettled like," replied Saunders, "he's for a' the world like a stirk wi' a horse cleg on him that he canna get at. He comes in an' sits doon at his desk, an' spreads oot his buiks, an' ye wad think that he's gaun to be at it the leevelang day. But afore ye hae time to turn roon' an' get at yer ain wark, the craitur'll be oot again an' awa' up to the hill wi' a buik aneath his oxter. Then he rises early in the mornin', whilk is no a guid sign o' a learned man, as I judge. What for should a learned man rise afore his parritch is made? There maun be something sair wrang," said Saunders Mowdiewort.

"Muckle ye ken aboot learned men. I suppose, ye think because ye carry up the Bible, that ye ken a' that's in't," returned Meg, with a sneer of her voice that might have turned milk sour. The expression of the emotions is fine and positive in the kitchens of the farm towns of Galloway.

"SWISH, SWISH!" steadily the white streams of milk shot into the pails. "JANGLE, JANGLE!" went the steel head chains of the cows. Occasionally, as Jess and Meg lifted their stools, they gave Flecky or Speckly a sound clap on the back with their hand or milking-pail, with the sharp command of "Stan' aboot there!" "Haud up!" "Mind whaur yer comin'!" Such expressions as these Jess and Meg could interject into the even tenor of their conversation, in a way that might have been disconcerting in dialogues conducted on other principles. But really the interruptions did not affect Ebie Farrish or any other of the byre-visiting young men, any more than the rattling of the chains, as Flecky and Speckly arranged their own business at the end devoted to imports. These sharp words of command were part of the nightly and morningly ceremony of the "milking" at every farm.

The cans could no more froth with the white reaming milk without this accompaniment of slaps and adjurations than Speckly, Flecky, and the rest could take their slow, thoughtfully considerate, and sober way from the hill pastures into the yard without Meg at the gate of the field to cry: "Hurley, Hurley, hie awa' hame!" to the cows themselves; and "Come awa' bye wi' them, fetch them, Roger!" to the short-haired collie, who knew so much better than to go near their flashing heels.

The conversation in the byre proceeded somewhat in this way:

Jess was milking her last cow, with her head looking sideways at Ebie, who stood plaiting Marly's tail in a newfangled fashion he had brought from the low end of the parish, and which was just making its way among young men of taste.

"Aye, ye'll say so, nae doot," said Jess, in reply to some pointed compliment of her admirer; "but I ken you fowk frae the laich end ower weel. Ye hae practeesed a' that kind o' talk on the lasses doon there, or ye wadna be sae gleg [ready] wi't to me, Ebie."

This is an observation which shows that Jess could not have eaten more effectively of the tree of knowledge, had she been born in Mayfair.

Ebie laughed a laugh half of depreciation, half of pleasure, like a cat that has its back stroked and its tail pinched at the same time.

"Na, na, Jess, it a' comes by natur'. I never likit a lassie afore I set my een on you," said Ebie, which, to say the least of it, was curious, considering that he had an assortment of locks of hair—black, brown, and lint-white—up in the bottom of his "kist" in the stable loft where he slept. He kept them along with his whipcord and best Sunday pocket knife, and sometimes he took a look at them when he had to move them in order to get his green necktie. "I never really likit a lass afore, Jess, ye may believe me, for I wasna a lad to rin after them. But whenever I cam' to Craig Ronald I saw that I was dune for."

"STAN' BACK, YE MUCKLE SLABBER!" said Jess, suddenly and emphatically, in a voice that could have been heard a hundred yards away. Speckly was pushing sideways against her as if to crowd her off her stool.

"Say ye sae, Ebie?" she added, as if she had not previously spoken, in the low even voice in which she had spoken from the first, and which could be heard by Ebie alone. In the country they conduct their love-making in water-tight compartments. And though Ebie knew very well that the Cuif was there, and may have suspected Jock Forrest, even after his apparent withdrawal, so long as they did not trouble him in his conversation with Jess, he paid no heed to them, nor indeed they to him. No man is his brother's keeper when he goes to the byre to plait cows' tails.

"But hoo div ye ken, or, raither, what gars ye think that ye're no the first that I hae likit, Jess?"

"Oh, I ken fine," said Jess, who was a woman of knowledge, and had her share of original sin.

"But hoo div ye ken?" persisted Ebie.

"Fine that," said Jess, diplomatically.

A DAUGHTER OF THE PICTS

"But tell us, Jess," said Ebie, who was in high good humour at these fascinating accusations.

"Oh," said Jess, with a quick gipsy look out of her fine dark eyes, "brawly I kenned on Saturday nicht that yon wasna the first time ye had kissed a lass!"

"Jess," said Ebie, "ye're a wunnerfu' woman!" which was his version of Ralph's "You are a witch." In Ebie's circle "witch" was too real a word to be lightly used, so he said "wunnerfu' woman."

He went on looking critically at Jess, as became so great a connoisseur of the sex.

"I hae seen, maybes, bonnier faces, as ye micht say—"

"HAUD AFF, WI' YE THERE; MIND WHAUR YER COMIN', YE MUCKLE SENSELESS NOWT!" said Jess to her Ayrshire Hornie, who had been treading on her toes.

"As I was sayin', Jess, I hae seen—"

"CAN YE NO UNNERSTAN', YE SENSELESS LUMP?" cried Jess, warningly; "I'll knock the heid aff ye, gin ye dinna drap it!" still to Hornie, of course.

But the purblind theorist went on his way: "I hae seen bonnier faces, but no mair takin', Jess, than yours. It's no aye beauty that tak's a man, Jess, ye see, an' the lassies that hae dune best hae been plain-favoured lassies that had pleasant expressions—"

"Tell the rest to Hornie gin ye like!" said Jess, rising viciously and leaving Ebie standing there dumfounded. He continued to hold Hornie's tail for some time, as if he wished to give her some further information on the theory of beauty, as understood in the "laich" end of the parish.

Saunders saw him from afar, and cried out to him down the length of the byre,

"Are ye gaun to mak' a watch-guard o' that coo's tail, Ebie?—ye look fell fond o't."

"Ye see what it is to be in love," said John Scott, the herd, who had stolen to the door unperceived and so had marked Ebie's discomfiture.

"He disna ken the difference between Jess hersel' an' Hornie!" said the Cuif, who was repaying old scores.

CHAPTER XIX
AT THE BARN END

In a little while the cows were all milked. Saunders was standing at the end of the barn, looking down the long valley of the Grannoch water. There was a sweet coolness in the air, which he vaguely recognized by taking off his hat.

"Open the yett!" cried Jess, from the byre door. Saunders heard the clank and jangle of the neck chains of Hornie and Specky and the rest, as they fell from their necks, loosened by Jess's hand. The sound grew fainter and fainter as Jess proceeded to the top of the byre where Marly stood soberly sedate and chewed her evening cud. Now Marly did not like Jess, therefore Meg always milked her; she would not, for some special reason of her own, "let doon her milk" when Jess laid a finger on her. This night she only shook her head and pushed heavily against Jess as she came.

"Hand up there, ye thrawn randy!" said Jess in byre tones.

And so very sulkily Marly moved out, looking for Meg right and left as she did so. She had her feelings as well as any one, and she was not the first who had been annoyed by the sly, mischievous gipsy with the black eyes, who kept so quiet before folk. As she went out of the byre door, Jess laid her switch smartly across Marly's loins, much to the loss of dignity of that stately animal, who, taking a hasty step, slipped on the threshold, and overtook her neighbours with a slow resentment gathering in her matronly breast.

When Saunders Mowdiewort heard the last chain drop in the byre, and the strident tones of Jess exhorting Marly, he took a few steps to the gate of the hill pasture. He had to pass along a short home-made road, and over a low parapetless bridge constructed simply of four tree-trunks laid parallel and covered with turf. Then he dropped the bars of the gate into the hill pasture with a clatter, which came to Winsome's ears as she stood at her window looking out into the night. She was just thinking at that moment what a good thing it was that she had sent back Ralph Peden's poem. So, in order to see whether this were so or not, she repeated it all over again to herself.

When he came back again to the end of the barn, Saunders found Jess standing there, with the wistful light in her eyes which that young woman of many accomplishments could summon into them as easily as she could smile. For Jess was a minx—there is no denying the fact. Yet even slow Saunders admitted that, though she was nothing to Meg, of course, still there was something original and attractive about her—like original sin.

Jess was standing with her head on one side, putting the scarlet head of a poppy among her black hair. Jess had strange tastes, which would be called artistic nowadays in some circles. Her liking was always BIZARRE and excellent, the taste of the primitive Galloway Pict from whom she was descended, or of that picturesque Glenkens warrior, who set a rowan bush on his head on the morning when he was to lead the van at the battle of the Standard. Scotland was beaten on that great occasion, it is true; but have the chroniclers, who complain of the place of Galloway men in the ranks, thought how much more terribly Scotland might have been beaten had Galloway not led the charge? But this is written just because Jess Kissock, a Galloway farm lassie, looked something like a cast back to the primitive Pict of the south, a fact which indeed concerns the story not at all, for Saunders Mowdiewort had not so much as ever heard of a Pict.

Jess did not regard Saunders Mowdiewort highly at any time. He was one of Meg's admirers, but after all he was a man, and one can never tell. It was for this reason that she put the scarlet poppy into her hair.

She meditated "I maybe haena Meg's looks to the notion o' some folk, but I mak' a heap better use o' the looks that I hae, an' that is a great maitter!"

"Saunders," said Jess softly, going up to the Cuif and pretending to pick a bit of heather off his courting coat. She did this with a caressing touch which soothed the widower, and made him wish that Meg would do the like. He began to think that he had never properly valued Jess.

"Is Meg comin' oot again?" Jess inquired casually, the scarlet poppy set among the blue-black raven's wings, and brushing his beard in a distracting manner.

Saunders would hare given a good deal to be able to reply in the affirmative, but Meg had dismissed him curtly after the milking, with the intimation that it was time he was making manseward. As for her, she was going within doors to put the old folks to bed.

After being satisfied on this point the manner of Jess was decidedly soothing. That young woman had a theory which was not quite complimentary either to the sense or the incorruptibility of men. It was by showing an interest in them and making them think that they (or at least the one being operated upon) are the greatest and most fascinating persons under the sun, almost anything can be done. This theory has been acted upon with results good and bad, in other places besides the barn end of Craig Ronald.

"They're a' weel at the Manse?" said Jess, tentatively.

"On aye," said Saunders, looking round the barn end to see if Meg could see him. Satisfied that Meg was safe in bed, Saunders put his hand on Jess's shoulder—the sleek-haired, candle-greased deceiver that he was.

"Jess, ye're bonny," said he.

"Na, na," said Jess, very demurely, "it's no me that's bonny—its Meg!"

Jess was still looking at him, and interested in getting all the rough wool off the collar of his homespun coat.

The Samson of the graveyard felt his strength deserting him.

"Davert, Jess lass, but it's a queer thing that it never cam across me that ye were bonny afore!"

Jess looked down. The Cuif thought that it was because she was shy, and his easy heart went out to her; but had he seen the smile that was wasted on a hopping sparrow beneath, and especially the wicked look in the black eyes, he might have received some information as to the real sentiments of girls who put red poppies in their hair in order to meet their sisters' sweethearts at the barn end.

"Is the young minister aye bidin' at the Manse?" asked Jess.

"Aye, he is that!" said Saunders, "he's a nice chiel' yon. Ye'll see him whiles ower by here. They say—that is Manse Bell says— that he's real fond o' yer young mistress here. Ken ye ocht aboot that, Jess?"

"Hoots, havers, our young mistress is no for penniless students, I wot weel. There'll be nocht in't, an' sae ye can tell Bell o' the Manse, gin you an' her is so chief [intimate]."

"Very likely ye're right. There'll be nocht in't, I'm thinkin'—at least on her side. But what o' the young man? D'ye think he's sair ta'en up aboot Mistress Winsome? Meg was sayin' so."

"Meg thinks there's naebody worth lookin' at in the warl' but hersel' and Mistress Winifred Charteris, as she ca's hersel'; but there's ithers thinks different."

"What hae ye against her, Jess? I thocht that she's a fell fine young leddy."

"Oh she's richt eneuch, but there's bonny lasses as weel as her; an' maybe, gin young Maister Peden comes ower by to Oraig Eonald to see a lass nnkenned o' a'—what faut wad there be in that?"

"Then it's Meg he comes to see, and no' the young mistress?" said the alarmed grave-digger.

"Maybes aye an' maybes no—there's bonny lasses forby Meg Kissock for them that hae gotten een in their heads."

"Wi' Jess! Is't yerself?" said Saunders.

Jess was discreetly silent.

"Ye'll no tell onybody, wull ye, Maister Mowdiewort?" she said anxiously.

To Saunders this was a great deal better than being called a "Cuif."

"Na, Jess, lass, I'll no tell a soul—no yin."

"No' even Meg-mind!" repeated Jess, who felt that this was a vital point.

So Saunders promised, though he had intended to do so on the first opportunity.

"Mind, if ye do, I'll never gie ye a hand wi' Meg again as lang as I leeve!" said Jess emphatically.

"Jess, d'ye think she likes me?" asked the widower in a hushed whisper.

"Saunders, I'm jnist sure o't," replied Jess with great readiness. "But she's no yin o' the kind to let on."

"Na," groaned Saunders, "I wuss to peace she was. But ye mind me that I gat a letter frae the young minister that I was to gie to Meg. But as you're the yin he comes to see, I maun as weel gie't direct to yoursel'."

"It wad be as weel," said Jess, with a strange sort of sea-fire like moonshine in her eyes.

Saunders passed over a paper to her readily, and Jess, with her hand still on his coat-collar, in a way that Meg had never used, thanked him in her own way.

"Juist bide a wee," she said; "I'll be wi' ye in a minute!"

Jess hurried down into the old square-plotted garden, which ran up to the orchard trees. She soon found a moss-rose bush from which she selected a bud, round which the soft feathery envelope was just beginning to curl back. Then she went round by the edge of the brook which keeps damp one side of the orchard, where she found some single stems of forget-me-nots, shining in the dusk like beaded turquoise. She pulled some from the bottom of the half-dry ditch, and setting the pale moss-rosebud in the middle, she bound the whole together with a striped yellow and green withe. Then snipping the stacks with her pocket scissors, she brought the posy to Saunders, with instructions to wrap it in a dock-leaf and never to let his hands touch it the whole way.

Saunders, dazed and fascinated, forgetful even of Meg and loyalty, promised. The glamour of Jess, the gypsy, was upon him.

"But what am I to say," he asked.

"Say its frae her that he sent the letter to; he'll ken brawly that Meg hadna the gumption to send him that!" said Jess candidly.

Saunders said his good-night in a manner which would certainly have destroyed all his chances with Meg had she witnessed the parting. Then he stolidly tramped away down the loaning.

Jess called after him, struck with a sudden thought. "See that ye dinna gie it to him afore the minister."

Then she put her hands beneath her apron and walked home meditating. "To be a man is to be a fool," said Jess Kissock, putting her whole experience into a sentence. Jess was a daughter of the cot; put then she was also a daughter of Eve, who had not even so much as a cot.

CHAPTER XX
"DARK-BROWED EGYPT"

As soon as Jess was by herself in the empty byre, to which she withdrew herself with the parcel which the faithful and trustworthy Cuif had entrusted to her, she lit the lantern which always stood in the inside of one of the narrow triangular wickets that admitted light into the byre. Sitting down on the small hay stall, she pulled the packet from her pocket, looked it carefully over, and read the simple address, "In care of Margaret Kissock." There was no other writing upon the outside.

Opening the envelope carefully, he let the light of the byre lantern rest on the missive. It was written in a delicate but strong handwriting—the hand of one accustomed to forming the smaller letters of ancient tongues into a current script. "To Mistress Winifred Charteris," it ran. "Dear Lady: That I have offended you by the hastiness of my words and the unforgivable wilfulness of my actions, I know, but cannot forgive myself. Yet, knowing the kindness of your disposition, I have thought that you might be better disposed to pardon me than I myself. For I need not tell you, what you already know, that the sight of you is dearer to me than the light of the morning. You are connected in my mind and heart with all that is best and loveliest. I need not tell now that I love you, for you know that I love the string of your bonnet. Nor am I asking for anything in return, save only that you may know my heart and not be angry. This I send to ease its pain, for it has been crying out all night long, 'Tell her— tell her!' So I have risen early to write this. Whether I shall send it or no, I cannot tell. There is no need, Winsome, to answer it, if you will only let it fall into your heart and make no noise, as a drop of water falls into the sea. Whether you will be angry or not I cannot tell, and, truth to tell you, sweetheart, I am far past caring. I am coming, as I said, to Craig Ronald to see your grandmother, and also, if you will, to see you. I shall not need you to tell me whether you are angered with a man's love or no; I shall know that before you speak to me. But keep a thought for one that loves you beyond all the world, and as if there were no world, and naught but God and you and him. For this time fare you well. Ralph Peden."

Jess turned it over with a curious look on her face. "Aye, he has the grip o't, an' she micht get him gin she war as clever as Jess Kissock; but him that can love yin weel can lo'e anither better, an' I can keep them sindry [asunder]. I saw him first, an' he spak to me first. 'Ye're no to think o' him,' said my mither. Think o' him! I hae thocht o' nocht else. Think of him! Since when is thinkin' a crime? A lass maun juist do the best she can for hersel', be she cotman's dochter or laird's. Love's a' yae thing— kitchen or byre, but or ben. See a lad, lo'e a lad, get a lad, keep a lad! Ralph Peden will kiss me afore the year's oot," she said with determination.

So in the corner of the byre, among the fragrant hay and fresh-cut clover, Jess Kissock the cottar's lass prophesied out of her wayward soul, baring her intentions to herself as perhaps her sister in boudoir hushed and perfumed might not have done. There are Ishmaels also among women, whose hand is against every woman, and who stand for their own rights to the man on whom they have set their love; and the strange thing is, that such are by no means the worst of women either.

Stranger still, so strong and dividing to soul and marrow is a clearly defined purpose and determinately selfish, that such women do not often fail. And indeed Jess Kissock, sitting in the hay- neuk, with her candle in the lantern throwing patterns on the cobwebby walls from the tiny perforations all round, made a perfectly correct prophecy. Ralph Peden did indeed kiss her, and that of his own free will as his love of loves within a much shorter space of time than a year.

Strangely also, Jess the gipsy, the dark-browed Pictess, was neither angry nor jealous when she read Ralph's letter to Winsome. According to all rules she ought to have been. She even tried to persuade herself that she was. But the sight of Ralph writing to Winsome gave no pang to her heart. Nor did this argue that she did not love really and passionately. She did; but Jess had in her the Napoleon instinct. She loved obstacles. So thus it was what she communed with herself, sitting with her hand on her brow, and her swarthy tangle of hair falling all about her face. All women have a pose in which they look best. Jess looked best leaning forward with her elbows on her knees. Had there been a fender at her father's fireside Jess would have often sat on it, for there is a dangerous species of girl that, like a cat, looks best sitting on a fender. And such a girl is always aware of the circumstance.

"He has written to Winsome," Jess communed with herself. "Well, he shall write to me. He loves her, he thinks; then in time he shall love me, and be sure perfectly o't. Let me see. Gin she had gotten this letter, she wadna hae answered it. So he'll come the morn, an' he'll no say a word to her aboot the letter. Na, he'll juist look if she's pleased like, and gin that gomeral Saunders gied him the rose, he'll no be ill to please eyther! But afore he gangs hame he shall see Jess Kissock, an' hear frae her aboot the young man frae the Castle!" Jess took another look at the letter." It's a bonny hand o' write," she said, "but Dominie Cairnochan learned me to write as weel as onybody, an' some day he'll write to me. I'se no be byre lass a' my life. Certes no. There's oor Meg, noo; she'll mairry some ignorant landward man, an' leeve a' her life in a cot hoose, wi' a dizzen weans tum'lin' aboot her! What yin canna learn, anither can," continued Jess. "I hae listened to graun' fowk speakin', an' I can speak as weel as onybody. I'll disgrace nane. Gin I canna mak' mysel' fit for kirk or manse, my name's no Jess Kissock. I'm nae country lump, to be left where I'm set doon, like a milkin' creepie [stool], an' kickit ower when they are dune wi' me."

It is of such women, born to the full power and passion of sex, and with all the delicate keenness of the feminine brain, utterly without principle or scruple, that the Cleopatras are made. For black-browed Egypt, the serpent of old Nile, can sit in a country byre, and read a letter to another woman. For Cleopatra is not history; she is type.

CHAPTER XXI
THE RETURN OF EBIE FARRISH

Now Ebie Farrish had been over at the Nether Crae seeing the lassies there in a friendly way after the scene in the byre, for Galloway ploughmen were the most general of lovers. Ebie considered it therefore no disloyalty to Jess that he would display his watch-guard and other accomplishments to the young maids at the Crae. Nor indeed would Jess herself have so considered it. It was only Meg who was so particular that she did not allow such little practice excursions of this kind on the part of her young men.

When Ebie started to go home, it was just midnight. As he came over the Grannoch bridge he saw the stars reflected in the water, and the long stretches of the loch glimmering pearl grey in the faint starlight and the late twilight. He thought they looked as if they were running down hill. His thoughts and doings that day and night had been earthly enough. He had no regrets and few aspirations. But the coolness of the twilight gave him the sense of being a better man than he knew himself to be. Ebie went to sit under the ministrations of the Reverend Erasmus Teends at twelve by the clock on Sunday. He was a regular attendant. He always was spruce in his Sunday blacks. He placed himself in the hard pews so that he could have a view of his flame for the time being. As he listened to the minister he thought sometimes of her and of his work, and of the turnip-hoeing on the morrow, but oftenest of Jess, who went to the Marrow kirk over the hills. He thought of the rise of ten shillings that he would ask at the next half- year's term, all as a matter of course—just as Robert Jamieson the large farmer, thought of the rent day and the market ordinary, and bringing home the "muckle greybeard "full of excellent Glenlivat from the Cross Keys on Wednesday. Above them both the Reverend Erasmus Teends droned and drowsed, as Jess Kissock said with her faculty for expression, "bummelin' awa like a bubbly-Jock or a bum-bee in a bottle."

But coming home in the coolness of this night, the ploughman was, for the time being, purged of the grosser humours which come naturally to strong, coarse natures, with physical frames ramping with youth and good feeding. He stood long looking into the lane water, which glided beneath the bridge and away down to the Dee without a sound.

He saw where, on the broad bosom of the loch, the stillness lay grey and smooth like glimmering steel, with little puffs of night wind purling across it, and disappearing like breath from a new knife-blade. He saw where the smooth satin plane rippled to the first water-break, as the stream collected itself, deep and black, with the force of the water behind it, to flow beneath the bridge. When Ebie Farrish came to the bridge he was a material Galloway ploughman, satisfied with his night's conquests and chewing the cud of their memory.

He looked over. He saw the stars, which were perfectly reflected a hundred yards away on the smooth expanse, first waver, then tremble, and lastly break into a myriad delicate shafts of light, as the water quickened and gathered. He spat in the water, and thought of trout for breakfast. But the long roar of the rapids of the Dee came over the hill, and a feeling of stillness with it, weird and remote. Uncertain lights shot hither and thither under the bridge, in strange gleams of reflection. The ploughman was awed. He continued to gaze. The stillness closed in upon him. The aromatic breath of the pines seemed to cool him and remove him from himself. He had a sense that it was Sabbath morning, and that he had just washed his face to go to church. It was the nearest thing to worship he had ever known. Such moments come to the most material, and are their theology. Far off a solitary bird whooped and whinnied. It sounded mysterious and unknown, the cry of a lost soul. Ebie Farrish wondered where he would go to when he died. He thought this over for a little, and then he concluded that it were better not to dwell on this subject. But the crying on the lonely hills awed him. It was only a Jack snipe from whose belated nest an owl had stolen two eggs. But it was Ebie Farrish's good angel. He resolved that he would go seldomer to the village public o' nights, and that he would no more find cakes and ale sweet to his palate. It was a foregone conclusion that on Saturday night he would be there, yet what he heard and saw on Grannoch Bridge opened his sluggish eyes. Of a truth there was that in the world which had not been there him before. It is to Jess Kissock's credit, that when Ebie was most impressed by the stillness and most under the spell of the night, he thought of her. He was only an ignorant, godless, good-natured man, who was no more moral than he could help; but it is both a testimonial and a compliment when such a man thinks of a woman in his best and most solemn moments.

At that moment Jess Kissock was putting Winsome Charteris's letter into her pocket.

There is no doubt that poor, ignorant Ebie, with his highly developed body and the unrestrained and irregular propensities of his rudimentary soul, was nearer the Almighty that night than his keen-witted and scheming sweetheart.

A trout leaped in the calm water, and Ebie stopped thinking of the eternities to remember where he had set a line. Far off a cock crew, and the well-known sound warned Ebie that he had better be drawing near his bed. He raised himself from the copestone of the parapet, and solemnly tramped his steady way up to the "onstead" of Craig Ronald, which took shape before him as he advanced like a low, grey-bastioned castle. As he entered the low square on his way across to the stable door he was surprised to notice a gleam of light in the byre. Ebie thought that some tramps were trespassing on the good nature of the mistress of the house, and he had the feeling of loyalty to his master's interests which distinguished the Galloway ploughman of an older time. He was mortally afraid of bogles, and would not have crossed the kirkyard after the glimmer of midnight without seeing a dozen corpse- candles; but tramps were quite another matter, for Ebie was not in the least afraid of mortal man—except only of Allan Welsh, the Marrow minister.

So he stole on tiptoe to the byre door, circumnavigating the "wicket," which poured across the yard its tell-tale plank of light. Standing within the doorway and looking over the high wooden stall, tenanted in winter by Jock, the shaggy black bull, Ebie saw Jess Kissock, lost in her dreams. The lantern was set on the floor in front of her. The candle had nearly burned down to the socket. Jess's eyes were large and brilliant. It seemed to Ebie Farrish that they were shining with light. Her red lips were pouted, and there was a warm, unwonted flush on her cheeks. In her dreams she was already mistress of a house, and considering how she would treat her servants. She would treat them kindly and well. She had heard her sister, who was servant at Earlston, tell how the ladies there treated their servants. Jess meant to do just the same. She meant to be a real lady. Ambition in a woman has a double chance, for adaptation is inborn along with it. Most men do not succeed very remarkably in anything, because at heart they do not believe in themselves. Jess did. It was her heritage from some Pict, who held back under the covert of his native woods so long as the Roman tortoise crept along, shelved in iron, but who drave headlong into a gap with all his men, when, some accident of formation showed the one chance given in a long day's march.

Ebie thought he had never seen Jess so beautiful. It had never struck him before that Jess was really handsomer than Meg. He only knew that there was a stinging wild-fruit fragrance about Jess and her rare favours he had never experienced in the company of any other woman. And he had a large experience.

Was it possible that she knew that he was out and was waiting for him? In this thought, which slowly entered in upon his astonishment, the natural Ebie forced himself to the front.

"Jess!" he exclaimed impulsively, taking a step within, the door. Instantly, as though some night-flying bat had flown against it, the candle went out—a breath wafted by him as lightly and as silently as a snowy owl flies home in the twilight. A subtle something, the influence of a presence, remained, which mingled strangely with the odours of the clover in the neuk, and the sour night-smell of the byre. Again there was a perfect silence. Without, a corncrake ground monotonously. A rat scurried along the rafter. Ebie in the silence and the darkness had almost persuaded himself that he had been dreaming, when his foot clattered against something which fell over on the cobble-stones that paved the byre. He stopped and picked it up. It was the byre lantern. The wick was still glowing crimson when he opened the little tin door. As he looked it drew slowly upward into a red star, and winked itself out. It was no dream. Jess had been in the byre. To meet whom? he asked himself.

Ebie went thoughtfully up-stairs, climbing the stable ladder as the first twilight of the dawn was slowly pouring up from beneath into a lake of light and colour in the east, as water gushes from a strong well-eye.

"Ye're a nice boy comin' to yer bed at this time o' the mornin'," said Jock Forrest from his bunk at the other side.

"Nicht-wanderin' bairns needs skelpin'!" remarked Jock Gordon, who had taken up his abode in a vacant stall beneath.

"Sleep yer ain sleeps, ye pair o' draft-sacks, in yer beds," answered Ebie Farrish without heat and simply as a conversational counter.

He did not know that he was quoting the earliest English classic. He had never heard of Chaucer.

"What wad Jess say?" continued Jock Forrest, sleepily.

"Ask her," said Ebie sharply.

"At any rate, I'm no gaun to be disturbit in my nicht's rest wi' the like o' you, Ebie Farrish! Ye'll eyther come hame in time o' nicht, or ye'll sleep elsewhere—up at the Crae, gin ye like."

"Mind yer ain business," retorted Ebie, who could think of nothing else to say.

Down below daft Jock Gordon, with some dim appropriateness was beginning his elricht croon of—

"The devil sat on his ain lum-tap,
Hech how—black and reeky—"

when Jock Forrest, out of all patience, cried out down to him: "Jock Gordon, gin ye begin yer noise at twa o'clock i' the mornin' I'll come down an' pit ye i' the mill-dam!"

"Maybes ye'll be cryin' for me to pit you i' the mill-dam some warm day!" said Jock Gordon grimly, "but I'se do naething o' the kind. I'll een bank up the fires an' gie ye a turn till ye're weel brandered. Ye'll girn for mill-dams then, I'm thinkin'!"

So, grumbling and threatening in his well-accustomed manner, Jock Gordon returned to the wakeful silence which he kept during the hours usually given to sleep. It was said, however, that he never really slept. Indeed, Ebie and Jock were ready to take their oath that they never went up and down that wooden ladder, from which three of the rounds were missing, without seeing Jock Gordon's eyes shining like a cat's out of the dark of the manger where, like an ape, he sat all night cross-legged.

CHAPTEK XXII
A SCARLET POPPY

IT was early afternoon at Craig Ronald. Afternoon is quite a different time from morning at a farm. Afternoon is slack-water in the duties of the house, at least for the womenfolk—except in hay and harvest, when it is full flood tide all the time, night and day. But when we consider that the life of a farm town begins about four in the morning, it will be readily seen that afternoon comes far on in the day indeed for such as have tasted the freshness of the morning.

In the morning, Winsome had seen that every part of her farm machinery was going upon well-oiled wheels. She had consulted her honorary factor, who, though a middle-aged man and a bachelor of long and honourable standing, enrolled himself openly and avowedly in the army of Winsome's admirers. He used to ask every day what additions had been made to the list of her conquests, and took much interest in the details of her costume. This last she mostly devised for herself with taste which was really a gift natural to her, but which seemed nothing less than miraculous to the maidens and wives of a parish which had its dressmaking done according to the canons of an art which the Misses Crumbcloth, mantua-makers at the Dullarg village, had learned twenty-five years before, once for all.

Now it was afternoon, and Winsome was once more at the bake-board. There were few things that Winsome liked better to do, and she daily tried the beauty of her complexion before the open fireplace, though her grandmother ineffectually suggested that Meg Kissock would do just as well.

While Winsome was rubbing her hands with dry meal, before beginning, she became conscious that some one was coming up the drive. So she was not at all astonished when a loud knock in the stillness of the afternoon echoed through the empty house and far down the stone passages.

It was Ralph Peden who knocked, as indeed she did not need to tell herself. She called, however, to Meg Kissock.

"Meg," she said, "there is the young minister come to see my grandmother. Go and show him into the parlour."

Meg looked at her mistress. Her reply was irrelevant. "I was born on a Friday," she said.

But notwithstanding she went, and received the young man. She took him into the parlour, where he was set down among strange voluted foreign shells with a pink flush within the wide mouth of every one of them. Here there was a scent of lavender and subtle essences in the air, and a great stillness. While he sat waiting, he could hear afar off the sound of rippling water. It struck a little chill over him that, after the letter he had sent, Winsome should not have come to greet him herself. From this he argued the worst. She might be offended, or—still more fatal thought—she and Meg might be laughing over it together.

A tall, slim girl entered the quiet parlour with a silent, catlike tread. She was at his side before he knew it. It was the girl whom he had met on his way to the Manse the first day of his arrival. Jess's experience as a maid to her ladyship has stood her in good stead. She had a fineness of build which even the housework of a farm could not coarsen. Besides, Winsome considered Jess delicate, and did not allow her to lift anything really heavy. So it happened that when Ralph Peden came Jess was putting the fresh flowers in the great bowls of low relief chinaware—roses from the garden and sprays of white hawthorn, which flowers late in Galloway, blue hyacinths and harebells massed together—yellow marigolds and glorious scarlet poppies, of which Jess with her taste of the savage was passionately fond. She had arranged some of these against a pale blue background of bunches of forget-me- nots, with an effect strangely striking in that cool, dusky room.

When Jess came in Ralph had risen instinctively. He shook hands heartily with her. As she looked up at him, she said:

"Do you remember me?"

Ralph replied with an eager frankness, all the more marked that he had expected Winsome instead of Jess Kissock: "Indeed, how could I forget, when you helped me to carry my books that night? I am glad to find you here. I had no idea that you lived here."

Which was indeed true, for he had not yet been able to grasp the idea that any but Winsome lived at Craig Ronald.

Jess Kissock, who knew that not many moments were hers before Meg might come in, replied:

"I am here to help with the house. Meg Kissock is my sister." She looked to see if there was anything in Ralph's eyes she could resent; but a son of the Marrow kirk had not been trained to respect of persons.

"I am sure you will help very much," he said, politely.

"I'm not as strong as my sister, you see, so that I'm generally in the house," said Jess, who was carrying two dishes of flowers at once across the room. At Ralph's feet one of them overset, and poured all its wealth of blue and white and splashed crimson over the floor.

Jess stooped to lift them, crying shame on her own awkwardness. Ralph kindly assisted her. As they stooped to gather them together, Jess put forward all her attractions. Her lithe grace never showed to more advantage. Yet, for all the impression she made on Ralph, she might as well have wasted her sweetness on Jock Gordon—indeed, better so, for Jock recognized in her something strangely kin to his own wayward spirit.

When the flowers were all gathered and put back:

"Now you shall have one for helping," said Jess, as she had once seen a lady in England do, and she selected a dark-red, velvety damask rose from the wealth which she had cut and brought out of the garden. Standing on tiptoe, she could scarcely reach his button-hole.

"Bend down," she said. Obediently Ralph bent, good-humouredly patient, to please this girl who had done him a good turn on that day which now seemed so far away—the day that had brought Craig Ronald and Winsome into his life.

But in spite of his stooping, Jess had some difficulty in pinning in the rose, and in order to steady herself on tiptoe, she reached up and laid a staying hand on his shoulder. As he bent down, his face just touched the crisp fringes of her dark hair, which seemed a strange thing to him.

But a sense of another presence in the room caused him to raise his eyes, and there in the doorway stood Winsome Charteris, looking so pale and cold that she seemed to be a thousand miles away.

"I bid you good-afternoon, Master Peden," said Winsome quietly; "I am glad you have had time to come and visit my grandmother. She will be glad to see you."

For some moments Ralph had no words to answer. As for Jess, she did not even colour; she simply withdrew with the quickness and feline grace which were characteristic of her, without a flush or a tremor. It was not on such occasions that her heart stirred. When she was gone she felt that things had gone well, even beyond her expectation.

When Ralph at last found his voice, he said somewhat falteringly, yet with a ring of honesty in his voice which for the time being was lost upon Winsome:

"You are not angry with me for coming to-day. You knew I would come, did you not?"

Winsome only said: "My grandmother is waiting for me. You had better go in at once."

"Winsome," said Ralph, trying to prolong the period of his converse with her, "you are not angry with me for writing what I did?"

Winsome thought that he was referring to the poem which had come to her by way of Manse Bell and Saunders Mowdiewort. She was indignant that he should try to turn the tables upon her and so make her feel guilty.

"I received nothing that I had any right to keep," she said.

Ralph was silent. The blow was a complete one. She did not wish him to write to her any more or to speak to her on the old terms of friendship. He thought wholly of the letter that he had sent by Saunders the day before, and her coldness and changed attitude were set down by him to that cause, and not to the embarrassing position in which Winsome had surprised him when she came into the flower-strewn parlour. He did not know that the one thing a woman never really forgives is a false position, and that even the best of women in such cases think the most unjust things. Winsome moved towards the inner door of her grandmother's room.

Ralph put out his hand as if to touch hers, but Winsome withdrew herself with a swift, fierce movement, and held the door open for him to pass in. He had no alternative but to obey.

CHAPTER XXIII
CONCERNING JOHN BAIRDIESON

"Guid e'en to ye, Maister Ralph," said the gay old lady within, as soon as she caught sight of Ralph. "Keep up yer heid, man, an' walk like a Gilchrist. Ye look as dowie as a yow [ewe] that has lost her lammie."

Walter Skirving from his arm-chair gave this time no look of recognition. He yielded his hand to Ralph, who raised it clay- chill and heavy even in the act to shake. When he let it drop, the old man held up his palm and looked at it.

"Hae ye gotten aneuch guid Gallawa' lear to learn ye no to rin awa frae a bonny lass yet, Maister Ralph?" said the old lady briskly. She had not many jokes save with Winsome and Meg, and she rode one hard when she came by it.

But no reply was needed.

"Aye, aye, weelna," meditated the old lady, leaning back and folding her hands like a mediaeval saint of worldly tendencies, "tell me aboot your faither." "He is very robust and strong in health of body," said Kalph.

"Ye leeve in Edinbra'?" said the old lady, with a rising inflection of inquiry.

"Yes," said Ralph, "we live in James's Court. My father likes to be among his people."

"Faith na, a hantle o' braw folk hae leeved in James's Court in their time. I mind o' the Leddy Partan an' Mistress Girnigo, the king's jeweller's wife haein' a fair even-doon fecht a' aboot wha was to hae the pick o' the hooses on the stair.—Winifred, ma lassie, come here an' sit doon! Dinna gang flichterin' in an' oot, but bide still an' listen to what Maister Peden has to tell us aboot his farther."

Winsome came somewhat slowly and reluctantly towards the side of her grandmother's chair. There she sat holding her hand, and looking across the room towards the window where, motionless and abstracted, Walter Skirving, who was once so bold and strong, dreamed his life away.

"I hardly know what to tell you first," said Ralph, hesitatingly.

"Hoot, tell me gin your faither and you bide thegither withoot ony woman body, did I no hear that yince; is that the case na?" demanded the lady of Craig Ronald with astonishing directness.

"It is true enough," said Ralph, smiling, "but then we have with us my father's old Minister's Man, John Bairdieson. John has us both in hands and keeps us under fine. He was once a sailor, and cook on a vessel in his wild days; but when he was converted by falling from the top of a main yard into a dock (as he tells himself), he took the faith in a somewhat extreme form. But that does not affect his cooking. He is as good as a woman in a house."

"An' that's a lee," said the old lady. "The best man's no as guid as the warst woman in a hoose!"

Winsome did not appear to be listening. Of what interest could such things be to her?

Her grandmother was by no means satisfied with Ralph's report. "But that's nae Christian way for folk to leeve, withoot a woman o' ony kind i' the hoose—it's hardly human!"

"But I can assure you, Mistress Skirving, that, in spite of what you say, John Bairdieson does very well for us. He is, however, terribly jealous of women coming about. He does not allow one of them within the doors. He regards them fixedly through the keyhole before opening, and when he does open, his usual greeting to them is, 'Noo get yer message dune an' be gaun!'"

The lady of Craig Ronald laughed a hearty laugh.

"Gin I cam' to veesit ye I wad learn him mainners! But what does he do," she continued, "when some of the dames of good standing in the congregation call on your faither? Does he treat them in this cavalier way?"

"In that case," said Ralph, "John listens at my father's door to hear if he is stirring. If there be no sign, John says, 'The minister's no in, mem, an' I could not say for certain when he wull be!' Once my father came out and caught him in the act, and when he charged John with telling a deliberate lie to a lady, John replied, 'A'weel, it'll tak' a lang while afore we mak' up for the aipple!'"

It is believed that John Bairdieson here refers to Eve's fatal gift to Adam.

"John Bairdieson is an ungallant man. It'll be from him that ye learned to rin awa'," retorted the old lady.

"Grandmother," interrupted Winsome, who had suffered quite enough from this, "Master Peden has come to see you, and to ask how you find yourself to-day."

"Aye, aye, belike, belike—but Maister Ralph Peden has the power o' his tongue, an' gin that be his errand he can say as muckle for himsel'. Young fowk are whiles rale offcecious!" she said, turning to Ralph with the air of an appeal to an equal from the unaccountabilities of a child.

Winsome lifted some stray flowers that Jess Kissock had dropped when she sped out of the room, and threw them out of the window with an air of disdain. This to some extent relieved her, and she felt better. It surprised Ralph, however, who, being wholly innocent and unembarrassed by the recent occurrence, wondered vaguely why she did it.

"Noo tell me mair aboot your faither," continued Mistress Skirving. "I canna mak' oot whaur the Marrow pairt o' ye comes in —I suppose when ye tak' to rinnin' awa'."

"Grandmammy, your pillows are not comfortable; let me sort them for you."

Winsome rose and touched the old lady's surroundings in a manner that to Ralph was suggestive of angels turning over the white- bosomed clouds. Then Ralph looked at his pleasant querist to find out if he were expected to go on. The old lady nodded to him with an affectionate look.

"Well," said Ralph, "my father is like nobody else. I have missed my mother, of course, but my father has been like a mother for tenderness to me."

"Yer grandfaither, auld Ralph Gilchrist, was sore missed. There was thanksgiving in the parish for three days after he died!" said the old lady by way of an anticlimax.

Winsome looked very much as if she wished to say something, which brought down her grandmother's wrath upon her.

"Noo, lassie, is't you or me that's haein' a veesit frae this young man? Ye telled me juist the noo that he had come to see me. Then juist let us caa' oor cracks, an' say oor says in peace."

Thus admonished, Winsome was silent. But for the first time she looked at Ralph with a smile that had half an understanding in it, which made that yonng man's heart leap. He answered quite at random for the next few moments.

"About my father—yes, he always takes up the Bibles when John Bairdieson preaches."

"What!" said the old lady.

"I mean, John Bairdieson takes up the Bibles for him when he preaches, and as he shuts the door, John says over the railing in a whisper,'Noo, dinna be losin' the Psalms, as ye did this day three weeks'; or perhaps,'Be canny on this side o' the poopit; the hinge is juist pitten on wi' potty [putty];' whiles John will walk half-way down the kirk, and then turn to see if my father has sat quietly down according to instructions. This John has always done since the day when some inward communing overcame my father before he began his sermon, and he stood up in the pulpit without saying a word till the people thought that he was in direct communion with the Almighty."

"There was nane o' thae fine abstractions aboot your grandfaither, Ralph Gilchrist—na, whiles he was taen sae that he couldna speak he was that mad, an' aye he gat redder an' redder i' the face, till yince he gat vent, and then the ill words ran frae him like the Skyreburn [Footnote: A Galloway mountain stream noted for sudden floods.] in spate."

"What else did John Bairdieson say to yer faither?" asked Winsome, for the first time that day speaking humanly to Ralph.

That young man looked gratefully at her, as if she had suddenly dowered him with a fortune. Then he paused to try (because he was very young and foolish) to account for the unaccountability of womankind.

He endeavoured to recollect what it was that he had said and what John Bairdieson had said, but with indifferent success. He could not remember what he was talking about.

"John Bairdieson said—John Bairdieson said—It has clean gone out of my mind what John Bairdieson said," replied Ralph with much shamefacedness.

The old lady looked at him approvingly. "Ye're no a Whig. There's guid bluid in ye," she said, irrelevantly.

"Yes, I do remember now," broke in Ralph eagerly. "I remember what John Bairdieson said. 'Sit doon, minister,' he said, 'gin yer ready to flee up to the blue bauks'" [rafters—said of hens going to rest at nights]; "'there's a heap o' folk in this congregation that's no juist sae ready yet.'"

Ralph saw that Winsome and her grandmother were both genuinely interested in his father.

"Ye maun mind that I yince kenned yer faither as weel as e'er I kenned a son o' mine, though it's mony an' mony a year sin' he was i' this hoose." Winsome looked curiously at her grandmother. "Aye, lassie," she said, "ye may look an' look, but the faither o' him there cam as near to bein' your ain faither—"

Walter Skirving, swathed in his chair, turned his solemn and awful face from the window, as though called back to life by his wife's words. "Silence, woman!" he thundered.

But Mistress Skirving did not look in the least put out; only she was discreetly silent for a minute or two after her husband had spoken, as was her wont, and then she proceeded:

"Aye, brawly I kenned Gilbert Peden, when he used to come in at that door, wi' his black curls ower his broo as crisp an' bonny as his son's the day."

Winsome looked at the door with an air of interest. "Did he come to see you, grandmammy?" she asked.

"Aye, aye, what else?—juist as muckle as this young man here comes to see me. I had the word o' baith o' them for't. Ralph Peden says that he comes to see me, an' sae did the faither o' him—"

Again Mistress Skirving paused, for she was aware that her husband had turned on her one of his silent looks.

"Drive on aboot yer faither an' John Rorrison," she said; "it's verra entertainin'."

"Bairdieson," said Winsome, correctingly.

Ralph, now reassured that he was interesting Winsome as well, went on more briskly. Winsome had slipped down beside her grandmother, and had laid her arm across her grandmother's knees till the full curve of her breast touched the spare outlines of the elder woman. Ralph wondered if Winsome would ever in the years to come be like her grandmother. He thought that he could love her a thousand times more then.

"My father," said Ralph, "is a man much beloved by his congregation, for he is a very father to them in all their troubles; but they give him a kind of adoration in return that would not be good for any other kind of man except my father. They think him no less than infallible. 'Dinna mak' a god o' yer minister,' he tells them, but they do it all the same."

Winsome looked as if she did not wonder.

"When I kenned yer faither," said the old dame, "he wad hae been nocht the waur o' a pickle mair o' the auld Adam in him. It's a rale usefu' commodity in this life—"

"Why, grandmother—" began Winsome.

"Noo, lassie, wull ye haud yer tongue? I'm sair deeved wi' the din o' ye! Is there ony yae thing that a body may say withoot bern' interruptit? Gin it's no you wi' yer 'Grandmither!' like a cheepin' mavis, it's him ower by lookin' as if ye had dung doon the Bible an' selled yersel' to Sawtan. I never was in sic a hoose. A body canna get their tongue rinnin' easy an' comfortable like, but it's 'Woman, silence!' in a yoice as graund an' awfu' as 'The Lord said unto Moses'—or else you wi' yer Englishy peepin' tongue, 'Gran'mither!' as terrible shockit like as if a body were gaun intil the kirk on Sabbath wi' their stockin's doon aboot their ankles!"

The little outburst seemed mightily to relieve the old lady. Neither of the guilty persons made any signs, save that Winsome extended her elbow across her grandmother's knee, and poised a dimpled chin on her hand, smiling as placidly and contentedly as if her relative's words had been an outburst of admiration. The old woman looked sternly at her for a moment. Then she relented, and her hand stole among the girl's clustering curls. The little burst of temper gave way to a semi-humorous look of feigned sternness.

"Ye're a thankless madam," she said, shaking her white-capped head; "maybe ye think that the fifth commandment says nocht aboot grandmithers; but ye'll be tamed some day, my woman. Mony's the gamesome an' hellicat [madcap] lassie that I hae seen brocht to hersel', an' her wings clippit like a sea-gull's i' the yaird, tethered by the fit wi' a family o' ten or a dizzen—"

Winsome rose and marched out of the room with all the dignity of offended youth at the suggestion. The old lady laughed a hearty laugh, in which, however, Ralph did not join.

"Sae fine an' Englishy the ways o' folk noo," she went on; "ye mauna say this, ye mauna mention that; dear sirse me, I canna mind them a'. I'm ower auld a Pussy Bawdrous to learn new tricks o' sayin' 'miauw' to the kittlins. But for a' that an' a' that, I haena noticed that the young folk are mair particular aboot what they do nor they waur fifty years since. Na, but they're that nice they manna say this and they canna hear that."

The old lady had got so far when by the sound of retreating footsteps she judged that Winsome was out of hearing. Instantly she changed her tone.

"But, young man," she said, shaking her finger at him as if she expected a contradiction, "mind you, there's no a lass i' twunty parishes like this lassie o' mine. An' dinna think that me an' my guidman dinna ken brawly what's bringin' ye to Craig Ronald. Noo, it's richt an' better nor richt—for ye're yer faither's son, an' we baith wuss ye weel. But mind you that there's sorrow comin' to us a'. Him an' me here has had oor sorrows i' the past, deep buried for mair nor twenty year."

"I thank you with all my heart," said Ralph, earnestly. "I need not tell you, after what I have said, that I would lay my life down as a very little thing to pleasure Winsome Charteris. I love her as I never thought that woman could be loved, and I am not the kind to change."

"The faither o' ye didna change, though his faither garred him mairry a Gilchrist—an' a guid bit lass she was. But for a' that he didna change. Na, weel do I ken that he didna change."

"But," continued Ralph, "I have no reason in the world to imagine that Winsome thinks a thought about me. On the contrary, I have some reason to fear that she dislikes my person; and I would not be troublesome to her—"

"Hoot toot! laddie, dinna let the Whig bluid mak' a pulin' bairn o' ye. Surely ye dinna expect a lass o' speerit to jump at the thocht o' ye, or drap intil yer moo' like a black-ripe cherry aff a tree i' the orchard. Gae wa' wi' ye, man! what does a blithe young man o' mettle want wi' encouragement—encouragement, fie!"

"Perhaps you can tell me—" faltered Ralph. "I thought—"

"Na, na, I can tell ye naething; ye maun juist find oot for yersel', as a young man should. Only this I wull say, it's only a cauldrife Whigamore that wad tak' 'No' for an answer. Mind ye that gin the forbears o' the daddy o' ye was on the wrang side o' Bothwell Brig that day—an' guid Westland bluid they spilt, nae doot, Whigs though they waur—there's that in ye that rode doon the West Port wi' Clavers, an' cried:

'Up wi' the bonnets o' bonny Dundee!'"

"I know," said Ralph with some of the stiff sententiousness which he had not yet got rid of, "that I am not worthy of your granddaughter in any respect—"

"My certes, no," said the sharp-witted dame, "for ye're a man, an' it's a guid blessin' that you men dinna get your deserts, or it wad be a puir lookoot for the next generation, young man. Gae wa' wi' ye, man; mind ye, I'll no' say a word in yer favour, but raither the ither way—whilk," smiled Mistress Skirving in the deep still way that she sometimes had in the midst of her liveliness, "whilk will maybe do ye mair guid. But I'm speakin' for my guid-man when I say that ye hae oor best guid-wull. We think that ye are a true man, as yer faither was, though sorely he was used by this hoose. It wad maybes be some amends," she added, as if to herself.

Then the dear old lady touched her eyes with a fine handkerchief which she took out of a little black reticule basket on the table by her side.

As Ralph rose reverently and kissed her hand before retiring, Walter Skirving motioned him near his chair. Then he drew him downward till Ralph was bending on one knee. He laid a nerveless heavy hand on the young man's head, and looked for a minute—which seemed years to Ralph—very fixedly on his eyes. Then dropping his hand and turning to the window, he drew a long, heavy breath.

Ralph Peden rose and went out.

CHAPTER XXIV
LEGITIMATE SPORT

As Ralph Peden went through the flower-decked parlour in which he had met Jess Kissock an hour before, he heard the clang of controversy, or perhaps it is more correct to say, he heard the voice of Meg Kissock raised to its extreme pitch of command.

"Certes, my lass, but ye'll no hoodwink me; ye hae dune no yae thing this hale mornin' but wander athort [about] the hoose wi' that basket o' flooers. Come you an' gie us a hand wi' the kirn this meenit! Ye dinna gang a step oot o' the hoose the day!"

Ralph did not think of it particularly at the time, but it was probably owing to this utilitarian occupation that he did not again see the attractive Jess on his way out. For, with all her cleverness, Jess was afraid of Meg.

Ralph passed through the yard to the gate which led to the hill. He was wonderfully comforted in heart, and though Winsome had been alternatively cold and kind, he was too new in the ways of girls to be uplifted on that account, as a more experienced man might have been. Still, the interview with the old people had done him good.

As he was crossing the brook which flows partly over and partly under the road at the horse watering-place, he looked down into the dell among the tangles of birch and the thick viscous foliage of the green-berried elder. There he caught the flash of a light dress, and as he climbed the opposite grassy bank on his way to the village, he saw immediately beneath him the maiden of his dreams and his love-verses. Now she leaped merrily from stone to stone; now she bent stealthily over till her palms came together in the water; now she paused to dash her hair back from her flushed face. And all the time the water glimmered and sparkled about her feet. With her was Andra Kissock, a bare-legged, bonnetless squire of dames. Sometimes he pursued the wily burn trout with relentless ferocity and the silent intentness of a sleuthhound. Often, however, he would pause and with his finger indicate some favourite stone to Winsome. Then the young lady, utterly forgetful of all else and with tremulous eagerness, delicately circumvented the red-spotted beauties.

Once throwing her head back to clear the tumbling avalanches of her hair, she chanced to see Ralph standing silent above. For a moment Winsome was annoyed. She had gone to the hill brook with Andra so that she might not need to speak further with Ralph Peden, and here he had followed her. But it did not need a second look to show her that he was infinitely more embarrassed than she. This is the thing of all others which is fitted to make a woman calm and collected. It allows her to take the measure of her opportunity and assures her of her superiority. So, with a gay and quipsome wave of the hand, in which Ralph was conscious of some faint resemblance to her grandmother, she called to him:

"Come down and help us to catch some trout for supper."

Ralph descended, digging his heels determinedly into the steep bank, till he found himself in the bed of the streamlet. Then he looked at Winsome for an explanation. This was something he had not practised in the water of Leith. Andra Kissock glared at him with a terrible countenance, in which contempt was supposed to blend with a sullen ferocity characteristic of the noble savage. The effect was slightly marred by a black streak of mud which was drawn from the angle of his mouth to the roots of his hair. Ralph thought from his expression that trout-fishing of this kind did not agree with him, and proposed to help Winsome instead of Andra.

This proposal had the effect of drawing a melodramatic "Ha! ha!" from that youth, ludicrously out of keeping with his usual demeanour. Once he had seen a play-acting show unbeknown to his mother, when Jess had taken him to Cairn Edward September fair.

So "Ha! ha!" he said with the look of smothered desperation which to the unprejudiced observer suggested a pain in his inside. "You guddle troot!" he cried scornfully, "I wad admire to see ye! Ye wad only fyle [dirty] yer shune an' yer braw breeks!"

Ralph glanced at the striped underskirt over which Winsome had looped her dress. It struck him with astonishment to note how she had managed to keep it clean and dry, when Andra was apparently wet to the neck.

"I do not know that I shall be of any use," he said meekly, "but I shall try."

Winsome was standing poised on a stone, bending like a lithe maid, her hands in the clear water. There had been a swift and noiseless rush underneath the stone; a few grains of sand rose up where the white under part of the trout had touched it as it glided beneath. Slowly and imperceptibly Winsome's hand worked its way beneath the stone. With the fingers of one hand she made that slight swirl of the water which is supposed by expert "guddlers" to fascinate the trout, and to render them incapable of resisting the beckoning fingers. Andra watched breathlessly from the bank above. Ralph came nearer to see the issue. The long, slender fingers, shining mellow in the peaty water, were just closing, when the stone on which Ralph was standing precariously toppled a little and fell over into the burn with a splash. The trout darted out and in a moment was down stream into the biggest pool for miles.

Winsome rose with a flush of disappointment, and looked very reproachfully towards the culprit. Ralph, who had followed the stone, stood up to his knees in the water, looking the picture of crestfallen humility.

Overhead on the bank Andra danced madly like an imp. He would not have dared to speak to Ralph on any other occasion, but guddling, like curling, loosens the tongue. He who fails or causes the failures of others is certain to hear very plainly of it from those who accompany him to this very dramatic kind of fishing.

"0' a' the stupid asses!" cried that young man. "Was there ever sic a beauty?—a pund wecht gin it was an ounce!—an' to fa' aff a stane like a six-months' wean!"

His effective condemnation made Winsome laugh. Ralph laughed along with her, which very much increased the anger of Andra, who turned away in silent indignation. It was hard to think, just when he had got the "prairie flower" of Craig Ronald (for whom he cherished a romantic attachment of the most desperate and picturesque kind) away from the house for a whole long afternoon at the fishing, that this great grown-up lout should come this way and spoil all his sport. Andra was moved to the extremity of scorn.

"Hey, mon!" he called to Ralph, who was standing in the water's edge with Winsome on a miniature bay of shining sand, looking down on the limpid lapse of the clear moss-tinted water slipping over its sand and pebbles—"hey, mon!" he cried.

"Well, Andra, what is it?" asked Winsome Charteris, looking up after a moment. She had been busy thinking.

"Tell that chap frae Enbro'," said Andra, collecting all his spleen into one tremendous and annihilating phrase—"him that tummilt aff the stane—that there's a feck o' paddocks [a good many frogs] up there i' the bog. He micht come up here an' guddle for paddocks. It wad be safer for the like o' him!" The ironical method is the favourite mode or vehicle of humour among the common orders in Galloway. Andra was a master in it.

"Andra," said Winsome warmly, "you must not—"

"Please let him say whatever he likes. My awkwardness deserves it all," said Ralph, with becoming meekness.

"I think you had better go home now," said Winsome; "it will soon be time for you to bring the kye home."

"Hae ye aneuch troots for the mistress's denner?" said Andra, who knew very well how many there were.

"There are the four that you got, and the one I got beneath the bank, Andra," answered Winsome.

"Nane o' them half the size o' the yin that he fleyed [frightened] frae ablow the big stane," said Andra Kissock, indicating the culprit once more with the stubby great toe of his left foot. It would have done Ralph too much honour to have pointed with his hand. Besides, it was a way that Andrew had at all times. He indicated persons and things with that part of him which was most convenient at the time. He would point with his elbow stuck sideways at an acute angle in a manner that was distinctly libellous. He would do it menacingly with his head, and the indication contemptuous of his left knee was a triumph. But the finest and most conclusive use of all was his great toe as an index-finger of scorn. It stuck out apart from all the others, red and uncompromising, a conclusive affidavit of evil conduct.

"It's near kye-time," again said Winsome, while Ralph yearned with a great yearning for the boy to betake himself over the moor. But Andra had no such intention.

"I'se no gaun a fit till I hae showed ye baith what it is to guddle. For ye mauna gang awa' to Embro" [elbow contemptuous to the north, where Andra supposed Edinburgh to lie immediately on the other side of the double-breasted swell of blue Cairnsmuir of Carsphairn], "an' think that howkin' (wi' a lassie to help ye) in among the gravel is guddlin'. You see here!" cried Andra, and before either Winsome or Ralph could say a word, he had stripped himself to his very brief breeches and ragged shirt, and was wading into the deepest part of the pool beneath the water-fall.

Here he scurried and scuttled for all the world like a dipper, with his breast showing white like that of the bird, as he walked along the bottom of the pool. Most of the time his head was beneath the water, as well as all the rest of his body. His arms bored their way round the intricacies of the boulders at the bottom. His brown and freckled hands pursued the trouts beneath the banks. Sometimes he would have one in each hand at the same time.

When he caught them he had a careless and reckless way of throwing them up on the bank without looking where he was throwing. The first one he threw in this way took effect on the cheek of Ralph Peden, to his exceeding astonishment.

Winsome again cried "Andra!" warningly, but Andra was far too busy to listen; besides, it is not easy to hear with one's head under water and the frightened trout flashing in lightning wimples athwart the pool.

But for all that, the fisherman's senses were acute, even under the water; for as Winsome and Ralph were not very energetic in catching the lively speckled beauties which found themselves so unexpectedly frisking upon the green grass, one or two of them (putting apparently their tails into their mouths, and letting go, as with the release of a steel spring) turned a splashing somersault into the pool. Andra did not seem to notice them as they fell, but in a little while he looked up with a trout in his hand, the peat-water running in bucketfuls from his hair and shirt, his face full of indignation.

"Ye're lettin' them back again!" he exclaimed, looking fiercely at the trout in his hand. "This is the second time I hae catched this yin wi' the wart on its tail!" he said. "D'ye think I'm catchin' them for fun, or to gie them a change o' air for their healths, like fine fowk that come frae Embro'!"

"Andra, I will not allow —" Winsome began, who felt that on the ground of Craig Ronald a guest of her grandmother's should be respected.

But before she had got further Andra was again under the water, and again the trout began to rain out, taking occasional local effect upon both of them.

Finally Andra looked up with an air of triumph. "It tak's ye a' yer time to grup them on the dry land, I'm thinkin'," said he with some fine scorn; "ye had better try the paddocks. It's safer." So, shaking himself like a water-dog, he climbed up on the grass, where he collected the fish into a large fishing basket which Winsome had brought. He looked them over and said, as he handled one of them:

"Oh, ye're there, are ye? I kenned I wad get ye some day, impidence. Ye hae nae business i' this pool ony way. Ye belang half a mile faurer up, my lad; ye'll bite aff nae mair o' my heuks. There maun be three o' them i' his guts the noo —"

Here Winsome looked a meaning look at him, upon which Andra said:

"I'm juist gaun. Ye needna tell me that it's kye-time. See you an' be hame to tak' in yer grannie's tea. Ye're mair likely to be ahint yer time than me!"

Haying sped this Parthian shaft, Andra betook himself over the moor with his backful of spoil.

CHAPTER XXV
BARRIERS BREAKING

"Andra is completely spoiled," exclaimed Winsome; "he is a clever boy, and I fear we have given him too much of his own will. Only Jess can manage him."

Winsome felt the reference to be somewhat unfortunate. It was, of course, no matter to her whether a servant lass put a flower in Ralph Peden's coat; though, even as she said it, she owned to herself that Jess was different from other servant maids, both by nature and that quickness of tongue which she had learned when abroad.

Still, the piquant resentment Winsome felt, gave just that touch, of waywardness and caprice which was needed to make her altogether charming to Ralph, whose acquaintance with women had been chiefly with those of his father's flock, who buzzed about him everywhere in a ferment of admiration.

"Your feet are wet," said Winsome, with charming anxiety.

Andra was assuredly now far over the moor. They had rounded the jutting point of rock which shut in the linn, and were now walking slowly along the burnside, with the misty sunlight shining upon them, with a glistering and suffused green of fresh leaf sap in its glow. So down that glen many lovers had walked before.

Ralph's heart beat at the tone of Winsome's inquiry. He hastened to assure her that, as a matter of personal liking, he rather preferred to go with his feet wet in the summer season.

"Do you know," said Winsome, confidingly, "that if I dared I would run barefoot over the grass even yet. I remember to this day the happiness of taking off my stockings when I came home from the Keswick school, and racing over the fresh grass to feel the daisies underfoot. I could do it yet."

"Well, let us," said Ralph Peden, the student in divinity, daringly.

Winsome did not even glance up. Of course, she could not have heard, or she would have been angry at the preposterous suggestion. She thought awhile, and then said:

"I think that, more than anything in the world, I love to sit by a waterside and make stories and sing songs to the rustle of the leaves as the wind sifts among them, and dream dreams all by myself."

Her eyes became very thoughtful. She seemed to be on the eve of dreaming a dream now.

Ralph felt he must go away. He was trespassing on the pleasaunce of an angel.

"What do you like most? What would you like best to do in all the world?" she asked him.

"To sit with you by the waterside and watch you dream," said Ralph, whose education was proceeding by leaps and bounds.

Winsome risked a glance at him, though well aware that it was dangerous.

"You are easily satisfied," she said; "then let us do it now."

So Ralph and Winsome sat down like boy and girl on the fallen trunk of a fir-tree, which lay across the water, and swung their feet to the rhythm of the wimpling burn beneath.

"I think you had better sit at the far side of that branch," said Winsome, suspiciously, as Ralph, compelled by the exigencies of the position, settled himself precariously near to her section of the tree-trunk.

"What is the matter with this?" asked Ralph, with an innocent look. Now no one counterfeits innocence worse than a really innocent man who attempts to be more innocent than he is.

So Winsome looked at him with reproach in her eyes, and slowly she shook her head. "It might do very well for Jess Kissock, but for me it will balance better if you sit on the other side of the branch. We can talk just as well."

Ralph had thought no more of Jess Kissock and her flower from the moment he had seen Winsome. Indeed, the posy had dropped unregarded from his button-hole while he was gathering up the trout. There it had lain till Winsome, who had seen it fall, accidentally set her foot on it and stamped it into the grass. This indicates, like a hand on a dial, the stage of her prepossession. A day before she had nothing regarded a flower given to Ralph Peden; and in a little while, when the long curve has at last been turned, she will not regard it, though a hundred women give flowers to the beloved.

"I told you I should come," said Ralph, beginning the personal tale which always waits at the door, whatever lovers may say when they first meet. Winsome was meditating a conversation about the scenery of the dell. She needed also some botanical information which should aid her in the selection of plants for a herbarium. But on this occasion Ralph was too quick for her. "I told you I should come," said Ralph boldly, "and so you see I am here," he concluded, rather lamely.

"To see my grandmother," said Winsome, with a touch of archness in her tone or in her look—Ralph could not tell which, though he eyed her closely. He wished for the first time that the dark-brown eyelashes which fringed her lids were not so long. He fancied that, if he could only have seen the look in the eyes hidden underneath, he might have risked changing to the other side of the unkindly frontier of fir-bough which marked him off from the land of promise on the farther side.

But he could not see, and in a moment the chances were past.

"Not only to see your grandmother, who has been very kind to me, but also to see you, who have not been at all kind to me," answered Ralph.

"And pray, Master Ralph Peden, how have I not been kind to you?" said Winsome with dignity, giving him the full benefit of a pair of apparently reproachful eyes across the fir-branch.

Now Ralph had strange impulses, and, like Winsome, certainly did not talk by rule.

"I do wish," he said complainingly, with his head a little to one side, "that you would only look at me with one eye at a time. Two like that are too much for a man."

This is that same Ralph Peden whose opinions on woman were written in a lost note-book which at this present moment is—we shall not say where.

CHAPTER XXVI
SUCH SWEET PERIL

Winsome looked away down the glen, and strove to harden her face into a superhuman indignation.

"That he should dare—the idea!"

But it so happened that the idea so touched that rare gift of humour, and the picture of herself looking at Ralph Peden solemnly with one eye at a time, in order at once to spare his susceptibilities and give the other a rest, was too much for her. She laughed a peal of rippling merriment that sent all the blackbirds indignant out of their copses at the infringement of their prerogative.

Ralph's humour was slower and a little grimmer than Winsome's, whose sunny nature had blossomed out amid the merry life of the woods and streams. But there was a sternness in both of them as well, that was of the heather and the moss hags. And that would in due time come out. It is now their day of love and bounding life. And there are few people in this world who would not be glad to sit just so at the opening of the flower of love. Indeed, it was hardly necessary to tell one another.

Laughter, say the French (who think that their l'amour is love, and so will never know anything), kills love. But not the kind of laughter that rang in the open dell which peeped like the end of a great green-lined prospect glass upon the glimmering levels of Loch Grannoch; nor yet the kind of love which in alternate currents pulsed to and fro between the two young people who sat so demurely on either side of the great, many-spiked fir-branch.

"Is not this nice?" said Winsome, shrugging her shoulders contentedly and swinging her feet.

Their laughter made them better friends than before. The responsive gladness in each other's eyes seemed part of the midsummer stillness of the afternoon. Above, a red squirrel dropped the husks of larch tassels upon them, and peered down upon them with his bright eyes. He was thinking himself of household duties, and had his own sweetheart safe at home, nestling in the bowl of a great beech deep in the bowering wood by the loch.

"I liked to hear you speak of your father to-day," said Winsome, still swinging her feet girlishly. "It must be a great delight to have a father to go to. I never remember father or mother."

Her eyes were looking straight before her now, and a depth of tender wistfulness in them went to Ralph's heart. He was beginning to hate the branch.

"My father," he said, "is often stern to others, but he has never been stern to me—always helpful, full of tenderness and kindness. Perhaps that is because I lost my mother almost before I can remember."

Winsome's wet eyes, with the lashes curving long over the under side of the dark-blue iris, were turned full on him now with the tenderness of a kindred pity.

"Do you know I think that your father was once kind to my mother. Grandmother began once to tell me, and then all at once would tell me no more—I think because grandfather was there."

"I did not know that my father ever knew your mother," answered Ralph.

"Of course, he would never tell you if he did," said the woman of experience, sagely; "but grandmother has a portrait in an oval miniature of your father as a young man, and my mother's name is on the back of it."

"Her maiden name?" queried Ralph.

Winsome Charteris nodded. Then she said wistfully: "I wish I knew all about it. I think it is very hard that grandmother will not tell me!"

Then, after a silence which a far-off cuckoo filled in with that voice of his which grows slower and fainter as the midsummer heats come on, Winsome said abruptly, "Is your father ever hard and— unkind?"

Ralph started to his feet as if hastily to defend his father. There was something in Winsome's eyes that made him sit down again—something shining and tender and kind.

"My father," he said, "is very silent and reserved, as I fear I too have been till I came down here" (he meant to say, "Till I met you, dear," but he could not manage it), "but he is never hard or unkind, except perhaps on matters connected with the Marrow kirk and its order and discipline. Then he becomes like a stone, and has no pity for himself or any. I remember him once forbidding me to come into the study, and compelling me to keep my own garret- room for a month, for saying that I did not see much difference between the Marrow kirk and the other kirks. But I am sure he could never be unkind or hurtful to any one in the world. But why do you ask, Mistress Winsome?"

"Because—because—" she paused, looking down now, the underwells of her sweet eyes brimming to the overflow—"because something grandfather said once, when he was very ill, made me wonder if your father had ever been unkind to my mother."

Two great tears overflowed from under the dark lashes and ran down Winsome's cheek. Ralph was on the right side of the branch now, and, strangely enough, Winsome did not seem to notice it. He had a lace-edged handkerchief in his hand which had been his mother's, and all that was loving and chivalrous in his soul was stirred at the sight of a woman's tears. He had never seen them before, and there is nothing so thrilling in the world to a young man. Gently, with a light, firm hand, he touched Winsome's cheek, instinctively murmuring tenderness which no one had ever used to him since that day long ago, when his mother had hung, with the love of a woman who knows that she must give up all, over the cot of a boy whose future she could not foresee.

For a thrilling moment Winsome's golden coronet of curls touched his breast, and, as he told himself after long years, rested willingly there while his heart beat at least ten times. Unfortunately, it did not take long to beat ten times.

One moment more, and without any doubt Ralph would have taken Winsome in his arms. But the girl, with that inevitable instinct which tells a woman when her waist or her lips are in danger— matters upon which no woman is ever taken by surprise, whatever she may pretend—drew quietly back. The time was not yet.

"Indeed, you must not, you must not think of me. You must go away. You know that there are only pain and danger before us if you come to see me any more."

"Indeed, I do not know anything of the kind. I am sure that my father could never be unkind to any creature, and I am certain that he was not to your mother. But what has he to do with us, Winsome?"

Her name sounded so perilously sweet to her, said thus in Ralph's low voice, that once again her eyes met his in that full, steady gaze which tells heart secrets and brings either life-long joys or unending regrets. Nor—as we look—can we tell which?

"I cannot speak to you now, Ralph," she said, "but I know that you ought not to come to see me any more. There must be something strange and wicked about me. I feel that there is a cloud over me, Ralph, and I do not want you to come under it."

At the first mention of his name from the lips of his beloved, Ralph drew very close to her, with that instinctive drawing which he was now experiencing. It was that irresistible first love of a man who has never wasted himself even on the harmless flirtations which are said to be the embassies of love.

But Winsome moved away from him, walking down towards the mouth of the linn, through the thickly wooded glen, and underneath the overarching trees, with their enlacing lattice-work of curving boughs.

"It is better not," she said, almost pleadingly, for her strength was failing her. She almost begged him to be merciful.

"But you believe that I love you, Winsome?" he persisted.

Low in her heart of hearts Winsome believed it. Her ear drank in every word. She was silent only because she was thirsty to hear more. But Ralph feared that he had fatally offended her.

"Are you angry with me, Winsome?" he said, bending from his masculine height to look under the lilac sunbonnet.

Winsome shook her head. "Not angry, Ralph, only sorry to the heart."

She stopped and turned round to him. She held out a hand, when Ralph took it in both of his. There was in the touch a determination to keep the barriers slight but sure between them. He felt it and understood.

"Listen, Ralph," she said, looking at him with shining eyes, in which another man would have read the love, "I want you to understand. There is a fate about those who love me. My mother died long ago; my father I never knew; my grandfather and grandmother are—what you know, because of me; Mr. Welsh, at the Manse, who used to love me and pet me when I was a little girl, now does not speak to me. There is a dark cloud all about me!" said Winsome sadly, yet bravely and determinedly.

Yet she looked as bright and sunshiny as her own name, as if God had just finished creating her that minute, and had left the Sabbath silence of thanksgiving in her eyes. Ralph Peden may be forgiven if he did not attend much to what she said. As long as Winsome was in the world, he would love her just the same, whatever she said.

"What the cloud is I cannot tell," she went on; "but my grandfather once said that it would break on whoever loved me— and—and I do not want that one to be you."

Ralph, who had kept her hand a willing prisoner, close and warm in his, would have come nearer to her.

He said: "Winsome, dear" (the insidious wretch! he thought that, because she was crying, she would not notice the addition, but she did)— "Winsome, dear, if there be a cloud, it is better that it should break over two than over one."

"But not over you," she said, with a soft accent, which should have been enough, for any one, but foolish Ralph was already fixed on his own next words:

"If you have few to love you, let me be the one who will love you all the time and altogether. I am not afraid; there will be two of us against the world, dear."

Winsome faltered. She had not been wooed after this manner before. It was perilously sweet. Little ticking pulses beat in her head. A great yearning came to her to let herself drift up on a sea of love. That love of giving up all, which is the precious privilege, the saving dowry or utter undoing of women, surged in upon her heart.

She drew away her hand, not quickly, but slowly and firmly, and as if she meant it. "I have come to a decision—I have made a vow," she said. She paused, and looked at Ralph a little defiantly, hoping that he would take the law into his own hands, and forbid the decision and disallow the vow.

But Ralph was not yet enterprising enough, and took her words a little too seriously. He only stood looking at her and waiting, as if her decision were to settle the fate of kingdoms.

Then Winsome emitted the declaration which has been so often made, at which even the more academic divinities are said to smile, "I am resolved never to marry!"

An older man would have laughed. He might probably have heard something like this before. But Ralph had no such experience, and he bowed his head as to an invincible fate—for which stupidity Winsome's grandmother would have boxed his ears.

"But I may still love you, Winsome?" he said, very quietly and gently.

"Oh, no, you must not—you must not love me! Indeed, you must not think of me any more. You must go away."

"Go away I can and will, if you say so, Winsome; but even you do not believe that I can forget you when I like."

"And you will go away?" said Winsome, looking at him with eyes that would have chained a Stoic philosopher to the spot.

"Yes," said Ralph, perjuring his intentions.

"And you will not try to see me any more—you promise?" she added, a little spiteful at the readiness with which he gave his word.

So Ralph made a promise. He succeeded in keeping it just twenty-four hours—which was, on the whole, very creditable, considering.

What else he might have promised we cannot tell—certainly anything else asked of him so long as Winsome continued to look at him.

Those who have never made just such promises, or listened to them being made—occupations equally blissful and equally vain—had better pass this chapter by. It is not for the uninitiated. But it is true, nevertheless.

So in silence they walked down to the opening of the glen. As they turned into the broad expanse of glorious sunshine the shadows were beginning to slant towards them. Loch Grannoch was darkening into pearl grey, under the lee of the hill. Down by the high-backed bridge, which sprang at a bound over the narrows of the lane, there was a black patch on the greensward, and the tripod of the gipsy pot could faintly be distinguished.

Ralph, who had resumed Winsome's hand as a right, pointed it out. It is strange how quickly pleasant little fashions of that kind tend to perpetuate themselves!

As Winsome's grandmother would have said, "It's no easy turnin' a coo when she gets the gate o' the corn."

Winsome looked at the green patch and the dark spot upon it. "Tell me," she said, looking up at him, "why you ran away that day?"

Ralph Peden was nothing if not frank. "Because," he said, "I thought you were going to take off your stockings!"

Through the melancholy forebodings which Winsome had so recently exhibited there rose the contagious blossom of mirth, that never could be long away even from such a fate-harassed creature as Winsome Charteris considered herself to be. "Poor fellow," she said, "you must indeed have been terribly frightened!"

"I was," said Ralph Peden, with conviction. "But I do not think I should feel quite the same about it now!"

They walked silently to the foot of the Craig Ronald loaning, where by mutual consent they paused.

Winsome's hand was still in Ralph's. She had forgotten to take it away. She was, however, still resolved to do her duty.

"Now you are sure you are not going to think of me any more?" she asked.

"Quite sure," said Ralph, promptly.

Winsome looked a little disappointed at the readiness of the answer. "And you won't try to see me any more?" she asked, plaintively.

"Certainly not," replied Ralph, who had some new ideas.

Winsome looked still more disappointed. This was not what she had expected.

"Yes," said Ralph, "because I shall not need to think of you again, for I shall never stop thinking of you; and I shall not try to see you again, because I know I shall. I shall go away, but I shall come back again; and I shall never give you up, though every friend forbid and every cloud in the heavens break!"

The gladness broke into his love's face in spite of all her gallant determination.

"But remember," said Winsome, "I am never going to marry. On that point I am quite determined."

"You can forbid me marrying you, Winsome dear," said Ralph, "but you cannot help me loving you."

Indeed on this occasion and on this point of controversy Winsome did not betray any burning desire to contradict him. She gave him her hand — still with the withholding power in it, however, which told Ralph that his hour was not yet come.

He bowed and kissed it — once, twice, thrice. And to him who had never kissed woman before in the way of love, it was more than many caresses to one more accustomed.

Then she took her way, carrying her hand by her side tingling with consciousness. It seemed as if Ebie Farrish, who was at the watering-stone as she passed, could read what was written upon it as plain as an advertisement. She put it, therefore, into the lilac sunbonnet and so passed by.

Ralph watched her as she glided, a tall and graceful young figure, under the archway of the trees, till he could no longer see her light dress glimmering through the glades of the scattered oaks.

CHAPTER XXVII
THE OPINIONS OF SAUNDERS
MOWDIEWORT UPON BESOMSHANKS

Ralph Peden kept his promise just twenty-four hours, which under the circumstances was an excellent performance. That evening, on his return to the manse, Manse Bell handed him, with a fine affectation of unconcern, a letter with the Edinburgh post-mark, which had been brought with tenpence to pay, from Cairn Edward. Manse Bell was a smallish, sharp-tongued woman of forty, with her eyes very close together. She was renowned throughout the country for her cooking and her temper, the approved excellence of the one being supposed to make up for the difficult nature of the other.

The letter was from his father. It began with many inquiries as to his progress in the special studies to which he had been devoting himself. Then came many counsels as to avoiding all entanglements with the erroneous views of Socinians, Erastians, and Pelagians In conclusion, a day was suggested on which it would be convenient for the presbytery of the Marrow kirk to meet in Edinburgh in order to put Ralph through his trials for license. Then it was that Ralph Peden felt a tingling sense of shame. Not only had he to a great extent forgotten to prepare himself for his examinations, which would be no great difficulty to a college scholar of his standing, but unconsciously to himself his mind had slackened its interest in his licensing. The Marrow kirk had receded from him as the land falls back from a ship which puts out to sea, swiftly and silently. He was conscious that he had paid far more attention to his growing volume of poems than he had done to his discourses for license; though indeed of late he had given little attention to either.

He went up-stairs and looked vaguely at his books. He found that it was only by an effort that he could at all think himself into the old Ralph, who had shaken his head at Calvin under the broom- bush by the Grannoch Water. Sharp penitence rode hard upon Ralph's conscience. He sat down among his neglected books. From these he did not rise till the morning fully broke. At last he lay down on the bed, after looking long at the ridge of pines which stood sharp up against the morning sky, behind which Craig Ronald lay. Then the underlying pang, which he had been crushing down by the night's work among the Hebrew roots, came triumphantly to the surface. He must leave the manse of Dullarg, and with it that solitary white farmhouse on the braeface, the orchard at the back of it, and the rose-clambered gable from which a dear window looked down the valley of the Grannoch, and up to the heathery brow of the Crae Hill.

So, unrefreshed, yet unconscious of the need of any refreshment, Ralph Peden rose and took his place at the manse table.

"I saw your candle late yestreen," said the minister, pausing to look at the young man over the wooden platter of porridge which formed the frugal and sufficient breakfast of the two.

Porridge for breakfast and porridge for supper are the cure-alls of the true Galloway man. It is not every Scot who stands through all temptation so square in the right way as morning and night to confine himself to these; but he who does so shall have his reward in a rare sanity of judgment and lightness of spirit, and a capacity for work unknown to countrymen of less Spartan habit.

So Ralph answered, looking over his own "cogfu' o' brose" as Manse Bell called them, "I was reading the book of Joel for the second time."

"Then you have," said the minister, "finished your studies in the Scripture character of the truly good woman of the Proverbs, with which you were engaged on your first coming here?"

"I have not quite finished," said Ralph, looking a little strangely at the minister.

"You ought always to finish one subject before you begin another," said Mr. Welsh, with a certain slow sententiousness.

By-and-bye Ralph got away from the table, and in the silence of his own room gave himself to a repentant and self-accusing day of study. Remorsefully sad, with many searchings of heart, he questioned whether indeed he were fit for the high office of minister in the kirk of the Marrow; whether he could now accept that narrow creed, and take up alone the burden of these manifold protestings. It was for this that he had been educated; it was for this that he had been given his place at his father's desk since ever he could remember.

Here he had studied in the far-off days of his boyhood strange deep books, the flavour of which only he retained. He had learned his letters out of the Bible—the Old Testament. He had gone through the Psalms from beginning to end before he was six. He remembered that the paraphrases were torn out of all the Bibles in the manse. Indeed, they existed only in a rudimentary form even in the great Bible in the kirk (in which by some oversight a heathen binder had bound them), but Allan Welsh had rectified this by pasting them up, so that no preacher in a moment of demoniac possession might give one out. What would have happened if this had occurred in the Marrow kirk it is perhaps better only guessing. At twelve Ralph was already far on in Latin and Greek, and at thirteen he could read plain narrative Hebrew, and had a Hebrew Bible of his own in which he followed his father, to the admiration of all the congregation.

Prigs of very pure water have sometimes been manufactured by just such means as this.

Sometimes his father would lean over and say, "My son, what is the expression for that in the original?" whereupon Ralph would read the passage. It was between Gilbert Peden and his Maker that sometimes he did this for pride, and not for information; but Ralph was his only son, and was he not training him, as all knew, in order that he might be a missionary apostle of the great truths of the protesting kirk of the Marrow, left to testify lonely and forgotten among the scanty thousands of Scotland, yet carrying indubitably the only pure doctrine as it had been delivered to the saints?

But, in spite of all, the lad's bent was really towards literature. The books of verses which he kept under lock and key were the only things that he had ever concealed from his father. Again, since he had come to man's estate, the articles he had covertly sent to the Edinburgh Magazine were manifest tokens of the bent of his mind. All the more was he conscious of this, that he had truly lived his life before the jealous face of his father's God, though his heart leaned to the milder divinity and the kindlier gospel of One who was the Bearer of Burdens.

Ralph lay long on his bed, on which he had lain down at full length to think out his plans, as his custom was. It did not mean to leave Winsome, this call to Edinburgh. His father would not utterly refuse his consent, though he might urge long delays. And, in any case, Edinburgh was but two days' journey from the Dullarg; two days on the road by the burnsides and over the heather hills was nothing to him. But, for all that, the aching would not be stilled. Hearts are strange, illogical things; they will not be argued with.

Finally, he rose with the heart of him full of the intention of telling Winsome at once. He would write to her and tell her that he must see her immediately. It was necessary for him to acquaint her with what had occurred. So, without further question as to his motive in writing, Ralph rose and wrote a letter to give to Saunders Mowdiewort. The minister's man was always ready to take a letter to Craig Ronald after his day's work was over.

His inclinations jumped cheerfully along with the shilling which Ralph—who had not many such—gave him for his trouble. Within a drawer, the only one in his room that would lock, on the top of Ralph's poems lay the white moss-rose and the forget-me-nots which, as a precious and pregnant emblem from his love, Saunders had brought back with him.

As Ralph sat at the window writing his letter to Winsome, he saw over the hedge beneath his window the bent form of Allan Welsh— his great, pallid brow over-dominating his face—walking slowly to and fro along the well-accustomed walk, at one end of which was the little wooden summer house in which was his private oratory. Even now Ralph could see his lips moving in the instancy of his unuttered supplication. His inward communing was so intense that the agony of prayer seemed to shake his frail body. Ralph could see him knit his hands behind his back in a strong tension of nerves. Yet it seemed a right and natural thing for Ralph to be immersed in his own concerns, and to turn away with the light tribute of a sigh to finish his love-letter—for, after all (say they), love is only a refined form of selfishness.

"Beloved," wrote Ralph, "among my many promises to you yester even, I did not promise to refrain from writing to you; or if I did, I ask you to put off your displeasure until you have read my letter. I am not, you said, to come to see you. Then will you come to meet me? You know that I would not ask you unless the matter were important. I am at a cross-roads, and I cannot tell which way to go. But I am sure that you can tell me, for your word shall be to me as the whisper of a kind angel. Meet me to-night, I beseech you, for ere long I must go very far away, and I have much to say to thee, my beloved! Saunders will bring any message of time or place safely. Believing that you will grant me this request—for it is the first time and may be the last—and with all my heart going out to thee, I am the man who truly loves thee.—RALPH PEDEN."

It was when Saunders came over from his house by the kirkyard that Ralph left his books and went down to find him. Saunders was in the stable, occupying himself with the mysteries of Birsie's straps and buckles, about which he was as particular as though he were driving a pair of bays every day.

"An' this is the letter, an' I'm to gie it to the same lass as I gied the last yin till? I'll do that, an' thank ye kindly," said Saunders, putting the letter into one pocket and Ralph's shilling into the other; "no that I need onything but white silver kind o' buckles friendship. It's worth your while, an' its worth my while —that's the way I look at it."

Ralph paused a moment. He would have liked to ask what Meg said, and how Winsome looked, and many other things about Saunders's last visit; but the fear of appearing ridiculous even to Saunders withheld him.

The grave-digger went on: "It's a strange thing—love—it levels a'. Noo there's me, that has had a wife an' burriet her; I'm juist as keen aboot gettin' anither as if I had never gotten the besom i' the sma' o' my back. Ye wad never get a besom in the sma' o' yer back?" he said inquiringly.

"No," said Ralph, smiling in spite of himself.

"Na, of course no; ye havna been mairrit. But bide a wee; she's a fell active bit lass, that o' yours, an' I should say"—here Saunders spoke with the air of a connoisseur—"I wad say that she micht be verra handy wi' the besom."

"You must not speak in that way," began Ralph, thinking of Winsome. But, looking at the queer, puckered face of Saunders, he came to the conclusion that it was useless to endeavour to impress any of his own reverence upon him. It was not worth the pains, especially as he was assuredly speaking after his kind.

"Na, of course no," replied Saunders, with a kind of sympathy for youth and inexperience in his tone; "when yer young an' gaun coortin' ye dinna think o' thae things. But bide a wee till ye gann on the same errand the second time, and aiblins the third time—I've seen the like, sir—an' a' thae things comes intil yer reckoning, so so speak."

"Really," said Ralph, "I have not looked so far forward."

Saunders breathed on his buckle and polished it with the tail of his coat, after which he rubbed it on his knee. Then he held it up critically in a better light. Still it did not please him, so he breathed on it once more.

"'Deed, an' wha could expect it? It's no in youth to think o' thae things—no till it's ower late. Noo, sir, I'll tell ye, when I was coortin' my first, afore I gat her, I could hae etten [eaten] her, an' the first week after Maister Teends mairrit us, I juist danced I was that fond o' her. But in anither month, faith, I thocht that she wad hae etten me, an' afore the year was oot I wussed she had. Aye, aye, sir, it's waur nor a lottery, mairriage—it's a great mystery."

"But how is it, then, that you are so anxious to get married again?" asked Ralph, to whom these conversations with the Cuif were a means of lightening his mind of his own cares.

"Weel, ye see, Maister Ralph," pursued the grave-digger, "I'm by inclination a social man, an' the nature o' my avocation, so to speak, is a wee unsocial. Fowk are that curious. Noo, when I gang into the square o' a forenicht, the lads 'll cry oot, 'Dinna be lookin' my gate, Saunders, an' wonnerin' whether I'll need a seven-fit hole, or whether a six-fit yin will pass!' Or maybe the bairns'll cry oot, 'Hae ye a skull i' yer pooch?' The like o' that tells on a man in time, sir."

"Without doubt," said Ralph; "but how does matrimony, for either the first or the second time, cure that?"

"Weel, sir, ye see, mairriage mak's a man kind o' independent like. Say, for instance, ye hae been a' day at jobs up i' the yaird, an' it's no been what ye micht ca' pleesant crunchin' through green wud an' waur whiles. Noo, we'll say that juist as a precaution, ye ken, ye hae run ower to the Black Bull for a gless or twa at noo's an' nan's" [now and then].

"*I* have run over, Saunders?" queried Ralph.

"Oh, it's juist a mainner o' speakin', sir; I was takin' a personal example. Weel, ye gang hame to the wife aboot the gloamin', an' ye open the door, an' ye says, says you, pleesant like, bein' warm aboot the wame,' Guid e'en to ye, guidwife, my dawtie, an' hoos a' thing been gaim wi' ye the day?' D'ye think she needs to luik roon' to ken a' aboot the Black Bull? Na, na, she kens withoot even turnin' her heid. She kenned by yer verra fit as ye cam' up the yaird. She's maybe stirrin' something i' the pat. She turns roon' wi' the pat-stick i' her haund. 'I'll dawtie ye, my man!' she says, an' WHANG, afore ye ken whaur ye are, the pat-stick is acquant wi' the side o' yer heid. 'I'll dawtie ye, rinnin' rakin' to the public-hoose wi' yer hard-earned shillin's. Dawtie!' quo' she; 'faith, the Black Bull's yer dawtie!'"

"But how does she know?" asked Ralph, in the interests of truth and scientific inquiry.

Saunders thought that he was speaking with an eye on the future. He lifted up his finger solemnly: "Dinna ye ever think that ye can gang intil a public hoose withoot yer wife kennin'. Na, it's no the smell, as an unmarrit man micht think; and peppermints is a vain thing, also ceenimons. It's juist their faculty—aye, that's what it is—it's a faculty they hae; an' they're a' alike. They ken as weel wi' the back o' their heids till ye, an' their noses fair stuffit wi' the cauld, whether ye hae been makin' a ca' or twa on the road hame on pay-nicht. I ken it's astonishin' to a single man, but ye had better tak' my word for't, it's the case. 'Whaur's that auchteenpence?' Betty used to ask; 'only twal an' sixpence, an' your wages is fourteen shillings—forbye your chance frae mourners for happen the corp up quick'—then ye hummer an' ha', an' try to think on the lee ye made up on the road doon; but it's a gye queery thing that ye canna mind o't. It's an odd thing hoo jooky [nimble] a lee is when ye want it in time o' need!"

Ralph looked so interested that Saunders quite felt for him.

"And what then?" said he.

"Then," said Saunders, nodding his head, so that it made the assertion of itself without any connection with his body—"then, say ye, then is juist whaur the besom comes in"—he paused a moment in deep thought—"i' the sma' o' yer back!" he added, in a low and musing tone, as of one who chews the cud of old and pleasant memories. "An' ye may thank a kind Providence gin there's plenty o' heather on the end o't. Keep aye plenty o' heather on the end o' the besom," said Saunders; "a prudent man aye sees to that. What is't to buy a new besom or twa frae a tinkler body, whan ye see the auld yin gettin' bare? Nocht ava, ye can tak' the auld yin oot to the stable, or lose it some dark nicht on the moor! O aye, a prudent man aye sees to his wife's besom." Saunders paused, musing. "Ye'll maybe no believe me, but often what mak's a' the hale differ atween a freendly turn up wi' the wife, that kind o' cheers a man up, an' what ye micht ca' an onpleesantness— is juist nae mair nor nae less than whether there's plenty o' heather on his wife's besom."

Saunders had now finished all his buckles to his satisfaction. He summed up thus the conclusion of his great argument: "A besom i' the sma' o' yer back is interestin' an' enleevinin', whan it's new an' bushy; but it's the verra mischief an' a' whan ye get the bare shank on the back o' yer heid—an' mind ye that."

"I am very much indebted to you for the advice, Saunders."

"Aye, sir," said Saunders, "it's sound! it's sound! I can vouch for that."

Ralph went towards the door and looked out. The minister was still walking with his hands behind his back. He did not in the least hear what Saunders had said. He turned again to him. "And what do you want another wife for, then, Saunders?"

"'Deed, Maister Ralph, to tell ye the Guid's truth, it's awfu' deevin' [deafening] leevin' wi' yin's mither. She's a awfu' woman to talk, though a rale guid mither to me. Forbye, she canna tak' the besom to ye like yer ain wife—the wife o' yer bosom, so to speak—when ye hae been to the Black Bull. It's i' the natur' o' things that a man maun gang there by whiles; but on the ither haund it's richt that he should get a stap ta'en oot o' his bicker when he comes hame, an' some way or ither the best o' mithers haena gotten the richt way o't like a man's ain wife."

"And you think that Meg would do it well?" said Ralph, smiling.

"Aye, sir, she Avad that, though I'm thinkin' that she wad be kindlier wi' the besom-shank than Jess; no that I wad for a moment expect that there wad be ony call for siclike," he said, with a look of apology at Ralph, which was entirely lost on that young man, "but in case, sir—in case—"

Ralph looked in bewilderment at Saunders, who was indulging in mystic winks and nods.

"You see, the way o't is this, sir: yin's mither—(an' mind, I'm far frae sayin' a word agin my ain mither—she's a guid yin, for a' her tongue, whilk, ye ken, sir, she canna help ony mair than bein' a woman;) but ye ken, that when ye come hame frae the Black Bull, gin a man has only his mither, she begins to flyte on [scold] him, an' cast up to him what his faither, that's i' the grave, wad hae said, an' maybe on the back o' that she begins the greetin'. Noo, that's no comfortable, ava. A man that gangs to the Black Bull disna care a flee's hin' leg what his faither wad hae said. He disna want to be grutten ower [wept over]; na, what he wants is a guid-gaun tongue, a wullin' airm, an' a heather besom no ower sair worn."

Ralph nodded in his turn in appreciative comment.

"Then, on the morrow's morn, when ye rub yer elbow, an' fin' forbye that there's something on yer left shoother-blade that's no on the ither, ye tak' a resolve that ye'll come straught hame the nicht. Then, at e'en, when ye come near the Black Bull, an' see the crony that ye had a glass wi' the nicht afore, ye naturally tak' a bit race by juist to get on the safe side o' yer hame. I'm hearin' aboot new-fangled folk that they ca' 'temperance advocates,' Maister Ralph, but for my pairt gie me a lang-shankit besom, an' a guid-wife's wullin airm!"

These are all the opinions of Saunders Mowdiewort about besom-shanks.

CHAPTER XXVIII
THAT GIPSY JESS

Saunders took Ralph's letter to Craig Ronald with him earlier that night than usual, as Ralph had desired him. At the high hill gate, standing directing the dogs to gather the cows off the hill for milking, he met Jess.

"Hae ye ouy news, Saunders?" she asked, running down to the little foot-bridge to meet him. Saunders took it as a compliment; and, indeed, it was done with a kind of elfish grace, which cast a glamour over his eyes. But Jess, who never did anything without a motive, really ran down to be out of sight of Ebie Farrish, who stood looking at her from within the stable door.

"Here's a letter for ye, Jess," Saunders said, importantly, handing her Ralph's letter. "He seemed rale agitatit when he brocht it in to me, but I cheered him up by tellin' him how ye wad dreel him wi' the besom-shank gin he waur to gang to the Black Bull i' the forenichts."

"Gang to the Black Bull!—what div ye mean, ye gomeril?— Saunders I mean; ye ken weel that Maister Peden wadna gang to ony Black Bull."

"Weel, na, I ken that; it was but a mainner o' speakin'; but I can see that he's fair daft ower ye, Jess. I ken the signs o' love as weel as onybody. But hoo's Meg—an' do ye think she likes me ony better?"

"She was speakin' aboot ye only this mornin'," answered Jess pleasantly, "she said that ye waur a rale solid, sensible man, no a young ne'er-do-weel that naebody kens whaur he'll be by the Martinmas term."

"Did Meg say that!" cried Saunders in high delight, "Ye see what it is to be a sensible woman. An' whaur micht she be noo?"

Now Jess knew that Meg was churning the butter, with Jock Forrest to help her, in the milk-house, but it did not suit her to say so. Jess always told the truth when it suited as well as anything else; if not, then it was a pity.

"Meg's ben the hoose wi' the auld fowk the noo," she said, "but she'll soon be oot. Juist bide a wee an' bind the kye for me."

Down the brae face from the green meadowlets that fringed the moor came the long procession of cows. Swinging a little from side to side, they came—black Galloways, and the red and white breed of Ayrshire in single file—the wavering piebald line following the intricacies of the path. Each full-fed, heavy-uddered mother of the herd came marching full matronly with stately tread, blowing her flower-perfumed breath from dewy nostrils. The older and staider animals—Marly, and Dumple, and Flecky—came stolidly homeward, their heads swinging low, absorbed in meditative digestion, and soberly retasting the sweetly succulent grass of the hollows, and the crisper and tastier acidity of the sorrel- mixed grass of the knolls. Behind them came Spotty and Speckly, young and frisky matrons of but a year's standing, who yet knew no better than to run with futile head at Roger, and so encourage that short-haired and short-tempered collie to snap at their heels. Here also, skirmishing on flank and rear, was Winsome's pet sheep, "Zachary Macaulay"—so called because he was a living memorial to the emancipation of the blacks. Zachary had been named by John Dusticoat, who was the politician of Cairn Edward, and "took in" a paper. He was an animal of much independence of mind. He utterly refused to company with the sheep of his kind and degree, and would only occasionally condescend to accompany the cows to their hill pasture. Often he could not be induced to quit poking his head into every pot and dish about the farm-yard. On these occasions he would wander uninvited with a little pleading, broken-backed bleat through every room in the house, looking for his mistress to let him suck her thumb or to feed him on oatcake or potato parings.

To-night he came down in the rear of the procession. Now and then he paused to take a random crop at the herbage, not so much from any desire for wayside refreshment, as to irritate Roger into attacking him. But Roger knew better. There was a certain imperiousness about Zachary such as became an emancipated black. Zachary rejoiced when Speckly or any of the younger or livelier kine approached to push him away from a succulent patch of herbage. Then he would tuck his belligerent head between his legs, and drive fore-and-aft in among the legs of the larger animals, often bringing them down full broadside with the whole of their extensive systems ignominiously shaken up.

By the time that Saunders had the cows safe into the byre, Jess had the letter opened, read, and resealed. She had resolved, for reasons of her own, on this occasion to give the letter to Winsome. Jess ran into the house, and finding Winsome reading in the parlour, gave her the letter in haste.

"There's a man waiting for the answer," she said, "but he can easy bide a while if it is not ready."

Winsome, seeing it was the handwriting she knew so well, that of the note-book and the poem, went into her own room to read her first love-letter. It seemed very natural that he should write to her, and her heart beat within her quickly and strongly as she opened it. As she unfolded it her eye seemed to take in the whole of the writing at once as if it were a picture. She knew, before she had read a word, that "beloved" occurred twice and "Winsome dear" twice, nor had she any fault to find, unless it were that they did not occur oftener.

So, without a moment's hesitation, she sat down and wrote only a line, knowing that it would be all-sufficient. It was her first love-tryst. Yet if it had been her twentieth she could not have been readier.

"I shall be at the gate of the hill pasture," so she wrote, "at ten o'clock to-night."

It was with a very tumultuous heart that she closed this missive, and went out quickly to give it to Jess lest she should repent. A day before, even, it had never entered her mind that by any possibility she could write such a note to a young man whom she had only known so short a time. But then she reflected that certainly Ralph Peden was not like any other young man; so that in this case it was not only right but also commendable. He was so kind and good, and so fond of her grandmother, that she could not let him go so far away without a word. She ought at least to go and tell him that he must never do the like again. But she would forgive him this time, after being severe with him for breaking his word, of course. She sighed when she thought of what it is to be young and foolish. Once the letter in Jess's hands, these doubts and fears came oftener to her. After a few minutes of remorse, she ran out in order to reclaim her letter, but Jess was nowhere to be seen. She was, in fact, at her mother's cottage up on the green, where she was that moment employed in coercing her brother Andra to run on a message for her. "When she went out of the kitchen with Winsome's reply in her pocket she made it her first duty to read it. This there was no difficulty in doing, for opening letters was one of Jess's simplest accomplishments. Then Jess knitted her black brows, and thought dark and Pictish thoughts. In a few moments she had made her dispositions. She was not going to let Winsome have Ralph without a struggle. She felt that she had the rude primogeniture of first sight. Besides, since she had no one to scheme for her, she resolved that she would scheme for herself. Shut in her mother's room she achieved a fair imitation of Winsome's letter, guiding herself by the genuine document spread out before her. She had thought of sending only a verbal message, but reflecting that Ralph Peden had probably never seen Winsome's handwriting, she considered it safer, choosing between two dangers, to send a written line.

"Meet me by the waterside bridge at ten o'clock," she wrote. No word more. Then arose the question of messengers. She went out to find Saunders Mowdiewort; she got him standing at the byre door, looking wistfully about for Meg. "Saunders," she said, "you are to take back this answer instantly to the young Master Peden."

"Na, na, Jess, what's the hurry? I dinna gang a fit till I hae seen Meg," said Saunders doggedly. "Your affairs are dootless verra important, but sae are mine. Your lad maun een wait wi' patience till I gang hame, the same as I hae had mony a day to wait. It's for his guid."

Jess stamped her foot. It was too irritating that her combinations should fail because of a Cuif whom she had thought to rule with a word, and upon whom she had counted without a thought.

She could not say that it was on Winsome's business, though she knew that in that case he would have gone at once on the chance of indirectly pleasuring Meg. She had made him believe that she herself was the object of Ralph Peden's affections. But Jess was not to be beaten, for in less than a quarter of an hour she had overcome the scruples of Andra, and despatched Jock Gordon on another message in another direction. Jess believed that where there is a will there are several ways: the will was her own, but she generally made the way some one else's. Then Jess went into the byre, lifting up her house gown and covering it with the dust- coloured milking overall, in which she attended to Speckly and Crummy. She had done her best—her best, that is, for Jess Kissock—and it was with a conscience void of offence that she set herself to do well her next duty, which happened to be the milking of the cows. She did not mean to milk cows any longer than she could help, but in the meantime she meant to be the best milker in the parish. Moreover, it was quite in accordance with her character that, in her byre flirtations with Ebie Farrish, she should take pleasure in his rough compliments, smacking of the field and the stable. Jess had an appetite for compliments perfectly eclectic and cosmopolitan. Though well aware that she was playing this night with the sharpest of edged tools, till her messengers should return and her combinations should close, Jess was perfectly able and willing to give herself up to the game of conversational give-and-take with Ebie Farrish. She was a girl of few genteel accomplishments, but with her gipsy charm and her frankly pagan nature she was fitted to go far.

CHAPTER XXIX
THE DAKK OF THE MOON AT
THE GKANNOCH BRIDGE

Over the manse of Dullarg, still and grey, with only the two men in it; over the low-walled rectangular farm steading of Craig Ronald, fell alike the midsummer night. Ten o'clock on an early July evening is in Galloway but a modified twilight. But as the sun went down behind the pines he sent an angry gleam athwart the green braes. The level cloud-band into which he plunged drew itself upward to the zenith, and, like the eyelid of a gigantic eye, shut down as though God in his heaven were going to sleep, and the world was to be left alone.

It was the dark of the moon, and even if there had been full moon its light would have been as completely shut out by the cloud canopy as was the mild diffusion of the blue-grey twilight. So it happened that, as Ralph Peden took his way to his first love- tryst, it was all that he could do to keep the path, so dark had it become. But there was no rain—hardly yet even the hint or promise of rain.

Yet under the cloud there was a great solitariness—the murmur of a land where no man had come since the making of the world. Down in the sedges by the lake a blackcap sang sweetly, waesomely, the nightingale of Scotland. Far on the moors a curlew cried out that its soul was lost. Nameless things whinnied in the mist-filled hollows. On the low grounds there lay a white mist knee-deep, and Ralph Peden waded in it as in a shallow sea. So in due time he came near to the place of his tryst.

Never had he stood so before. He stilled the beating of his heart with his hand, so loud and riotous it was in that silent place. He could hear, loud as an insurrection, the quick, unequal double- knocking in his bosom.

A grasshopper, roosting on a blade of grass beneath, his feet, tumbled off and gave vent to his feelings in a belated "chirr." Overhead somewhere a raven croaked dismally and cynically at intervals. Ralph's ears heard these things as he waited, with every sense on the alert, at the place of his love-tryst.

He thrilled with the subtle hope of strange possibilities. A mill-race of pictures of things sweet and precious ran through his mind. He saw a white-spread table, with Winsome seated opposite to himself, tall, fair, and womanly, the bright heads of children between them. And the dark closed in. Again he saw Winsome with her head on his arm, standing looking out on the sunrise from the hilltop, whence they had watched it not so long ago. The thought brought him to his pocket-book. He took it out, and in the darkness touched his lips to the string of the lilac sunbonnet. It surely must be past ten now, he thought. Would she not come? He had, indeed, little right to ask her, and none at all to expect her. Yet he had her word of promise—one precious line. What would he say to her when she came? He would leave that to be settled when his arms were about her. But perhaps she would be colder than before. They would sit, he thought, on the parapet of the bridge. There were no fir-branches to part them with intrusive spikes. So much at least should be his.

But then, again, she might not come at all! What more likely than that she had been detained by her grandmother? How could he expect it? Indeed, he told himself he did not expect it. He had come out here because it was a fine night, and the night air cooled his brain for his studies. His heart, hammering on his life's anvil, contradicted him. He could not have repeated the Hebrew alphabet. His head, bent a little forward in the agony of listening, whirled madly round; the ambient darkness surrounding all.

There! He heard a footstep. There was a light coming down the avenue under the elders. At last! No, it was only the glow-worms under the leaves, shining along the grass by the wayside. The footstep was but a restless sheep on the hillside. Then some one coughed, with the suppressed sound of one who covers his mouth with his hand. Ralph was startled, but almost laughed to think that it was still only the lamb on the other side of the wall moving restlessly about in act to feed. Time and again the blood rushed to his temples, for he was sure that he heard her coming to him. But it was only the echo of the blood surging blindly through his own veins, or some of the night creatures fulfilling their love-trysts, and seeking their destinies under the cloud of night.

Suddenly his whole soul rose in revolt against him. Certainly now he heard a light and swift footstep. There was a darker shape coming towards him against the dim, faint grey glimmer of the loch. It was his love, and she had come out to him at his bidding. He had dreamed of an angel, and lo! now he should touch her in the hollow night, and find that she was a warm, breathing woman.

Wrapped from head to foot in a soft close shawl, she came to him. He could see her now, but only as something darker against the canopy of the night. So, in the blissful dark, which makes lovers brave, he opened his arms to receive her. For the first time in his life he drew them to him again not empty.

The thrill electric of the contact, the yielding quiescence of the girl whom he held to his breast, stilled his heart's tumultuous beating. She raised her head, and their lips drew together into a long kiss. What was this thing? It was a kiss in which he tasted a strange alien flavour even through the passion of it. A sense of wrong and disappointment flowed round Ralph's heart. So on the bridge in the darkness, where many lovers had stood ever since the first Pict trysted his dark-browed bride by the unbridged water, the pair stood very still. They only breathed each other's breath. Something familiar struck on Ralph's senses. He seemed to be standing silent in the parlour at Craig Ronald—not here, with his arms round his love—and somehow between them there rose unmistakable the perfume of the flower which for an hour he had carried in his coat on the day that he and she went a-fishing.

"Beloved," he said tenderly, looking down, "you are very good to me to come!"

For all reply a face was held close pressed to his. The mists of night had made her cheek damp. He passed his hand across the ripples of her hair. Half hidden by the shawl he could feel the crisping of the curls under his fingers.

It was harder in texture than he had fancied Winsome's hair would be. He half smiled that he had time at such a moment to think such a thing. It was strange, however. He had thought a woman's hair was like floss silk— at least Winsome's, for he had theorized about none other.

"Winsome, dear!" he said, again bending his head to look down, "I have to go far away, and I wanted to tell you. You are not angry with me, sweetest, for asking you to come? I could not go without bidding you good-bye, and in the daytime I might not have seen you alone. You know that I love you with all my life and all my heart. And you love me—at least a little. Tell me, beloved!"

Still there was no answer. Ralph waited with some certitude and ease from pain, for indeed the clasping arms told him all he wished to know.

There was a brightness low down in the west. Strangely and slowly the gloomy eyelid of cloud which had fallen athwart the evening lifted for a moment its sullen fringe; a misty twilight of lurid light flowed softly over the land. The shawl fell back like a hood from off the girl's shoulders. She looked up throbbing and palpitating. Ralph Peden was clasping Jess Kissock in his arms. She had kept her word. He had kissed her of his own free will, and that within a day. Her heart rejoiced over Winsome. "So much, at least, she cannot take from me."

Ralph Peden's heart stopped beating for a tremendous interval of seconds. Then the dammed-back blood-surge drave thundering in his ears. He swayed, and would have fallen but for the parapet of the bridge and the clinging arms about his neck. All his nature and love in full career stopped dead. The shock almost unhinged his soul and reason. It was still so dark that, though he could see the outline of her head and the paleness of her face, nothing held him but the intense and vivid fascination of her eyes. Ralph would have broken away, indignant and amazed, but her arms and eyes held him close prisoner, the dismayed turmoil in his own heart aiding.

"Yes, Ralph Peden," Jess Kissock said, cleaving to him, "and you hate me because it is I and not another. You think me a wicked girl to come to you in her place. But you called her because you loved her, and I have come because I loved you as much. Have I not as much right? Do not dream that I came for aught but that. Have I not as good a right to love as you?"

She prisoned his face fiercely between her hands, and held him off from her as if to see into his soul by the light of the lingering lake of ruddy light low in the west.

"In your Bible where is there anything that hinders a woman from loving? Yet I know you will despise me for loving you, and hate me for coming in her place."

"I do not hate you!" said Ralph, striving to go without rudely unclasping the girl's hands. Her arms fell instantly again about his neck, locking themselves behind.

"No, you shall not go till you have heard all, and then you can cast me into the loch as a worthless thing that you are better rid of."

Through his disappointment and his anger, Ralph was touched. He would have spoken, but the girl went on:

"No, you do not hate me—I am not worth it. You despise me, and do you think that is any better? I am only a cottar's child. I have been but a waiting-maid. But I have read how maids have loved the kings and the kings loved them. Yes, I own it. I am proud of it. I have schemed and lain awake at nights for this. Why should I not love you? Others have loved me without asking my leave. Why should I ask yours? And love came to me without your leave or my own that day on the road when you let me carry your books."

She let her arms drop from his neck and buried her face in her hands, sobbing now with very genuine tears. Ralph could not yet move away, even though no longer held by the stringent coercion of this girl's arms. He was too grieved, too suddenly and bitterly disappointed to have any fixed thought or resolve. But the good man does not live who can listen unmoved to the despairing catch of the sobbing in a woman's throat. Then on his hands, which he had clasped before him, he felt the steady rain of her tears; his heart went out in a great pity for this wayward girl who was baring her soul to him.

The whole note and accent of her grief was of unmistakable feeling. Jess Kissock had begun in play, but her inflammable nature kindled easily into real passion. For at least that night, by the bridge of the Grannoch water, she believed that her heart was broken.

Ralph put his hand towards her with some unformed idea of sympathy. He murmured vague words of comfort, as he might have done to a wailing child that had hurt itself; but he had no idea how to still the tempestuous grief of a passion-pale woman.

Suddenly Jess Kissock slipped down and clasped him about the knees. Her hair had broken from its snood and streamed a cloud of intense blackness across her shoulders. He could see her only weirdly and vaguely, as one may see another by the red light of a wood ember in the darkness. She seemed like a beautiful, pure angel, lost by some mischance, praying to him out of the hollow pit of the night.

"I carried your burden for you once, the day I first saw you. Let me carry your burden for you across the world. If you will not love me, let me but serve you. I would slave so hard! See, I am strong—"

She seized his hands, gripping thorn till his fingers clave together with the pressure.

"See how I love you!" her hands seemed to say. Then she kissed his hands, wetting them with the downfalling of her tears.

The darkness settled back thicker than before. He could not see the kneeling woman whose touch he felt. He strove to think what he should do, his emotions and his will surging in a troubled maelstrom about his heart.

But just then, from out of the darkness high on the unseen hill above them, there came a cry—a woman's cry of pain, anger, and ultimate danger: "Ralph, Ralph, come to me—come!" it seemed to say to him. Again and again it came, suddenly faltered and was silenced as if smothered—as though a hand had been laid across a mouth that cried and would not be silent.

Ralph sprang clear of Jess Kissock in a moment. He knew the voice. He would have known it had it come to him across the wreck of worlds. It was his love's voice. She was calling to him—Ralph Peden—for help. Without a thought for the woman whose despairing words he had just listened to, he turned and ran, plunging into the thick darkness of the woods, hillward in the direction of the cry. But he had not gone far when another cry was heard—not the cry of a woman this time, but the shorter, shriller, piercing yell of a man at the point of death—some deadly terror at his throat, choking him. Mixed with this came also unearthly, wordless, inhuman howlings, as of a wild beast triumphing. For a dozen seconds these sounds dominated the night. Then upon the hill they seemed to sink into a moaning, and a long, low cry, like the whining of a beaten dog. Lights gleamed about the farm, and Ralph could vaguely see, as he sprang out of the ravine, along which he and Winsome had walked, dark forms flitting about with lanterns. In another moment he was out on the moor, ranging about like a wild, questing hound, seeking the cause of the sudden and hideous outcry.

CHAPTEE XXX
THE HILL GATE

There was no merry group outside Winsome's little lattice window this night, as she sat unclad to glimmering white in the quiet of her room. In her heart there was that strange, quiet thrill of expectancy—the resolve of a maiden's heart, when she knows without willing that at last the flood-gates of her being must surely be raised and the great flood take her to the sea. She did not face the thought of what she would say. In such a case a man plans what he will say, and once in three times he says it. But a woman is wiser. She knows that in that hour it will be given her what she shall speak.

"I shall go to him," said Winsome to herself; "I must, for he is going away, and he has need of me. Can I let him go without a word?"

Though Ralph had done no noble action in her sight or within her ken, yet there was that about him which gave her the knowledge that she would be infinitely safe with him even to the world's end. Winsome wondered how she could so gladly go, when she would not have so much as dreamed of stealing out at night to meet any other, though she might have known him all her life. She did not know, often as she had heard it read, that "perfect love casteth out fear." Then she said to herself gently, as if she feared that the peeping roses at the window might hear, "Perhaps it is because I love him." Perhaps it was. Happy Winsome, to have found it out so young!

The curtain of the dark drew down. Moist airs blew into the room, warm with the scent of the flowers of a summer night. Honeysuckle and rose blew in, and quieted the trembling nerves of the girl going to meet her first love.

"He has sair need o' me!" she said, lapsing as she sometimes did into her grandmother's speech. "He will stand before me," she said, "and look so pale and beautiful. Then I will not let him come nearer—for a while—unless it is very dark and I am afraid."

She glanced out. It promised to be very dark, and a tremour came over her. Then she clad herself in haste, drawing from a box a thin shawl of faded pale blue silk with a broad crimson edge, which she drew close about her shoulders. The band of red lying about her neck forced forward her golden tresses, throwing them about her brow so that they stood out round her face in a changeful aureole of fine-spun gold. She took a swift glance in the mirror, holding her candle in her hand. Then she laughed a nervous little laugh all to herself. How foolish of her! Of course, it would be impossible for him to see her. But nevertheless she put out her light, and went to the door smiling. She had no sense of doing that which she ought not to do; for she had been accustomed to her liberty in all matters whatsoever, ever since she came to Craig Ronald, and in the summer weather nothing was more common than for her to walk out upon the moor in the dewy close of day. She shut the door quietly behind her, and set her foot on the silent elastic turf, close cropped by many woolly generations. The night shut down behind her closer than the door. The western wind cooled her brain, and the singing in her heart rose into a louder altar-song. A woman ever longs to be giving herself. She rejoices in sacrifice. It is a pity that she so often chooses an indifferently worthy altar. Yet it is questionable whether her own pleasure in the sacrifice is any the less.

At the gate of the yard, which had been left open and hung backward perilously upon its hinges, she paused.

"That is that careless girl, Jess!" she said, practical even at such a moment.

And she was right—it was Jess who had so left it. Indeed, had she been a moment sooner, she might have seen Jess flit by, taking the downward road which led through the elder—trees to the waterside. As it was, she only shut the gate carefully, so that no night- wandering cattle might disturb the repose of her grandparents, laid carefully asleep by Meg in their low-ceilinged bedroom.

The whole farm breathed from its walls and broad yard spaces the peaceful rise and fall of an infant's repose. There was no sound about the warm and friendly place save the sleepy chunner of a hen on the bauks of the peat-house, just sufficiently awake to be conscious of her own comfort.

The hill road was both stony and difficult, but Winsome's light feet went along it easily and lightly. On not a single stone did she stumble. She walked so gladsomely that she trod on the air. There were no rocks in her path that night. Behind her the light in the west winked once and went out. Palpable darkness settled about her. The sigh of the waste moorlands, where in the haggs the wild fowl were nestling and the adders slept, came down over the well-pastured braes to her.

Winsome did not hasten. Why hasten, when at the end of the way there certainly lies the sweet beginning of all things. Already might she be happy in the possession of certainties? It never occurred to her that Ralph would not be at the trysting-place. That a messenger might fail did not once cross her mind. But maidenly tremours, delicious in their uncertainty, coursed along her limbs and through all her being. Could any one have seen, there was a large and almost exultant happiness in the depths of her eyes. Her lips were parted a little, like a child that waits on tiptoe to see the curtain rise on some wondrous and long- dreamed-of spectacle.

Soon against the darker sky the hill dyke stood up, looking in the gloom massive as the Picts' Wall of long ago. It followed irregularly the ridgy dips and hollows downward, till it ran into the in tenser darkness of the pines. In a moment, ere yet she was ready, there before her was the gate of her tryst. She paused, affrighted for the first time. She listened, and there was no sound. A trembling came over her and an uncertainty. She turned, in act to flee.

But out of the dark of the great dyke stepped a figure cloaked from head to heel, and while Winsome wavered, tingling now with shame and fear, in an instant she was enclosed within two very strong arms, that received her as in a snare a bird is taken.

Suddenly Winsome felt her breath shorten. She panted as if she could not get air, like the bird as it nutters and palpitates.

"Oh, I ought not to have come!" &he said, "but I could not help it!"

There was no word in answer, only a closer folding of the arms that cinctured her. In the west the dusk was lightening and the eyelid of the night drew slowly and grimly up.

When for the first time she looked shyly upward, Winsome found herself in the arms of Agnew Greatorix. Wrapped in his great military cloak, with a triumphant look in his handsome face, he smiled down upon her.

Great Lord of Innocence! give now this lamb of thine thy help!

The leaping soul of pure disembodied terror stood in Winsome's eyes. Fascinated like an antelope in the coils of a python she gazed, her eyes dilating and contracting—the world whirling about her, the soul of her bounding and panting to burst its bars.

"Winsome, my darling!" he said, "you have come to me. You are mine"—bending his face to hers.

Not yet had the power to speak or to resist come back to her, so instant and terrible was her surprise. But at the first touch of his lips upon her cheek the very despair brought back to her tenfold her own strength. She pushed against him with her hands, straining him from her by the rigid tension of her arms, setting her face far from his, but she was still unable to break the clasp of his arms about her.

"Let me go! let me go!" she cried, in a hoarse and labouring whisper.

"Gently, gently, fair and softly, my birdie," said Greatorix; "surely you have not forgotten that you sent for me to meet you here. Well, I am here, and I am not such a fool as to come for nothing!"

The very impossibility of words steeled Winsome's heart,

"*I* send for you!" cried Winsome; "I never had message or word with you in my life to give you a right to touch me with your little finger. Let me go, and this instant, Agnew Greatorix!"

"Winsome, sweetest girl, it pleases you to jest. Have not I your own letter in my pocket telling me where to meet you? Did you not write it? I am not angry. You can play out your play and pretend you do not care for me as much as you like; but I will not let you go. I have loved you too long, though till now you were cruel and would give me no hope. So when I got your letter I knew it was love, after all, that had been in your eyes as I rode away."

"Listen," said Winsome eagerly; "there is some terrible mistake; I never wrote a line to you —"

"It matters not; it was to me that your letter came, brought by a messenger to the castle an hour ago. So here I am, and here you are, my beauty, and we shall just make the best of it, as lovers should when the nights are short."

He closed his arms about her, forcing the strength out of her wrists with slow, rude, masculine muscles. A numbness and a deadness ran through her limbs as he compelled her nearer to him. Her head spun round with the fear of fainting. With a great effort she forced herself back a step from him, and just as she felt the breath of his mouth upon hers her heart made way through her lips.

"Ralph! Ralph! Help me—help! Oh, come to me!" she cried in her extremity of terror and the oncoming rigour of unconsciousness.

The next moment she dropped limp and senseless into the arms of Agnew Greatorix. For a long moment he held her up, listening to the echoes of that great cry, wondering whether it would wake up the whole world, or if, indeed, there were none to answer in that solitary place.

But only the wild bird wailed like a lost soul too bad for heaven, too good for hell, wandering in the waste forever.

Agnew Greatorix laid Winsome down on the heather, lifeless and still, her pure white face resting in a nest of golden curls, the red band of her mother's Indian shawl behind all.

But as the insulter stooped to take his will of her lips, now pale and defenceless, something that had been crouching beastlike in the heather for an hour, tracking and tracing him like a remorseless crawling horror, suddenly sprang with a voiceless rush upon him as he bent over Winsome's prostrate body—gripped straight at his throat and bore him backward bareheaded to the ground.

So unexpected was the assault that, strong man as Greatorix was, he had not the least chance of resistance. He reeled at the sudden constriction of his throat by hands that hardly seemed human, so wide was their clutch, so terrible the stringency of their grasp. He struck wildly at his assailant, but, lying on his back with the biting and strangling thing above him, his arms only met on one another in vain blows. He felt the teeth of a great beast meet in his throat, and in the sudden agony he sent abroad the mighty roar of a man in the grips of death by violence. But his assailant was silent, save for a fierce whinnying growl as of a wild beast greedily lapping blood.

It was this terrible outcry ringing across the hills that brought the farm steading suddenly awake, and sent the lads swarming about the house with lanterns. But it was Ralph alone who, having heard the first cry of his love and listened to nothing else, ran onward, bending low with a terrible stitch in his side which caught his breath and threw him to the ground almost upon the white-wrapped body of his love. Hastily he knelt beside her and laid his hand upon her heart. It was beating surely though faintly.

But on the other side, against the gray glimmer of the march dyke, he could see the twitchings of some great agony. At intervals there was the ghastly, half-human growling and the sobbing catch of some one striving for breath.

A light shone across the moor, fitfully wavering as the searcher cast its rays from side to side. Ralph glanced behind him with the instinct to carry his love away to a place of safety. But he saw the face of Meg Kissock, with slow Jock Forrest behind her carrying a lantern. Meg ran to the side of her mistress.

"Wha's dune this?" she demanded, turning fiercely to Ralph. "Gin ye—"

"I know nothing about it. Bring the lantern here quickly," he said, leaving Winsome in the hands of Meg. Jock Forrest brought the lantern round, and there on the grass was Agnew Greatorix, with daft Jock Gordon above him, his sinewy hands gripping his neck and his teeth in his throat.

Ralph pulled Jock Gordon off and flung him upon the heather, where Jock Forrest set his foot upon him, and turned the light of the lantern upon the fierce face of a maniac, foam-flecked and blood- streaked. Jock still growled and gnashed his teeth, and struggled in sullen fury to get at his fallen foe. With his hat Ralph brought water from a deep moss-hole and dashed it upon the face of Winsome. In a little while, she began to sob in a heartbroken way. Meg took her head upon her knees, and soothed her mistress, murmuring tendernesses. Next he brought water to throw over the face and neck of Greatorix, which Jock Gordon in his fury had made to look like nothing human.

The rest might wait. It was Ralph's first care to get Winsome home. Kneeling down beside her he soothed her with whispered words, till the piteous sobbing in her throat stilled itself. The ploughman was at this moment stolidly producing pieces of rope from his pockets and tying up Jock Gordon's hands and feet; but after his first attempts again to fly at Greatorix, and his gasps of futile wrath when forced into the soft moss of the moor by Jock Forrest's foot, he had not offered to move.

His paroxysm was only one of the great spasms of madness which sometimes come over the innocently witless. He had heard close by him the cries of Winsome Charteris, whom he had worshipped for years almost in the place of the God whom he had not the understanding to know. The wonder rather was that he did not kill Greatorix outright. Had it happened a few steps nearer the great stone dyke, there is little doubt but that Jock Gordon would have beat out the assailant's brains with a ragged stone.

Winsome had not yet awakened enough to ask how all these things came about. She could only cling to Meg, and listen to Ralph whispering in her ear.

"I can go home now," she said earnestly.

So Ralph and Meg helped her up, Ralph wrapping her in her great crimson-barred shawl.

Ralph would have kissed her, but Winsome, standing unsteadily clasping Meg's arm, said tenderly:

"Not to-night. I am not able to bear it."

It was almost midnight when Ralph and the silent Jock Forrest got Agnew Greatorix into the spring-cart to be conveyed to Greatorix Castle.

He lay with his eyes closed, silent. Ralph took Jock Gordon to the manse with him, determined to tell the whole to Mr. Welsh if necessary; but if it were not necessary, to tell no one more than he could help, in order to shelter Winsome from misapprehension. It says something for Ralph that, in the turmoil of the night and the unavailing questionings of the morning, he never for a moment thought of doubting his love. It was enough for him that in the depths of agony of body or spirit she had called out to him. All the rest would be explained in due time, and he could wait. Moreover, so selfish is love, that he had never once thought of Jess Kissock from the moment that his love's cry had pealed across the valley of the elder-trees and the plain of the water meadows.

When he brought Jock Gordon, hardly yet humanly articulate, into the kitchen of the manse, the house was still asleep. Then Ralph wakened Manse Bell, who slept above. He told her that Jock Gordon had taken a fit upon the moor, that he had found him ill, and brought him home. Next he went up to the minister's room, where he found Mr. Welsh reading his Bible. He did not know that the minister had watched him both come and go from his window, or that he had remained all night in prayer for the lad, who, he misdoubted, was in deep waters.

As soon as Jock Gordon had drunk the tea and partaken of the beef ham which Manse Bell somewhat grumblingly set before him, he said:

"Noo, I'll awa'. The tykes'll be after me, nae doot, but it's no in yin o' them to catch Jock Gordon gin yince he gets into the Dungeon o' Buchan."

"But ye maun wait on the minister or Maister Peden. They'll hae muckle to ask ye, nae doot!" said Bell, who yearned for news.

"Nae doot, nae doot!" said daft Jock Gordon, "an' I hae little to answer. It's no for me to tie the rape roond my ain craig [neck]. Na, na, time aneu' to answer when I'm afore the sherra at Kirkcudbright for this nicht's wark."

With these words Jock took his pilgrim staff and departed for parts unknown. As he said, it was not bloodhounds that could catch Jock Gordon on the Rhinns of Kells.

In the morning there was word come to the cot-house of the Kissocks that Mistress Kissock was wanted up at the castle to nurse a gentleman who had had an accident when shooting. Mistress Kissock was unable to go herself, but her daughter Jess went instead of her, having had some practice in nursing, among other experiences which she had gained in England. It was reported that she made an excellent nurse.

CHAPTEE XXXI
THE STUDY OF THE MANSE OF DULLARG

IT was growing slowly dusk again when Ralph Peden returned from visiting Craig Ronald along the shore road to the Dullarg and its manse. He walked briskly, as one who has good news. Sometimes he whistled to himself—breaking off short with a quick smile at some recollection. Once he stopped and laughed aloud. Then he threw a stone at a rook which eyed him superciliously from the top of a turf dyke. He made a bad shot, at which the black critic wiped the bare butt of his bill upon the grass, uttered a hoarse "A-ha!" of derision, and plunged down squatty among the dock- leaves on the other side.

As Ralph turned up the manse loaning to the bare front door, he was conscious of a vague uneasiness, the feeling of a man who returns to a house of gloom from a world where all things have been full of sunshine. It was not the same world since yesterday. Even he, Ralph Peden, was not the same man. But he entered the house with that innocent affectation of exceeding ease which is the boy's tribute to his own inexperience. He went up the stairs through the dark lobby and entered Allan Welsh's study. The minister was sitting with his back to the window, his hands clasped in front of him, and his great domed forehead and emaciated features standing out against the orange and crimson pool of glory where the sun had gone down.

Ralph ostentatiously clattered down his armful of books on the table. The minister did not speak at first, and Ralph began his explanation.

"I am sorry," he said, hesitating and blushing under the keen eyes of his father's friend. "I had no idea I should have been detained, but the truth is—"

"I ken what the truth is," said Allan Welsh, quietly. "Sit down, Ralph Peden. I have somewhat to say to you."

A cold chill ran through the young man's veins, to which succeeded a thrill of indignation. Was it possible that he was about to reproach him, as a student in trials for the ministry of the Marrow kirk, with having behaved in any way unbecoming of an aspirant to that high office, or left undone anything expected of him as his father's son?

The minister was long in speaking. Against the orange light of evening which barred the window, his face could not be seen, but Ralph had the feeling that his eyes, unseen themselves, were reading into his very soul. He sat down and clenched his hands under the table,

"I was at the Bridge of Grannoch this day," began the minister at last. "I was on my way to visit a parishioner, but I do not conceal from you that I also made it my business to observe your walk and conversation."

"By what right do you so speak to me?" began Ralph, the hotter blood of his mother rising within him.

"By the right given to me by your father to study your heart and to find out whether indeed it is seeking to walk in the more perfect way. By my love and regard for you, I hope I may also say."

The minister paused, as if to gather strength for what he had yet to say. He leaned his head upon his hand, and Balph did not see that his frail figure was shaken with some emotion too strong for his physical powers, only kept in check by the keen and indomitable will within.

"Ralph, my lad," Allan Welsh continued, "do not think that I have not foreseen this; and had jour father written to inform me of his intention to send you to me, I should have urged him to cause you to abide in your own city. What I feared in thought is in act come to pass. I saw it in your eyes yestreen."

Kalph's eyes spoke an indignant query.

"Ralph Peden," said the minister, "since I came here, eighteen years ago, not a mouse has crept out of Craig Ronald but I have made it my business to know it. I am no spy, and yet I need not to be told what happened yesterday or to-day."

"Then, sir, you know that I have no need to be ashamed."

"I have much to say to you, Ralph, which I desire to say by no means in anger. But first let me say this: It is impossible that you can ever be more to Winifred Charteris than you are to-day."

"That is likely enough, sir, but I would like to know why in that case I am called in question." "Because I have been, more than twenty years ago, where you are to-day, Ralph Peden, I—even I— have seen eyes blue as those of Winsome Charteris kindle with pleasure at my approach. Yes, I have known it. And I have also seen the lids lie white and still upon these eyes, and I am here to warn you from the primrose way; and also, if need be, to forbid you to walk therein."

His voice took a sterner tone with the last words.

Ralph bowed his head on the table and listened; but there was no feeling save resentment and resistance in his heart.

The minister went on in a level, unemotional tone, like one telling a tale of long ago, of which the issues and even the interests are dead and gone.

"I do not look now like a man on whom the eye of woman could ever rest with the abandonment of love. Yet I, Allan Welsh, have seen 'the love that casteth out fear.'"

After a pause the high, expressionless voice took up the tale.

"Many years ago there were two students, poor in money but rich in their mutual love. They were closer in affection than twin brothers. The elder was betrothed to be married to a beautiful girl in the country; so he took down his friend with him to the village where the maid dwelt to stand by his side and look upon the joy of the bridegroom. He saw the trysted (betrothed) of his friend. He and she looked into one another's eyes and were drawn together as by a power beyond them. The elder was summoned suddenly back to the city, and for a week he, all unthinking, left the friends of his love together glad that they should know one another better. They walked together. They spoke of many things, ever returning back to speak of themselves. One day they held a book together till they heard their hearts beat audibly, and in the book read no more that day.

"Upon the friend's return he found only an empty house and distracted parents. Bride and brother had fled. Word came that they had been joined by old Joseph Paisley, the Gretna Green 'welder,' without blessing of minister or kirk. Then they hid themselves in a little Cumbrian village, where for six years the unfaithful friend wrought for his wife—for so he deemed her— till in the late bitterness of bringing forth she died, that was the fairest of women and the unhappiest."

The minister ceased. Outside the rain had come on in broad single drops, laying the dust on the road. Ralph could hear it pattering on the broad leaves of the plane-tree outside the window. He did not like to hear it. It sounded like a woman's tears.

But he could not understand how all this bore on his case. He was silenced and awed, but it was with the sight of a soul of a man of years and approved sanctity in deep apparent waters of sorrow.

The minister lifted his head and listened. In the ancient woodwork of the manse, somewhere in the crumbling wainscoting, the little boring creature called a death-watch ticked like the ticking of an old verge watch. Mr. Welsh broke off with a sudden causeless auger very appalling in one so sage and sober in demeanour.

"There's that beast again!" he said; "often have I thought it was ticking in my head. I have heard it ever since the night she died—"

"I wonder at a man like you," said Ralph, "with your wisdom and Christian standing, caring for a worm—"

"You're a very young man, and when you are older maybe you'll wonder at a deal fewer things," answered the minister with a kind of excited truculence very foreign to his habit, "for I myself am a worm and no man," he added dreamily. "And often I tried to kill the beast. Ye see thae marks—" he broke off again—"I bored for it till the boards are a honeycomb, but the thing aye ticks on."

"But, Mr. Welsh," said Ralph eagerly, with some sympathy in his voice, "why should you trouble yourself about this story now—or I, for the matter of that? I can understand that Winsome Charteris has somehow to do with it, and that the knowledge has come to you in the course of your duty; but even if, at any future time, Winsome Charteris were aught to me or I to her—the which I have at present only too little hope of—her forbears, be they whomsoever they might, were no more to me than Julius Caesar. I have seen her and looked into her eyes. What needs she of ancestors that is kin to the angels?"

Something like pity came into the minister's stern eyes as he listened to the lad. Once he had spoken just such wild, heart-eager words.

"I will answer you in a sentence," he said. "I that speak with you am the cause. I am he that has preached law and the gospel—for twenty years covering my sin with the Pharisee's strictness of observance. I am he that was false friend but never false lover— that married without kirk or blessing. I am the man that clasped a dead woman's hand whom I never owned as wife, and watched afar off the babe that I never dared to call mine own. I am the father of Winifred Oharteris, coward before man, castaway before God. Of my sin two know besides my Maker—the father that begot you, whose false friend I was in the days that were, and Walter Skirving, the father of the first Winifred whose eyes this hand closed under the Peacock tree at Crossthwaite."

The broad drops fell on the window-panes in splashes, and the thunder rain drummed on the roof.

The minister rose and went out, leaving Ralph Peden sitting in the dark with the universe in ruins about him. The universe is fragile at twenty-one.

And overhead the great drops fell from the brooding thunder-clouds, and in the wainscoting of Allan Welsh's study the death-watch ticked.

CHAPTER XXXII
OUTCAST AND ALIEN FROM
THE COMMONWEALTH

"Moreover," said the minister—coming in an hour afterwards to take up the interrupted discussion—"the kirk of the Marrow overrides all considerations of affection or self-interest. If you are to enter the Marrow kirk, you must live for the Marrow, and fight for the Marrow, and, above all, you must wed for the Marrow—"

"As you did, no doubt," said Ralph, somewhat ungenerously.

Ralph had remained sitting in the study where the minister had left him.

"No, for myself," said the minister, with a certain firmness and high civility, which made the young man ashamed of himself, "I am no true son of the Marrow. I have indeed served the Marrow kirk in her true and only protesting section for twenty-five years; but I am only kept in my position by the good grace of two men—of your father and of Walter Skirving. And do not think that they keep their mouths sealed by any love for me. Were there only my own life and good name to consider, they would speak instantly, and I should be deposed, without cavil or word spoken in my own defence. Nay, by what I have already spoken, I have put myself in your hands. All that you have to do is simply to rise in your place on the Sabbath morn and tell the congregation what I have told you— that the minister of the Marrow kirk in Dullarg is a man rebuking sin when his own hearthstone is unclean—a man irregularly espoused, who wrongfully christened his own unacknowledged child."

Allan Welsh laid his brow against the hard wood of the study table as though to cool it.

"No," he continued, looking Ralph in the face, as the midnight hummed around, and the bats softly fluttered like gigantic moths outside, "your father is silent for the sake of the good name of the Marrow kirk; but this thing shall never be said of his own son, and the only hope of the Marrow kirk—the lad she has colleged and watched and prayed for—not only the two congregations of Edinburgh and the Dullarg contributing yearly out of their smallest pittances, but the faithful single members and adherents throughout broad Scotland—many of whom are coming to Edinburgh at the time of our oncoming synod, in order to be present at it, and at the communion when I shall assist your father."

"But why can not I marry Winsome Charteris, even though she be your daughter, as you say?" asked Ralph.

"O young man," said the minister, "ken ye so little about the kirk o' the Marrow, and the respect for her that your father and myself cherish for the office of her ministry, that ye think that we could permit a probationer, on trials for the highest office within her gift, to connect himself by tie, bond, or engagement with the daughter of an unblest marriage? That wouald be winking at a new sin, darker even, than the old." Then, with a burst of passion—"I, even I, would sooner denounce it myself, though it cost me my position! For twenty years I have known that before God I was condemned. You have seen me praying—yes, often—all night, but never did you or mortal man hear me praying for myself."

Ralph held out his hand in sympathy. Mr. Welsh did not seem to notice it. He went on:

"I was praying for this poor simple folk—the elect of God—their minister alone a castaway, set beyond the mercy of God by his own act. Have I not prayed that they might never be put to shame by the knowledge of the minister's sin being made a mockery in the courts of Belial? And have I not been answered?"

Here we fear that Mr. Welsh referred to the ecclesiastical surroundings of the Reverend Erasmus Teends.

"And I prayed for my poor lassie, and for you, when I saw you both in the floods of deep waters. I have wept great and bitter tears for you twain. But I am to receive my answer and reward, for this night you shall give me your word that never more will you pass word of love to Winsome, the daughter of Allan Charteris Welsh. For the sake of the Marrow kirk and the unstained truth delivered to the martyrs, and upheld by your father one great day, you will do this thing."

"Mr. Welsh," said the young man calmly, "I cannot, even though I be willing, do this thing. My heart and life, my honour and word, are too deeply engaged for me to go back. At whatever cost to myself, I must keep tryst and pledge with the girl who has trusted me, and who for me has to-night suffered things whose depths of pain and shame I know not yet."

"Then," said the minister sternly, "you and I must part. My duty is done. If you refuse my appeal, you are no true son of the Marrow kirk, and no candidate that I can recommend for her ministry. Moreover, to keep you longer in my house and at my board were tacitly to encourage you in your folly."

"It is quite true," replied Ralph, unshaken and undaunted, "that I may be as unfit as you say for the office and ministry of the Marrow kirk. It is, indeed, only as I have thought for a long season. If that be so, then it were well that I should withdraw, and leave the place for some one worthier."

"I wonder to hear ye, Ralph Peden, your father's son," said the minister, "you that have been colleged by the shillings and sixpences of the poor hill folk. How will ye do with these?"

"I will pay them back," said Ralph.

"Hear ye, man: can ye pay back the love that hained and saved to send them to Edinburgh? Can ye pay back the prayers and expectations that followed ye from class to class, rejoicing in your success, praying that the salt of holiness might be put for you into the fountains of earthly learning? Pay back, Ralph Peden?—I wonder sair that ye are not shamed!"

Indeed, Ralph was in a sorrowful quandary. He knew that it was all true, and he saw no way out of it without pain and grief to some. But the thought of Winsome's cry came to him, heard in the lonesome night. That appeal had severed him in a moment from all his old life. He could not, though he were to lose heaven and earth, leave her now to reproach and ignominy. She had claimed him only in her utter need, and he would stand good, lover and friend to be counted on, till the world should end.

"It is true what you say," said Ralph; "I mourn for it every word, but I cannot and will not submit my conscience and my heart to the keeping even of the Marrow kirk." ¬

"Ye should have thought on that sooner," interjected the minister grimly.

"God gave me my affections as a sacred trust. This also is part of my religion. And I will not, I cannot in any wise give up hope of winning this girl whom I love, and whom you above all others ought surely to love."

"Then," said the minister, rising solemnly with his hand outstretched as when he pronounced the benediction, "I, Allan Welsh, who love you as my son, and who love my daughter more than ten daughters who bear no reproach, tell you, Ralph Peden, that I can no longer company with you. Henceforth I count you as a rebel and a stranger. More than self, more than life, more than child or wife, I, sinner as I am, love the honour and discipline of the kirk of the Marrow. Henceforth you and I are strangers."

The words fired the young man. He took up his hat, which had fallen upon the floor.

"If that be so, the sooner that this house is rid of the presence of a stranger and a rebel the better for it, and the happier for you. I thank you for all the kindness you have shown to me, and I bid you, with true affection and respect, farewell!"

So, without wailing even to go up-stairs for anything belonging to him, and with no further word on either side, Ralph Peden stepped into the clear, sobering midnight, the chill air meeting him like a wall. The stars had come out and were shining frosty-clear, though it was June.

And as soon as he was gone out the minister fell on his knees, and so continued all the night praying with his face to the earth.

CHAPTER XXXIII
JOCK GORDON TAKES A HAND

Whatever is too precious, too tender, too good, too evil, too shameful, too beautiful for the day, happens in the night. Night is the bath of life, the anodyne of heartaches, the silencer of passions, the breeder of them too, the teacher of those who would learn, the cloak that shuts a man in with his own soul. The seeds of great deeds and great crimes are alike sown in the night. The good Samaritan doeth his good by stealth; the wicked one cometh and soweth his tares among the wheat. The lover and the lustful person, the thief and the thinker, the preacher and the poacher, are abroad in the night. In factories and mills, beside the ceaseless whirl of machinery, stand men to whom day is night and night day. In cities the guardians of the midnight go hither and thither with measured step under the drizzling rain. No man cares that they are lonely and cold. Yet, nevertheless, both light and darkness, night and day, are but the accidents of a little time. It is twilight— the twilight of the morning and of the gods—that is the true normal of the universe. Night is but the shadow of the earth, light the nearness of the central sun. But when the soul of man goeth its way beyond the confines of the little multiplied circles of the system of the sun, it passes at once into the dim twilight of space, where for myriads of myriad miles there is only the grey of the earliest God's gloaming, which existed just so or ever the world was, and shall be when the world is not. Light and dark, day and night, are but as the lights of a station at which the train does not stop. They whisk past, gleaming bright but for a moment, and the world which came out of great twilight plunges again into it, perhaps to be remade and reillumined on some eternal morning.

It is good for man, then, to be oftentimes abroad in the early twilight of the morning. It is primeval-instinct with possibilities of thought and action. Then, if at all, he will get a glimpse into his soul that may hap to startle him. Judgment and the face of God justly angry seem more likely and actual things than they do in the city when the pavements are thronged and at every turning some one is ready for good or evil to hail you "fellow."

So Ralph Peden stepped out into the night, the sense of injustice quick upon him. He had no plans, but only the quick resentments of youth, and the resolve to stay no longer in a house where he was an unwelcome guest. He felt that he had been offered the choice between his career and unfaithfulness to the girl who had trusted him. This was not quite so; but, with the characteristic one- sidedness of youth, that was the way that he put the case to himself.

It was the water-shed of day and night when Ralph set out from the Dullarg manse. He had had no supper, but he was not hungry. Naturally his feet carried him in the direction of the bridge, whither he had gone on the previous evening and where amid an eager press of thoughts he had waited and watched for his love. When he got there he sat down on the parapet and looked to the north. He saw the wimples of the lazy Grannoch Lane winding dimly through their white lily beds. In the starlight the white cups glimmered faintly up from their dark beds of leaves. Underneath the bridge there was only a velvety blackness of shadow.

What to do was now the question. Plainly he must at once go to Edinburgh, and see his father. That was the first certainty. But still more certainly he must first see Winsome, and, in the light of the morning and of her eyes, solve for her all the questions which must have sorely puzzled her, at the same time resolving his own perplexities. Then he must bid her adieu. Right proudly would he go to carve out a way for her. He had no doubts that the mastership in his old school, which Dr. Abel had offered him a month ago, would still be at his disposal. That Winsome loved him truly he did not doubt. He gave no thought to that. The cry across the gulf of air from the high march dyke by the pines on the hill, echoing down to the bridge in the valley of the Grannoch, had settled that question once for all.

As he sat on the bridge and listened to the ripple of the Grannoch lane running lightly over the shallows at the Stepping Stones, and to the more distant roar of the falls of the Black Water, he shaped out a course for himself and for Winsome. He had ceased to call her Winsome Charteris. "She," he called her—the only she. When next he gave her a surname he would call her Winsome Peden. Instinctively he took off his hat at the thought, as though he had opened a door and found himself light-heartedly and suddenly in a church.

Sitting thus on the bridge alone and listening to the ocean-like lapse of his own thoughts, as they cast up the future and the past like pebbles at his feet, he had no more thought of fear for his future than he had that first day at Craig Ronald, under the whin- bushes on the ridge behind him, on that day of the blanket-washing so many ages ago. He was so full of love that it had cast out fear.

Suddenly out of the gloom beneath the bridge upon which he was sitting, dangling his legs, there came a voice.

"Maister Ralph Peden, Maister Ralph Peden."

Ralph nearly fell backward over the parapet in his astonishment.

"Who is that calling on me?" he asked in wonder.

"Wha but juist daft Jock Gordon? The hangman haesna catchit him yet, an' thank ye kindly—na, nor ever wull."

"Where are you, Jock, man?" said Ralph, willing to humour the instrument of God.

"The noo I'm on the shelf o' the brig; a braw bed it maks, if it is raither narrow. But graund practice for the narrow bed that I'll get i' the Dullarg kirkyaird some day or lang, unless they catch puir Jock and hang him. Na, na," said Jock with a canty kind of content in his voice, "they may luik a lang while or they wad think o' luikin' for him atween the foundation an' the spring o' the airch. An' that's but yin o' Jock Gordon's hidie holes, an' a braw an' guid yin it is. I hae seen this bit hole as fu' o' pairtricks and pheasants as it could hand, an' a' the keepers and their dowgs smellin', and them could na find it oot. Na, the water taks awa' the smell."

"Are ye not coming out, Jock?" queried Ralph.

"That's as may be," said Jock briefly. "What do ye want wi' Jock?"

"Come up," said Ralph; "I shall tell you how ye can help me. Ye ken that I helped you yestreen."

"Weel, ye gied me an unco rive aff that blackguard frae the Castle, gin that was a guid turn, I ken na!"

So grumbling, Jock Gordon came to the upper level of the bridge, paddling unconcernedly with his bare feet and ragged trousers through the shallows.

"Weel, na—hae ye a snuff aboot ye, noo that I am here? No—dear sirce, what wad I no do for a snuff?"

"Jock," said Ralph, "I shall have to walk to Edinburgh. I must start in the morning."

"Ye'll hae plenty o' sillar, nae doot?" said Jock practically.

Ralph felt his pockets. In that wild place it was not his custom to carry money, and he had not even the few shillings which were in his purse at the manse.

"I am sorry to say," he said, "that I have no money with me."

"Then ye'll be better o' Jock Gordon wi' ye?" said Jock promptly.

Ralph saw that it would not do to be saddled with Jock in the city, where it might be necessary for him to begin a new career immediately; so he gently broke the difficulties to Jock.

"Deed na, ye needna be feared; Jock wadna set a fit in a toon. There's ower mony nesty imps o' boys, rinnin' an' cloddin' stanes at puir Jock, forby caa'in' him names. Syne he loses his temper wi' them an' then he micht do them an injury an' get himsel' intil the gaol. Na, na, when Jock sees the blue smoor o' Auld Reeky gaun up into the lift he'll turn an' gae hame."

"Well, Jock," said Ralph, "it behooves me to see Mistress Winsome before I go. Ye ken she and I are good friends."

"So's you an' me; but had puir Jock no cried up till ye, ye wad hae gane aff to Embra withoot as muckle as 'Fairguide'en to ye, Jock.'"

"Ah, Jock, but then you must know that Mistress Charteris and I are lad and lass," he continued, putting the case as he conceived in a form that would suit it to Jock's understanding.

"Lad an' lass! What did ye think Jock took ye for? This is nane o' yer Castle tricks," he said; "mind, Jock can bite yet!"

Ralph laughed.

"No, no, Jock, you need not be feared. She and I are going to be married some day before very long"—a statement made entirely without authority.

"Hoot, hoot!" said Jock, "wull nocht ser' ye but that ava—a sensible man like you? In that case ye'll hae seen the last o' Jock Gordon. I canna be doin' wi' a gilravage o' bairns aboot a hoose—"

"Jock," said Ralph earnestly, "will you help me to see her before I go?"

"'Deed that I wull," said Jock, very practically. "I'll gaun an' wauken her the noo!"

"You must not do that," said Ralph, "but perhaps if you knew where Meg Kissock slept, you might tell her."

"Certes, I can that," said Jock; "I can pit my haund on her in a meenit. But mind yer, when ye're mairret, dinna expect Jock Gordon to come farther nor the back kitchen."

So grumbling, "It couldna be expeckit—I canna be doin' wi' bairns ava'—"Jock took his way up the long loaning of Craig Ronald, followed through the elderbushes by Ralph Peden.

CHAPTER XXXIV
THE DEW OF THEIR YOUTH

Jock made his way without a moment's hesitation to the little hen-house which stood at one end of the farm steading of Craig Ronald. Up this he walked with his semi-prehensile bare feet as easily as though he were walking along the highway. Up to the rigging of the house he went, then along it—setting one foot on one side and the other on the other, turning in his great toes upon the coping for support. Thus he came to the gable end at which Meg slept. Jock leaned over the angle of the roof and with his hand tapped on the window.

"Wha's there? "said Meg from her bed, no more surprised than if the knock had been upon the outer door at midday.

"It's me, daft Jock Gordon," said Jock candidly.

"Gae wa' wi' ye, Jock! Can ye no let decent fowk sleep in their beds for yae nicht?"

"Ye maun get up, Meg," said Jock.

"An' what for should I get up?" queried Meg indignantly. "I had ancuch o' gettin' up yestreen to last me a gye while."

"There's a young man here wantin' to coort your mistress!" said Jock delicately.

"Haivers!" said Meg, "hae ye killed another puir man?"

"Na, na, he's honest—this yin. It's the young man frae the manse. The auld carle o' a minister has turned him oot o' hoose an' hame, and he's gaun awa' to Enbra'. He says he maun see the young mistress afore he gangs—but maybe ye ken better, Meg."

"Gae wa' frae the wunda, Jock, and I'll get up," said Meg, with a brevity which betokened the importance of the news.

In a little while Meg was in Winsome's room. The greyish light of early morning was just peeping in past the little curtain. On the chair lay the lilac-sprigged muslin dress of her grandmother's, which Winsome had meant to put on next morning to the kirk. Her face lay sideways on the pillow, and Meg could see that she was softly crying even in her sleep. Meg stood over her a moment. Something hard lay beneath Winsome's cheek, pressing into its soft rounding. Meg tenderly slipped it out. It was an ordinary memorandum-book written with curious signs. On the pillow by her lay the lilac sunbonnet.

Meg put her arms gently round Winsome, saying:

"It's me, my lamb. It's me, your Meg!"

And Meg's cheek was pressed against that of Winsome, moist with sleep. The sleeper stirred with a dovelike moaning, and opened her eyes, dark with sleep and wet with the tears of dreams, upon Meg.

"Waken, my bonnie; Meg has something that she maun tell ye."

So Winsome looked round with the wild fear with which she now started from all her sleeps; but the strong arms of her loyal Meg were about her, and she only smiled with a vague wistfulness, and said:

"It's you, Meg, my dear!"

So into her ear Meg whispered her tale. As she went on, Winsome clasped her round the neck, and thrust her face into the neck of Meg's drugget gown. This is the same girl who had set the ploughmen their work and appointed to each worker about the farm her task. It seems necessary to say so.

"Noo," said Meg, when she had finished, "ye ken whether ye want to see him or no!"

"Meg," whispered Winsome, "can I let him go away to Edinburgh and maybe never see me again, without a word?"

"Ye ken that best yersel'," said Meg with high impartiality, but with her comforting arms very close about her darling.

"I think," said Winsome, the tears very near the lids of her eyes, "that I had better not see him. I—I do not wish to see him—Meg," she said earnestly; "go and tell him not to see me any more, and not to think of a girl like me—"

Meg went to Winsome's little cupboard wardrobe in the wall and took down the old lilac-sprayed summer gown which she had worn when she first saw Ralph Peden.

"Ye had better rise, my lassie, an' tak' that message yersel'!" said Meg dryly.

So obediently Winsome rose. Meg helped her to dress, holding silently her glimmering white garments for her as she had done when first as a fairy child she came to Craig Ronald. Some of them were a little roughly held, for Meg could not see quite so clearly as usual. Also when she spoke her speech sounded more abruptly and harshly than was its wont.

At last the girl's attire was complete, and Winsome stood ready for her morning walk fresh as the dew on the white lilies. Meg tied the strings of the old sunbonnet beneath her sweet chin, and stepped back to look at the effect; then, with sudden impulsive movement, she went tumultuously forward and kissed her mistress on the cheek.

"I wush it was me!" she said, pushing Winsome from the room.

The day was breaking red in the east when Winsome stepped out upon the little wooden stoop, damp with the night mist, which seemed somehow strange to her feet. She stepped down, giving a little familiar pat to the bosom of her dress, as though to advertise to any one who might be observing that it was her constant habit thus to walk abroad in the dawn.

Meg watched her as she went. Then she turned into the house to stop the kitchen clock and out to lock the stable door.

Through the trees Winsome saw Ralph long before he saw her. She was a woman; he was only a naturalist and a man. She drew the sunbonnet a little farther over her eyes. He started at last, turned, and came eagerly towards her.

Jock Gordon, who had remained about the farm, went quickly to the gate at the end of the house as if to shut it.

"Come back oot o' that," said Meg sharply.

Jock turned quite as briskly.

"I was gaun to stand wi' my back til't, sae that they micht ken there was naebody luikin'. D'ye think Jock Gordon haes nae mainners?" he said indignantly.

"Staun wi' yer back to a creel o' peats, Jock; it'll fit ye better!" ooserved Meg, giving him the wicker basket with the broad leather strap which was used at Craig Ronald for bringing the peats in from the stack.

Winsome had not meant to look at Ralph as she came up to him. It seemed a bold and impossible thing for her ever again to come to him. The fear of a former time was still strong upon her.

But as soon as she saw him, her eyes somehow could not leave his face. He dropped his hat on the grass beneath, as he came forward to meet her under the great branches of the oak-trees by the little pond. She had meant to tell him that he must not touch her —she was not to be touched; yet she went straight into his open arms like a homing dove. Her great eyes, still dewy with the warm light of love in them, never left his till, holding his love safe in his arms, he drew her to him and upon her sweet lips took his first kiss of love.

"At last!" he said, after a silence.

The sun was rising over the hills of heather. League after league of the imperial colour rolled westward as the level rays of the sun touched it.

"Now do you understand, my beloved?" said Ralph. Perhaps it was the red light of the sun, or only some roseate tinge from the miles of Galloway heather that stretched to the north, but it is certain that there was a glow of more than earthly beauty on Winsome's face as she stood up, still within his arms, and said:

"I do not understand at all, but I love you."

Then, because there is nothing more true and trustful than the heart of a good woman, or more surely an inheritance from the maid-mother of the sinless garden than her way of showing that she gives her all, Winsome laid her either hand on her lover's shoulders and drew his face down to hers—laying her lips to his of her own free will and accord, without shame in giving, or coquetry of refusal, in that full kiss of first surrender which a woman may give once, but never twice, in her life.

This also is part of the proper heritage of man and woman, and whoso has missed it may attain wealth or ambition, may exhaust the earth—yet shall die without fully or truly living.

A moment they stood in silence, swaying a little like twin flowers in the wind of the morning. Then taking hands like children, they slowly walked away with their faces towards the sunrise. There was the light of a new life in their eyes. It is good sometimes to live altogether in the present. "Sufficient unto the day is the good thereof," is a proverb in all respects equal to the scriptural original.

For a little while they thus walked silently forward, and on the crest of the ridge above the nestling farm Ralph paused to take his last look of Craig Ronald. Winsome turned with him in complete comprehension, though as yet he had told her no word of his projects. Nor did she think of any possible parting, or of anything save of the eyes into which she did not cease to look, and the lover whose hand it was enough to hold. All true and pure love is an extension of God—the gladness in the eyes of lovers, the tears also, bridals and espousals, the wife's still happiness, the delight of new-made homes, the tinkle of children's laughter. It needs no learned exegete to explain to a true lover what John meant when he said, "For God is love." These things are not gifts of God, they are parts of him.

It was at this moment that Meg Kissock, having seen them stand a moment still against the sky, and then go down from their hilltop towards the north, unlocked the stable door, at which Ebie Fairrish had been vainly hammering from within for a quarter of an hour. Then she went indoors and pulled close the curtains of Winsome's little room. She came out, locked the bedroom door, and put the key in her pocket. Her mistress had a headache. Meg was a treasure indeed, as a thoughtful person about a household often is.

As Winsome and Ralph went down the farther slope of the hill, towards the road that stretched away northward across the moors, they fell to talking together very practically. They had much to say. Before they had gone a mile the first strangeness had worn off, and the stage of their intimacy may be inferred from the fact that they were only at the edge of the great wood of Grannoch bank, when Winsome reached the remark which undoubtedly Mother Eve made to her husband after they had been some time acquainted:

"Do you know, I never thought I should talk to any one as I am talking to you?"

Ralph allowed that it was an entirely wonderful thing—indeed, a belated miracle. Strangely enough, he had experienced exactly the same thought. "Was it possible?" smiled Winsome gladly, from under the lilac sunbonnet.

Such wondrous and unexampled correspondence of impression proved that they were made for one another, did it not? At this point they paused. Exercise in the early morning is fatiguing. Only the unique character of these refreshing experiences induces us to put them on record.

Then Winsome and Ralph proceeded to other and not less extraordinary discoveries. Sitting on a wind-overturned tree- trunk, looking out from the edge of the fringing woods of the Grannoch bank towards the swells of Cairnsmuir's green bosom, they entered upon their position with great practicality. Nature, with an unusual want of foresight, had neglected to provide a back to this sylvan seat, so Ralph attended to the matter himself. This shows that self-help is a virtue to be encouraged.

Ralph had some disinclination to speak of the terrors of the night which had forever rolled away. Still, he felt that the matter must be cleared up; so that it was with doubt in his mind that he showed Winsome the written line which had taken him to the bridge instead of to the hill gate.

"That's Jess Kissock's writing!" Winsome said at once. Ralph had the same thought. So in a few moments they traced the whole plot to its origin. It was a fit product of the impish brain of Jess Kissock. Jess had sent the false note of appointment to Ralph by Andra, knowing that he would be so exalted with the contents that he would never doubt its accuracy. Then she had despatched Jock Gordon with "Winsome's real letter to Greatorix Castle; in answer to the supposed summons, which was genuine enough, though not meant for him, Agnew Greatorix had come to the hill gate, and Jess had met Ralph by the bridge to play her own cards as best she could for herself.

"How wicked!" said Winsome, "after all."

"How foolish!" said Ralph, "to think for a moment that any one could separate you and me."

But Winsome bethought herself how foolishly jealous she had been when she found Jess putting a flower into Ralph's coat, and Jess's plot did not look quite so impossible as before.

"I think, dear," said Ralph, "you must after this make your letters so full of your love, that there can be no mistake whom they are intended for."

"I mean to," said Winsome frankly.

There was also some fine scenery at this point.

But there was no hesitation in Ralph Peden's tone when he settled down steadily to tell her of his hopes.

Winsome sat with her eyes downcast and her head a little to one side, like a bright-eyed bird listening.

"That is all true and delightful," she said, "but we must not be selfish or forget."

"We must remember one another!" said Ralph, with the absorption of newly assured love.

"We are in no danger of forgetting one another," said that wise woman in counsel; "we must not forget others. There is your father—you have not forgotten him."

With a pang Ralph remembered that there was yet something that he could not tell Winsome. He had not even been frank with her concerning the reason of his leaving the manse and going to Edinburgh. She only understood that it was connected with his love for her, which was not approved of by the minister of the Marrow kirk.

"My father will be as much pleased with you as I," said Ralph, with enthusiasm.

"No doubt," said Winsome, laughing; "fathers always are with their sons' sweethearts. But you have not forgotten something else?"

"What may that be?" said Ralph doubtfully.

"That I cannot leave my grandfather and grandmother at Craig Ronald as they are. They have cared for me and given me a home when I had not a friend. Would you love me as you do, if I could leave them even to go out into the world with you?"

"No," said Ralph very reluctantly, but like a man.

"Then," said Winsome bravely, "go to Edinburgh. Fight your own battle, and mine," she added.

"Winsome," said Ralph, earnestly, for this serious and practical side of her character was an additional and unexpected revelation of perfection, "if you make as good a wife as you make a sweetheart, you will make one man happy."

"I mean to make a man happy," said Winsome, confidently.

The scenery again asserted its claim to attention. Observation enlarges the mind, and is therefore pleasant.

After a pause, Winsome said irrelevantly.

"And you really do not think me so foolish?"

"Foolish! I think you are the wisest and—"

"No, no." Winsome would not let him proceed. "You do not really think so. You know that I am wayward and changeable, and not at all what I ought to be. Granny always tells me so. It was very different when she was young, she says. Do you know," continued Winsome thoughtfully, "I used to be so frightened, when I knew that you could read in all these wise books of which I did not know a letter? But I must confess—I do not know what you will say, you may even be angry—I have a note-book of yours which I kept."

But if Winsome wanted a new sensation she was disappointed, for Ralph was by no means angry.

"So that's where it went?" said Ralph, smiling gladly.

"Yes," said Winsome, blushing not so much with guilt as with the consciousness of the locality of the note-book at that moment, which she was not yet prepared to tell him. But she consoled herself with the thought that she would tell him one day.

Strangely however, Ralph did not seem to care much about the book, so Winsome changed the subject to one of greater interest.

"And what else did you think about me that first day?—tell me," said Winsome, shamelessly.

It was Ralph's opportunity.

"Why, you know very well, Winsome dear, that ever since the day I first saw you I have thought that there never was any one like you—"

"Yes?" said Winsome, with a rising inflection in her voice.

"I ever thought you the best and the kindest—"

"Yes?" said Winsome, a little breathlessly.

"The most helpful and the wisest—"

"Yes?" said Winsome.

"And the most beautiful girl I have ever seen in my life!"

"Then I do not care for anything else!" cried Winsome, clapping her hands. She had been resolving to learn Hebrew five minutes before.

"Nor do I, really," said Ralph, speaking out the inmost soul that is in every young man.

As Ralph Peden sat looking at Winsome the thought came sometimes to him—but not often—"This is Allan Welsh's daughter, the daughter of the woman whom my father once loved, who lies so still under the green sod of Crossthwaite beneath the lea of Skiddaw."

> He looked at her eyes, deep blue like the depths of the Mediterranean Sea, and, like it, shot through with interior light.

"What are you thinking of?" asked Winsome, who had also meanwhile been looking at him.

"Of your eyes, dear!" said Ralph, telling half the truth—a good deal for a lover.

Winsome paused for further information, looking into the depths of his soul. Ralph felt as though his heart and judgment were being assaulted by storming parties. He looked into these wells of blue and saw the love quivering in them as the broken light quivers, deflected on its way through clear water to a sea bottom of golden sand.

"You want to hear me tell you something wiser," said Ralph, who did not know everything; "you are bored with my foolish talk."

And he would have spoken of the hopes of his future.

"No, no; tell me—tell me what you see in my eyes," said Winsome, a little impatiently.

"Well then, first," said truthful Ralph, who certainly did not flinch from the task, "I see the fairest thing God made for man to see. All the beauty of the world, losing its way, stumbled, and was drowned in the eyes of my love. They have robbed the sunshine, and stolen the morning dew. The sparkle of the light on the water, the gladness of a child when it laughs because it lives, the sunshine which makes the butterflies dance and the world so beautiful—all these I see in your eyes."

"This story is plainly impossible. This practical girl was not one to find pleasure in listening to flattery. Let us read no more in this book." This is what some wise people will say at this point. So, to their loss will they close the book. They have not achieved all knowledge. The wisest woman would rather hear of her eyes than of her mind. There are those who say the reverse, but then perhaps no one has ever had cause to tell them concerning what lies hid in their eyes.

Many had wished to tell Winsome these things, but to no one hitherto had been given the discoverer's soul, the poet's voice, the wizard's hand to bring the answering love out of the deep sea of divine possibilities in which the tides ran high and never a lighthouse told of danger.

"Tell me more," said Winsome, being a woman, as well as fair and young. These last are not necessary; to desire to be told about one's eyes, it is enough to be a woman.

Ralph looked down. In such cases it is necessary to refresh the imagination constantly with the facts. As in the latter days wise youths read messages from the quivering needle of the talking machine, so Ralph read his message flash by flash as it pulsated upward from a pure woman's soul.

"Once you would not tell me why your eyelashes were curled up at the ends," said this eager Columbus of a new continent, drawing the new world nearer his heart in order that his discoveries might be truer, surer, in detail more trustworthy. "I know now without telling. Would you like to know, Winsome?"

Winsome drew a happy breath, nestling a little closer—so little that no one but Ralph would have known. But the little shook him to the depths of his soul. This it is to be young and for the first time mastering the geography of an unknown and untraversed continent. The unversed might have thought that light breath a sigh, but no lover could have made the mistake. It is only in books, wordy and unreal, that lovers misunderstand each other in that way.

"I know," said Ralph, needing no word of permission to proceed, "it is with touching your cheek when you sleep."

"Then I must sleep a very long time!" said Winsome merrily, making light of his words.

"Underneath in the dark of either eye," continued Ralph, who, be it not forgotten, was a poet, "I see two young things like cherubs."

"I know," said Winsome; "I see myself in your eyes—you see yourself in mine."

She paused to note the effect of this tremendous discovery.

"Then," replied Ralph, "if it be indeed my own self I see in your eyes, it is myself as God made me at first without sin. I do not feel at all like a cherub now, but I must have been once, if I ever was like what I see in your eyes."

"Now go on; tell me what else you see," said Winsome.

"Your lips—" began Ralph, and paused.

"No, six is quite enough," said Winsome, after a little while, mysteriously. She had only two, and Ralph only two; yet she said with little grammar and no sense at all, "Six is enough."

But a voice from quite other lips came over the rising background of scrub and tangled thicket.

"Gang on coortin'," it said; "I'm no lookin', an' I canna see onything onyway."

It was Jock Gordon. He continued:

"Jock Scott's gane hame till his breakfast. He'll no bother ye this mornin', sae coort awa'."

CHAPTEE XXXV
SUCH SWEET SORROW

WINSOME and Ralph laughed, but Winsome sat up and put straight her sunbonnet. Sunbonnets are troublesome things. They will not stick on one's head. Manse Bell contradicts this. She says that her sunbonnet never comes off, or gets pushed back. As for other people's, lasses are not what they were in her young days.

"I must go home," said Winsome; "they will miss me."

"You know that it is 'good-bye,' then," said Ralph.

"What!" said Winsome, "shall I not see you to-morrow?" the bright light of gladness dying out of her eye. And the smile drained down out of her cheek like the last sand out of the sand-glass.

"No," said Ralph quietly, keeping his eyes full on hers, "I cannot go back to the manse after what was said. It is not likely that I shall ever be there again."

"Then when shall I see you?" said Winsome piteously. It is the cry of all loving womanhood, whose love goes out to the battle or into the city, to the business of war, or pleasure, or even of money- getting. "Then when shall I see you. again?" said Winsome, saying a new thing. There is nothing new under the sun, yet to lovers like Winsome and Ralph all things are new.

There was a catch in her throat. A salter dew gathered about her eyes, and the pupils expanded till the black seemed to shut out the blue.

Very tenderly Ralph looked down, and said, "Winsome, my dear, very soon I shall come again with more to ask and more to tell."

"But you are not going straight away to Edinburgh now? You must get a drive to Dumfries and take the Edinburgh coach."

"I cannot do that," said Ralph; "I must walk all the way; it is nothing."

Winsome looked at Ralph, the motherly instinct that is in all true love surging up even above the lover's instinct. It made her clasp and unclasp her hands in distress, to think of him going away alone over the waste moors, from the place where they had been so happy.

"And he will leave me behind!" she said, with a sudden fear of the loneliness which would surely come when the bright universe was emptied of Ralph.

"Had it only been to-morrow, I could have borne it better," she said. "Oh, it is too soon! How could he let us be so happy when he was going away from me?"

Winsome knew even better than Ralph that he must go, but the most accurate knowledge of necessity does not prevent the resentful feeling in a woman's heart when one she loves goes before his time.

But the latent motherhood in this girl rose up. If he were truly hers, he was hers to take care of. Therefore she asked the question which every mother asks, and no sweetheart who is nothing but a sweetheart has ever yet asked:

"Have you enough money?"

Ralph blushed and looked most unhappy, for the first time since the sun rose.

"I have none at all," he said; "my father only gave me the money for my journey to the Dullarg, and Mr. Welsh was to provide me what was necessary—" He stopped here, it seemed such a hard and shameful thing to say. "I have never had anything to do with money," he said, hanging down his head.

Now Winsome, who was exceedingly practical in this matter, went forward to him quickly and put an arm upon his shoulder.

"My poor boy!" she said, with the tenderest and sweetest expression on her face. And again Ralph Peden perceived that there are things more precious than much money.

"Now bend your head and let me whisper." It was already bent, but it was in his ear that Winsome wished to speak.

"No, no, indeed I cannot, Winsome, my love; I could not, indeed, and in truth I do not need it."

Winsome dropped her arms and stepped back tragically. She put one hand over the other upon her breast, and turned half way from him.

"Then you do not love me," she said, purely as a coercive measure.

"I do, I do—you know that I do; but I could not take it," said Ralph, piteously.

"Well, good-bye, then," said Winsome, without holding out her hand, and turning away.

"You do not mean it; Winsome, you cannot be cruel, after all. Come back and sit down. We shall talk about it, and you will see—"

Winsome paused and looked at him, standing so piteously. She says now that she really meant to go away, but she smiles when she says it, as if she did not quite believe the statement herself. But something—perhaps the look in his eyes, and the thought that, like herself, he had never known a mother—made her turn. Going back, she took his hand and laid it against her cheek.

"Ralph," she said, "listen to me; if I needed help and had none I should not be proud; I would not quarrel with you when you offered to help me. No, I would even ask you for it! BUT THEN I LOVE YOU." It was hardly fair. Winsome acknowledges as much herself; but then a woman has no weapons but her wit and her beauty—which is, seeing the use she can make of these two, on the whole rather fortunate than otherwise.

Ralph looked eager and a little frightened.

"Would you do that really?" he asked eagerly.

"Of course I should!" replied Winsome, a little indignantly.

Ralph took her in his arms, and in such a masterful way, that first she was frightened and then she was glad. It is good to feel weak in the arms of a strong man who loves you. God made it so when he made all things well.

"My lassie!" said Ralph for all comment.

Then fell a silence so prolonged that a shy squirrel in the boughs overhead resumed his researches upon the tassels and young shoots of the pine-tops, throwing down the debris in a contemptuous manner upon Winsome and Ralph, who stood below, listening to the beating of each other's hearts.

Finally Winsome, without moving, produced apparently from regions unknown a long green silk purse with three silver rings round the middle.

As she put it into Ralph's hand, something doubtful started again into his eyes, but Winsome looked so fierce in a moment, and so decidedly laid a finger on his lips, that perforce he was silent.

As soon as he had taken it, Winsome clapped her hands (as well as was at the time possible for her—it seemed, indeed, altogether impossible to an outsider, yet it was done), and said:

"You are not sorry, dear—you are glad?" with interrogatively arched eyebrows.

"Yes," said Ralph, "I am very glad." As indeed he might well be.

"You see," said the wise young woman, "it is this way: all that is my very own. *I* am your very own, so what is in the purse is your very own."

Logic is great—greatest when the logician is distractingly pretty; then, at least, it is sure to prevail—unless, indeed, the opponent be blind, or another woman. This is why they do not examine ladies orally in logic at the great colleges.

We have often tried to recover Ralph's reply, but the text is corrupt at this place, the context entirely lost. Experts suspect a palimpsest.

Perhaps we linger overly long on the records; but there is so much called love in the world, which is no love, that there may be some use in dwelling upon the histories of a love which was fresh and tender, sweet and true. It is at once instruction for the young, and for the older folk a cast back into the days that were. If to any it is a mockery or a scorning, so much the worse—for of them who sit in the scorner's chair the doom is written.

Winsome and Ralph walked on into the eye of the day, hand in hand, as was their wont. They crossed the dreary moor, which yet is not dreary when you came to look at it on such a morning as this.

The careless traveller glancing at it as he passed might call it dreary; but in the hollows, miniature lakes glistened, into which the tiny spurs of granite ran out flush with the water like miniature piers. The wind of the morning waking, rippled on the lakelets, and blew the bracken softly northward. The heather was dark rose purple, the "ling" dominating the miles of moor; for the lavender-grey flush of the true heather had not yet broken over the great spaces of the south uplands.

So their feet dragged slower as they drew near to that spot where they knew they must part. There was no thought of going back. There was even little of pain.

Perfect love had done its work. All frayed and secondhand loves may be made ashamed by the fearlessness of these two walking to their farewell trysting-place, lonely amid the world of heather. Only daft Jock Gordon above them, like a jealous scout, scoured the heights—sometimes on all-fours, sometimes bending double, with his long arms swinging like windmills, scaring even the sheep and the deer lest they should come too near. Overhead there was nothing nearer them than the blue lift, and even that had withdrawn itself infinitely far away, as though the angels themselves did not wish to spy on a later Eden. It was that midsummer glory of love-time, when grey Galloway covers up its flecked granite and becomes a true Purple Land.

If there be a fairer spot within the four seas than this fringe of birch-fringed promontory which juts into westernmost Loch Ken, I do not know it. Almost an island, it is set about with the tiniest beaches of white sand. From the rocks that look boldly up the loch the heather and the saxifrage reflect themselves in the still water. To reach it Winsome led Ralph among the scented gall-bushes and bog myrtle, where in the marshy meadows the lonely grass of Parnassus was growing. Pure white petals, veined green, with spikelets of green set in the angles within, five-lobed broidery of daintiest gold stitching, it shone with so clear a presage of hope that Ralph stooped to pick it that he might give it to Winsome.

She stopped him.

"Do not pull it," she said; "leave it for me to come and look at— when— when you are gone. It will soon wither if it is taken away; but give me some of the bog myrtle instead," she added, seeing that Ralph looked a little disappointed.

Ralph gathered some of the narrow, brittle, fragrant leaves. Winsome carefully kept half for herself, and as carefully inserted a spray in each pocket of his coat.

"There, that will keep you in mind of Galloway!" she said. And indeed the bog myrtle is the characteristic smell of the great world of hill and moss we call by that name. In far lands the mere thought of it has brought tears to the eyes unaccustomed, so close do the scents and sights of the old Free Province—the lordship of the Picts—wind themselves about the hearts of its sons.

"We transplant badly, we plants of the hills. You must come back to me," said Winsome, after a pause of wondering silence.

Loch Ken lay like a dream in the clear dispersed light of the morning, the sun shimmering upon it as through translucent ground glass. Teal and moor-hen squattered away from the shore as Winsome and Ralph climbed the brae, and stood looking northward over the superb levels of the loch. On the horizon Cairnsmuir showed golden tints through his steadfast blue.

Whaups swirled and wailed about the rugged side of Bennan above their heads. Across the loch there was a solitary farm so beautifully set that Ralph silently pointed it out to Winsome, who smiled and shook her head.

"The Shirmers has just been let on a nineteen years' lease," she said, "eighteen to run."

So practical was the answer, that Ralph laughed, and the strain of his sadness was broken. He did not mean to wait eighteen years for her, fathers or no fathers.

Then beyond, the whole land leaped skyward in great heathery sweeps, save only here and there, where about some hill farm the little emerald crofts and blue-green springing oatlands clustered closest. The loch spread far to the north, sleeping in the sunshine. Burnished like a mirror it was, with no breath upon it. In the south the Dee water came down from the hills peaty and brown. The roaring of its rapids could faintly be heard. To the east, across the loch, an island slept in the fairway, wooded to the water's edge.

It were a good place to look one's last on the earth, this wooded promontory, which might indeed have been that mountain, though a little one, from which was once seen all the kingdoms of the earth and the glory of them. For there are no finer glories on the earth than red heather and blue loch, except only love and youth.

So here love and youth had come to part, between the heather that glowed on the Bennan Hill and the sapphire pavement of Loch Ken.

For a long time Winsome and Ralph were silent—the empty interior sadness, mixed of great fear and great hunger, beginning to grip them as they stood. Lives only just twined and unified were again to twain. Love lately knit was to be torn asunder. Eyes were to look no more into the answering eloquence of other eyes.

"I must go," said Ralph, looking down into his betrothed's face.

"Stay only a little," said Winsome. "It is the last time."

So he stayed.

Strange, nervous constrictions played at "cat's cradle" about their hearts. Vague noises boomed and drummed in their ears, making their own words sound strange and empty, like voices heard in a dream.

"Winsome!" said Ralph.

"Ralph!" said Winsome.

"You will never for a moment forget me?" said Winsome Charteris.

"You will never for a moment forget me?" said Ralph Peden.

The mutual answer taken and given, after a long silence of soul and body in not-to-be-forgotten communion, they drew apart.

Ralph went a little way down the birch-fringed hill, but turned to look a last look. Winsome was standing where he had left her. Something in her attitude told of the tears steadily falling upon her summer dress. It was enough and too much.

Ralph ran back quickly.

"I cannot go away, Winsome. I cannot bear to leave you like this!"

Winsome looked at him and fought a good fight, like the brave girl she was. Then she smiled through her tears with the sudden radiance of the sun upon a showery May morning when the white hawthorn is coming out.

At this a sob, dangerously deep, rending and sudden, forced itself from Ralph's throat. Her smile was infinitely more heart-breaking than her tears. Ralph uttered a kind of low inarticulate roar at the sight—being his impotent protest against his love's pain. Yet such moments are the ineffaceable treasures of life, had he but known it. Many a man's deeds follow his vows simply because his lips have tasted the salt water of love's ocean upon the face of the beloved.

"Be brave, Winsome," said Ralph; "it shall not be for long."

Yet she was braver than he, had he but known it; for it is the heritage of the woman to be the stronger in the crises which inevitably wait upon love and love's achievement.

Winsome bent to kiss, with a touch like a benediction, not his lips now but his brow, as he stood beneath her on the hill slope.

"Go," she said; "go quickly, while I have the strength. I will be brave. Be thou brave also. God be with thee!"

So Ralph turned and fled while he could. He dared not trust himself to look till he was past the hill and some way across the moor. Then he turned and looked back over the acres of heather which he had put between himself and his love.

Winsome still stood on the hill-top, the sun shining on her face. In her hand was the lilac sunbonnet, making a splash of faint pure colour against the blonde whiteness of her dress. Ralph could just catch the golden shimmer of her hair. He knew but he could not see how it crisped and tendrilled about her brow, and how the light wind blew it into little cirrus wisps of sun-flossed gold. The thought that for long he should see it no more was even harder than parting. It is the hard things on this earth that are the easiest to do. The great renunciation is easy, but it is infinitely harder to give up the sweet, responsive delight of the eye, the thought, the caress. This also is human. God made it.

The lilac sunbonnet waved a little heartless wave which dropped in the middle as if a string were broken. But the shining hair blew out, as a waft of wind from the Bennan fretted a moving patch across the loch.

Ralph flung out his hand in one of the savage gestures men use when they turn bewildered and march away, leaving the best of their lives behind them.

So shutting his eyes Ralph plunged headlong into the green glades of the Kenside and looked no more. Winsome walked slowly and sedately back, not looking on the world any more, but only twining and pulling roughly the strings of her sunbonnet till one came off. Winsome threw it on the grass. What did it matter now? She would wear it no longer. There was none to cherish the lilac sunbonnet any more.

CHAPTER XXXVI
OVER THE HILLS AND FAR AWA'

Winsome came back to a quiet Craig Ronald. The men were in the field. The farmsteading was hushed, Meg not to be seen, the dogs silent, the bedroom blind undrawn when she entered to find the key in the door. She went within instantly and threw herself down upon the bed. Outside, the morning sun strengthened and beat on the shining white of the walls of Craig Ronald, and on Ralph far across the moors.

Winsome must wait. We shall follow Ralph. It is the way of the world at any rate. The woman always must wait and nothing said. With the man are the keen interests of the struggle, the grip of opposition, the clash of arms. With the woman, naught worth speaking of—only the silence, the loneliness, and waiting.

Ralph went northward wearing Winsome's parting kiss on his brow like an insignia of knighthood. It meant much to one who had never gone away before. So simple was he that he did not know that there are all-experiencing young men who love and sail away, clearing as they go the decks of their custom-staled souls for the next action.

He stumbled, this simple knight, blindly into the ruts and pebbly water courses down which the winter rains had rushed, tearing the turf clean from the granite during the November and February rains.

So he journeyed onward, heedless of his going.

To him came Jock Gordon, skipping like a wild goat down the Bennan side.

"Hey, mon, d'ye want to drive intil Loch Ken? Ye wad mak' braw ged-bait. Haud up the hill, breest to the brae."

Through his trouble Ralph heard and instinctively obeyed. In a little while he struck the beautiful road which runs north and south along the side of the long loch of Ken. Now there are fairer bowers in the south sunlands. There are Highlands and Alp-lands of sky-piercing beauty. But to Galloway, and specially to the central glens and flanking desolations thereof, one beauty belongs. She is like a plain girl with beautiful eyes.

There is no country like her in the world for colour—so delicately fresh in the rain- washed green of her pasture slopes, so keen the viridian [Footnote: Veronese green] of her turnip-fields when the dew is on the broad, fleshy, crushed leaves, so tender and deep the blue in the hollow places. It was small wonder that Ralph had set down in the note-book in which he sketched for future use all that passed under his eye:

> "Hast thou seen the glamour that follows
>   The falling of summer rain-
> The mystical blues in the hollows,
>   The purples and greys on the plain?"

It is true that all these things were but the idle garniture of a tale that had lost its meaning to Ralph this morning; but yet in time the sense that the beauty and hope of life lay about him stole soothingly upon his soul. He was glad to breathe the gracious breaths of spraying honeysuckle running its creamy riot of honey-drenched petals over the hedges, and flinging daring reconnaissances even to the tops of the dwarf birches by the wayside.

So quickly Nature eased his smart, that—for such is the nature of the best men, even of the very best—at the moment when Winsome threw herself, dazed and blinded with pain, upon her low white bed in the little darkened chamber over the hill at Craig Ronald, Ralph was once more, even though with the gnaw of emptiness and loss in his heart, looking forward to the future, and planning what the day would bring to him on which he should return.

Even as he thought he began to whistle, and his step went lighter, Jock Gordon moving silently along the heather by his side at a dog's trot. Let no man think hardly of Ralph, for this is the nature of the man. It was not that man loves the less, but that with him in his daring initiative and strenuous endeavour the future lies.

The sooner, then, that he could compass and overpass his difficulties the more swiftly would his face be again set to the south, and the aching emptiness of his soul be filled with a strange and thrilling expectancy. The wind whistled in his face as he rounded the Bennan and got his first glimpse of the Kells range, stretching far away over surge after surge of heather and bent, through which, here and there, the grey teeth of the granite shone. It is no blame to him that, as he passed on from horizon to horizon, each step which took him farther and farther from Craig Ronald seemed to bring him nearer and nearer to Winsome. He was going away, yet with each mile he regained the rebounding spirit of youth, while Winsome lay dazed in her room at Craig Ronald. But let it not be forgotten that he went in order that no more she might so lie with the dry mechanic sobs catching ever and anon in her throat. So the world is not so ill divided, after all. And, being a woman, perhaps Winsome's grief was as dear and natural to her as Ralph's elastic hopefulness.

Soon Ralph and Jock Gordon were striding across the moors towards Moniaive. Ralph wished to breakfast at one of the inns in New Galloway, but this Jock Gordon would not allow. He did not like that kind o' folk, he said.

"Gie's tippens, an' that'll serve brawly," said Jock.

Ralph drew out Winsome's purse; he looked at it reverently and put it back again. It seemed too early, and too material a use of her love-token.

"Nae sillar in't?" queried Jock. "How's that? It looks brave and baggy."

"I think I will do without for the present," said Ralph.

"Aweel," said Jock, "ye may, but I'm gaun to hae my breakfast a' the same, sillar or no sillar."

In twenty minutes he was back by the dykeside, where he had left Ralph sitting, twining Winsome's purse through his fingers, and thinking on the future, and all that was awaiting him in Edinburgh town.

Jock seemed what he had called Winsome's purse—baggy.

Then he undid himself. From under the lower buttons of his long russet "sleeved waistcoat" with the long side flaps which, along with his sailor-man's trousers, he wore for all garment, he drew a barn-door fowl, trussed and cooked, and threw it on the ground. Now came a dozen farles of cake, crisp and toothsome, from the girdle, and three large scones raised with yeast.

Then followed, out of some receptacle not too strictly to be localized, half a pound of butter, wrapped in a cabbage-leaf, and a quart jug of pewter.

Ralph looked on in amazement.

"Where did you get all these?" he asked.

"Get them? Took them!" said Jock succinctly. "I gaed alang to Mistress MacMorrine's, an' says I, 'Guid-mornin' till ye, mistress, an' hoo's a' wi' ye the day?' for I'm a ceevil chiel when folks are ceevil to me."

"'Nane the better for seein' you, Jock Gordon,' says she, for she's an unceevil wife, wi' nae mair mainners nor gin she had just come ower frae Donnachadee—the ill-mainnered randy.

"'But,' says I, 'maybe ye wad be the better o' kennin' that the kye's eatin' your washin' up on the loan. I saw Provost Weir's muckle Ayreshire halfway through wi' yer best quilt,' says I.

"She flung up her hands.

"'Save us!' she cries; 'could ye no hae said that at first?'

"An' wi' that she ran as if Auld Hornie was at her tail, screevin' ower the kintra as though she didna gar the beam kick at twa hunderweicht guid."

"But was that true, Jock Gordon?" asked Ralph, astounded.

"True!—what for wad it be true? Her washin' is lyin' bleachin', fine an' siccar, but she get a look at it and a braw sweet. A race is guid exercise for ony yin that its as muckle as Luckie MacMorrine."

"But the provisions—and the hen?" asked Ralph, fearing the worst.

"They were on her back-kitchen table. There they are now," said Jock, pointing with his foot, as though that was all there was to say about the matter.

"But did you pay for them?" he asked.

"Pay for them! Does a dowg pay for a sheep's heid when he gangs oot o' the butcher's shop wi' yin atween his teeth, an' a twa-pund wecht playin' dirl on his hench-bane? Pay for't! Weel, I wat no! Didna yer honour tell me that ye had nae sillar, an' sae gaed it in hand to Jock?"

Ralph started up. This might be a very serious matter. He pulled out Winsome's purse again. In the end he tried first there was silver, and in the other five golden guineas in a little silken inner case. One of the guineas Ralph took out, and, handing it to Jock, he bade him gather up all that he had stolen and take his way back with them. Then he was to buy them from Luckie MacMorrine at her own price.

"Sic a noise aboot a bit trifle!" said Jock. "What's aboot a bit chuckle an' a heftin' o' cake? Haivers!"

But very quickly Ralph prevailed upon him, and Jock took the guinea. At his usual swift wolf's lope he was out of sight over the long stretches of heather and turf so speedily that he arrived at the drying-ground on the hillside before Luckie MacMorrine, handicapped by her twenty stone avoirdupois, had perspired thither.

Jock met her at the gate.

"Noo, mistress," exclaimed Jock, busily smoothing out the wrinkles and creases of a fine linen sheet, with "E. M. M." on the corner, "d'ye see this?

I juist gat here in time, and nae mair. Ye see, thae randies o' kye, wi' their birses up, they wad sune hae seen the last o' yer bonny sheets an' blankets, gin I had letten them."

Mistress MacMorrine did not waste a look on the herd of cows, but proceeded to go over her washing with great care. Jock had just arrived in time to make hay of it, before the owner came puffing up the road. Had she looked at the cows curiously it might have struck her that they were marvellously calm for such ferocious animals. This seemed to strike Jock, for he went after them, throwing stones at them in the manner known as "henchin'" [jerking from the side], much practised in Galloway, and at which Jock was a remarkable adept. Soon he had them excited enough for anything, and pursued them with many loud outcryings till they were scattered far over the moor.

When he came back he said: "Mistress MacMorrine, I ken brawly that ye'll be wushin' to mak' me some sma' recompense for my trouble an' haste. Weel, I'll juist open my errand to ye. Ye see the way o't was this: There is twa gentlemen shooters on the moors, the Laird o' Balbletherum an' the Laird o' Glower-ower-'em-twa respectit an' graund gentlemen. They war wantin' some luncheon, but they were that busy shootin' that they hadna time to come, so they says to me, 'Jock Gordon, do ye ken an honest woman in this neighbourhood that can supply something to eat at a reasonable chairge?' 'Yes,' says I, 'Mistress MacMorrine is sic a woman, an' nae ither.' 'Do ye think she could pit us up for ten days or a fortnight?' says they. 'I doot na', for she's weel plenisht an' providit,' I says. 'Noo, I didna ken but ye micht be a lang time detained wi' the kye (as indeed ye wad hae been, gin I hadna come to help ye), an' as the lairds couldna be keepit, I juist took up the bit luncheon that I saw on your kitchie table, an' here it is, on its way to the wames o' the gentlemen—whilk is an honour till't.'"

Mistress MacMorrine did not seem to be very well pleased at the unceremonious way in which Jock had dealt with the contents of her larder, but the inducement was too great to be gainsaid.

"Ye'll mak' it reasonable, nae doot," said Jock, "sae as to gie the gentlemen a good impression. There's a' thing in a first impression."

"Tak' it till them an' welcome—wi' the compliments o' Mrs. MacMorrine o' the Blue Bell, mind an' say till them. Ye may consider it a recognition o' yer ain trouble in the matter o' the kye; but I will let the provost hear o't on the deafest side o' his heid when he ca's for his toddy the nicht."

"Thank ye, mistress," said Jock, quickly withdrawing with his purchases; "there's nocht like obleegements for makin' freends."

At last Ralph saw Jock coming at full speed over the moor.

He went forward to him anxiously.

"Is it all right?" he asked.

"It's a' richt, an' a' paid for, an' mair, gin ye like to send Jock for't; an' I wasna to forget Mistress MacMorrine's compliments to ye intil the bargain."

Ralph looked mystified.

"Ye wadna see the Laird o' Balbletherum? Did ye?" said Jock, cocking his impudent, elvish head to the side.

"Who is he?" asked Ralph.

"Nor yet the Laird o' Glower—ower—'em?"

"I have seen nobody from the time you went away," said Ralph.

"Then we'll e'en fa' to. For gin thae twa braw gentlemen arena here to partake o' the guid things o' this life, then there's the mair for you an' Jock Gordon."

Jock never fully satisfied Ralph's curiosity as to the manner in which he obtained this provender. Luckie Morrine bestowed it upon him for services rendered, he said; which was a true, though somewhat abbreviated and imperfect account of the transaction.

What the feelings of the hostess of the Blue Bell were when night passed without the appearance of the two lairds, for whom she had spread her finest sheets, and looked out her best bottles of wine, we have no means of knowing. Singularly enough, for some considerable time thereafter Jock patronized the "Cross Keys" when he happened to be passing that way. He "preferred it to the Blue Bell," he said.

—

CHAPTER XXXVII
UNDER THE BED HEATHER

So refreshed, Ralph and Jock passed on their way. All the forenoon they plodded steadily forward. From Moniaive they followed the windings of a flashing burn, daching and roaring in a shallow linn, here and there white with foam and fretting, and again dimpling black in some deep and quiet pool. Through the ducal village of Thornhill and so northward along the Nithside towards the valley of the Menick they went. The great overlapping purple folds of the hills drew down about these two as they passed. Jock Gordon continually scoured away to either side like a dog fresh off the leash. Ralph kept steadily before him the hope in his heart that before long the deep cleft would be filled up and that for always.

It so happened that it was night when they reached the high summit of the Leadhills and the village of Wanlockhead gleamed grey beneath them. Ralph proposed to go down and get lodgings there; but Jock had other intentions.

"What for," he argued, "what for should ye pay for the breadth of yer back to lie doon on? Jock Gordon wull mak' ye juist as comfortable ablow a heather buss as ever ye war in a bed in the manse. Bide a wee!"

Jock took him into a sheltered little "hope," where they were shut in from the world of sheep and pit-heads.

With his long, broad-bladed sheath-knife Jock was not long in piling under the sheltered underside of a great rock over which the heather grew, such a heap of heather twigs as Ralph could hardly believe had been cut in so short a time. These he compacted into an excellent mattress, springy and level, with pliable interlacings of broom.

"Lie ye doon there, an' I'll mak' ye a bonnie plaidie," said Jock.

There was a little "cole" or haystack of the smallest sort close at hand. To this Jock went, and, throwing off the top layer as possibly damp, he carried all the rest in his arms and piled it on Ralph till he was covered up to his neck.

"We'll mak' a' snod [neat] again i' the mornin'!" he said. "Noo, we'll theek [thatch] ye, an' feed ye!" said Jock comprehensively. So saying, he put other layers of heather, thinner than the mattress underneath, but arranged in the same way, on the top of the hay.

"Noo ye're braw an' snug, are ye na'? What better wad ye hae been in a three-shillin' bed?"

Then Jock made a fire of broken last year's heather. This he carefully watched to keep it from spreading, and on it he roasted half a dozen plover's eggs which he had picked up during the day in his hillside ranging. On these high moors the moor-fowls go on laying till August. These being served on warmed and buttered scones, and sharpened with a whiff of mordant heather smoke, were most delicious to Ralph, who smiled to himself, well pleased under his warm covering of hay and overthatching of heather.

After each egg was supplied to him piping hot, Jock would say:

"An' isna that as guid as a half-croon supper?"

Then another pee-wit's egg, delicious and fresh—

"Luckie Morrine couldna beat that," said Jock.

There was a surprising lightness in the evening air, the elastic life of the wide moorland world settling down to rest for a couple of hours, which is all the night there is on these hill-tops in the crown of the year.

Jock Gordon covered himself by no means so elaborately as he had provided for Ralph, saying: "I hae covered you for winter, for ye're but a laddie; the like o' me disna need coverin' when the days follow yin anither like sheep jumpin' through a slap."

Ralph was still asleep when the morning came. But when the young sun looked over the level moors—for they were on the very top of the heathery creation—Jock Gordon made a little hillock of dewy heather to shelter Ralph from the sun. He measured at the same time a hand's breadth in the sky, saying to himself, "I'll wakken the lad when he gets to there!" He was speaking of the sun.

But before the flood of light overtopped the tiny break-water and shot again upon Ralph's face, he sat up bewildered and astonished, casting a look about him upon the moorland and its crying birds.

Jock Gordon was just coming towards him, having scoured the face of the ridge for more plover's eggs.

"Dinna rise," said Jock, "till I tak' awa' the beddin'. Ye see," continued the expert in camping out on hills, "the hay an' the heather gets doon yer neck an' mak's ye yeuk [itch] an' fidge a' day. An' at first ye mind that, though after a while gin ye dinna yeuk, ye find it michty oninterestin'!"

Ralph sat up. Something in Jock's bare heel as he sat on the grass attracted his attention.

"Wi', Jock," he said, infinitely astonished, "what's that in yer heel?"

"Ou!" said Jock, "it's nocht but a nail!"

"A nail!" said Ralph; "what are ye doin' wi' a nail in yer foot?"

"I gat it in last Martinmas," he said.

"But why do you not get it out? Does it not hurt?" said Ralph, compassionating.

"'Deed did it awhile at the first," said Jock, "but I got used to it. Ye can use wi' a'thing. Man's a wunnerful craitur!"

"Let me try to pull it out," said Ralph, shivering to think of the pain he must have suffered.

"Na, na, ye ken what ye hae, but ye dinna ken what ye micht get. I ken what I hae to pit up wi', wi' a nail in my fit; but wha kens what it micht be gin I had a muckle hole ye could pit yer finger in? It wadna be bonny to hae the clocks howkin' [beetles digging] and the birdies biggin' their nests i' my heel! Na, na, it's a guid lesson to be content wi' yer doon-settin', or ye may get waur!"

It was in the bright morning light that these two took the Edinburgh road, which clambered down over the hillsides by the village of Leadhills into the valley of the Clyde. Through Abingdon and Biggar they made their way, and so admirable were Jock's requisitioning abilities that Winsome's green purse was never once called into action.

When they looked from the last downward step of the Mid-Lothian table-land upon the city of Edinburgh, there was a brisk starting of smoke from many chimneys, for the wives of the burgesses were kindling their supper fires, and their husbands were beginning to come in with the expectant look of mankind about meal-time.

"Come wi' me, Jock, and I'll show ye Edinburgh, as ye have showed me the hills of heather!" This was Ralph's invitation.

"Na," said Jock, "an' thank ye kindly a' the same. There's muckle loons there that micht snap up a guid-lookin' lad like Jock, an' ship him ontill their nesty ships afore he could cry 'Mulquarchar and Craignell!' Jock Gordon may be a fule, but he kens when he's weel aff. Nae Auld Reekies for him, an' thank ye kindly. When he wants to gang to the gaol he'll steal a horse an' gang daicent! He'll no gang wi' his thoom in his mooth, an' when they say till him, 'What are ye here for?' be obleeged to answer, 'Fegs, an' I dinna ken what for!' Na, na, it wadna be mensefu' like ava'. A' the Gordons that ever was hae gaen to the gaol—but only yince. It's aye been a hangin' maitter, an' Jock's no the man to turn again the rule an' custom o' his forebears. 'Yince gang, yince hang,' is Jock's motto."

Ralph did not press the point. But he had some unexpected feeling in saying good-bye to Jock. It was not so easy. He tried to put three of Winsome's guineas into his hand, but Jock would have none of them.

"ME wi' gowden guineas!" he said. "Surely ye maun hae an ill-wull at puir Jock, that wusses ye weel; what wad ony body say gin I poo'ed out sic a lump of gowd? 'There's that loon Jock been breakin' somebody's bank,' an' then 'Fare-ye-weel, Kilaivie,' to Jock's guid name. It's gane, like his last gless o' whusky, never to return."

"But you are a long way from home, Jock; how will you get back?"

"Hoots, haivers, Maister Ralph, gin Jock has providit for you that needs a' things as gin ye war in a graund hoose, dinna be feared for Jock, that can eat a wamefu' o' green heather-taps wi' the dew on them like a bit flafferin' grouse bird. Or Jock can catch the muir-fowl itsel' an' eat it ablow a heather buss as gin he war a tod [fox]. Hoot awa' wi' ye! Jock can fend for himsel' brawly. Sillar wad only tak' the edge aff his genius."

"Then is there nothing that I can bring you from Edinburgh when I come again?" said Ralph, with whom the coming again was ever present.

"'Deed, aye, gin ye are so ceevil—it's richt prood I wad be o' a boxfu' o' Maister Cotton's Dutch sneeshin'—him that's i' the High Street—they say it's terrible graund stuff. Wullie Hulliby gat some when he was up wi' his lambs, an' he said that, after the first snifter, he grat for days. It maun be graund!"

Ralph promised, with gladness to find some way of easing his load of debt to Jock.

"Noo, Maister Ralph, it's a wanchancy [uncertain] place, this Enbra', an' I'll stap aff an' on till the morrow's e'en here or hereaboots, for sae it micht be that ye took a notion to gang back amang kent fowk, whaur ye wad be safe an' soun'."

"But, Jock," urged Ralph, "ye need not do that. I was born and brought up in Edinburgh!"

"That's as may be; gin I bena mista'en, there's a byous [extraordinary] heap o' things has happened since then. Gang yer ways, but gin ye hae message or word for Jock, juist come cannily oot, an' he'll be here till dark the morn."

CHAPTER XXXVIII
BEFORE THE REFORMER'S CHAIR

"The Lord save us, Maister Ralph, what's this?" said John Bairdieson, opening the door of the stair in James's Court. It was a narrow hall that it gave access to, more like a passage than a hall. "Hoo hae ye come? An' what for didna Maister Welsh or you write to say ye war comin'? An' whaur's a' the buiks an' the gear?" continued John Bairdieson.

"I have walked all the way, John," said Ralph. "I quarrelled with the minister, and he turned me to the door."

"Dear sirce!" said John anxiously, "was't ill-doing or unsound doctrine?"

"Mr. Welsh said that he could not company with unbelievers."

"Then it's doctrine—wae's me, wae's me! I wuss it had been the lasses. What wull his faither say? Gin it had been ill-doin', he micht hae pitten it doon to the sins o' yer youth; but ill- doctrine he canna forgie. O Maister Ralph, gin ye canna tell a lee yersel', wull ye no haud yer tongue—I can lee, for I'm but an elder—an' I'll tell him that at a kirn [harvest festival] ye war persuaded to drink the health o' the laird, an' you no bein' acquant wi' the strength o' Glenlivat—"

"John, John, indeed I cannot allow it. Besides, you're a sailor- man, an' even in Galloway they do not have kirns till the corn's ripe," replied Ralph with a smile.

"Aweel, can ye no say, or let me say for ye, gin ye be particular, that ye war a wee late oot at nicht seein' a bit lassie—or ocht but the doctrine? It wasna anything concernin' the fundamentals o' the Marrow, Maister Ralph, though, surely," continued John Bairdieson, whose elect position did not prevent him from doing his best for the interests of his masters, young and old. Indeed, to start with the acknowledged fact of personal election sometimes gives a man like John Bairdieson an unmistakable advantage. Ralph went to his own room, leaving John Bairdieson listening, as he prayed to be allowed to do, at the door of his father's room.

In a minute or two John Bairdieson came up, with a scared face.

"Ye're to gang doon, Maister Ralph, an' see yer faither. But, O sir, see that ye speak lown [calm] to him. He hasna gotten sleep for twa nichts, an' he's fair pitten by himsel' wi' thae ill-set Conformists—weary fa' them! that he's been in the gall o' bitterness wi'."

Ralph went down to his father's study. Knocking softly, he entered. His father sat in his desk chair, closed in on every side. It had once been the pulpit of a great Reformer, and each time that Gilbert Peden shut himself into it, he felt that he was without father or mother save and except the only true and proper Covenant-keeping doctrine in broad Scotland, and the honour and well-being of the sorely dwindled Kirk of the Marrow.

Gilbert Peden was a noble make of a man, larger in body though hardly taller than his son. He wore a dark-blue cloth coat with wide flaps, and the immense white neckerchief on which John Bairdieson weekly expended all his sailor laundry craft. His face was like his son's, as clear-cut and statuesque, though larger and broader in frame and mould. There was, however, a coldness about the eye and a downward compression of the lips, which speaks the man of narrow though fervid enthusiasms.

Ralph went forward to his father. As he came, his father stayed him with the palm of his hand, the finger-tips turned upward.

"Abide, my son, till I know for what cause you have left or been expelled from the house of the man to whom I committed you during your trials for license. Answer me, why have you come away from the house of Allan Welsh like a thief in the night?"

"Father," said Ralph, "I cannot tell you everything at present, because the story is not mine to tell. Can you not trust me?"

"I could trust you with my life and all that I possess," said his father; "they are yours, and welcome; but this is a matter that affects your standing as a probationer on trials in the kirk of the Marrow, which is of divine institution. The cause is not mine, my son. Tell me that the cause of your quarrel had nothing to do with the Marrow kirk and your future standing in it, and I will ask you no more till you choose to tell me of your own will concerning the matter."

The Marrow minister looked at his son with a gleam of tenderness forcing its way through the sternness of his words.

But Ralph was silent.

"It was indeed in my duty to the Marrow kirk that Mr. Welsh considered that I lacked. It was for this cause that he refused to company further with me."

Then there came a hardness as of grey hill stone upon the minister's face. It was not a pleasant thing to see in a father's face.

"Then," he said slowly, "Ralph Peden, this also is a manse of the Marrow kirk, and, though ye are my own son, I cannot receive ye here till your innocence is proven in the presbytery. Ye must stand yer trials."

Ralph bowed his head. He had not been unprepared for something like this, but the pain he might have felt at another time was made easier by a subtle anodyne. He hardly seemed to feel the smart as a week before he might have done. In some strange way Winsome was helping him to bear it—or her prayers for him were being answered.

John Bairdieson broke into the study, his grey hair standing on end, and the shape of the keyhole cover imprinted on his brow above his left eye. John could see best with his left eye, and hear best with his right ear, which he had some reason to look upon as a special equalization of the gifts of Providence, though not well adapted for being of the greatest service at keyholes.

"Save us, minister!" he burst out; "the laddie's but a laddie, an' na doot his pranks hae upset guid Maister Welsh a wee. Lads will be lads, ye ken. But Maister Ralph's soond on the fundamentals—I learned him the Shorter Questions mysel', sae I should ken—forbye the hunner an' nineteenth Psalm that he learned on my knee, and how to mak' a Fifer's knot, an' the double reef, an' a heap o' usefu' knowledge forbye; an' noo to tak' it into your heid that yer ain son's no soond in the faith, a' because he has fa'en oot wi' a donnert auld carle—"

"John," said the minister sternly, "leave the room! You have no right to speak thus of an honoured servant of the kirk of the Marrow."

Ralph could see through the window the light fading off the Fife Lomonds, and the long line of the shore darkening under the night into a more ethereal blue.

There came to him in this glimpse of woods and dewy pastures overseas a remembrance of a dearer shore. The steading over the Grannoch Loch stood up clear before him, the blue smoke going straight up, Winsome's lattice standing open with the roses peeping in, and the night airs breathing lovingly through them, airing it out as a bed-chamber for the beloved.

The thought made his heart tender. To his father he said:

"Father, will you not take my word that there is nothing wicked or disgraceful in what I have done? If it were my own secret, I would gladly tell you at once; but as it is, I must wait until in his own time Mr. Welsh communicates with you."

The minister, sitting in the Reformer's seat, pulling at his stern upper lip, winced; and perhaps had it not been for the pulpit the human in him might have triumphed. But he only said:

"I am quite prepared to support you until such time as at a meeting of the presbytery the matter be tried, but I cannot have in a Marrow Manse one living under the fama of expulsion from the house of a brother minister in good standing."

"Thank you, father," said his son, "for your kind offer, but I do not think I shall need to trouble you."

And so with these words the young man turned and went out proudly from the father's sight, as he had gone from the manse of the other minister of the Marrow kirk.

As he came to the outside of the door, leaving his father sitting stately and stern in the Reformer's pulpit, he said, in the deeps of his heart:

"God do so to me, and more also, if I ever seek again to enter the Marrow kirk, if so be that, like my father, I must forget my humanity in order worthily to serve it!"

After he had gone out, the Reverend Gilbert Peden took his Bible and read the parable of the prodigal son. He closed the great book, which ever lay open before him, and said, as one who both accuses and excuses himself:

"But the prodigal son was not under trials for license in the kirk of the Marrow!"

At the door, John Bairdieson, his hair more than ever on end, met Ralph. He held up his hands.

"It's an awfu'—like thing to be obleegit to tell the hale truth! O man, couldna ye hae tell't a wee bit lee? It wad hae saved an awfu' deal o' fash! But it's ower late now; ye can juist bide i' the spare room up the stair, an' come an' gang by door on the Castle Bank, an' no yin forbye mysel' 'ill be a hair the wiser. I, John Bairdieson, 'll juist fetch up yer meals the same as ordinar'. Ye'll be like a laddie at the mastheid up there; it'll be braw an' quate for the studyin'!"

"John, I am much obliged to you for your kind thought," said Ralph, "but I cannot remain in his house against my father's expressed wish, and without his knowledge."

"Hear till him! Whaur else should he bide but in the hoose that he was born in, an' his faither afore him? That would be a bonny like story. Na, na, ye'll juist bide, Maister Ralph, an'—"

"I must go this very night," said Ralph. "You mean well, John, but it cannot be. I am going down to see my uncle, Professor Thriepneuk."

"Leave yer faither's hoose to gang to that o' a weezened auld—"

"John!" said Ralph, warningly.

"He's nae uncle o' yours, onygate, though he married your mother's sister. An' a sair life o't she had wi' him, though I doot na but thae dochters o' his sort him to richts noo."

So, in spite of John Bairdieson's utmost endeavours, and waiting only to put his clothes together, Ralph took his way over to the Sciennes, where his uncle, the professor, lived in a new house with his three daughters, Jemima, Kezia, and Keren-happuch. The professor had always been very kind to Ralph. He was not a Marrow man, and therefore, according to the faith of his father, an outcast from the commonwealth. But he was a man of the world of affairs, keen for the welfare of his class at the University College—a man crabbed and gnarled on the surface, but within him a strong vein of tenderness of the sort that always seems ashamed of catching its possessor in a kind action.

To him Ralph knew that he could tell the whole story. The Sciennes was on the very edge of the green fields. The corn-fields stretched away from the dyke of the Professor's garden to the south towards the red-roofed village of Echo Bank and the long ridge of Liberton, crowned by the square tower on which a stone dining-room table had been turned up, its four futile legs waving in the air like a beetle overset on its back.

CHAPTER XXXIX
JEMIMA, KEZIA, AND LITTLE KEREN-HAPPUCH

Ralph found the professor out. He was, indeed, engaged in an acrimonious discussion on the Wernerian theory, and at that moment he was developing a remarkable scientific passion, which threatened to sweep his adversaries from the face of the earth in the debris of their heresies.

Within doors, however, Ralph found a very warm welcome from his three cousins—Jemima, Kezia, and Keren-happuch. Jemima was tall and angular, with her hair accurately parted in the middle, and drawn in a great sweep over her ears—a fashion intended by Nature for Keren-happuch, who was round of face, and with a complexion in which there appeared that mealy pink upon the cheeks which is peculiar to the metropolis. Kezia was counted the beauty of the family, and was much looked up to by her elder and younger sisters.

These three girls had always made much of Ralph, ever since he used to play about the many garrets and rooms of their old mansion beneath the castle, before they moved out to the new house at the Sciennes. They had long been in love with him, each in her own way; though they had always left the first place to Kezia, and wove romances in their own heads with Ralph for the central figure. Jemima, especially, had been very jealous of her sisters, who were considerably younger, and had often spoken seriously to them about flirting with Ralph. It was Jemima who came to the door; for, in those days, all except the very grandest persons thought no more of opening the outer than the inner doors of their houses.

"Ralph Peden, have you actually remembered that there is such a house as the Sciennes?" said Jemima, holding up her face to receive the cousinly kiss.

Ralph bestowed it chastely. Whereupon followed Kezia and little Keren-happuch, who received slightly varied duplicates.

Then the three looked at one another. They knew that this Ralph had eaten of the tree of knowledge.

"That is not the way you kissed us before you went away," said outspoken Kezia, who had experience in the matter wider than that of the others, looking him straight in the eyes as became a beauty.

For once Ralph was thoroughly taken aback, and blushed richly and long.

Kezia laughed as one who enjoyed his discomfiture.

"I knew it would come," she said. "Is she a milkmaid? She's not the minister's daughter, for he is a bachelor, you said!"

Jemima and Keren-happuch actually looked a little relieved, though a good deal excited. They had been standing in the hall while this conversation was running its course.

"It's all nonsense, Kezia; I am astonished at you!" said Jemima.

"Come into the sitting-parlour," said Kezia, taking Ralph's hand; "we'll not one of us bear any malice if only you tell us all about it."

Jemima, after severe consideration, at last looked in a curious sidelong way to Ralph.

"I hope," she said, "that you have not done anything hasty."

"Tuts!" said Kezia, "I hope he has. He was far too slow before he went away. Make love in haste; marry at leisure—that's the right way."

"Can I have the essay that you read us last April, on the origin of woman?" asked Keren-happuch unexpectedly. "You won't want it any more, and I should like it."

Even little Keren-happuch had her feelings.

The three Misses Thriepneuks were a little jealous of one another before, but already they had forgotten this slight feeling, which indeed was no more than the instinct of proprietorship which young women come to feel in one who has never been long out of their house, and with whom they have been brought up.

But in the face of this new interest they lost their jealousy of one another; so that, in place of presenting a united front to the enemy, these three kindly young women, excited at the mere hint of a love-story, vied with one another which should be foremost in interest and sympathy. The blush on Ralph's face spoke its own message, and now, when he was going to speak, his three cousins sat round with eager faces to listen.

"I have something to tell, girls," said Ralph, "but I meant to tell it first to my uncle. I have been turned out of the manse of Dullarg, and my father will not allow me to live in his house till after the meeting of the presbytery."

This was more serious than a love-story, and the bright expression died down into flickering uncertainty in the faces of Jemima, Kezia, and Keren-happuch.

"It's not anything wrong?" asked Jemima, anxiously.

"No, no," said Ralph quickly, "nothing but what I have reason to be proud enough of. It is only a question of the doctrines and practice of the Marrow kirk—"

"Oh!" said all three simultaneously, with an accent of mixed scorn and relief. The whole matter was clear to them now.

"And of the right of the synod of the Marrow kirk to control my actions," continued Ralph.

But the further interest was entirely gone from the question.

"Tell us about HER," they said in unison.

"How do you know it is a 'her'?" asked Ralph, clumsily trying to put off time, like a man.

Kezia laughed on her own account, Keren-happuch, because Kezia laughed, but Jemima said solemnly:

"I hope she is of a serious disposition."

"Nonsense! *I* hope she is pretty," said Kezia.

"And *I* hope she will love me," said little Keren-happuch.

Ralph thought a little, and then, as it was growing dark, he sat on the old sofa with his back to the fading day, and told his love-story to these three sweet girls, who, though they had played with him and been all womanhood to him ever since he came out of petticoats, had not a grain of jealousy of the unseen sister who had come suddenly past them and stepped into the primacy of Ralph's life.

When he was half-way through with his tale he suddenly stopped, and said:

"But I ought to have told all this first to your father, because he may not care to have me in his house. There is only my word for it, after all, and it is the fact that I have not the right to set foot in my own father's house."

"We will make our father see it in the right way," said Jemima quietly.

"Yes," interposed Kezia, "or I would not give sixpence for his peace of mind these next six months."

"It is all right if you tell us," said little Keren-happuch, who was her father's playmate. Jemima ruled him, Kezia teased him—the privilege of beauty—but it was generally little Keren-happuch who fetched his slippers and sat with her cheek against the back of his hand as he smoked and read in his great wicker chair by the north window.

There was the sound of quick nervous footsteps with an odd halt in their fall on the gravel walk outside. The three girls ran to the door in a tumultuous greeting, even Jemima losing her staidness for the occasion. Ralph could hear only the confused babble of tongues and the expressions, "Now you hear, father—" "Now you understand—" "Listen to me, father—" as one after another took up the tale.

Ralph retold the story that night from the very beginning to the professor, who listened silently, punctuating his thoughts with the puffs of his pipe.

When he had finished, there was an unwonted moisture in the eyes of Professor Thriepneuk—perhaps the memory of a time when he too had gone a-courting.

He stretched the hand which was not occupied with his long pipe to Ralph, who grasped it strongly.

"You have acted altogether as I could have desired my own son to act; I only wish that I had one like you. Let the Marrow Kirk alone, and come and be my assistant till you see your way a little into the writer's trade. Pens and ink are cheap, and you can take my classes in the summer, and give me quietness to write my book on 'The Abuses of Ut with the Subjunctive.'"

"But I must find lodgings—" interrupted Ralph.

"You must find nothing—just bide here. It is the house of your nearest kin, and the fittest place for you. Your meat's neither here nor there, and my lasses—"

"They are the best and kindest in the world," said Ralph.

The professor glanced at him with a sharp, quizzical look under his eyebrows. He seemed as if he were about to say something, and then thought better of it and did not. Perhaps he also had had his illusions.

As Ralph was going to his room that night Kezia met him at the head of the stairs. She came like a flash from nowhere in particular.

"Good-night, Ralph," she said; "give your Winsome a kiss from me—the new kind—like this!"

Then Kezia vanished, and Ralph was left wondering, with his candle in his hand.

CHAPTER XL
A TRIANGULAR CONVERSATION

It was the day of the fast before the Communion in the Dullarg. The services of the day were over, and Allan Welsh, the minister of the Marrow kirk, was resting in his study from his labours. Manse Bell came up and knocked, inclining her ear as she did so to catch the minister's low-toned reply.

"Mistress Winifred Charteris frae the Craig Ronald to see ye, sir."

Allan Welsh commanded his emotion without difficulty—what of it he felt—as indeed he had done for many years.

He rose, however, with his hand on the table as though for support, as Winsome came in. He received her in silence, bending over her hand with a certain grave reverence.

Winsome sat down. She was a little paler but even lovelier in the minister's eyes than when he had seen her before. The faint violet shadows under her lower lids were deeper, and gave a new depth to her sapphire eyes whose irises were so large that the changeful purple lights in them came and went like summer lightnings.

It was Winsome who first spoke, looking at him with a strange pity and a stirring of her soul that she could not account for. She had come unwillingly on her errand, disliking him as the cause of her lover's absence—one of the last things a woman learns to forgive. But, as she looked on Allan Welsh, so bowed and broken, his eyes fallen in, looking wistfully out of the pain of his life, her heart went out to him, even as she thought that of a truth he was Ralph Peden's enemy.

"My grandfather," she said, and her voice was low, equable, and serious, "sent me with a packet to you that he instructed me only to give into your own hands."

Winsome went over to the minister and gave him a sealed parcel. Allan Welsh took it in his hand and seemed to weigh it.

"I thank you," he said, commanding his voice with some difficulty. "And I ask you to thank Walter Skirving for his remembrance of me. It is many years since we were driven apart, but I have not forgotten the kindness of the long ago!"

He opened the parcel. It was sealed with Walter Skirving's great seal ring which he wore on his watch-chain, lying on the table before him as he kept his never-ending vigil. There was a miniature and a parcel of letters within.

It was the face of a fair girl, with the same dark-blue eyes of the girl now before him, and the same golden hair—the face of an earlier but not a fairer Winifred. Allan Welsh set his teeth, and caught at the table to stay his dizzying head. The letters were his own. It was Walter Skirving's stern message to him. From the very tomb his own better self rose in judgment against him. He saw what he might have been—the sorrow he had wrought, and the path of ultimate atonement.

He had tried to part two young lovers who had chosen the straight and honest way. It was true that his duty to the kirk which had been his life, and which he himself was under condemnation according to his own standard, had seemed to him to conflict with the path he had marked out for Ralph.

But his own letters, breaking from their brittle confining band, poured in a cataract of folded paper and close-knit writing which looked like his own self of long ago, upon the table before him. He was condemned out of his own mouth.

Winsome sat with her face turned to the window, from which she could see the heathery back of a hill which heaved its bulk between the manse and the lowlands at the mouth of the Dee. There was a dreamy look in her eyes, land her heart was far away in that Edinburgh town from which she had that day received a message to shake her soul with love and pity.

The minister of the Dullarg looked up.

"Do you love him?" he asked, abruptly and harshly.

Winsome looked indignant and surprised. Her love, laid away in the depths of her heart, was sacred, and not thus to be at the mercy of every rude questioner. But as her eye rested on Allan Welsh, the unmistakable accent of sincerity took hold on her—that accent which may ask all things and not be blamed.

"I do love him," she said—"with all my heart."

That answer does not vary while God is in his heaven.

The eye of Allan Welsh fell on the miniature. The woman he had loved so long ago took part in the conversation.

"That is what you said twenty years ago!" the unseen Winsome said from the table.

"And he loves you?" he asked, without looking up.

"If I did not believe it, I could not live!"

Allan Welsh glanced with a keen and sudden scrutiny at Winsome Charteris; but the clearness of her eye and the gladness and faith at the bottom of it satisfied him as to his thought.

This Ralph Peden was a better man than he. A sad yearning face looked up at him from the table, and a voice thrilled in his ears across the years—

"So did not you!"

"You know," said Allan Welsh, again untrue to himself, "that it is not for Ralph Peden's good that he should love you." The formal part of him was dictating the words.

"I know you think so, and I am here to ask you why," said Winsome fearlessly.

"And if I persuade you, will you forbid him?" said Allan Welsh, convinced of his own futility.

Winsome's heart caught the accent of insincerity. It had gone far beyond forbidding love or allowing it with Ralph Peden and herself.

"I shall try!" she said, with her own sweet serenity. But across the years a voice was pleading their case. As the black and faded ink of the letters flashed his own sentences across the minister's eye, the soul God had put within him rose in revolt against his own petty and useless preaching.

"So did not you" persisted the voice in his ear. "Me you counselled to risk all, and you took me out into the darkness, lighting my way with love. Did ever I complain—father lost, mother lost, home lost, God well nigh lost—all for you; yet did I even regret when you saw me die?"

"Think of the Marrow kirk," said the minister. "Her hard service does not permit a probationer, before whom lies the task of doctrine and reproof, to have father or mother, wife or sweetheart."

"And what did you," said the voice, "in that past day, care for the Marrow kirk, when the light shone upon me, and you thought the world, and the Marrow kirk with it, well lost for love's sake and mine?"

Allan Welsh bowed his head yet lower.

Winsome Charteris went over to him. His tears were falling fast on the dulled and yellowing paper.

Winsome put her hands on his shoulder.

"Is that my mother's picture?" she said, hardly knowing what she said.

Allan Welsh put his hand greedily about it, he could not let it go.

"Will you kiss me for your mother's sake?" he said.

And then, for the first time since her babyhood, Winsome Charteris, whose name was Welsh, kissed her father.

There were tears on her mother's miniature, but through them the face of the dead Winifred seemed to smile well pleased.

"For my mother's sake!" said Winsome again, and kissed him of her own accord on the brow.

Thus Walter Skirving's message was delivered.

CHAPTER XLI
THE MEETING OF THE SYNOD

With the vestry of the Marrow kirk in Bell's Wynd the synod met, and was constituted with prayer. Sederunt, the Reverend Gilbert Peden, moderator, minister of the true kirk of God in Scotland, commonly called the Marrow Kirk, in which place the synod for the time being was assembled; the Reverend Allan Welsh, minister of the Marrow kirk in Dullarg, clerk of the synod; John Bairdieson, synod's officer. The minutes of the last meeting having been read and approved of, the court proceeded to take up business. Inter alia the trials of Master Ralph Peden, some time student of arts and humanity in the College of Edinburgh, were a remit for this day and date. Accordingly, the synod called upon the Reverend Allan Welsh, its clerk, to make report upon the diligence, humility, and obedience, as well as upon the walk and conversation of the said Ralph Peden, student in divinity, now on trials for license to preach, the gospel.

Allan Welsh read all this gravely and calmly, as if the art of expressing ecclesiastical meaning lay in clothing it in as many overcoats as a city watchman wears in winter.

The moderator sat still, with a grim earnestness in his face. He was the very embodiment of the kirk of the Marrow, and though there were but two ministers with no elders there that day to share the responsibility, what did that matter?

He, Gilbert Peden, successor of all the (faithful) Reformers, was there to do inflexible and impartial justice.

John Bairdieson came in and sat down. The moderator observed his presence, and in his official capacity took notice of it.

"This sederunt of the synod is private," he said. "Officer, remove the strangers."

In his official capacity the officer of the court promptly removed John Bairdieson, who went most unwillingly.

The matter of the examination of probationers comes up immediately after the reading of the minutes in well-regulated church courts, being most important and vital.

"The clerk will now call for the report upon the life and conduct of the student under trials," said the moderator.

The clerk called upon the Reverend Allan Welsh to present his report. Then he sat down gravely, but immediately rose again to give his report. All the while the moderator sat impassive as a statue.

The minister of Dullarg began in a low and constrained voice. He had observed, he said, with great pleasure the diligence and ability of Master Ralph Peden, and considered the same in terms of the remit to him from the synod. He was much pleased with the clearness of the candidate upon the great questions of theology and church government. He had examined him daily in his work, and had confidence in bearing testimony to the able and spiritual tone of all his exercises, both oral and written.

Soon after he began, a surprised look stole over the face of the moderator. As Allan Welsh went on from sentence to sentence, the thin nostrils of the representative of the Reformers dilated. A strange and intense scorn took possession of him. He sat back and looked fixedly at the slight figure of the minister of Dullarg bending under the weight of his message and the frailty of his body. His time was coming.

Allan Welsh sat down, and laid his written report on the table of the synod.

"And is that all that you have to say?" queried the moderator, rising.

"That is all," said Allan Welsh.

"Then," said the moderator, "I charge it against you that you have either said too much or too little: too much for me to listen to as the father of this young man, if it be true that you extruded him, being my son and a student of the Marrow kirk committed to your care, at midnight from your house, for no stated cause; and too little, far too little to satisfy me as moderator of this synod, when a report not only upon diligence and scholarship, but also upon a walk and conversation becoming the gospel, is demanded."

"I have duly given my report according to the terms of the remit," said Allan Welsh, simply and quietly.

"Then," said the moderator, "I solemnly call you to account as the moderator of this synod of the only true and protesting Kirk of Scotland, for the gravest dereliction of your duty. I summon you to declare the cause why Ralph Peden, student in divinity, left your house at midnight, and, returning to mine, was for that cause denied bed and board at his father's house."

"I deny your right, moderator, to ask that question as an officer of this synod. If, at the close, you meet me as man to man, and, as a father, ask me the reasons of my conduct, some particulars of which I do not now seek to defend, I shall be prepared to satisfy you."

"We are not here convened," said the moderator, "to bandy compliments, but to do justice—"

"And to love mercy," interjected John Bairdieson through the keyhole.

"Officer," said the moderator, "remove that rude interrupter."

"Aye, aye, sir," responded the synod officer promptly, and removed the offender as much as six inches.

"You have no more to say?" queried the moderator, bending his brows in threatening fashion.

"I have no more to say," returned the clerk as firmly. They were both combative men; and the old spirit of that momentous conflict, in which they had fought so gallantly together, moved them to as great obstinacy now that they were divided.

"Then," said the moderator, "there's nothing for't but another split, and the Lord do so, and more also, to him whose sin brings it about!"

"Amen!" said Allan Welsh.

"You will remember," said the moderator, addressing the minister of Dullarg directly, "that you hold your office under my pleasure. There is that against you in the past which would justify me, as moderator of the kirk of the Marrow, in deposing you summarily from the office of the ministry. This I have in writing under your own hand and confession."

"And I," said the clerk, rising with the gleaming light of war in his eye, "have to set it against these things that you are guilty of art and part in the concealment of that which, had you spoken twenty years ago, would have removed from the kirk of the Marrow an unfaithful minister, and given some one worthier than I to report on the fitness of your son for the ministry. It was you, Gilbert Peden, who made this remit to me, knowing what you know. I shall accept the deposition which you threaten at your hands, but remember that co-ordinately the power of this assembly lies with me—you as moderator, having only a casting, not a deliberative vote; and know you, Gilbert Peden, minister and moderator, that I, Allan Welsh, will depose you also from the office of the ministry, and my deposition will stand as good as yours."

"The Lord preserve us! In five meenetes there'll be nae Marrow Kirk" said John Bairdieson, and flung himself against the door; but the moderator had taken the precaution of locking it and placing the key on his desk.

The two ministers rose simultaneously. Gilbert Peden stood at the head and Allan Welsh at the foot of the little table. They were so near that they could have shaken hands across it. But they had other work to do.

"Allan Welsh," said the moderator, stretching out his hand, "minister of the gospel in the parish of Dullarg to the faithful contending remnant, I call upon you to show cause why you should not be deposed for the sins of contumacy and contempt, for sins of person and life, confessed and communicate under your hand."

"Gilbert Peden," returned the minister of the Dullarg and clerk to the Marrow Synod, looking like a cock-boat athwart the hawse of a leviathan of the deep, "I call upon you to show cause why you should not be deposed for unfaithfulness in the discharge of your duty, in so far as you have concealed known sin, and by complicity and compliance have been sharer in the wrong."

There was a moment's silence. Gilbert Peden knew well that what his opponent said was good Marrow doctrine, for Allan Welsh had confessed to him his willingness to accept deposition twenty years ago.

Then, as with one voice, the two men pronounced against each other the solemn sentence of deposition and deprivation:

"In the name of God, and by virtue of the law of the Marrow Kirk,
I solemnly depose you from the office of the ministry."

John Bairdieson burst in the door, leaving the lock hanging awry with the despairing force of his charge.

"Be merciful, oh, be merciful!" he cried; "let not the Philistines rejoice, nor the daughter of the uncircumcised triumph. Let be! let be! Say that ye dinna mean it! Oh, say ye dinna mean it! Tak' it back—tak' it a' back!"

There was the silence of death between the two men, who stood lowering at each other.

John Bairdieson turned and ran down the stairs. He met Ralph and Professor Thriepneuk coming up.

"Gang awa'! gang awa'!" he cried. "There's nae leecense for ye noo. There's nae mair ony Marrow Kirk! There's nae mair heaven and earth! The Kirk o' the Marrow, precious and witnessing, is nae mair!"

And the tears burst from the old sailor as he ran down the street, not knowing whither he went.

Half-way down the street a seller of sea-coal, great and grimy, barred his way. He challenged the runner to fight. The spirit of the Lord came upon John Bairdieson, and, rejoicing that a foe withstood him, he dealt a buffet so sore and mighty that the seller of coal, whose voice could rise like the grunting of a sea beast to the highest windows of the New Exchange Buildings, dropped as an ox drops when it is felled. And John Bairdieson ran on, crying out: "There's nae kirk o' God in puir Scotland ony mair!"

CHAPTER XLII
PURGING AND RESTORATION

It was the Lord's day in Edinburgh town. The silence in the early morning was something which could be felt—not a footstep, not a rolling wheel. Window-blinds were mostly down—on the windows provided with them. Even in Bell's Wynd there was not the noise of the week. Only a tinker family squabbled over the remains of the deep drinking of the night before. But then, what could Bell's Wynd expect—to harbour such?

It was yet early dawn when John Bairdieson, kirk officer to the little company of the faithful to assemble there later in the day, went up the steps and opened the great door with his key. He went all round the church with his hat on. It was a Popish idea to take off the head covering within stone walls, yet John Bairdieson was that morning possessed with the fullest reverence for the house of God and the highest sense of his responsibility as the keeper of it.

He was wont to sing:

> "Rather in
> My God's house would I keep a door
> Than dwell in tents of sin."

That was the retort which he flung across at Taminas Laidlay, the beadle of the Established Kirk opposite, with all that scorn in the application which was due from one in John Bairdieson's position to one in that of Tammas Laidlay.

But this morning John had no spirit for the encounter. He hurried in and sat down by himself in the minister's vestry. Here he sat for a long season in deep and solemn thought.

"I'll do it!" he said at last.

It was near the time when the minister usually came to enter into his vestry, there to prepare himself by meditation and prayer for the services of the sanctuary. John Bairdieson posted himself on the top step of the stairs which led from the street, to wait for him. At last, after a good many passers-by, all single and all in black, walking very fast, had hurried by, John's neck craning after every one, the minister appeared, walking solemnly down the street with his head in the air. His neckcloth was crumpled and soiled—a fact which was not lost on John.

The minister came up the steps and made as though he would pass John by without speaking to him; but that guardian of the sanctuary held out his arms as though he were wearing sheep.

"Na, na, minister, ye come na into this Kirk this day as minister till ye be lawfully restored. There are nae ministers o' the kirk o' the Marrow the noo; we're a body without a heid. I thocht that the Kirk was at an end, but the Lord has revealed to me that the Marrow Kirk canna end while the world lasts. In the nicht season he told me what to do."

The minister stood transfixed. If his faithful serving-man of so many years had turned against him, surely the world was at an end. But it was not so.

John Bairdieson went on, standing with his hat in his hand, and the hairs of his head erect with the excitement of unflinching justice.

"I see it clear. Ye are no minister o' this kirk. Mr. Welsh is no minister o' the Dullarg. I, John Bairdieson, am the only officer of the seenod left; therefore I stand atween the people and you this day, till ye hae gane intil the seenod hall, that we ca' on ordinary days the vestry, and there, takkin' till ye the elders that remain, ye be solemnly ordainit ower again and set apairt for the office o' the meenistry."

"But I am your minister, and need nothing of the sort!" said
Gilbert Peden. "I command you to let me pass!"

"Command me nae commands! John Bairdieson kens better nor that. Ye are naither minister nor ruler; ye are but an elder, like mysel'— equal among your equals; an' ye maun sit amang us this day and help to vote for a teachin' elder, first among his equals, to be set solemnly apairt."

The minister, logical to the verge of hardness, could not gainsay the admirable and even-handed justice of John Bairdieson's position. More than that, he knew that every man in the congregation of the Marrow Kirk of Bell's Wynd would inevitably take the same view.

Without another word he went into the session-house, where in due time he sat down and opened the Bible.

He had not to wait long, when there joined him Gavin MacFadzean, the cobbler, from the foot of Leith Walk, and Alexander Taylour, carriage-builder, elders in the kirk of the Marrow; these, forewarned by John Bairdieson, took their places in silence. To them entered Allan Welsh.

Then, last of all, John Bairdieson came in and took his own place. The five elders of the Marrow kirk were met for the first time on an equal platform. John Bairdieson opened with prayer. Then he stated the case. The two ex-ministers sat calm and silent, as though listening to a chapter in the Acts of the Apostles. It was a strange scene of equality, only possible and actual in Scotland.

"But mind ye," said John Bairdieson, "this was dune hastily, and not of set purpose—for ministers are but men—even ministers of the Marrow kirk. Therefore shall we, as elders of the kirk, in full standing, set apairt two of our number as teaching elders, for the fulfilling of ordinances and the edification of them that believe. Have you anything to say? If not, then let us proceed to set apairt and ordain Gilbert Peden and Allan Welsh."

But before any progress could be made, Allan Welsh rose.
John Bairdieson had been afraid of this.

"The less that's said, the better," he said hastily, "an' it's gottin' near kirk-time. We maun get it a' by or then."

"This only I have to say," said Allan Welsh, "I recognize the justice of my deposition. I have been a sinful and erring man, and I am not worthy to teach in the pulpit any more. Also, my life is done. I shall soon lay it down and depart to the Father whose word I, hopeless and castaway, have yet tried faithfully to preach."

Then uprose Gilbert Peden. His voice was husky with emotion. "Hasty and ill-advised, and of such a character as to bring dishonour on the only true Kirk in Scotland, has such an action been. I confess myself a hasty man, a man of wrath, and that wrath unto sin. I have sinned the sin of anger and presumption against a brother. Long ere now I would have taken it back, but it is the law of God that deeds once done cannot be undone; though we seek repentance carefully with tears, we cannot put the past away."

Thus, with the consecration and the humility of confession Gilbert Peden purged himself from the sin of hasty anger.

"Like Uzzah at the threshing-floor of Nachon," he went on, "I have sinned the sin of the Israelite who set his hand to the ox-cart to stay the ark of God. It is of the Lord's mercy that I am not consumed, like the men of Beth-shemesh."

So Gilbert Peden was restored, but Allan Welsh would not accept any restoration.

"I am not a man accepted of God," he said. And even Gilbert Peden said no word.

"Noo," said John Bairdieson, "afore this meetin' scales [is dismissed], there is juist yae word that I hae to say. There's nane o' us haes wives, but an' except Alexander Taylour, carriage- maker. Noo, the proceedings this mornin' are never to be jince named in the congregation. If, then, there be ony soond of this in the time to come, mind you Alexander Taylour, that it's you that'll hae to bear the weight o't!"

This was felt to be fair, even by Alexander Taylour, carriage- maker.

The meeting now broke up, and John Bairdieson went to reprove Margate Truepenny for knocking with her crutch on the door of the house of God on the Sabbath morning.

"D'ye think," he said, "that the fowk knockit wi' their staves on the door o' the temple in Jerusalem?"

"Aiblins," retorted Margate, "they had feller [quicker] doorkeepers in thae days nor you, John Bairdieson."

The morning service was past. Gilbert Peden had preached from the text, 'Greater is he that ruleth his spirit than he that taketh a city."

"Oor minister is yin that looks deep intil the workings o' his ain heart," said Margate, as she hirpled homeward.

But when the church was empty and all gone home, in the little vestry two men sat together, and the door was shut. Between them they held a miniature, the picture of a girl with a flush of rose on her cheek and a laughing light in her eyes. There was silence, but for a quick catch in the stronger man's breathing, which sounded like a sob. Gilbert Peden, who had only lost and never won, and Allan Welsh, who had both won and lost, were forever at one. There was silence between them, as they looked with eyes of deathless love at the picture which spoke to them of long ago.

Walter Skirving's message, which Winsome had brought to the manse of Dullarg, had united the hearts estranged for twenty years. Winsome had builded better than she knew.

CHAPTER XLIII
THREADS DRAWN TOGETHER

Winsome took her grandmother out one afternoon into the rich mellow August light, when the lower corn-fields were glimmering with misty green shot underneath with faintest blonde, and the sandy knowes were fast yellowing. The blithe old lady was getting back some of her strength, and it seemed possible that once again she might be able to go round the house without even the assistance of an arm.

"And what is this I hear," said Mistress Skirving, "that the daft young laird frae the Castle has rin' aff wi' that cottar's lassie, Jess Kissock, an' marriet her at Gretna Green. It's juist no possible."

"But, grandma, it is quite true, for Jock Gordon brought the news. He saw them postin' back from Gretna wi' four horses!"

"An' what says his mither, the Lady Elizabeth?"

"They say that she's delighted," said Winsome.

"That's a lee, at ony rate!" said the mistress of Craig Ronald, without a moment's hesitation. She knew the Lady Elizabeth,

"They say," said Winsome, "that Jess can make them do all that she wants at the Castle."

"Gin she gars them pit doon new carpets, she'll do wonders," said her grandmother, acidly. She came of a good family, and did not like mesalliances, though she had been said to have made one herself.

But there was no misdoubting the fact that Jess had done her sick nursing well, and had possessed herself in honourable and lawful wedlock of the Honourable Agnew Greatorix—and that too, apparently with the consent of the Lady Elizabeth.

"What took them to Gretna, then?" said Winsome's grandmother.

"Well, grandmammy, you see, the Castle folk are Catholic, and would not have a minister; an' Jess, though a queer Christian, as well as maybe to show her power and be romantic, would have no priest or minister either, but must go to Gretna. So they're back again, and Jock Gordon says that she'll comb his hair. He has to be in by seven o'clock now," said Winsome, smiling.

"Wha's ben wi' yer grandfaither?" after a pause, Mistress Skirving asked irrelevantly.

"Only Mr. Welsh from the manse," said Winsome. "I suppose he came to see grandfather about the packet I took to the manse a month ago. Grandmother, why does Mr. Welsh come so seldom to Craig Ronald?" she asked.

But her grandmother was shaking in a strange way.

"I have not heard any noise," she said. "You had better go in and see."

Winsome stole to the door and looked within. She saw the minister with his head on the swathed knees of her grandfather. The old man had laid his hand upon the grey hair of the kneeling minister. Awed and solemnised, Winsome drew back.

She told her grandmother what she had seen, and the old lady said nothing for the space of a quarter of an hour. At the end of that time she said:

"Help me ben."

And Winsome, taking her arm, guided her into the hushed room where her husband sat, still holding his hand on the head of Allan Welsh.

Something in the pose of the kneeling man struck her—a certain helpless inclination forward.

Winsome ran, and, taking Allan Welsh by the shoulders, lifted him up in her strong young arms.

He was dead. He had passed in the act of forgiveness.

Walter Skirving, who had sat rapt and silent through it all as though hardly of this world, now said clearly and sharply:

"'For if ye forgive men their trespasses, so also shall your heavenly Father forgive you.'"

Walter Skirving did not long survive the man, in hatred of whom he had lived, and in unity with whom he had died. It seemed as though he had only been held to the earth by the necessity that the sun of his life should not go down upon his wrath. This done, like a boat whose moorings are loosed, very gladly he went out that same night upon the ebb tide. The two funerals were held upon the same day. Minister and elder were buried side by side one glorious August day, which was a marvel to many. So the Dullarg kirk was vacant, and there was only Manse Bell to take care of the property. Jonas Shillinglaw came from Cairn Edward and communicated the contents of both Walter Skirving's will and of that of Allan Welsh to those whom it concerned. Jonas had made several journeys of late both to the manse as well as to the steading of Craig Ronald. Walter Skirving left Craig Ronald and all of which he died possessed to Winsome Charteris, subject to the approval of her grandmother as to whom she might marry. There was a recent codicil. "I desire to record my great satisfaction that Winifred Charteris or Welsh is likely to marry the son of my old friend Gilbert Peden, minister of the Marrow kirk in Edinburgh; and hearing that the young man contemplates the career of letters, I desire that, if it be possible, in the event of their marriage, they come to abide at Craig Ronald, at least till a better way be opened for them. I commend my wife, ever loving and true, to them both; and in the good hope of a glorious resurrection I commit myself to Him who made me."

Allan Welsh left all his goods and his property to Ralph Peden, "being as mine own son, because he taught me to know true love, and fearlessness and faith unfeigned. Also because one dear to him brought me my hope of forgiveness."

There was indeed need of Ralph at Craig Ronald. Mistress Skirving cried out incessantly for him. Meg begged Winsome to let her look every day at the little miniature Ralph had sent her from Edinburgh. The Cuif held forth upon the great event every night when he came over to hold the tails of Meg's cows. Jock Forrest still went out, saying nothing, whenever the Cuif came in, which the Cuif took to be a good sign. Only Ebie Fairrish, struck to the heart by the inconstancy of Jess, removed at the November term back again to the "laigh end" of the parish, and there plunged madly into flirtations with several of his old sweethearts. He is reported to have found in numbers the anodyne for the unfaithfulness of one. As for what Winsome thought and longed for, it is better that we should not begin to tell, not having another volume to spare.

Only she went to the hill-top by the side of Loch Ken and looked northward every eventide; and her heart yearned within her.

CHAPTER XLIV
WINSOME'S LAST TRYST

It was the morn before a wedding, and there had been a constant stir all night all about the farmsteading, for a brand-new world was in the making. Such a marrying had not been for years. The farmers' sons for miles around were coming on their heavy plough- horses, with here and there one of better breed. Long ago in the earliest morning some one had rung the bell of the little kirk of the Dullarg. It came upon the still air a fairy tinkle, and many a cottar and many a shepherd turned over with a comfortable feeling: "This is the Sabbath morn; I need not rise so soon to-day." But all their wives remembered, and turned them out with wifely elbow.

It was Winsome Charteris's wedding day. The flower of all the countryside was to wed the young Edinburgh lad who had turned out so great a poet. It was the opinion of the district that her "intended" had unsettled the thrones of all the great writers of the past by his volume of poems, which no one in the parish had read; but the fame of whose success had been wafted down upon the eastern breezes which bore the snell bite of the metropolis upon their front.

"Tra-la-la-la!" chanted the cocks of Craig Ronald.

"Tra-la-la-la-la!" airily sang the solitary bird which lived up among the pine woods, where, in the cot of Mistress Kissock, Ralph Peden occupied the little bedroom which Meg had got ready for him with such care and honour.

"Tra-la-la-laa!" was echoed in the airiest diminuendo from the far-away leader of the harem at the Nether Orae. His challenge crossed the wide gulf of air above Loch Grannoch, from which in the earliest morning the mists were rising.

Ralph Peden heard all three birds. He had a delightfully comfortable bedroom, and the flowers on the little white-covered table have come from the front square of Mistress Kissock's garden. There was a passion-flower on his table, which somehow reminded him of a girl who had put poppies in hair of the raven's wing hue. It had not grown in the garden of the cot.

Yet Ralph was out in the earliest dawn, listening to the sighing of the trees and taking in the odour of the perfume from the pines on the slope.

Ralph did not write any poem this morning, though the Muses were abroad in the stillness of the dawn. His eyes were on a little window once more overclambered by the June roses. His poem was down there, and it was coming to him.

How eagerly he looked, his eyes like telescopes! Then his heart thrilled. In the cool flood of slanting morning sunshine which had just overflowed the eastern gable of the house, some one swiftly crossed the court-yard of the farm. In a moment the sun, winking on a pair of tin pails, told him that Meg Kissock was going to the well. From the barn end some one stepped out by her side and walked to the well. Then, as they returned, it was not the woman who was carrying the winking pails. At the barn end they drew together in the shadow for a long minute, and then again Ralph saw Meg's back as she walked sedately to the kitchen door, the cans flashing rhythmically as she swung them. So high was he above them that he could even notice the mellow dimple of diffused light from the water in the bright pail centring and scattering the morning sunlight as it swayed.

Presently the one half of the blue kitchen door became black. It had been opened. Ralph's heart gave a great bound. Then the black became white and glorified, for framed within it appeared a slender shape like a shaft of light. Ralph's eyes did not leave the figure as it stepped out and came down by the garden edge.

Along the top of the closely-cut hawthorn a dot of light moved. It was but a speck, like the paler centre of the heather bells. Ralph ran swiftly down the great dyke in a manner more natural to a young man than dignified in a poet. In a minute he came to the edge of the glen in which Andra Kissock had guddled the trouts. That flash of layender must pass this way. It passed and stayed.

So in the cool translucence of morning light the lovers met in this quiet glade, the great heather moors above them once more royally purple, the burnie beneath singing a gentle song, the birds vying with each other in complicated trills of pretended artlessness.

It was purely by chance that Winsome Charteris passed this way. And a kind Providence, supplemented on Ralph's side by some activity and observation, brought him also to the glen of the elders that June morning. Yet there are those who say that there is nothing in coincidence.

When Winsome, moving thoughtfully onward, gently waving a slip of willow in her hand, came in sight of Ralph, she stood and waited. Ralph went towards her, and so on their marriage morn these two lovers met.

It was like that morning on which by the lochside they parted, yet it was not like it.

With that prescience which is a sixth sense to women, Winsome had slipped on the old sprigged gown which had done duty at the blanket-washing so long ago, and her hair, unbound in the sun, shone golden as it flowed from beneath the lilac sunbonnet. As for Ralph, it does not matter how he was dressed. In love, dress does not matter a brass button after the first corner is turned—at least not to the woman.

"Sweet," said Ralph, "you are awake?"

Winsome looked up with eyes so glorious and triumphant that a blind man could scarce have doubted the fact.

"And you love me?" he continued, reading her eyes. With her old ripple of laughter she lightened the strain of the occasion.

"You are a silly boy," she said; "but you'll learn. I have come out to gather flowers," she added, ingenuously. "I shall expect you to help. No—no—and nothing else."

Had Ralph been in a fit condition to observe Nature this morning, it might have occurred to him that when girls come out to gather flowers for somewhat extensive decoration, they bring with them at least a basket and generally also their fourth best pair of scissors. Winsome had neither. But he was not in a mood for careful inductions.

The morning lights sprayed upon them as they went hither and thither gathering flowers—dew-drenched hyacinths, elastic wire- strung bluebells the colour of the sky when the dry east wind blows, the first great red bushes of the ling. Now it is a known fact that, in order properly to gather flowers, the collectors must divide and so quarter the ground.

"But this was not a scientific expedition," said Ralph, when the folly of their mode of proceeding was pointed out to him.

It was manifestly impossible that they could gather flowers walking with the palm of Ralph's left hand laid on the inside of Winsome's left arm. The thing cannot be done. At least so Ralph admitted afterwards.

"No," said Ralph, "but you made me promise to keep my shoulders back, and I am trying to to do it now."

And his manner of assisting Winsome to gather her flowers for her wedding bouquet was, when you come to think of it, admirably adapted for keeping the shoulders back.

"Meg waked me this morning," said Winsome suddenly.

"She did, did she?" remarked Ralph ineffectively, with a quick envy of Meg. Then it occurred to him that he had no need to envy Meg. And Winsome blushed for no reason at all.

Then she became suddenly practical, as the protective instinct teaches women to be on these occasions.

"You have not seen your study," she said.

"No," said Ralph, "but I have heard enough about it. It has occupied sixteen pages in the last three letters."

Ralph considered the study a good thing, but he had his views upon the composition of love-letters.

"You are an ungrateful boy," said Winsome sternly, "and I shall see that you get no more letters—not any more!"

"I shall never want any, little woman," cried Ralph joyously, "for I shall have you!"

It was a blessing that at this moment they were passing under the dense shade of the great oaks at the foot of the orchard. Winsome had thought for five minutes that it would happen about there. It happened.

A quarter of an hour later they came out into the cool ocean of leaf shadow which lay blue upon the grass and daisies. Winsome now carried the sunbonnet over her arm, and in the morning sunshine her uncovered head was so bright that Ralph could not gaze at it long. Besides, he wanted to look at the eyes that looked at him, and one cannot do everything at once.

"This is your study," she said, standing back to let him look in. It was a long, low room with an outside stair above the farthermost barn, and Winsome had fitted it up wondrously for Ralph. It opened off the orchard, and the late blossoms scattered into it when the winds blew from the south.

They stood together on the topmost step. There was a desk and one chair, and a low window-seat in each of the deep windows.

"You will never be disturbed here," said Winsome.

"But I want to be disturbed," said Ralph, who was young and did not know any better.

"Now go in," said Winsome, giving him a little push in the way that, without any offence, a proximate wife may. "Go in and study a little this morning, and see how you like it."

Ralph considered this as fair provocation, and turned, with bonds and imprisonment in his mind. But Winsome had vanished.

But from beneath came a clear voice out of the unseen:

"If you don't like it, you can come round and tell me. It will not be too late till the afternoon. Any time before three!"

A mere man is at a terrible disadvantage in word play of this kind. On this occasion Ralph could think of nothing better than—

"Winsome Charteris, I shall pay you back for this!"

Then he heard what might either have been a bell ringing for the fairies' breakfast, or a ripple of the merriest earthly laughter very far away.

Then he sat down to study.

It took him quite an hour to arrive at a conclusion; but when reached it was a momentous one. It was, that it is a mistake to be married in summer, for three o'clock in the afternoon is such a long time in coming.

CHAPTER XLV
THE LAST OF THE LILAC SUNBONNET

Craig Ronald lies bright in a dreaming day in mid-September. The reapers are once more in the fields. Far away there is a crying of voices. The corn-fields by the bridge are white with a bloomy and mellow whiteness. Some part of the oats is already down. Close into the standing crop there is a series of rhythmic flashes, the scythes swinging like a long wave that curls over here and there. Behind the line of flashing steel the harvesters swarm like ants running hither and thither crosswise, apparently in aimless fashion.

Up through the orchard comes a girl, tall and graceful, but with a touch of something nobler and stiller that does not come to girlhood. It is the seal of the diviner Eden grace which only comes with the after Eden pain.

Winsome Peden carries more than ever of the old grace and beauty; and the eyes of her husband, who has been finishing the proofs of his next volume and at intervals looking over the busy fields to the levels of Loch Grannoch, tell her so as she comes.

But suddenly from opposite sides of the orchard this girl with the gracious something in her eyes is borne down by simultaneous assault. Shrieking with delight, a boy and a girl, dressed in complete defensive armour of daisies, and wielding desperate arms of lath manufactured by Andra Kissock, their slave, rush fiercely upon her. They pull down their quarry after a brisk chase, who sinks helplessly upon the grass under a merciless fire of caresses.

It is a critical moment. A brutal and licentious soldiery are not responsible at such moments. They may carry sack and rapine to unheard of extremities.

"You young barbarians, be careful of your only mother—unless you have a stock of them!" calls a voice from the top of the stairs which lead to the study.

"Father's come out—hurrah! Come on, Allan!" shouts Field-Marshal Winifred the younger who is leader and commander, to her army whose tottery and chubby youth does not suggest the desperation of a forlorn hope. So the study is carried at the point of the lath, and the banner of the victors—a cross of a sort unknown to heraldry, marked on a white ground with a blue pencil—is planted on the sacred desk itself.

Winsome the matron comes more slowly up the stairs.

"Can common, uninspired people come in?" she says, pausing at the top.

She looks about with a motherly eye, and pulls down the blind of the window into which the sun has been streaming all the morning. It is one of the advantages of such a wife that her husband, especially the rare literary variety, may be treated as no more than the eldest but most helpless of the babes. It is also true that Ralph had pulled up the blind in order that he might the better be able to see his wife moving among the reapers. For Winsome was more than ever a woman of affairs.

She stood in the doorway, looking in spite of the autumn sun and the walk up from the corn-field, deliriously cool. She fanned herself with a broad rhubarb-leaf—an impromptu fan plucked by the way. She sat down on the ledge of the upper step of Ralph's study, as she often did when she worked or rested. Ralph was again within, reclining on a window-seat, while the pack of reckless banditti swarmed over him.

"Have the rhymes been behaving themselves this morning?" Winsome said, looking across at Ralph as only a wife of some years' standing can look at her husband—with love deepened into understanding, and tempered with a spice of amusement and a wide and generous tolerance—the look of a loving woman to whom her husband and her husband's ways are better than a stage play. Such a look is a certificate of happy home and an ideal life, far more than all heroics. The love of the after-years depends chiefly on the capacity of a wife to be amused by her husband's peculiarities—and not to let him see it.

"There are three blanks," said Ralph, a little wistfully. "I have written a good deal, but I dare not read it over, lest it should be nothing worth."

This was a well-marked stage in Ralph's composition, and it was well that his wife had come.

"I fear you have been dreaming, instead of working," she said, looking at him with a kind of pitying admiration. Ralph, too, had grown handsomer, so his wife thought, since she had him to look after. How, indeed, could it be otherwise?

She rose and went towards him.

"Sun down, now, children, and play on the grass," she said. "Sun, chicks—off with you—shoo!" and she flirted her apron after them as she did when she scattered the chickens from the dairy door. The pinafored people fled shrieking across the grass, tumbling over each other in riotous heaps.

Then Winsome went over and kissed her husband. He was looking so handsome that he deserved it. And she did not do it too often. She was glad that she had made him wear a beard. She put one of her hands behind his head and the other beneath his chin, tilting his profile with the air of a connoisseur. This can only be done in one position.

"Well, does it suit your ladyship?" said Ralph.

She gave him a little box on the ear.

"I knew," he said, "that you wanted to come and sit on my knee!"

"I never did," replied Winsome with animation, making a statement almost certainly inaccurate upon the face of it.

"That's why you sent away the children," he went on, pinching her ear.

"Of all things in this world," said Winsome indignantly, "commend me to a man for conceit!"

"And to winsome wives for wily ways!" said her husband instantly. To do him justice, he did not often do this sort of thing.

"Keep the alliteration for the poems," retorted Winsome. "Truth will do for me."

After a little while she said, without apparent connection:

"It is very hot."

"What are they doing in the hay-field?" asked Ralph.

"Jock Forrest was leading and they were cutting down the croft very steadily. I think it looks like sixty bushels to the acre," she continued practically; "so you shall have a carpet for the study this year, if all goes well."

"That will be famous!" cried Ralph, like a schoolboy, waving his hand. It paused among Winsome's hair.

"I wish you would not tumble it all down," she said; "I am too old for that kind of thing now!"

The number of times good women perjure themselves is almost unbelievable.

But the recording angel has, it is said, a deaf side, otherwise he would need an ink-eraser. Ralph knew very well what she really meant, and continued to throw the fine-spun glossy waves over her head, as a miser may toss his gold for the pleasure of the cool, crisp touch.

"Then," continued Winsome, without moving (for, though so unhappy and uncomfortable, she sat still—some women are born with a genius for martyrdom), "then I had a long talk with Meg."

"And the babe?" queried Ralph, letting her hair run through his fingers.

"And the babe," said Winsome; "she had laid it to sleep under a stock, and when we went to see, it looked so sweet under the narrow arch of the corn! Then it looked up with big wondering eyes. I believe he thought the inside of the stook was as high as a temple."

"It is not I that am the poet!" said Ralph, transferring his attention for a moment from her hair.

"Meg says Jock Forrest is perfectly good to her, and that she would not change her man for all Greatorix Castle."

"Does Jock make a good grieve?" asked Ralph.

"The very best; he is a great comfort to me," replied his wife. "I get far more time to work at the children's things—and also to look after my Ursa Major!"

"What of Jess?" asked Ralph; "did Meg say?"

"Jess has taken the Lady Elizabeth to call on My Lord at Bowhill! What do you think of that? And she leads Agnew Greatorix about like a lamb, or rather like a sheep. He gets just one glass of sherry at dinner," said Winsome, who loved a spice of gossip—as who does not?

"There is a letter from my father this morning," said Ralph, half turning to pick it off his desk; "he is well, but he is in distress, he says, because he got his pocket picked of his handkerchief while standing gazing in at a shop window wherein books were displayed for sale, but John Bairdieson has sewed another in at the time of writing. They had a repeating tune the other day, and the two new licentiates are godly lads, and turning out a credit to the kirk of the Marrow."

"And that is more than ever you would have done, Ralph," said his wife candidly.

"Kezia is to be married in October, and there is a young man coming to see little Keren-happuch, but Jemima thinks that the minds of both of her younger sisters are too much set on the frivolous things of this earth.

The professor has received a new kind of snuff from Holland which Kezia says is indistinguishable in its effects from pepper—one of his old students brought it to him—and that's all the news," said Ralph, closing up the letter and laying it on the table.

"Has Saunders Moudiewort cast his easy affections on any one this year yet?" Ralph asked, returning to the consideration of Winsome's hair.

Saunders was harvesting at present at Craig Ronald. The mistress of the farm laughed.

"I think not," she said; "Saunders says that his mother is the most' siccar' housekeeper that he kens of, and that after a while ye get to mind her tongue nae mair nor the mill fanners."

"That's just the way with me when you scold me," said Ralph.

"Very well, then, I must go to the summer seat and put you out of danger," replied Winsome. "Since you are so imposed upon, I shall see if the grannymother has done with her second volume. She never gets dangerous, except when she is kept waiting for the third."

But before they had time to move, the rollicking storm-cloud of younglings again came tumultuously up the stairs—Winifred far in front, Allan toddling doggedly in the rear.

"See what granny has put on my head!" cried Mistress Winifred the youngest, whose normal manner of entering a room suggested a revolution.

"Oo" said Allan, pointing with his chubby finger, "yook, yook! mother's sitting on favver's knee-rock-a-by, favver, rock-a-by!"

But Ralph had no eyes for anything but the old sunbonnet in which, the piquant flower face of Mistress Five-year-old Winifred was all but lost. He stooped and kissed it, and the face under it. It was frayed and faded, and it had lost both strings.

Then he looked up and kissed the wife who was still his sweetheart, for the love the lilac sunbonnet had brought to them so many years ago was still fresh with the dew of their youth.